BELIEVE
LIKE A CHILD

PAIGE DEARTH

ISBN: 1461105676
ISBN-13: 9781461105671

SOME DIRT ON THE AUTHOR:

Born and raised in Plymouth Meeting, a small town west of Philadelphia, Paige Dearth was a victim of child rape and spent her early years yearning for a better life. To escape the unwanted attentions of her molester, a pedophile uncle who lived with the family, she married at the age of nineteen and moved with her new husband to Chula Vista, California. After two years of marriage during which she struggled to make ends meet, she became pregnant, only to discover that her husband was a heroin addict. Paige waited for the birth of her daughter and when the baby was just eight months old, moved back to Pennsylvania. With no formal education or money to fall back on, she courageously set out to pick up the pieces of her shattered life and make it whole once more.

Living through the fear and isolation of her youth, Paige developed the ability to create stories that would help her cope and finally put them to use by embarking on a series of novels. *Believe Like A Child*, the author's debut offering, is the darkest version of who she could have become, had fate not intervened in the nick of time. It presents a fine balance between what lives on in her imagination and the evil that lurks in the real world.

CONNECT WITH PAIGE:

Visit her website at www.paigedearth.com

Friend Paige on Facebook at www.facebook.com/paigedearth

Dedication

This book is dedicated to my daughter, Sweetpea, the love of my life.

Thank you for putting the Ivy Eye to the words on these pages.

~Mom

Acknowledgements

Thanks to my husband, my Remo. You saved my life. I am never alone, knowing that you believe in me with such certainty. You are the greatest idea guy ever born! I will always love you.

Thanks to the Big E for coming over to the dark side with your eyes wide open.

My appreciation and love to my real-life Ebby. I will never forget what you did for me.

Thanks to Debbie (Flyers Pin Lady) and Deneen for being my first Facebook friends.

Finally, thanks to my entire family for all of your love and support.

~Paige

How It All Began

lessa awoke in the middle of the night to find her nightgown bunched up around her chest and her uncle's fingers between her legs. Just seven years old, she was scared and confused by what her so-called protector was doing to her and pretended to still be asleep, hoping it would make him stop. Alessa didn't know if what he was doing was right or wrong; all she knew was that it filled her with dread. Ten minutes later, she felt as if she were going to explode right there in her uncle's bed from the terror welling up inside her. She pretended to be just waking up, and gathered the courage to look up at him with wide, terrified eyes.

"Just lie back and be quiet," he rasped. "I'll make you feel really good."

Then he placed his thick, wet mouth, still stinking of cigars, over hers and continued to explore her undeveloped body until he had finally entered her. Alessa was young, but knew instinctively that no one would believe her, if she reported what her uncle had just done to her.

Alessa was the youngest of four children and the only introvert in the group. While her family was loud and opinionated, she was quiet and timid. And because she was so different from the rest of them, she often found herself watching the chaos that ensued during family gatherings from the periphery, like an outsider who didn't belong. She wondered why God had placed her with them. She couldn't relate to her parents; nor did she share any of the qualities that characterized her siblings. In the constant arguing and heated debates that they had with each other, the seven-year-old found herself lost and forgotten.

Alessa lacked all of the right characteristics for becoming anything important in life. Shy and unexceptional, with rarely a smile to light up her solemn expression, she led people to believe she was a miserable little child. Her lank hair and large, serious brown eyes made her look homely. Her small frame was always draped in threadbare hand-me-downs that were always too big for her and never seemed to sit on her the way they did on her two older sisters. The youngest in the family, she stood in stark contrast to her siblings—Anna, the firstborn, and Rosabella—and Anthony, the brother who came between the two. All three flaunted thick black hair, beautiful brown eyes and radiant olive complexions. From the time she was very young, Alessa had known she was not like the rest of them. The sheer force of their outgoing personalities appealed to all and overshadowed her meek demeanor. Simply put, Alessa was forgettable.

Their maternal grandmother, who they called Grammy, lived with the family and since their mother, Caterina, was the youngest of fourteen siblings, they always had people visiting. Being an insignificant part of such a large family was unbearable for the solitary seven-year-old. She would listen to them argue with each other over the most trivial matters, as they spent hours sitting around the kitchen table, drinking coffee and passing judgment on people they knew, bitterly criticizing the way they lived their lives or raised their children. As each of these evenings drew to a close, someone would invariably stomp out of the house either in a fit of silent rage or screaming at another family member. The constant friction was traumatic for the little girl, a fact that no one else in her family sensed or understood. Turmoil was what her family thrived on, whereas all she wanted was to be in the company of people who would make her feel she belonged.

Alessa found an ally in Grammy who, given the limited number of bedrooms in their house, shared one with her. The child loved sleeping with Grammy whose very presence instilled in her a sense of security amid the ominous darkness teeming with imaginary monsters that settled around her bed at night. Every evening, when it was time for bed, Alessa would snuggle up close, her small arm linked as tightly as a vice through her grandmother's. As Alessa lay beside her, Grammy would go through her rosary beads and murmur her evening prayers, assuring her granddaughter that monsters didn't exist.

Alessa's grandmother was a happy woman. Her cheerful face was framed by short, curly gray hair and her skin felt as soft and smooth as silk. The matriarch of the family, she was a gentle soul, loved and respected because of her kindness to others. She often invited neighbors and relatives to their home so she could provide them with a hot meal. Even though she wasn't a wealthy woman, she believed in sharing what God had provided her. She would knit for hours on end so she could gift afghans in the winter to people she knew. Alessa would squeeze in beside her grandmother, as she sat knitting on her rocking chair, and often find herself dozing off, lulled by the sound of her infinitely soothing voice. In her company, Alessa always felt tranquil and completely at peace.

The family was poor and enjoyed few luxuries. One of Alessa's most memorable ones was the weeklong vacation she had taken with her grandmother in Atlantic City, New Jersey, as a five-year-old. At the Chalfonte-Haddon Hall Hotel where they stayed, the child had felt as though she were in heaven. Wearing the new bathing suit her grandmother had bought her, she had played on the beach, building sand castles and jumping the waves. She had loved eating in the elegant dining room where she could choose whatever delicacies she wanted from the dessert table. The waiters were nice to her and attentive to their every need. Grammy had let her order Shirley Temples that were served in tall glasses with crushed ice and topped with a cherry. The vacation in Atlantic City was Alessa's only good childhood memory. She would relive that week a million times in her mind, as she grew older and found less and less to look forward to.

When Alessa was six years old her grandmother died. Unable to imagine life without her, the child was devastated by her loss and felt there was no longer a place in her home that she could call safe. She felt bereft and abandoned without her ally, but soon found solace in a new one. It was her Uncle Danny who held and comforted her through her bereavement. She felt special and deeply loved because of the kindness he showered upon her during those dark days following Grammy's death.

Everyone loved her Uncle Danny. He was extremely popular, a family icon, the man with all the money, and everyone sought his company. He often told stories about the mafia and most people secretly believed he worked for them. But eventually, Alessa realized, they were just stories concocted to make everyone live in awe of him. Uncle Danny's tales were so persuasive that most people who knew him ended up giving him far more respect than he deserved. He wielded a lot of clout and everyone around him automatically bowed to his demands.

Six long months after her grandmother had passed away and shortly after her Uncle Danny's live in girlfriend died tragically in a car accident, he moved in with Alessa's family.

"After all," Caterina told her husband, "we need the money. We can't keep this house going and raise the kids, if we don't get some help."

It was she, in fact, who had invited her brother to move in with them. Danny promptly accepted the offer and before they knew it, he had taken over one of the four bedrooms in their house and, along with it, Alessa's life.

When her uncle first moved in, the little girl was excited at the prospect of having him there. Uncle Danny loved her more than anyone else in the family did and was almost a substitute for her grandmother. He had an air of confidence about him that made Alessa feel utterly safe when she was by his side. He was generous and loving with her and made her feel special, like she was the only person on earth.

Grief-stricken and vulnerable and still fearful of the monsters that lurked in her imagination, she turned to Uncle Danny who found the perfect reason to console her. Shortly after he moved into her house, Alessa's uncle invited her to sleep in his bed. Just as she had done with her grandmother, the child would link her arm through his as she lay waiting to fall asleep. For the next several months, Alessa slept peacefully next to her protector, unafraid that the monsters of the night would attack her—until the night he raped her.

Alessa's parents knew that their youngest child had been sleeping in Danny's bed, but any concern they might have had over the situation was silenced when the income from their new tenant promptly alleviated their anxieties about how they would pay their bills. Caterina chose to believe her brother was in the mafia, a fact she took great pride in. She had a twisted view of reality and of the world in general. As far as she was concerned, the world revolved around this overgrown beast, her older brother. After all, he was paying her 750 dollars a month just to live in their house, a sum Alessa's whole family lived off. Her parents didn't go to work. Her father couldn't, because he had been disabled in combat during the war; and her mother just wouldn't, claiming she "needed" to stay home with the kids.

Until Uncle Danny moved in, the family had survived solely on welfare. In middle class circles, they were known as poor white trash. Alessa was the golden goose Caterina needed to indulge her unwillingness to work and keep her finances afloat. In a short period of time, the child became the ultimate sacrificial lamb, the bargaining chip her family could use to retain their home, buy the things they needed, and maintain the lifestyle they could ill afford otherwise.

The first time Alessa's uncle raped her, she felt isolated and helpless. The abuse became more frequent thereafter. It did occur to the child that she should tell her mother about her uncle's behavior, but Danny enjoyed a certain standing both in her family and in the neighborhood where they lived and she was not confident about being taken seriously. By abusing her, he had stripped her of all confidence and she felt entirely defenseless, unable to resist his assaults, and at times, she felt like it was her who had caused the abuse.

What confused Alessa even more was her uncle's assertion that whatever took place between them was a natural thing shared between two people who loved each other. After that first night, she had started sleeping in her own bed, but Uncle Danny would still wake her up in the middle of the night to quench his own sick desires. His six-foot-four-inch, two-hundred-and-seventy-five-pound body would crush her small frame so she could barely breathe in her tiny single bed.

About a year after he had started having his way with her, she woke up one night as he was thrusting his tongue into her vagina. She was still too young for pubic hair and Uncle Danny told her how much he liked her bald pussy. He was groaning and inserting his fingers inside her and grabbing at the small nipples on her completely flat chest. When he was sufficiently aroused, he shoved his penis in her face and ordered her to suck on it. When she hesitated, he grabbed the back of her head, forced her mouth open, pushed his penis between her small pink lips and repeated his order.

There were other occasions, when he would jam his thick fingers between her legs just to wake her up and have sex with her. He would be gentle, at first, but when his sexual excitement got the better of him, he would forget it was just a small child lying below him. He would ram himself further and further into her until he came. Her groin ached and she would feel as though his penis were encroaching right into spaces that lay beyond her ribcage. Her vagina was sore for days afterward, making it painful for her to urinate.

Sometimes, when the family was out, leaving the two of them alone at home, Uncle Danny would find her on the sofa watching television and tell her to unzip her pants. He would remove all of her clothing with slow deliberation and proceed to do whatever he was in the mood for that night.

When there was no one else in the house, he would groan and talk loudly during sex. Breathing heavily into her ear, he would tell her how much he loved her wet pussy and that she was the love of his life. He would grunt with each thrust as he ravaged her insides, finding his peculiar form of gratification between the small legs of a child. By the time Alessa was nine years old, this had become a nightly ritual for her uncle.

Year after year, the child lived cocooned in her own misery, feeling like a freak in every way imaginable. She had gradually come to understand that what her uncle was doing to her was far from normal or natural, but few options lay before her. With each passing year, she despised him more and withdrew further into herself. That monstrous being had come to consume her thoughts and her life, terrorizing her just like the imaginary monsters of the night had once done.

After she turned twelve, Uncle Danny wanted more from her. One night, she woke up to his customary groping. It was the middle of summer and the house had no air conditioning, except for the window units in her parents' and uncle's rooms. The heat was stifling and a thin film of sweat covered her small body, clad in old, worn baby-doll pajamas that were frayed around the neck and along the hem of the shirt. The pajamas, which she had worn for the last four summers, were too small for her now and barely covered her body. At twelve, Alessa knew she was too old to be wearing baby-doll pajamas. But she also knew there were many other things she shouldn't be doing, including putting up with her uncle's sick demands.

Uncle Danny quickly stripped off her baby-doll pajamas and commanded her to turn over and lie flat on her belly. As she complied, he slipped into the bed behind her. Wrapping his arm around her waist and pulling her up so that her weight rested on her knees, he slowly began to push his penis into her rectum. Little by little, he inched himself inside her until his penis was fully engulfed by her young, tender tissue.

This was the worst and most painful experience of all for Alessa. The other times had hurt too, especially in the beginning, but they were nothing compared to the pain she suffered at that moment. She felt mortified and humiliated. If she could have died there and then, she thought, it would have been a great release for her. She could smell her own feces and had to hold back the vomit that was threatening to gush forth from her mouth. The excruciating pain, as he ripped through her, was like fire scorching her insides. She was afraid he would tear her in half.

Through his harsh breathing, she heard him repeat, "This is good and tight." He kept telling her he loved her, until he came. Finally, he collapsed next to her on the tiny bed that barely had enough room for one person. She cried that night, until the tears wouldn't come anymore. And even when she finally fell asleep, there was no shelter from her pain. She dreamed of faceless men touching her, pawing her all over with their filthy hands. She couldn't escape the horrendous nightmare she was living through, not even in her sleep.

That terrible night, it finally dawned on her that the monsters she had always feared lived under her bed had never existed. The only real monster had a name: Uncle Danny, the ogre who had stripped her of her innocence and left nothing, but an empty shell. Her childhood, her very life, had been stolen from her. She no longer knew who she was; nor did she dare to contemplate her future. She had learned that life was flawed and just making it through each day would take all her strength and challenge her powers of endurance. Her rough childhood, robbed of its innocence, would arm her with the resilience to hold onto her sanity later in life.

Despite her moments of dark despair, Alessa had faith that she would eventually rise above the sordidness of her life and come through. Her belief in herself had been instilled early in life by her beloved grandmother who had chosen her name for her, imagining that she had seen something unique and exciting in the newborn. Alessa meant "defender of mankind". That is how her grandmother had visualized her when she looked into the baby's eyes and probed her soul. Despite Caterina's attempts to undermine her youngest child at every opportunity, Alessa's grandmother had been firm in her belief that one day, her favorite grandchild would be strong and resilient and the inspiration for many; but, most importantly, she would be a force to reckon with.

Chapter One

Caterina's foul temperament probably had as much to do with nurture as nature. Alessa's mother had stopped going to school after fourth grade so that she could work to help her parents pay their bills. Not only did the decision deprive her of an education, it also robbed her of all ambition and drive. Caterina had only one asset to fall back on: her good looks. And she was content to get by on them. Her body was lean, with curves that many women envied, and her legs were long and shapely. Her smile was inviting and she had jet-black hair, with a touch of curl, that fell in all the right places. Her deep olive complexion gave her an exotic look that men adored. There was no denying that she was a beautiful woman and since she was dirt poor and had nothing else to fall back on, she had no qualms about using that beauty to get everything she desired.

Caterina's lack of education had not stood in the way of mastering the art of manipulation. She could muster sympathy from a complete stranger in the street. She cried the blues about how poor they were and how her four kids needed to eat. Yet, no matter how much she complained, Caterina always looked great. She didn't wear expensive clothes, but her outfits were always new, perfectly accessorized with matching jewelry, sunglasses, shoes and purses. And she never left the house without her makeup in place.

As an adolescent, Alessa would always face the brunt of her mother's criticism, directed primarily at her lack of looks. Caterina often nagged her daughter, insisting that she wouldn't look quite so homely, if she just wore some makeup and fixed her hair. It never occurred to Alessa to retort that she and her siblings had always been less privileged than their mother, when it came to matching outfits, manicured nails and decent haircuts. The children rarely received new clothes and continued to use the same underwear, until the elastic on their panties and bras wore out. None of the children even owned their own toothbrush; they shared one between

1

the four of them. But it hardly mattered, because Caterina didn't provide them with toothpaste anyway. Only Caterina's bathroom boasted of such luxury. Naturally, the children's teeth were in poor condition. Alessa did the best she could with the little she had to work with, often sneaking up to her mother's bathroom to steal a squirt of toothpaste or deodorant before school.

Caterina disciplined her children by hitting them with a wooden spoon. She would bolt off in a huff to find it, so she could come back and beat the hell out of them for some misdemeanor or bad behavior. On one occasion, when she was beating her son, Anthony, the wooden spoon split into two. Unfazed, Caterina moved on to a metal spoon as the weapon of choice. As she struck one of her children with the spoon, she would scold him or her for whatever infraction the child had been guilty of and always ended her last three thrashings with, "I'll show you!"

Alessa's life during these years was a hollow one. The advantages of beauty, dignity, self-confidence and an appealing personality eluded her. What she lacked in looks and charisma, she made up for in maturity and in the ability to withdraw into her own mind. She had a vivid imagination and lived through the stories she heard other children narrate at school that spoke of the abundance of love they enjoyed at home and the fun they had with their own families. Alessa's classmates all had lives that were very different from hers. Through them and their description of their lives at home, she would build a beautiful imaginary world for herself.

But in reality, Alessa could never be carefree like the other kids her age. She had forgotten what it was to be a child. She had stopped believing in Santa Claus. Her reality was harsh and dark. From a very early age, she knew how different she was from the others and could never feel comfortable in her own skin.

The years of rape and abuse at the hands of her Uncle Danny had inadvertently taught her how to be a survivor. Deep in her soul, she knew that she would, one day, escape the nightmare she was living through, before it consumed her. She was determined that some day, she would have all the things she dreamed of, including real love and a family.

Shortly after her uncle sodomized her the first time, Alessa set herself the goal of escaping from his clutches. She summoned up the nerve to confide in her mother and tell her what had been happening. Terrified of Caterina's reaction, however, she practiced the conversation in her head for weeks before she actually gathered the courage to speak to her. Then, when she felt the moment was just right, she approached her mother who was in the kitchen, cooking dinner for the family. Waves of nausea rose from Alessa's stomach into the back of her throat. She could feel her heart pounding inside her chest as she approached her mother slowly.

Caterina saw her daughter standing idly in the kitchen and snapped, "What's wrong with you?"

"Mom," Alessa blurted out, "Uncle Danny has been doing things to me."

"What are you talking about? What kinds of things?" her mother asked angrily.

"He has been coming into my bedroom at night and doing things to me."

"What the fuck are you trying to say, girl?" Caterina's voice rose in indignation. "Everyone knows that Uncle Danny loves you. You don't complain when he brings you candy and things that you want, do you? Now, all of a sudden, he's doing things to you, is he? Don't you have the sense to realize that he is just being affectionate, because he loves you so much? Even your brother and sisters are jealous of how much attention he pays to you."

Caterina was screaming now and Alessa could feel herself begin to shut down. She was terrified that her mother would report everything back to Uncle Danny. She began to back out of the kitchen, sorry that she had made the mistake of confiding in her mother. Caterina hadn't even bothered to sit her down and question her in depth on this matter. Clearly, she did not care to understand or even acknowledge what her youngest child had just told her.

Instead, she went on, "Your Uncle Danny adores you. So when you hurl such accusations at him, you sound like a dirty little pig with a filthy little mind! You're rotten to the core! Go to your room right now before I get the spoon out and give you a good beating! That would straighten you out. And don't you go repeating this shit to people or they'll think something is wrong with *you*. You sound like a stupid little idiot by spewing out that stuff about Uncle Danny. He is good to us and helps out around here. We would never have been able to keep this house, if it weren't for him. Do you want to live on the streets? That's what we'd be doing, if he weren't here, helping us! *That's* what family is for. Now get out of my sight before I get really mad!"

It suited Caterina to live in denial. Accustomed to manipulating every situation in her life to get what she wanted, she preferred to ignore reality, even if it were staring her in the face, so long as it did not fit into her scheme of things. Certainly, she wouldn't allow herself to recognize the implications of what her daughter was telling her about her own brother, because that would mean having to do something about it, namely, ordering him out of the home. That would mean 750 dollars less every month. There was no way Caterina was going to give up easy income. The alternative would be to go out and get an actual job to support her family. She much preferred to pretend that Alessa was fabricating malicious tales and continue to collect her rent check.

Alessa turned and went back to her room, where she threw herself on the bed and cried. She was shocked and hurt that her mother not only refused to believe her, but seemed not to care about the situation at all. Instead, she had done her best to demoralize her daughter and threatened her with a beating. Alone in her misery, Alessa couldn't think of a single soul who might help her. She had no one to lean on, no one to talk to; she only had herself. She was determined to get away from this nightmare, get away from her uncle, away from all the pain and anguish he was causing her. She wanted to have nothing to do with the mother who had rejected her with such scorn. As soon as she was old enough, she would leave this house and never look back. She was desperate to believe she could escape this darkness and that there would be more to her life than this rotten place she called home.

Chapter Two

For a while, even school didn't offer Alessa a break from her misery. In junior high school, she had few friends. In fact, she had no real friends at all. Given her situation at home, she had always felt too much of an outcast to even try and make friends.

Alessa made her first friend when she was least expecting it. One afternoon, right before Easter break, she was in the school bathroom, washing her hands before going outside to where her creepy Uncle Danny was waiting to pick her up. Rhonda, one of the girls she knew from gym class, started talking to her. "Hey Alessa, how are you?" she asked. "Listen, there's this party tonight at the valley woods. They're getting a keg of beer and I wanted to know if you'd go with me. I live near your house. So I can come over and we can walk there together."

Stunned that someone was actually asking her to go somewhere, Alessa tried to remain calm as she replied, "Yeah, sure. Give me your phone number. I'll ask my mom and call you."

She was thrilled to be invited to a party. Even at the age of fourteen, she had never been to a party with teenagers and beer.

The moment she got home, she asked her mother about it.

"Who is this Rhonda girl?" Caterina asked at once. "How come I've never heard of her before?"

Alessa explained that she knew Rhonda from gym class. Just then, Anthony walked in on the conversation.

"Just let her go, Mom," he said. "She's like a little mutant. She doesn't have any friends and maybe, if she goes to the party, she will get some eventually."

Caterina agreed and told Alessa to be home by ten o'clock or she'd give her a beating.

Alessa ran to her bedroom to find something to wear. Of course, her selection was limited. She picked out her best jeans, a pair of hand-me-downs from her sister, Rosabella. The back pockets were slightly torn, but they would pass. Besides, she thought they fit her perfectly. Over them, she wore a plain black tee shirt, faded beyond its life, since it too, was a hand-me-down and had been washed so many times it had lost its shape. At least she wouldn't stand out in her outfit. Hopefully, if there was a God, she would just blend in with the rest of the crowd. Her hair wasn't much better than it used to be when she was younger. Although she had never actually had it cut and styled by a professional, it barely reached her shoulders. It was naturally curly and could have looked stylish with a professional cut and a little hair product to boost its shape and sheen.

When Rhonda arrived at Alessa's house, Caterina was surprisingly pleasant and warm. It was in her nature to go to great lengths to make people love and admire her, even if it happened to be her daughter's fourteen-year-old girlfriend. Rhonda was wearing a pair of brand new Jordache jeans and a new tube top with a rainbow on the front. Her long shiny brown hair was pulled back from her face in a perfect braid running down the center of her back. She wore a silver necklace, with a round turquoise pendant, the size of a quarter, dangling from it. Rhonda looked beautiful and Alessa immediately noticed the look of disapproval directed at her as her new friend silently assessed her appearance.

As the girls were preparing to leave, Uncle Danny entered the room walking towards them. Alessa wanted to scream, she could feel the evil lurking inside of him. This was the only friend who had ever come to her house and she started to sweat as he inched up and stood just a little too close to her. He turned and looked Rhonda over as if he knew a secret, shaking his head with his lips curled in a cruel smile. He turned to Caterina and opened his mouth as if he were going to say something, but instead dropped his head in disgust and walked over to his chair and sat down.

As they opened the door to leave, Caterina reminded her, "Alessa, don't forget your curfew."

Walking out the door, Alessa looked over at her Uncle Danny sitting in his chair in front of the television. As she closed the door behind her, she did not miss the scowl on his face. It not only signaled his obvious displeasure that he was being deprived of his pound of flesh, but hinted at the tortures that awaited her in her bedroom later.

Chapter Three

Once they were some distance from the house, Rhonda turned to Alessa and said, "Okay, let's spruce you up a bit. Turn around."

Alessa eagerly complied. Her new friend tugged hard on the back of the shapeless black tee shirt, twisting the fabric into a knot. Alessa was amazed at how snugly the shirt now fit and at the way she had gathered it at the back so that it was short enough in the front to expose the top of her navel. Then Rhonda turned Alessa around to face her and reached into her purse. She applied a dab of blue eyeshadow on her eyelids and defined her top and lower eyelids with black eyeliner. She took out two bobby pins from her purse and pinned Alessa's hair back on the sides. As a final touch, she rolled on bubble gum lip gloss. Then she looked critically at Alessa and said, "There, now we can go."

They were headed for a keg party at the Rope, which was located in a small wooded area in Plymouth Meeting, the small town in Pennsylvania where the girls lived. As they walked the mile or so to the place, Alessa asked her new friend, "Why do they call it 'the rope'?"

"Because there's a creek that runs through the woods in the place where we hang out and someone tied a thick rope on a big branch overhanging the creek. When people are fucked up, they jump on the rope and swing. Problem is, you have to make sure you get off before it stops swinging, because the creek is a ten-foot drop. It's so fucking cool! Wait until you see it."

When they arrived, a crowd of twenty other teenagers had already gathered. They were all standing in a loose circle around a keg of beer that stood in the center of the dirt floor. Alessa was terrified that the crowd of teenagers would either reject her because she didn't fit in or find out what she was doing with her Uncle Danny. Instead, they seemed not to notice her at all. Rhonda greeted several of the boys who immediately closed in and circled around her. Alessa noticed how the girls stared at her friend and whispered to each other, giggling and poking one another. Clearly, they had an issue with Rhonda. Must be jealousy, Alessa concluded.

Then Rhonda came over, grabbed her by the hand and led her to the keg. The girls filled up two plastic cups with beer and Rhonda offered up a toast: "To new friends!" she said. "We are going to have so much fun together." Alessa sipped at the beer while her friend chugged it down and filled another glass for herself. As the night wore on, Alessa watched as Rhonda worked the boys in the wooded area. They were all clearly enamored by her. And she sure was a beauty! Alessa sat on a log and took it all in.

Finally, one of the other girls came over and sat on the log with her. "You know that Rhonda is a slut, right?" she remarked.

"No, I didn't know that," Alessa responded.

"Well, if you hang with her, everyone is going to think you're a slut too."

Alessa looked at the girl she was meeting for the first time and said, "Maybe I am a slut too, what's wrong with being a slut? Just because people have sex doesn't mean they're bad. Maybe you should try it sometime. Another thing: Rhonda is my friend. So you should stop saying mean things about her to me. You and those girls are just jealous of her."

Enraged by the tone of Alessa's voice, the stranger lifted her hand and slapped her across the face, sending her flying backward off the log. The girl came around to where she lay sprawled on her back, reached down and pulled her to her feet by the collar of her tee shirt. Then she backhanded her across the face again. Alessa collapsed on the dirt and lay flat on her back. After a swift kick to her right thigh, the girl straddled her, looking down at her with a sinister grin. Alessa could now make out that the girl's two front teeth weren't real. Denise moved to the side of Alessa and stood, watching her with malice. She picked herself up, stunned, but kept her eyes on the ground, afraid to make eye contact with her assailant. She was petrified by the violence she had faced. She hadn't seen it coming and regretted that she hadn't just kept her mouth shut and her opinions to herself.

When Alessa finally looked up at the girl to gauge what her intentions were, Rhonda ran over with two of the boys who had been hanging all over her and said sharply, "Denise, cut her a break. She doesn't even know you!"

The girl called Denise just stared back at Rhonda with contempt.

"Come on, Denise," one of the boys cut in, "she's a loser. Just leave her alone. Look at her! She's scared to death. You made your point."

Studying Alessa, Denise seemed satisfied that she had terrorized her sufficiently. Then she turned back to the crowd of teenagers.

The boy who had spoken up turned to Rhonda and said, "Come on, Rho! Let's go into the woods."

Rhonda turned and followed a trail that led into the woods, leaving Alessa there by herself with the other kids who had gathered around to gawk at the scene that had taken place.

Her thigh still throbbing from Denise's kick and her face burning from the slaps she had received, Alessa went over to the keg and filled herself a fresh cup of beer. She stood there and guzzled the beer until it was gone. Then she filled another glass and walked back to the log she had been sitting on earlier. She sat alone and continued to drink her beer, trying to absorb what had just happened.

One of the boys came over and sat beside her. He was tall and thin, with black hair that came down to his shoulders. He had a nice smile and his voice was husky and tender when he spoke. "Hey," he said, "I'm Carl. You doing okay?"

"Yeah, I guess," Alessa conceded. "I'm not really sure why that girl got so mad. She was talking shit on Rhonda. So I defended her. Next thing I knew, she's pounding on me. Who is she?"

"Her name is Denise. Nobody fucks with her. She can kick most of the guys' asses here." Carl lowered his voice to a soft, deep whisper. "She's a really good fighter. She learned how to fight, after she got her ass kicked in seventh grade and lost two of her front teeth. She took boxing and karate lessons. She's fucking crazy and you should never disagree with anything she says. No matter what crazy shit she tells you, just pretend to agree with it. That's what the rest of us do; we let her think she's right."

"I wish I'd known," Alessa said regretfully.

"What did you say to her that made her freak out on you?" he persisted.

"She called Rhonda a slut and I stuck up for her."

"Oh, that will do it!" Carl was shaking his head from side to side, indicating to Alessa that she was guilty of a serious infraction. "Denise can't stand Rhonda, but doesn't mess with her, because she knows all the boys will stick up for her. She just hates her."

"Why does she hate her so much?"

"Rhonda gets a lot of attention from the guys in our group," Carl explained. "She will do shit that the other girls won't."

"Like what?" Alessa asked.

"You know, she'll mess around with us." He looked at Alessa for a moment, then said, "Rho will have sex with any one of us, if we want her to. She likes to have sex and that pisses the other girls off, because they're all a bunch of prudes. So Rhonda gets more attention from us guys then the other girls do." He went on, "Not to mention that she is hot and has great tits!"

Alessa blushed at his description of her new friend's breasts, but a smile broke out on her face, nonetheless. "So, is that why she went into the woods with that other guy?" she couldn't help asking.

"Pretty much. She'll be back, though. In the meantime, you want to smoke a joint?"

"I don't know. I've never smoked a joint."

Carl reached into his shirt pocket, pulled out a joint and lit it. He took a long, hard drag on it and held his breath. Then he handed it to Alessa who mimicked what he had just done.

Denise was watching them as she walked over to Alessa. "Gimme a hit," she said with authority.

Alessa had no idea what she was talking about and Carl quickly leaned over and explained, "She wants some of the joint."

Alessa quickly handed the joint to Denise. Afraid to even look at her, she kept her eyes fixed on the ground.

"You know, we're cool now," Denise said, handing back the joint. "You just pissed me off with what you said before. So are we cool?"

Alessa lifted her head and looked at her. "Yeah, we're cool," she replied, though she wanted to scream: *sure we're cool! Fuck you and the horse you rode in on, you bitch bull dike! I have survived torture and pain from the inside out and you are nothing more than a walking piece of shit!*

She would never dare say all that aloud to Denise for fear of provoking her into violence again, but in her mind, she was free to think it and find refuge from Denise's fury.

Alessa had been sitting with Carl on the log and talking for an hour by the time Rhonda reappeared. Her hair was tousled and the rainbow on her tube top now sat off-center.

"You doing okay?" she asked Alessa, throwing Carl a suspicious glance.

"She's doing fine, Rho," he retorted. "Fix your tube top, will ya?"

Rhonda looked down at herself and giggled as she readjusted the rainbow to center it on her perfect, B-cup breasts. When it was time to leave the Rope and walk home, Carl got up and accompanied the two girls to the end of the woods. Here he stopped. Rhonda looked at him, nodded and moved off to wait for Alessa at some distance from the spot.

Carl looked down at Alessa and said, "I liked talking to you tonight. You're pretty cool."

With that, he bent down and kissed her. Alessa was seasoned and knew just how to kiss him back. As he felt the depth of her kiss, Carl reached down between her legs and gently drew his hand across the outside of her jeans. She had been touched, rubbed, jabbed and banged there so many times before, but this touch was different. Alessa was confused and unsure as to whether it was the effect of the joint she had smoked or the presence of Carl that was causing a rush of excitement to flow through her veins, making her dizzy and warm inside.

Just then, Rhonda called out, "Let's go, Alessa! We need to get home."

Alessa said goodbye to Carl, turned and ran toward the place where her friend was waiting for her. On their way home, Rhonda asked, "Carl is pretty cool, huh?"

"Yeah, I like him. At least, he was willing to talk to me, while you were off with that guy. So what were you doing in the woods with him anyway?"

Rhonda beamed and turned to Alessa excitedly. "Giving him a blow job. Uh, you know what a blow job is, don't you?"

Alessa thought to herself: *yeah, I have been giving them since I was eight years old*! But instead, she said, "Yeah, I know what it is. You sucked his dick, right?"

Rhonda laughed at her friend's candor while Alessa thought to herself, if giving a blow job made Rhonda a slut, maybe she was a slut too.

On their way home, they talked incessantly with each other. Rhonda had observed there was something different about this girl. Unlike the other girls in her grade, Alessa didn't seem jealous of her or disgusted with her for going off to have sex in the woods. This girl seemed to understand her. Rhonda liked her and knew instinctively that they would become the best of friends.

When they got to Alessa's house, Rhonda said, "I'll call you tomorrow. There's another party at the Rope. If you want to come, you can."

Relieved that she finally had a person her own age to hang out with, Alessa answered, "That would be great! I had fun tonight—after my ass-beating was over anyway."

The two girls giggled and hugged and Alessa headed back into her house of horrors.

Chapter Four

---◼---

Going to the Rope became a regular weekend event for Alessa and Rhonda. By summer, they had come to depend on each other. Rhonda was generous with her clothes and makeup. Alessa readily accepted all the help she could get to improve her appearance.

Meanwhile, things hadn't changed much for her at home. Uncle Danny was still the pedophile he had always been, except that now, he was meaner, because he resented her growing friendship with Rhonda.

"That Rhonda is trouble," he would tell his sister, Caterina. "You shouldn't let Alessa go out with her."

For the first time in Alessa's life, however, her mother's ignorance and self-absorption worked in her favor. Caterina couldn't care less, as long as her daughter stayed out of her hair and didn't get into trouble. But she did use the opportunity to warn her to behave.

"Don't you go doing things with any boys," Caterina warned.

"What things, Mom?"

"Like letting them touch you where they shouldn't. Don't you come home and tell me you're pregnant; if you do, I'll kill you."

The thought of pummeling her mother to death flashed through Alessa's mind for an instant. It was ironic how worried Caterina professed to be about "boys", when her own brother had been raping her daughter since she was a child. Alessa loathed her mother for her failure or unwillingness to see the truth and for not only doubting her word, but threatening to beat her, if she made another allegation against her Uncle Danny. And now, the selfish fool, Caterina was suddenly concerned about Alessa's sex life! Although she was only fourteen, Alessa knew that her mother was a nut job, a self-centered woman who would never be able to help anyone other than herself. However, it didn't matter quite as much, ever since she had found comfort in her friendship with Rhonda.

Alessa slept over at Rhonda's place whenever she could, denying Uncle Danny the opportunity to embark every night on his free sexual adventure. She and Rhonda confided in each other, but kept her relationship with her uncle a deep, dark secret. Noticing that Alessa had grown closer to Carl, Rhonda promised not to "do him", out of loyalty to her friend. By the end of summer, Alessa and Carl were taking off their clothes and making out in the woods on a blanket that all the Rope kids used. While they were into a lot of heavy petting and engaging in oral sex, neither of them considered that as officially having sex, because they hadn't had intercourse yet. Alessa always told Rhonda everything she did in the woods with Carl.

Lying in her friend's bed one Saturday night after a party at the Rope, Alessa was taken aback when Rhonda asked her, "So when are you going to have real sex with him?"

"I don't know," she replied uncertainly. "He keeps asking me, but I'm afraid of getting pregnant. My mother threatened to kill me, if I did."

"Have you had an orgasm yet?" Rhonda asked.

Alessa shook her head vigorously. Rhonda turned on her side to face her. Then she tugged Alessa's underwear away to the side and began to caress her between her legs. Alessa started to experience the sensation that often gripped her when she was with Carl. As Rhonda continued teasing her with her feather-soft touch, her friend began craving for more. When Rhonda's fingers stilled for just a few seconds, Alessa thought she would go insane. At fourteen, Rhonda was an expert. She knew exactly how to drive her girlfriend to the brink of sexual insanity and leave her hovering there. Alessa looked up at Rhonda with crazed eyes that begged her to continue with what she had been doing or she would surely die.

Rhonda reached down and began to caress her softly again. At the same time, she leaned in to kiss Alessa's lips, parting them lightly with her probing tongue. With Rhonda still fondling her, the two kissed. Alessa's back arched and her body felt electrified, weightless with a desire she had never known before. At just the right moment, Rhonda slipped her fingers into her. With infinite gentleness, she slid them in and out until Alessa couldn't take it anymore and her first orgasm exploded within her. Rhonda rolled onto her back and stared up at the ceiling.

"That is an orgasm," she announced.

Alessa's response was barely audible. "That was the most incredible feeling I've ever had in my whole life!"

14

Rhonda giggled, proud to have given her friend her first orgasm, and they talked into the night until they had both fallen asleep.

The next morning, after showering and eating breakfast, they headed down to the playground at Plymouth Elementary School. There was a dodgeball game on and Rhonda quickly joined the crowd, throwing and catching the ball for her team. Alessa wasn't particularly athletic and decided to sit it out. Carl was there too. As she watched him play, she realized how much she liked him. He had been so nice to her all summer and Alessa wondered to herself if Carl could ever make her feel the way Rhonda had the night before.

After the game was over Alessa, Rhonda, Carl and half a dozen other boys and girls walked over to the Plymouth Meeting Mall for lunch at Roy Rogers. Alessa was truly happy when she was with Rhonda and Carl; her friendships with them ensured that the rest of the group accepted her. When she was with the two of them, she felt like a normal teenager.

After lunch, Rhonda and Alessa went into the Gap and laughed as they tried on jeans and tee shirts. Alessa enjoyed the experience, because she didn't get new clothes too often. Even when she did get a new shirt or a pair of pants, it was never two items at the same time. And there was no way her mother would ever buy her clothes from the Gap; she only shopped at K-Mart in Norristown.

Having got used to the idea of not receiving new clothes from Caterina, Alessa had ceased to long for them. Accepting the limitations of her reality was what kept her sane and enabled her to see the truth in other people. Alessa had no doubts at all that her mother was self-centered, her father little more than a shadow and her uncle a perverted asshole. This was a situation she would have to come to terms with on her own, for her siblings weren't around often enough to help her through it. In fact, other than Rosabella, she hardly knew them. She had come to understand that Rhonda was her true confidante, even though she could never bring herself to disclose what her Uncle Danny had been doing to her all her life.

Alessa had dinner at Rhonda's that night. Her friend lived with her mother, Zoe, who was single. Alessa thought she was the coolest woman on earth. Quite unlike her own mother, Zoe was charming and beautiful and had long, curly, light brown hair. Dressed in tie-dye shirts and jeans, she had an elegance about her that mesmerized Alessa. To her, Zoe seemed like she was always barefoot, happy and engrossed in all the music that the girls loved. When they were with her, they ate fish sticks and French fries, TV dinners and Ellio's pizza. In this hideaway, Alessa was able to enjoy all the luxuries her own mother had insisted were "too damn expensive to buy." Zoe was also the first person who told her that she had pretty eyes.

"Your eyes are warm, Alessa," she had said, "because they are such a light brown. It's like I can see into your soul. You have a good soul, Alessa. I can see it."

Alessa loved Zoe almost from the moment she met her. Whenever she was at Rhonda's house, watching Hitchcock and eating Jiffy Pop popcorn—another food Caterina had condemned as a waste of money—she felt like she belonged. Her nights with Rhonda and Zoe ensured that she was safe from her Uncle Danny and even though Zoe had a different guy friend sleeping over every weekend, they were all very nice to the girls.

Over time, Alessa became a permanent fixture at Rhonda's house on weekends. Her friend had become aware of how different she was during the week—more withdrawn and sad. The Monday morning before Easter break, while they were changing for gym class, Rhonda noticed a bruise on Alessa's inner thigh. It hadn't escaped her that her friend just wasn't herself that day, and decided to ask her about the mark on her thigh.

"I don't know," Alessa replied, averting her gaze.

Sensing that something was wrong and that she was not willing to discuss it, Rhonda let the subject drop. Alessa would never have confessed to anyone that the bruise had come from her Uncle Danny's big fingers burrowing into her thigh the night before. For the first time, she had made an attempt to resist him, knowing that he would use brute force to get his way anyway, by locking her thighs together. Uncle Danny hadn't been in the mood to tolerate any resistance, however. He had grabbed her thin thighs and forced them apart.

"After all, I own you," he had said to Alessa when he was finished with her.

By Easter break, the two young teens had been friends for a year. They shared everything with each other—except Carl. Alessa hadn't yet had intercourse with him. Nor had she had an orgasm since her first one with Rhonda. She didn't dare tell her friend why she couldn't have an orgasm with Carl. Alessa knew it was because every time he touched her, she thought of her uncle. Over the last six months, Carl had grown so insistent about having sex that it didn't seem like it would be special anymore, when it did eventually happen.

At a party at the Rope over Easter break, Alessa and Carl were in the woods, making out. They were both naked. Drunker than usual, Carl was sexually charged. His passion was obvious as they kissed and touched each other, breathing heavily and enjoying the moment. Carl said what he always did. "Come on, Alessa, let's make love."

"No, Carl," she answered, "I don't want to get pregnant. Plus, I want it to be special."

"Oh come on, Alessa, just a little bit," he urged, climbing on top of her.

Alessa started giggling. "No, Carl, stop it," she said, "and you know why too. Come on, stand up and I'll give you a blow job."

Carl was too drunk to pay attention. He stayed on top of her and, without warning, entered her with a quick, hard thrust. Alessa was startled and scared. Why would Carl do this to her? She had told him firmly that she didn't want to. She tried to push him off, but Carl pinned her arms above her head and his strong thighs held her legs in place, as he thrust into her over and over again until he was satisfied.

When it was over, he came to his senses and realized what he had done. "Oh my God, Alessa!" he exclaimed remorsefully. "I am so sorry. I was just so excited I couldn't stop myself. Please don't hate me. Please…"

Although the experience wasn't foreign to her, Alessa was surprised by what had just happened. Catching her breath, she said, "It's okay, Carl. I just can't let myself get pregnant."

Just then, a thought struck her. Her gut began to twist and her lungs felt so constricted it was hard to take a breath. If Carl could get her pregnant, so could her Uncle Danny! Alessa began to heave, as her stomach gave way to fear and anxiety. She would rather die, if her disgusting uncle made her pregnant! Her Uncle Danny, the pig of all pigs, scum of the earth.

Confused, Carl didn't know how to deal with the situation. He supported Alessa by the shoulders, until she had finished wretching. Then dressing quickly, he helped her to put her clothes on and guided her gently out of the woods and back to the Rope. Alessa looked over at the others, boys and girls laughing and yelling, a bunch of teenagers having fun, and realized, once again, how different she was. There was no doubt in her mind that she was damaged goods, scarred forever by her childhood. She would never be like the others. She wondered if she could ever enjoy peace of mind, having experienced nothing, but turmoil for seven long years from the time her uncle had chosen her as his sex toy. And as she watched her peers, drunk and a bit out of control, she wondered if she would ever feel as happy and carefree as they did.

Deep down, Alessa was aware that no normal girl her age would have reacted the way she had. She had actually assured Carl it was okay that he had forced himself on her. She knew her response was perverse. But so imprisoned had she become by now to sexual abuse, it didn't elicit the response it would have from a normal teenage girl emerging from a forced sexual encounter. Alessa knew how fucked up she was for being less upset about being violated than about getting pregnant. She felt like a mutant.

When Rhonda saw how pale her friend was, she ran over to her and had her sit on one of the logs. Denise, the bully, was staring at Alessa, a nasty smile playing on her lips. Alessa caught her eye and thought to herself, "Please God, not tonight. Do not let Denise beat my fucking ass tonight."

Carl read the fear in her eyes and followed her gaze. Then he caught the malicious look in Denise's eyes. Stepping in front of Alessa, he blocked her view. Whispering to Rhonda that it was time for them to leave, he helped Alessa to her feet and walked her out of the Rope. Although there was silence between them, Rhonda guessed something had gone terribly wrong. But she kept her questions to herself, waiting to ask them when she was alone with Alessa.

Rhonda detected that Carl was being unusually attentive to her friend and figured they had had a fight earlier. Or perhaps, Alessa had found out that he was getting blow jobs from some of the other girls at school. She had no idea, of course, that he had been cheating. Technically speaking, they weren't in an exclusive relationship; nor had they said as much to each other.

When the three of them reached Alessa's house, Carl turned to her and kissed her on the cheek. "I'll call you tomorrow, okay?" he asked.

"Yeah, fine," she answered.

Once he had left, Rhonda asked, "How about if I sleep over at your house tonight? Do you think your mom would mind?"

Comforted by the thought of her friend staying with her, Alessa replied, "I'm sure she wouldn't. Let's go and ask her."

Rhonda followed her friend into the house. Caterina was perched on her usual sofa in the living room, watching television. Alessa's father was in a recliner on the left and Uncle Danny overwhelmed his recliner on the right. Both men were smoking big fat cigars and Rhonda cringed at the pungent smell and cloudiness of the smoke filled room.

Caterina said, "Well, you're home early. What happened?"

"Nothing happened," Alessa replied. "Rhonda and I were just tired. Would it be okay if she slept over tonight?" Her tone was pleading.

Caterina turned her head away. Alessa knew she didn't like her to have friends sleep over; she had enough mouths to feed already. Her mother now said, "I guess it's okay if Rhonda's mom says she can."

Quickly, Alessa guided her friend through the smoked-filled room and into the kitchen, from where Rhonda could call her mother. As she passed Uncle Danny, she could see his jaws tighten with rage. For an instant, she wanted to curl her fingers into a fist and punch him in the face so that his hated features were obliterated forever into a soggy mass of flesh. He knew tonight was going to be a sexless one for him and the thought was obviously pissing him off.

Chapter Five

Out of earshot in Alessa's bedroom, Rhonda turned to her. "What happened tonight?" she inquired. "Did you and Carl have a fight?"

Alessa explained how the boy had forced himself on her while making out.

Rhonda was incredulous. "What a piece of shit!" she exclaimed angrily. "He's going to be real sorry he did that to you!"

"It's okay, Rhonda," Alessa replied. "I don't really care about the sex part. I'm just worried about getting pregnant. He didn't use a rubber."

For some odd reason, she felt the need to defend Carl. Rhonda calmed down a bit, once she had understood what was upsetting Alessa. But she was still intent on warning Carl that if he ever forced himself on her friend again, she would kill him. And it was time she confronted him about the blow jobs he was also getting from other girls at school.

Rhonda managed to alleviate Alessa's worries about being pregnant, assuring her that it wasn't a big deal. Even if the worst happened, she could always get an abortion. Carl would have to pay for it, of course. Alessa managed to put the evening's events, along with Carl and Uncle Danny, away in her mind for the time being and just focused on enjoying Rhonda's company.

They were listening to Lynyrd Skynyrd on Alessa's radio when Rhonda remarked, "Your Uncle Danny is kind of creepy. Whenever I'm around, he looks at me weird. I noticed he always has this mean expression when he is looking at you. What's up with him?"

"He's just a miserable prick," Alessa blurted out, with more anger in her voice than she had intended to reveal. "I ignore him and you should too. I don't really give a fuck what he thinks. My family is just plain fucked up."

21

Rhonda laughed as she thought about her own family—her mother. Zoe was a good person and Rhonda loved her very much. But she did have some peculiarities too, starting with all the men she brought home. That, of course, was how Rhonda had sexually matured way ahead of her time and become promiscuous as a young teenager. Zoe was very open about sex and her daughter had never felt uncomfortable about being sexually active. She knew about birth control, abortions, adoptions and all the other things that women far older than her were usually aware of. Rhonda had never needed to worry about getting pregnant, because she had been on the pill since she had started her period at the age of twelve. Of course, Zoe had advised her not to tell the boys she was on the pill; that was the only way she could convince them to use a rubber.

"After all," Rhonda's mother explained, "the pill may prevent pregnancy, but it doesn't prevent disease."

Alessa was aware that her friend's knowledge and experience of sex went far beyond her fourteen years. She envied Rhonda for having a mother who cared enough about her daughter to teach her things she needed to know. Even if the "things" involved methods of having protected sex.

On Sunday night, Alessa was lying in bed trying to sleep, when she heard Uncle Danny creep into her bedroom. This man, she thought, was someone she had adored before he began abusing her seven years ago. Now he was the most despicable creature in the world, where she was concerned. He slipped under her covers and began undressing her with his large, rough hands. As he licked at her breasts, which were small for a fourteen-year-old's, the sweat from his forehead dripped onto her chest, making her skin crawl. The unpleasant sensation paled in comparison, however, to the feeling of rug burn that her young skin suffered as his fat belly rubbed against it when he climbed on top of her and began thrusting his penis inside her. She stared up at the ceiling, mentally trying to escape this hell, until he collapsed on her like a dead whale. Everything about him repulsed her—his look, his smell, his touch. Just the fact that he breathed at all enraged her.

"You know," Alessa ventured, "I think we need to stop this. I could get pregnant. How would I explain that to Mom?"

Uncle Danny sat up on the edge of the small bed. "You will never need to explain anything, because I'm sterile. So if you ever get pregnant, it certainly won't be by me. You think I'm stupid or something? I know what you're trying to do. You're looking for a reason to break this thing off. Well, listen good: you will always belong to me, until you move out of here or I die, whichever comes first. If you tell your mother about us, she will never believe you anyway. I'm her brother. She will always believe me over you. And if you try any tricks, I will deny everything. Don't start any shit with me. I have been good to you all your life. I have bought you things and paid for stuff you needed. If it weren't for me, your mom and dad would have lost this house. You're an ungrateful little bitch!"

With that, he rose to his big cinderblock feet and thumped out of the bedroom. Alessa lay there and thought to herself: *what the hell does "sterile" mean?* She would ask Rhonda at school.

"Hey Rhonda," she called out, when she saw her friend the next morning.

"Hey Alessa, what's going on?"

"Nothing's going on. Just another stupid Monday. I hate Mondays."

Rhonda moved up close to prevent anyone passing by from overhearing what she had to say. "When is your period due?" she asked. "You will want to keep an eye on the date, because they won't do abortions after you've been pregnant for a while. *If* you are pregnant, which I doubt."

"It's due in a week. By the way, do you know what it means when a man is sterile?" Alessa asked.

"Yeah, it means they can't get women pregnant, because their fish are dead," Rhonda giggled.

"Their fish are dead? What does *that* mean?"

"Their sperm doesn't have whatever it takes to get a girl pregnant. Why? Who is sterile?" Rhonda asked, barely suppressing curiosity.

"No one we know," Alessa quickly replied. "I heard my parents talking about one of their friends last night and they said he was sterile and I just figured you would know what that meant." This answer put a halt to their conversation.

As Alessa left Rhonda to rush to her first-period class, she thought to herself: *so the fucking bastard can't get me pregnant? That's why he never wears rubbers or even cares if I get my period. Motherfucker!* She knew she would just have to wait until next week to see if she got her period. If she didn't, she would take care of it. For now, she would try to put it out of her mind and avoid Carl at all costs. She didn't feel like seeing him again. She was annoyed with him and his lack of self-control. Even though he had been nice to her afterward, she couldn't risk it happening again. Besides, she had wanted it to be special; he had taken even that away from her. Hell, she hadn't even had an orgasm with him yet!

A week later, Alessa got her period and squealed with delight when she saw Rhonda in the cafeteria at lunch. The two girls hugged and Rhonda told her she would give her a couple of condoms, just in case she decided she wanted to do it with Carl again. Alessa agreed that it was a good idea to have condoms, but silently doubted that she would be using them with Carl. In fact, since the last time with him, she had lost all desire to see him. She neither missed him nor wanted to be around him. It was as if her feelings for him had been shut off in an instant, like water from a spigot.

Alessa kept Carl at a distance for the next week. Finally, he approached her at school and asked, "What's going on? Are you avoiding me? I said I was sorry. What the hell do you want from me?"

"Nothing. I have been busy lately. That's all," Alessa lied.

They stood in the hallway next to her school locker, looking at one another awkwardly. Both of them knew their fling was over. Carl was relieved. He liked being with whomever he wanted and not having to sneak around in case Alessa found out. Alessa herself had no feelings at all about the matter. She just wanted to be free of him. Carl had gone too far and she thought he was weak and selfish. After all, she hadn't been a prude; they had been enjoying themselves until Mr. Can't-Hold-Back-Any-Longer had lost control and gone ahead to satisfy his own desire.

Unable to handle the tension between them another second, Carl said, "Well, I guess I'll see you later."

As she watched him walk away, a feeling of peace settled over Alessa. She was not confrontational; nor was she used to telling people what she thought of them. Not even those who hurt her. She was raised to silently accept whatever shit people chose to dish out to her.

She saw Rhonda in the cafeteria and told her about what had happened with Carl.

Rhonda listened intently. Then she said, "Whatever, fuck him! You don't need him anyway. Besides, it sounds like you're glad that you two aren't dating anymore. On to bigger and better. Did I say 'bigger'?" Rhonda giggled.

The two girls fell into conversation after that and discussed what the upcoming weekend would bring. Alessa found her friend's presence immensely comforting. Rhonda always seemed to understand her and knew what would be the right thing to say in a given situation. In Rhonda, Alessa had found a piece of her own self that was missing—a wise, but wild soul, with the courage to soar to heights beyond anyone's imagination. Rhonda wasn't fearful of anything or anyone. Alessa wanted so much to be like her, to have her confidence and her ability to stay grounded. Most of all, she longed for the strength she admired in her friend.

When Friday night came, Rhonda and Alessa headed down to the Rope for a keg party. The party was already in full swing by the time they got there. The guys were tapping the keg. The girls were all huddled together like a pack of morons, Alessa thought. These girls were so ridiculous. They sat around, drinking beer and gossiping about everyone. Every now and then, they would make out with one of the guys for ten minutes so they could run back to their circle and tell the rest of the drones whether or not the boy was a good kisser.

As Rhonda and Alessa were filling their first beer, they saw Carl approaching from one of the paths to the Rope. It was dark by then and they could make out that he was walking with someone. When they reached the opening, Rhonda and Alessa recognized Carl's companion; it was Denise. *Oh God*, Alessa thought to herself, *the last thing I need is Carl turning Denise against me.*

Denise seemed different that night. She was quieter than usual. And then Alessa saw that Carl was holding her hand. Having noticed Alessa staring at the two of them, Denise smirked at her, as if to say, "Fuck you!"

Rhonda was oblivious to what was going on. She was drinking her second beer already and the boys were flocking to her like flies to shit. Alessa wandered into the woods to pee, but just as she found her spot, she heard footsteps coming down the path behind her. She paused and saw Denise approaching. As Denise drew closer and sensed Alessa's fear, her face brightened with gleeful malice. Denise liked the girls to be scared of her; it was the only power she could exercise over her limited, pathetic existence.

She now walked up and stood so close to Alessa that she actually caught a whiff of Carl's musky cologne. It was a sweet, masculine aroma that made her gut twist in knots. Suddenly, she felt on edge.

Denise broke the silence. "Listen, bitch," she said. "Carl asked me out and we're together now. If I ever find out that you're with him again, I will kill you. I had told you before that you were a slut; someone like Carl isn't going to stay hooked up with a slut."

With one quick motion, she poked her fingers into Alessa's sternum, causing her to stumble backward.

It was clear that Denise drew energy off Alessa's fear. It made her swell with delusions of power. She stepped closer and asked, "You got a problem with that, don't you? You wish you could kick my ass, don't you? I know you want to hit me. So go ahead, do it."

"No Denise, I don't want to hit you," Alessa replied. "I hope that you and Carl are happy together. Really."

Denise looked at her, inched closer and punched her in the stomach. Alessa doubled over in pain and tried to catch her breath.

"You're so fucking pathetic!" Denise declared. "Little Miss Innocent, living in her perfect little world!"

With that, she slapped Alessa across the face, turned on her heel and yelled, "Later!" as she walked back down the trail to the Rope.

Alessa gathered herself and finished peeing, before she returned to the Rope. All she could think about was the "perfect little world" Denise had referred to. She realized that she had become so skillful at hiding the truth about her life that others thought it was perfect. Alessa's stomach was sore and her face was still stinging from Denise's slap.

The moment Rhonda saw her, she knew something was wrong. Rushing over to her friend, she asked, "Where were you? I saw Denise come off the same trail about five minutes ago. What happened? Are you okay?"

"Yeah, I'm fine. Just a quick shot to the stomach and a hard slap to the face. The way I see it, I got off easy." Alessa tried to smile and make light of it and ease Rhonda's worry, but it wasn't working.

"Why did she hit you?"

"Because, apparently, she and Carl are going out now and I was being warned to keep off her turf. She's an ugly, rotten bitch and has to threaten people to keep them away from her man. I hate her, Rhonda! She's a fucking bully! She's like a guy, you know. She's so rough she's more like a boy. I really don't see why Carl would even want to be with her."

Rhonda looked at her. Then she said something that would stay with her for the rest of her life.

"Alessa, you're a very special person. Inside you, there is energy, a force waiting to come out. People see it. People can sense it, when they are around you. You have an appeal that's different, an attractiveness that makes others wonder what makes you tick. You are a mystery to people and that intimidates them. It's what you are on the inside that makes people like Denise jealous and fearful of you. There is a power, a quiet storm within you and people sense that. Before I got to know you, I had seen it too. It's why no one really talks to you. You have something they all lack and that's heart and soul."

"I have no idea what you're talking about," Alessa said. She had never given it any thought.

"Someday, you will know what I'm talking about. I don't know how, but you will finally wake up and see the person that everyone else does."

Rhonda's words penetrated deep. They made Alessa nervous and uncomfortable. Suddenly, she realized that Rhonda was describing a survivor. Although she never thought about it, Alessa understood now that this was exactly what she was. What she didn't know was that being a survivor was exactly what had got her through each day. For the first time in her life, she was aware of her inner strength and her dormant power. This awareness was the precious gift Rhonda would give her and one for which Alessa would be eternally grateful.

Chapter Six

By the time Alessa's sixteenth birthday came around, she and Rhonda were closer than ever. They had come to care for each other deeply. However, Alessa still hadn't told Rhonda the truth about Uncle Danny. While he continued with his pedophile ways and did whatever he pleased to her as she lay in her bed, Alessa had mastered a form of passive self-defense; she had learned how to retreat deep into her own mind and lock herself in so that she remained unaffected by it all. However, spending a great deal of time with Rhonda and her mother had taught her to become more outspoken. She looked upon them as family and found a mother in the warm and big-hearted Zoe, who sensed something was not quite right with Alessa and went out of her way to give her the feeling of security and belonging that her own parents could not. She enjoyed the hours she spent at their house, all the more so, because it allowed her to escape momentarily from her Uncle Danny's clutches.

Having enough to contend with at home, Alessa hadn't had the heart to hook up with any of the other boys after her break up with Carl. They hadn't talked in almost a year. Carl didn't even dare make eye contact with her anymore. He was still going steady with Denise and knew only too well there would be hell to pay, if he so much as acknowledged Alessa's existence in his girlfriend's presence. Denise, for her part, always seemed on edge when Alessa was around. She would mock her in the presence of others, especially when Rhonda was off in the woods with one of the boys.

As for the other girls at the Rope, Alessa found them as annoying as ever. The gossiping bitches that they were, none of them would really talk to her, other than to say "Hi" to her on occasion. And even when they did, the expression in their eyes left no doubt that they were being judgmental.

Once in a while, one of them would yell out, "Hey Alessa, maybe you should grow a pair of tits so that Rhonda's shirts fit you better. What's wrong? Don't you have any clothes of your own? Parents too poor to buy them for you? Is that why you have to wear Rhonda's stuff? You're such a loser!"

Rhonda would urge Alessa to ignore them attributing their rudeness to their stupidity. Still, it wasn't easy being constantly made fun of by the others. Denise would feed into the girls' meanness. When Alessa showed up one evening at the Rope wearing a new pair of sneakers that her mother had bought her at K-Mart, Denise was over whispering to all the little drones. Suddenly, they all broke out in song.

"Bobos," they crooned, "they make your feet feel fine; Bobos, they cost a dollar ninety-nine!"

"Hey Alessa!" Denise yelled. "We love your Bobos! They look like you bought them from the Salvation Army!"

The little bitches didn't know that Alessa's feet had been crammed into the same pair of shoes for the last two years. She had begged her mother for a pair of sneakers that fit her. Caterina had reluctantly agreed to get them for her, but only after the sole on the front of one of her sneakers separated from the rest of the shoe and kept getting caught beneath her foot, tripping up Alessa constantly as she moved around the house. Even then, her mother scolded her that if she hadn't been so hard on things, she could have made them last longer. When Alessa reminded her mother she had worn the sneakers for two years, Caterina glared at her.

"Just shut up!" she snapped. "You act like you're so deprived. With all of you around, it isn't easy to pay the bills, you know! What do you think money grows on—trees? You're an ungrateful child; that's what you are!"

It was at times like these that Alessa was grateful to have Rhonda in her life. She was the only person on earth who never judged her or treated her badly. Rhonda was just as glad to have found a friend like Alessa. In her own way, Rhonda was just as much of an outcast as Alessa. The boys only liked her because she put out and the girls hated her precisely for that reason. Rhonda and Alessa were good for each other. Both knew their friendship would last forever. They would talk about getting married and having children. They planned their weddings together and decided how each would be the other's maid of honor.

Rhonda talked about going to cosmetology school and becoming a famous hairdresser, one that the movie stars would flock to. And Alessa believed her friend could do anything she set her mind on. Rhonda had certainly helped her with her hair and the little makeup she had taken to wearing. Unlike Rhonda, however, Alessa never dared to dream about what she would be, when she grew up. Without a clue as to what her options were—and they seemed pretty limited—and demoralized by her mother's claim that she wasn't good at anything except whining, she had no expectations of herself. Shackled by her circumstances, she had never set herself a goal and lacked the courage and motivation to develop new interests, learn new things or take up a hobby. Only once, when Alessa was feeling especially self-assured after a weekend with Rhonda and Zoe, had she declared to her mother, "When I grow up, I want to be an engineer."

Caterina had stopped in her tracks and put her hands on her hips combatively. "Do you know how smart you have to be to become an engineer?" she had sneered. "You'd be better off picking something else." Killing any hope that Alessa might have had for a future, her mother had concluded, "All you need to worry about is graduating from high school and getting a job."

She had believed her mother. She had thought to herself: *my mother is right. I'm not smart enough to be an engineer.* She didn't even know what an engineer was anyway. She had just overheard another kid in her math class say he wanted to be an engineer and the teacher had seemed very impressed. So she had used the same line to impress Caterina.

Alessa looked forward to being at Rhonda's house on the weekends. She loved to sleep there. Her friend had the greatest room ever, with posters of Led Zeppelin all over her pale green walls and white furniture, with silver accents. Her bed sheets felt satin-soft and sleeping under her comforter was like being under a cloud. Everything was so beautiful and well maintained. Nothing was secondhand or mismatched. When Alessa slept there, she felt like a princess. She wanted all the things that Rhonda enjoyed, but for the time being, she was just grateful that Rhonda was generous enough to share them with her.

One Saturday night, after getting back from a party at the Rope, the two girls were lying in Rhonda's room, talking, when Zoe came in and sat on the edge of the bed. She didn't have any of her men friends over that evening. To Alessa, that meant her night at Rhonda's place would be that much more enjoyable.

"Tonight, it's just us, girls," Zoe announced. "My date cancelled, but we're going to meet for lunch tomorrow."

An hour later, they were all still lying on the bed, talking and laughing. Listening to Zoe describe her adventures with her newest male friend, the two girls giggled hard till their bellies ached. Alessa thought she could listen to Zoe forever, but the doorbell suddenly interrupted their chatter. Zoe got up to answer the door, leaving the two girls wondering who could possibly be visiting at eleven-thirty p.m.

The girls could hear Zoe's voice getting progressively louder as the conversation with the unexpected visitor drew on. Assuming it was one of the neighbors, Alessa and Rhonda went out into the living room. An unknown woman stood at the front door, her right foot propped on the threshold. Her right hand was splayed across the door jamb, preventing Zoe from shutting the door. Rhonda's mother was telling the visitor she was sorry, that she hadn't known "he" was married. *This must be the wife of one of her men friends*, Alessa decided.

The girls had just come up behind Zoe when, without warning, the stranger pulled out a gun and shot a bullet off in her direction. It zinged past Zoe, grazing her right forearm. Before any of them could react, Rhonda was lying on the floor, with blood oozing out of the left side of her chest.

Zoe lunged forward, grabbed hold of the gun in the woman's hand and used it to maneuver her arm so that it was pointing down. She struggled to subdue the visitor, but when the gun went off a second time, its muzzle was pointing down at Rhonda. The bullet pierced the girl's stomach. Screaming with anguish and terror, Alessa tried to pull her friend away from the madwoman.

By now, the visitor had realized what she had done and gazed down at her victim with a stunned expression; instead of Zoe, she had wounded a young girl who now lay on the floor, her life bleeding away. Zoe seized the opportunity. With one fist to the face, she knocked out the woman who now lay unconscious on the porch. Then she quickly shut and locked the door and rushed over to her daughter. Zoe put her arms around Rhonda and held her as tight as she could. She rocked her back and forth in her arms, trying to awaken her. Then she felt something cold crawling down her skin and stared at it; her daughter's blood was streaming down her arm and seeping into her shirt. Alessa got up and dialed 911, but it was already too late. When the first ambulance arrived with a team of paramedics, Rhonda was pronounced dead. The first bullet had penetrated her heart, killing her instantly. Alessa stood there in a state of shock, not knowing what to do next. There was only one thing she was certain of: she wanted Rhonda back.

Another ambulance arrived to take Zoe and Alessa to the hospital. While Zoe's injury was serious, it wasn't life threatening. Alessa sat in the emergency room, overcome by a sense of loneliness she hadn't felt in years. Caterina showed up soon after. From the way she plowed through the emergency room doors, Alessa could tell she was angry as hell. The minute she laid eyes on her daughter, Caterina demanded to know what kind of trouble she had gotten herself into.

"I shouldn't have let you hang around with her!" she thundered. "Someone told me Rhonda's mother was a whore and now look what you have got yourself into! Do you have any idea how upset you've made me? You are such a disappointment! You better hope you're not in trouble with the police. They'll lock you up forever, if you are involved with a murder!"

As Caterina continued on her tirade, Alessa couldn't help thinking what a truly ugly person her mother was. Here she was, grieving over the loss of her only friend in the world, and all her mother could rant about was the possibility of her being in trouble with the police! Alessa's sorrow began to boil over into rage. Just at the moment she feared she'd explode, if her mother uttered one more word, a nurse walked in to quiet Caterina. Of course, the attempt to silence her only enraged her further.

She stepped up to the bed where Alessa lay and yelled, "When I get you home, you are going to be so sorry! And stop that crying! I really don't understand why you always have to be so melodramatic! From now on, no more sleepovers! And you don't go out with friends either!"

The nurse looked from Caterina to Alessa and back in disbelief. It disturbed her to see this woman being so cruel to her own child. She turned to Alessa and inquired, "Are you doing okay, honey?"

"Yeah, she's doing fine," Caterina cut in. "She should thank her lucky stars she's alive. That Zoe woman is a whore and now look at what she's gone and done to her kid!"

"For Christ's sake, lady!" the nurse exclaimed indignantly. "Pull yourself together! Your daughter has just been through a lot. She witnessed her friend getting killed for no good reason. Maybe, as her mother, you should consider how she might be feeling and try to comfort her instead of yelling at her."

"Don't you tell me what to do!" Caterina raged back at the nurse. "She isn't *your* child! You have no idea what she is like! So mind your own goddamn business before I call the doctor and complain to him about how disrespectful you are!" She turned to her daughter. "Now get dressed, Alessa," she commanded. "I'm taking you home right now!"

In a fog of confusion and grief, the teenager did exactly as she was told.

On their way out, Caterina and her daughter passed the room where Zoe had been taken. As Alessa's eyes met hers, Zoe got up and approached her. Between sobs, she managed to say, "God, Alessa, my baby is gone! I don't know what to do now!"

"I know, Zoe," Alessa said, trying to comfort her, "I loved her so much."

About to hug Zoe, the teenager felt her mother's vicious pinch on the underside of her upper arm. Alessa screamed out in pain.

"What did I just tell you about not talking to her?" Caterina said bitingly. "She doesn't even care that her daughter is dead. Look at her, with her boobs hanging out of her shirt for the world to see! You are not to go anywhere near her again. Do you understand me, Alessa?"

Her daughter could only nod, as she looked at her friend's mother with love and sadness. She hoped that one day, Zoe would forgive her for being born to a monster like Caterina.

Chapter Seven

<u>**W**</u>hen they reached Caterina's car, Alessa was still sobbing. Her mother ducked inside the car quickly and settled herself. Checking her makeup in the rearview mirror, she continued her verbal assault.

"You see what happens when a woman is a bad mother? The way I see it, that woman killed her daughter! I should never have let you hang around with that Rhonda girl!"

Her blood boiling now, Alessa yelled back, "I love them both! And Zoe wouldn't have let her brother rape Rhonda for nine years and pretended not to know!"

Caterina's response to that was to backhand Alessa, making her lip bleed. "You little bitch!" she hissed. "You're a fucking liar! Just you wait till I get you home! Then I'll break your fucking head! My brother would never do anything to hurt you! You'll burn in hell for talking such filth about him!"

Frightened by what she had just blurted out to her mother and the violent reaction it had provoked, Alessa sat in silence, until they got home. She wondered if she really would burn in hell, not for the accusations she had leveled at her uncle, but for the filthy acts she had been engaging in with him. Once they were in the house, she rushed to her bedroom and began to take off her clothes that were still wet and stained with Rhonda's blood.

She had just stripped down to her underwear, when her mother stormed into the room holding her favorite weapon—the metal spoon. She charged at Alessa with such speed and force that the girl had no time to defend herself against the first blow to her bare thigh. Caterina pulled back the spoon and started to swing again. This time, however, Alessa blocked the blow with her hands and flinched as the spoon cracked across her knuckles. She flung herself on the bed, trying to shield her body as her mother's blows landed randomly. One struck her on the side of her face, another on her ankle bone and several others on her back.

Having worn herself out, Caterina finally stopped, her hand dropping to the side with the spoon dangling from it. Glaring at her daughter, she screamed, "Now let's see if you dare talk back to me again! If you ever say another disgusting word about your Uncle Danny again, I will kill you! And don't even dream of going to that girl's funeral either! You're punished, until I give you my permission to go out again. Do you hear me?" With that, she rained three final blows on Alessa, screaming, "I'll show you!" Then she turned and left her daughter's bedroom.

Rosabella came in about twenty minutes later to see how her younger sister was doing and found her crying silently under the worn covers. She helped Alessa put on her pajamas, then gave her an extra sheet when she noticed her shivering.

Rosabella told Alessa, "I'm sorry about what happened to your friend. Mom is just fucking crazy. I can't wait to get out of this house." As Rosabella got Alessa settled she couldn't help but notice all the fresh bruises from the metal spoon. Rosabella felt sorry for her sister, as she knew too well what a monster Caterina was and hated her for it.

The weeks that followed were hell for Alessa. As her mother had decreed, she wasn't allowed to go to Rhonda's funeral. She wasn't allowed to go out anywhere at all. Just to school and back. Nor could she receive phone calls. Not that it mattered. Not a soul had tried to contact her—except for Zoe. When she called one night and asked to speak with Alessa, Caterina was not in a particularly genial mood.

"Listen, lady," she spat out, "Alessa is not your child. Why don't you call some of those boyfriends you have? Your daughter is dead, because you are a tramp. I don't want you calling my daughter again. Call someone your own age."

Alessa's enforced stay at home meant that once again, her Uncle Danny had her at his mercy seven nights a week. He was becoming rougher with her as he got older, slapping her hard and pinching her nipples before he was fully aroused. Sometimes, he yanked cruelly at her hair or gripped her by the neck as if he were going to choke her to death. Her life descended into unrelenting darkness once more, tumbling down into the cold, bottomless pit from which she had begun to escape after she met Rhonda.

Danny tortured Alessa mercilessly for having dared complain to Caterina about him. He laughed at his niece scornfully, reminding her that his adoring sister would never believe her. Her siblings were, by now, young adults and had moved out of the house as soon as they could afford to. Rosabella was the last one to go. The previous month, she had moved to a small apartment in Norristown that she was sharing with a friend. Alessa, however, had been grounded for months now and still wasn't allowed out of the house, other than to go to school.

The weekend before Alessa's seventeenth birthday, her parents went off to Atlantic City. Shortly after they had pulled out of the driveway, Uncle Danny went into Alessa's bedroom. He stood in front of her, dropped his pants, pushed his pelvis out and said, "Play with it." She held his penis and began to whack him off. After a few minutes, he stopped her and said, "Blow me now." When he was done, he looked down at her and said, "This is going to be a great weekend, don't cha think?"

Alessa would have given anything to die. Nothing brought her more comfort than the thought of leaving this world. She hated her family, her very existence. Now she had to endure an entire weekend of that fucking bastard wanting to blow a load off several times a day. She hated him with a passion. She tried to focus on the good times she had enjoyed with Rhonda, thinking about the fun they had together and the memories they had shared. Rhonda had loved Alessa and believed in her. Now she was alone again, with nothing but her demons to torment her.

On the Saturday morning after her parents left for Atlantic City, Alessa went out to the kitchen, only to find her Uncle Danny gorging himself at the kitchen table.

"My friends are coming over tonight to play poker," he announced with a gleam of anticipation in his eyes. "I expect you to be nice to them and not give me any shit."

"I won't get in your way," Alessa assured him. "I'll keep to my room."

"No, you *won't* stay in your room," Danny told her. "You will be out here with us. I promised them you would be 'nice' to all of them. What I mean is, you will do whatever they want you to. Do you understand?"

"Are you talking about sex?" Alessa shrieked.

"Well, I'm certainly not talking about serving them coffee and donuts. I'm talking about being a nice girl and doing what they ask you to do.

Nobody's going to hurt you, for Christ's sake! They just want to mess around a little. I want you to wear a tee shirt and panties tonight. That's it. Nothing else."

The room started to close in on Alessa as the reality of what was about to happen sunk in. Her legs went weak and she felt utterly defenseless. Her mind reeled, searching for an answer, trying to find a way out of this unimaginable situation. She thought for a moment of calling Rosabella, but what if her sister didn't believe her either? Alessa went into her bedroom and sat on the edge of her bed. What was she going to do now? How could she get out of this mess? She did not reflect on how her uncle could do this to her. He was the devil himself. He could do anything to her and get away with it.

Then it came to her. She would sneak out and go see Zoe. She would tell her everything. Zoe would help her decide what to do. Alessa got dressed and snuck out of the house while her uncle was taking his weekly shower. He was a disgusting pig who proclaimed that showering once a week was enough. That was the reason why there was a sweet, rotting smell about him all the time. Alessa ran the mile and a half to Zoe's house.

She knocked frantically on Zoe's door and had to wait for nearly ten minutes before it was finally opened. Her friend's mother seemed a different person from the one Alessa had known. Zoe's once beautiful hair was matted and tangled in knots. There were dark circles under her bloodshot eyes and the skin on her cheeks hung loose, as if she had aged a hundred years. Her clothes were stained and almost falling off her thin frame. Zoe reached out and took Alessa in her arms. Then she broke down in tears. The two of them stood at the front door, clinging to each other desperately, as though the floor would fall out from under them, if either one of them let go.

When they finally separated just to look at each other, Zoe said, "God, Alessa, I miss her so much! I can't go on without her. I swear I didn't know he was married!"

Alessa comforted her by telling her how much she herself missed her friend and how, without Rhonda there, life sucked. Finally, Zoe brought Alessa inside the house. They sat at the kitchen table and talked about Rhonda and everything that had happened that terrible night which would change their lives forever.

Zoe said, "Your mother is a real cunt. I don't know how you can stand her."

"I can't," Alessa said firmly. "You have no idea how much I hate her." She needed to tell her what was going on. She had kept it to herself for a long time and she had no one else in the world to turn to. "Zoe," she began, "I have something to tell you. I'm really scared, because I don't know how you will react and I wouldn't be able to bear it, if you ended up despising me."

Zoe looked at Alessa in bewilderment. "I could never hate you, Alessa," she said gently. "You are a wonderful person. Rhonda loved you deeply. You are the only real girlfriend she ever had. She told me all the time how she had always wanted a friend like you. Whatever you have to tell me will be fine."

There was no holding back now. "My Uncle Danny has been having sex with me since I was seven years old," Alessa blurted out. "Now, things are getting much worse. My parents are away for the weekend and he is having friends over for a poker game tonight. He made it clear that I would have to 'be nice' to all of them once they arrived."

Zoe's face went completely blank for a few seconds. She wondered what she could possibly say to make this child feel safe. She wanted to make her feel like a normal kid her age. She wanted to help Alessa understand that she had nothing to be mortified about. Nothing of what had happened to her was her fault.

After a long pause, she asked, "Have you told your mother?"

"I tried. Twice. Once, when I was much younger and again, the night Rhonda died. Both times, my mother defended my uncle and called me a liar. I'm so scared, Zoe! I can't have sex with them. They're a bunch of old men. I've put up with my uncle for the last ten years. I just can't do it, Zoe!"

Alessa was now crying bitterly. Her chest heaved with raw emotion as she grappled with the thought of what her uncle's friends would do to her. Her tears welled up from deep inside her, from the very depths of her soul. Zoe took the girl in her arms and held her for a long, long time. Both were sobbing, Zoe for the loss of her daughter and the pain this young girl in her arms had endured and Alessa, for all she had been denied in her short life and for the suffering she had borne.

Zoe managed a weak smile. "You can live here, Alessa," she told her.

This had always been Alessa's cherished dream. She knew, however, that Caterina would come home in a couple of days and discover that her daughter had not only defied her orders and left the house, but run away from home and taken shelter with Zoe, of all people.

"There is nothing I want more in the world than to stay here with you," Alessa said earnestly. "I wish you were my mother. But I know that when my mom comes home, this is the first place where she will come looking for me. She knows that Rhonda was the only person in my life, outside of my family. She will just make your life miserable, Zoe. In the end, I'll just have to go back to living with her and my uncle.

"If only I could get away from here and live somewhere where no one could find me until I was eighteen! That's just a year from now. After that, no one can tell me what to do. I would be able to come back and stay with you then, if you'd let me. I just need to get away for one year, Zoe. That's all." Alessa hesitated. "I can go to Philadelphia and live in the city for a year. I can get a job and find a small apartment. No one will need to know where I am and they will never think to look for me there."

"You need to finish high school, Alessa," Zoe reminded her.

"I can get my GED later. Right now, I don't really care about a high school diploma. I just need to get out of here before tonight," Alessa pleaded.

Zoe searched for a different solution, but in vain. Finally, she said, "Okay. I want you to go into Rhonda's room and pack her duffle bag with some of her clothes. Take whatever you want. Make sure you take her down coat, just in case. I'm going to run to the bank now and get you some cash to get you started. I also want you to take Rhonda's cell phone. This way, you and I can keep in touch and I will be able to help you."

As terrified as Alessa was of what she was about to do, she was relieved to be finally getting away from her uncle and her pathetic existence.

After Zoe had left for the bank, Alessa went into Rhonda's bedroom. It was just as they had left it that awful night. The bed was unmade and the orange soda and cookies still sat on top of the dresser. Alessa experienced a deep sense of loss as she looked around and remembered how safe she had once felt in this very room. Now, it was like looking at a picture in a book. She longed for that same sense of security, but all that she could feel here now was pain.

Zoe returned before she had finished packing and handed her an envelope. Inside was 2,000 dollars—in cash.

"A place in the city will be expensive," Zoe explained. "This should keep you going long enough to find a job. I called and made you a reservation for two nights at the Travelodge Motel in Philadelphia. It's located on Race Street. Here's the address. The reservation is under my name—Zoe. I will drop you off at the Norristown train station; you need to take the train to Thirtieth Street Station and get a cab from there to the hotel. Tomorrow, you'll have to find a more permanent place to stay. I only booked the hotel room for two nights. If they come looking for you, I don't want them finding out that I have a room being charged to my credit card in the city, when I am living right here in my home." Zoe paused for breath. "Here," she said, "take Rhonda's school identification so that you have something with you, in case they ask to see it at the Travelodge." Zoe thrust the card into Alessa's palm.

The two of them carried the large duffle bag Alessa had packed with some of Rhonda's clothes out to Zoe's car and placed it in the trunk. Alessa placed the envelope with the 2,000 dollars inside a small purse Rhonda had always used. When they got to the Norristown train station, Zoe helped Alessa up to the platform. The two turned to face each other and clung together in a long, final embrace, neither of them wanting to let go, both feeling, unreasonably, that if they held on long enough, Rhonda might reappear and join them.

They were both crying as Zoe turned to leave the platform.

Alessa called out, "I love you, Zoe. Thank you for everything!"

Zoe turned back and cupped the young girl's face in her hands. "I love you too, honey. I am so very sorry for all that you have gone through with your uncle. I wish there was a way I could help you heal. You are a very special young woman. Great things are in store for you. I know it doesn't seem like it now, but some day, you will know just how special you are. Promise me that you will always carry Rhonda in your heart."

"I promise, Zoe," Alessa said. "Rhonda will live in my heart forever."

At that moment, the train entered the station and came to a stop. Alessa turned and boarded it, thinking how lucky she was to have known Zoe.

Chapter Eight

A lessa arrived at the Travelodge Motel on Race Street on Saturday afternoon, completely worn out. It had been an exhausting morning and she knew the hardest task still lay ahead: finding a permanent place to live in the next day and a half. Outside the Travelodge, she noticed a crowd of men standing off to the side of the building next door. They all looked lost and lonely. Many wore shabby old clothes and were unshaven. She looked at the sign above the door outside which they waited: St. John's Hospice. It was a shelter for homeless men and a soup kitchen. Alessa held her small purse closer against her body, worried that those men might try and snatch it from her and take all of her money.

As she passed them, though, it was evident that her presence hadn't even registered with them. Relieved that she was invisible to these men, Alessa entered the Travelodge, one door down from the shelter. Once inside the lobby, she felt safe and couldn't wait to get to her room and rest, before starting her search for an apartment. The woman behind the counter wore black pants, a white blouse and a black vest. The vest had food stains on the front that resembled baby vomit. The dark ring around the open collar of her white blouse turned Alessa's stomach. The woman's fingernails were painted, but the polish had begun to chip.

"What do you want?" she asked Alessa with a sneer.

"I have a reservation for Zoe."

The woman grunted and blew her nose. Then she slowly moved down the counter to where the keys and paper work were kept. Reaching for a key, she turned to Alessa again. "You look a bit young. I'd like to make it clear that we don't tolerate parties or prostitution at this lodge. You understand?"

"I understand. You don't have to worry about me."

The woman handed Alessa a key and pointed to a room only ten feet from where she was standing. Alessa unlocked the door and stepped inside. It wasn't the greatest room she had seen, but it did look like it had been cleaned. The tub in the bathroom had mold around the edges, but overall, there was nothing about the place that Alessa couldn't handle.

She put her duffle bag on the dresser and lay down on the bed, stretching her thin frame across it. Her room had a window that faced the street, where she could still see the men lined up, waiting to be allowed into the shelter. Even with the window closed, the noise of the city was audible. It seemed as though the walls were made of cardboard. Alessa could hear people passing through the lobby and could clearly decipher their conversations. Still, she reveled in the fact that she was there, in that rundown place, instead of being at home with a bunch of old perverts. She fell asleep on the bed, the noise of people milling about outside her door and window making her feel as if she wasn't all alone.

She woke up an hour later, completely disoriented. She could not recall where she was. Her heart pounded in her chest. Soon enough, however, the reality of her situation came flooding back to her and she felt paralyzed with fear. Pushing her apprehensions aside, she stepped out into the lobby and picked up the free copy of a local newspaper that lay on a battered wooden table off to the side of the reception area. She began to look through it and found a small listing of apartments for rent. New to the city, she turned to the woman behind the desk and asked for a map.

"Here," the woman said, handing it to her, "that'll be a dollar fifty."

Alessa handed over the money and took the newspaper and the map back to her room.

She sat in the dimly lit room with its cream walls and scoured the section for apartment rentals. Most of them were well above 600 dollars a month. There was only one she thought she might be able to afford on Dauphin Street in North Philadelphia. The rent was 300 dollars and included utilities. She pulled out Rhonda's cell phone and dialed the phone number listed.

A woman with a husky voice answered. "Hello?"

"Hi, my name is Alessa. I'm calling about the apartment you have for rent."

"Yeah, whatta you want to know?"

"Is the apartment available? Can I come to see it?"

Clearly unimpressed, the woman asked, "Yeah, when do you want to come?"

"How about now? I'm on Race Street and I can be there within the hour," Alessa said excitedly.

"Okay, I'll be here. Knock on the front door."

Alessa hung up, feeling hopeful. She quickly combed her hair and washed her face. Then she stepped out again. Rushing through the lobby, she noticed a woman in very high heels and a short denim skirt that was ripped to the tops of her thighs. The woman turned to eye Alessa before going back to talking to a short, heavy man who was staring at her almost completely exposed breasts. Alessa heard the woman behind the desk yell out, "What did I tell you? Get the fuck outta here! We don't want any whores around!"

Alessa was out the lobby door before she could hear the woman in the mini skirt respond. She hailed a taxi and gave the driver the address.

He looked at her and asked, "Why do you want to go there?"

"I am going to see an apartment that I might be able to rent," she said, full of energy.

"Whatever, kid."

Within fifteen minutes, the taxi had turned onto Dauphin Street and pulled over a block later. The neighborhood was seedy. Alessa noticed that several of the houses were boarded up with plywood, while others appeared to be lived in. They were old row homes that stood three stories high. Trash lay piled on the streets and everywhere she looked, there were teenagers hanging out on corners. Alessa started to feel a little uneasy when the taxi driver turned to her for his fare. She asked him if he could wait for her and he agreed, but told her if she took longer than fifteen minutes, he would be gone.

The groups of teenagers were already staring at the taxi, watching to see who would get out. As she stepped out onto the curb and looked at the house that could be her new home, she caught sight of an old woman peering through a ripped curtain in the first floor window. She climbed the four broken cement steps to the wooden porch which was rotting and felt like it was going to give way beneath her feet. Then she knocked softly on the door. She knew the woman had seen her arrive and now she quickly threw open the door.

"Hi, I'm Alessa. I called about the apartment," Alessa told her cheerfully.

"I'm Lea, the owner and the landlady. Come on in. The apartment is on the second floor, third door to the left."

Alessa went up to the next level of the house with the old woman trailing behind her. When she got to the third door, she noticed what was written in black marker on the wall next to it: Apartment 2C. The woman unlocked the door and Alessa stepped into a small room. About ten feet into the room, there was a kitchen sink mounted on the wall, with three cabinets hanging over it. To the right of the sink was a small refrigerator. Against the far wall stood a rectangular metal table flanked by two wooden chairs. Alessa's stomach dropped when she stepped up to the sink and saw the filth inside it. There were half-empty soup cans and some waterlogged Cheerios floating around the bottom in a quarter-inch of dirty brown water.

When she opened the refrigerator, the handle came off. The old woman told her it could be easily fixed. Food had spilled inside the refrigerator. There was something round and moldy on the top shelf. It smelled like the corpse of a small animal left there to die. A single naked light bulb hung from the middle of the ceiling, casting a glow around the room that resembled horror movie lighting.

Alessa stepped through the door that stood between the refrigerator and the kitchen table, into a small bedroom with a single bed. The mattress was worn and stained. The walls were painted gray. Across from the bed was a four-drawer dresser standing against the wall. The bedroom floor was linoleum throughout and looked like it hadn't been cleaned since the house was built. A curtain strung between two nails hung over another doorway off the bedroom. When Alessa walked through, she saw a toilet that had rings of black inside and a tub that was overrun by mold and mildew.

The apartment was a slum, an absolutely disgusting mess, but Alessa figured it was the best she could do for 300 dollars a month.

She turned to Lea. "It's kind of dirty and it needs some work."

The old woman was defiant. "Listen," she said, "it doesn't look like you're in a position to be too picky. Either you want it or you don't. If you want it, I need 900 dollars. That's 300 for security, 300 for last month's rent and 300 for first month's rent. Let me know what you want to do."

Alessa stared at Lea and realized that she was not as old as she had first assumed. She stood five foot tall and had a rounded body. She was missing several teeth and those that had survived were rotting. Alessa could smell the stench of her breath, even from three feet away. Lea's housecoat was stained with food and on her feet were old, ripped slippers. Alessa suddenly remembered Rhonda and a smile hovered on her lips as she thought of the things her friend would have said about Lea's appearance. She could hear her say, "Look at that old bat. She hasn't seen a toothbrush since she finished teething and the bitch needs a hot bath, new clothes and an attitude adjustment." It reminded Alessa how much she missed her friend.

Lea left her standing in the dingy apartment. It was barely an apartment at all and certainly not a place you would call home. As Alessa stood in the center of the kitchen, she felt a chill pass through her. This was where she would live now. The inside of her apartment was almost scarier than what she had seen out on the street. She was certain, however, that this could be no worse than the house of horrors she had fled.

Alessa would have to leave the Travelodge in the morning. She needed a place to go to and it looked like this was it. It was the only apartment she could afford. She figured if it didn't work out, she could look for a new place later. Besides, even this shit-hole was costing her 900 dollars just to move in. She knew now that anything nicer would not be affordable. She had less than 1,100 dollars to live on, until she found a job. She would move in the next day and start looking for a job on Monday morning.

She went down to Lea's apartment and knocked on her door. The old lady opened the door and asked, "You decide?"

"Yes, I'll take it. I need to move in tomorrow, though."

"Fine with me, honey," Lea replied. "I need 900 hundred in cash now. I don't want any pets. And no boyfriends here. You pay each month, as you go. If you don't pay one month, you'll find your stuff on the sidewalk. I don't take any shit and I don't put up with a lot of noise. Another thing: the streets are crawling with hoodlums. Don't bring any of them in here. You got it?"

"I got it," Alessa answered politely.

When she stepped off the broken-down porch and into the sunlight, a feeling of relief surged through her. She noticed that the taxi driver hadn't waited. Panic began to rise in her as she started looking up and down the eight- hundred block of Dauphin Street.

Lea opened her window and rasped, "The bus stop is at the end of the block on Fifth. A bus should be there in five minutes. So you better get moving. It'll take you back into the city. Mind your business and they will leave you alone."

Alessa thought: *who will leave me alone?*

As she started down the street, she saw exactly whom Lea had been referring to. There were eight teenagers standing at the stop. They were laughing and pushing each other. As she got closer, she noticed they were all teenage boys. There was one middle aged woman sitting on the bench off to the side. They all lapsed into silence as she approached and her heart started racing at the memory of Lea's last words of advice. When she got to the bus stop, Alessa stood facing the street and tried not to make eye contact with the boys.

From behind her, she could hear them, though.

One of the boys yelled, "Look what we got here: pork, the other white meat."

The crowd started laughing. Alessa was vulnerable and she knew it. She looked over at the woman sitting on the bench. Then she walked slowly toward her and sat down beside her, assuming that her proximity to the woman would spare her further attention from the boys.

The moment she sat down, the woman looked at her and said, "If you looking for protection from me, honey, you've come to the wrong place. I don't get involved. I leave them alone and they leave me alone."

Alessa didn't acknowledge the woman. She sat there quietly and slipped into the special space in her head, the silent place she had discovered when she was seven years old. It was how she coped. She had been using that place all through her life and she was happy that it now belonged to her. After all, it was there that she had learned to separate mind and soul from body. It was there that she had become resilient and emerged a survivor. A few minutes later, the Septa bus pulled to a stop and Alessa got on, but only after the boys had done so.

When she got back to the Travelodge, Alessa went straight to her room and locked the door behind her. She undressed and took a lukewarm shower, as the Travelodge didn't seem to be very generous with their supply of hot water. She started planning out her next steps while washing herself. She would, she decided, get up early the next morning and head over to her apartment. She would buy the *Philadelphia Inquirer* and go through the "Help Wanted" section. Once she was through with that, she would spend the day cleaning her new apartment.

By the time she was dressed, it was almost five-thirty p.m. Famished from not having eaten all day, Alessa headed out to Chinatown, where colorful signs and lights lined the streets. The aroma of the food was simply irresistible and made her mouth water. Having no clue as to which restaurant would be the right one to choose, Alessa followed three young couples into the House of Chen. She was greeted by a short Asian woman in her mid-fifties, who seated her immediately at a table in the small first floor dining room.

After dinner, Alessa walked back to the motel, slowly taking in the sights of the city. Although it was, for the most part, dirty and life seemed fast-paced, people seemed to enjoy being there anyway. On her way back, she passed the homeless men lined up for the night at St. John's Hospice. They were chatting among themselves and sharing stories. They may not have had a home to return to, but Alessa got the impression that they had each other and drew comfort from that fact. She wondered if her perception was based on reality or merely the outcome of her desire to believe that these broken people had something to fall back on, a form of bonding and kinship that would provide them with emotional sustenance. As she watched them, she wondered if these destitute men could find friends and a sense of family in each other's company, maybe she too could, one day, find the happiness that continued to elude her.

Alessa went back into the Travelodge to call Zoe and tell her about the progress she had made since they parted ways at the Norristown train station. Zoe sounded pleased that Alessa had found an apartment so quickly.

"Did anyone from my family get in touch with you and ask about me?" Alessa asked a little apprehensively.

"No," Zoe replied. "I haven't heard a word from them. But Alessa, I want you to be careful. I don't know much about the city, but I do know that North Philadelphia has a reputation for being tough. Don't trust anyone and keep your door locked at night."

"Okay, Zoe, I will," Alessa reassured her. "I'll call you tomorrow night after I get settled into the apartment. Maybe you'll be able to come over and visit me soon. We could spend some time together in the city."

"Sure, that sounds nice," Zoe said.

When she had hung up the phone, Alessa changed into Rhonda's favorite tee shirt. It was a garment she had slept in many times, but wearing it now, she felt closer to her dead friend. She slid under the covers and fell asleep to the sounds of the television on the dresser at the foot of her bed. She didn't dream at all that night. She was finally about to start a new life for herself—with a clean slate. No one here knew who she was or of her shortcomings. Tomorrow, Sunday, was offering her the chance to start anew.

She woke up the next morning, brimming with excitement. Ready to get her new life on track, she prepared for the new day that, she wanted to believe, would mark the beginning of progress and hope. She was sure some part of her life, at least, was going to get better.

Chapter Nine

———————■———————

Carrying her purse and her duffle bag, Alessa checked out of the Travelodge and took the bus to Dauphin Street. When she got to her apartment building, she climbed to the top of the steps where Lea was waiting for her with two keys—one for the front door and the other for her apartment. Propped next to the door of Lea's apartment were a bucket, a mop and cleaning detergents.

Lea motioned toward them and said, "Here is some stuff you can use to clean up the place with. Just make sure I get it all back after you're done. That stuff cost money, ya know."

Alessa's heart felt light as she took everything up to the second floor. She unlocked the door to her first apartment and stepped inside the filthy, dingy kitchen. Nothing could break her spirit today. If necessary, she would scrub and clean until her hands fell off. This was her home now. For the first time ever, Alessa was in charge of her life and it was an invigorating feeling.

When she finished cleaning several hours later and looked at her watch, it was already two-thirty p.m. Remembering that she had nothing but a donut and a cup of coffee she bought from the street vendor outside the Travelodge, she quickly put her clothes away, locked the door and headed for the Dauphin Mini Market she had spotted while getting off at the bus stop. It was only two blocks from her new home and she was sure she could find a quick bite to eat there. On the way, she walked past groups of young people. Some of them looked like teenagers, but others seemed to be in their twenties. It was immediately obvious to her that other than Lea, she was the only white person on Dauphin Street.

As she navigated her way through small clusters of people, Alessa heard the guys heckling her and felt the girls looking her up-and-down with morbid hatred. Ignoring everyone around her and clinging to her purse, she pushed ahead in the direction of the mini mart. *Don't let them see that you're afraid*, she kept telling herself. *If they find out, they'll bother you even more.* Easier said than done, though. These people were intimidating, to say the least. No one smiled at her. On the contrary, everyone looked like they wanted to bash her brains in. Once inside the mini mart, which now seemed a safer haven than a ten-by-twelve-foot room reeking of rotting cheese, Alessa bought just enough groceries for the next three or four days, mindful of the fact that she would run out of money if she went overboard.

Having paid for her purchases, she made her way through the heavy glass door protected with black iron bars, only to come up against a wall of six teenagers who stood barring her way. The tallest of them, a gangly guy with gold front teeth, slithered closer and said, "Whatcha got there, girl? You gonna cook me somethin' good to eat? I could use some loving and I ain't never had me none of that white meat before." He turned to his friends and asked, "You think this young girl is sweeter than the meat we get around here?"

One of the boys yelled back, "I don't know, Tag, but after you have some of it, I'll get me some too!"

Alessa's heart was pounding so hard she thought it would jump out of her chest. She frantically looked around and noticed an elderly black woman coming out of the mini mart. Alessa prayed she would stand up for her, but the woman didn't so much as acknowledge either the girl or the boys who were heckling her; it was as if they were all invisible.

Trying to sound self-assured and assertive, Alessa said to the boys, "I have to go. Please let me through. I have had enough shit this weekend and I just can't take anymore. Please just leave me alone."

At her words, the tall black guy laughed and said, "You go on tonight, girl. We want you to settle into the neighborhood, but we'll be around and looking to test out watcha got between those fine legs of yours."

He moved to the side and Alessa bolted through. She ran all the way to her apartment building, holding her breath until she was safely inside with her groceries. Once she had shut the front door behind her, she took a deep, ragged breath. She realized this would be tougher than she had initially thought. These people made Denise from the Rope look like a fucking saint.

Alessa cooked herself macaroni and cheese and drank her orange soda as she plotted her job hunt plan for Monday morning. Judging by the apparently aimless young people who hung around the neighborhood, it didn't look like there was much by way of employment near where she was living.

In the morning, she had to change buses once to get back into Philadelphia, putting in applications everywhere from McDonald's in Center City to a drugstore in South Philly. She was thankful she could use Rhonda's cell phone number on her applications as a call-back number. After putting in her last application at Wendy's, she got a newspaper to guide her through her search the following day. She caught the last bus back to North Philadelphia and raced back to her apartment from the bus stop, desperate to dodge the group of guys who had scared the shit out her the day before.

After she was settled in for the evening, she dialed Zoe's number. Alessa's heart fluttered at the sound of her voice when she answered the call.

"Hi Zoe, it's me."

"Hey, listen. Your mom was here looking for you. She is mad as hell. She said that if I saw you, I was to tell you to get home. I don't think she suspected anything, but she kept eyeing me up and watching my reaction. She finally left, but said she would be back to see if you had come by."

"Oh God, Zoe, I'm sorry! My mom is a monster and she gets really ugly with people sometimes. Just keep telling her you haven't seen me, okay?"

"Okay, but you'll need to be careful. She didn't seem worried that you were gone, but angry as hell that you weren't there."

"Yeah, because I'm her meal ticket and she knows it. Uncle Danny gets to have whatever he wants from me and she knows that as long as he's happy, he will keep on living there and paying her rent. I don't know which one of them I hate more—my uncle or my mother."

Zoe had no words to console her. She was out of her element in this situation. She would have done anything to protect her own daughter from the kind of situation Alessa had been trapped in. She couldn't imagine a mother turning a blind eye to what was happening to her child in her own home.

Finally, Zoe said, "Listen, sweetheart. You need to focus on the future. You can't waste time thinking about your mother and your uncle anymore. They are scumbags by anybody's standards. You need to focus on yourself. Did you manage to find any work today?"

"No, not really," Alessa replied. "I put in a lot of applications and everyone said they would call, if they were interested. I have some more places to go to tomorrow and I will just keep on applying until I find something."

"Good. Keep up the good work. You deserve all great things in life, Alessa, and some day, you will have them. I'm sure of it. I need to go now. I'll talk to you soon."

"Zoe? I wanted to thank you for what you've done for me over the last few days. Also, for all the fun times we had with Rhonda. I didn't have anyone to turn to on Saturday and you really came through for me. You didn't have to do what you did and I'll always remember your kindness."

"No problem," Zoe said, trying to sound brisk. But her voice broke as she said, "I am glad I could help you, Alessa. Good night, sweetheart."

Alessa lay on her bed and cried. For the first time in years, she started brooding over the things that her Uncle Danny had done to her. Things she had grown so accustomed to and reconciled herself to with such passive acceptance that she had almost lost all sense of the tragedy her life had turned into because of it. But now, all alone, she was able to weep for the years she had lost, the childhood that had been destroyed forever and the loneliness and sense of alienation it had created, leaving a permanent ache in her heart. She thought of the hollow place that separated her from her mother, Caterina, who, irony of ironies, was the youngest of fourteen children, while her own daughter, Alessa, sat all alone in a strange apartment, with no one to help her, except for Zoe, the very woman Caterina had abused and maligned.

Someday, Alessa hoped to have a family of her own. She would love and cherish her children, keeping them close and safe. She would be the mother that Caterina had been incapable of being, because selfishness had prevented her from becoming anything to anyone. For Alessa, the healing process had already begun. She was about to find out who she was and what she was made of. She was no longer the little girl at the mercy of the world, waiting to take orders and please others. Or so she thought.

Chapter Ten

———————————————————————

The next day, Alessa was back on the bus that would take her into Center City. She visited a couple of fast-food restaurants and low-end retail stores to fill out more applications. By the end of the day, she was exhausted. She could barely remember the names of all the stores she had applied to, but had a feeling that one was bound to call back. As she boarded the bus to Dauphin Street, she noticed the boys who had heckled her outside the mini mart sitting in the back. They began to hoot and holler at her, as she picked a seat as close to the driver as she could get. The other people riding the bus pretended to be oblivious to her predicament. No one wanted to get involved, and in the process, divert the boys' attention to themselves.

The bus began to empty as they drew closer to Dauphin Street. The boys crept closer to where Alessa was sitting. Her palms began to sweat, as the tall boy they called Tag yelled out, "So now, how about some of that sweet meat we been talkin' 'bout? Hell girl, we even been dreamin' about what you got waiting for us between those legs. Why don't you do us a favor and pull that skirt up and show us what you got goin' on under there. If you let each of us take a turn at giving you a feel up under that skirt, we'll leave you alone—for now. Deal?"

To Alessa's embarrassment and relief, she threw up all over herself. The boys started laughing and howling at her. One of Tag's drones hollered, "You stupid bitch! We ain't want nothing from you now. But next time we come to see you, if you throw up, we'll make you eat that motherfuckin' slop."

Alessa heard soft laughter from a couple of rows ahead of her on the other side of the bus. When she looked over, a young black woman was watching her. She went on laughing quietly to herself, as the boys withdrew to the back of the bus, still taunting Alessa about what was to come.

She looked at the young woman with wide, imploring eyes, hoping for some compassion, an empathetic response to her plight. But she just turned away and continued to look out the front window of the bus. Alessa realized that on the streets of North Philadelphia, no one had any mercy to spare. It seemed as though people were just plain relieved not to be a target themselves.

Alessa put little effort into cleaning the vomit off the front of her outfit. She figured it would serve as a form of protection, like wearing garlic around her neck to keep the vampires away. No one wanted her "sweet meat", if it meant going through a layer of puke to get to it. *Motherfuckers*, Alessa thought, *I hope they all choke in their sleep. Fucking bastards.* Just because she was young, white and poor didn't mean she had any lack of experience in knowing how to hate. She just hated these guys. All she wanted was to be left alone so she could restart her life.

When she got off the bus, Alessa practically ran to her apartment. She saw the young black woman watching her from the bus and wondered if she were right in assuming that just maybe, there was a hint of empathy in her eyes, but she didn't stick around to find out for sure.

At four o'clock that afternoon, her cell phone rang. Alessa looked at the screen and noticed a 215 area code. She knew it wasn't Zoe and quickly answered, hoping it was a job offer.

"Hello?"

"Hi, I'm Brady, the manager of the Dollar Store. You applied for a position here."

"Hi. Yes, I did."

"Okay. Well, can you come in tomorrow at ten a.m. for an interview?"

"Of course. I will see you at ten. Thank you."

"Yeah, see you at ten." The phone went dead.

Alessa was ecstatic that she had been called for an interview within just two days of submitting her applications. She called Zoe and told her about it. Zoe gave her some pointers on her interview: what to wear, not to repeat "like" after every few words, refrain from chewing gum and a bunch of other things that Alessa believed would give her the edge she needed to nail the job.

She caught the nine o'clock bus to the Dollar Store on Broad Street. She wasn't sure what to expect; this was the first job interview she'd ever been to. She was nervous and eager to get on with it. She arrived well ahead of the scheduled time and ducked into a local coffee shop to wait until it was closer to ten o'clock. Shortly before ten, she got up and walked over to the store.

As she entered, two women in their late twenties were working the registers in front. There was a guy around the same age stocking shelves. None of them seemed to notice her as she walked in. She approached the woman at the register closest to her and said, "Hi, my name is Alessa. I'm here for an interview with Mr. Brady."

One of the woman said, "Yeah, he's in the office in the back. Walk down this aisle. The door is on the far right. He's an asshole. Good luck."

Alessa's whole world was filled with assholes. Would one more matter?

She knocked on the office door and out popped a small, pudgy man in his mid-fifties. He was no more than five feet tall and the bulge around his stomach thrust through his shirt so that rolls of fat flowed over one another and were visible through the gaps between the buttons. His eyes, sunken deep into their sockets, were set too close together and sleaze seemed to ooze from his pores. The smell of stale coffee filled the air when he spoke, making Alessa's stomach gurgle in disgust.

"Yeah, you Alessa?" Brady asked.

"I am. Nice to meet you."

Alessa held out her hand and received a limp handshake. Brady led her into his office and shut the door behind them. She sat on an overused chair with torn upholstery, making a mental note not to touch her face until she had thoroughly washed her hands.

"So, have you ever worked retail before?"

"No, but I really want to learn. I'm sure I can be good at it. I'm very good with people," Alessa lied.

Brady sized her up. "You know, we are open from eight a.m. to nine p.m. every day. So your hours will vary. You have any issues with that?"

"No, I am available any time. The more hours I can get, the better."

Brady read over her application and said, "I see you will be seventeen this Saturday. You in high school?"

Alessa lied again. "No. Actually, I am studying for my GED. My parents died in a car accident a few months ago. They didn't have any money. So I needed to quit high school to get a job to support myself. I don't have any other family."

"Yeah, that's too bad. As long as you don't let your personal issues screw up my scheduling, I don't care. I can start you tomorrow, if you want.

The job pays minimum wage. I can probably give you forty hours a week. There are no benefits, but you get a half hour for lunch and two fifteen-minute breaks for an eight-hour shift. I need you on second shift for the rest of this week, including Saturday. Second shift is noon to closing. I'll have one of the other girls teach you how to close."

Alessa was so excited she readily agreed to all his conditions.

As she was on her way out, one of the cashiers asked, "So, are you gonna work here?"

"Yes, I start tomorrow on the second shift."

"Good," the woman responded. "We need someone to cover that awful shift. Since we have seniority, you had better get used to working it."

Alessa left feeling relieved that she had found a job. Minimum wage was enough to cover her rent and still leave her with a couple hundred dollars a month for groceries. Things were starting to fall into place for her. She got off the city bus at Fifth and Dauphin. Then she noticed the young black woman she had seen on the bus the day before.

Alessa approached her and said, "Hello."

The young woman was stunningly beautiful. Her skin, not much darker than Alessa's olive tone, was flawless. She had beautiful almond-shaped eyes, a slender nose and full pink lips. Her hair was jet black and shoulder length, with soft brown highlights. She was thin, with perfectly shaped breasts, and a plunging neckline showed off their fullness.

The young black girl looked Alessa up and down before deciding to respond. "Hi. Ain't you that girl who puked on the bus the other day?"

Alessa blushed, feeling a bit of a fool. "Yeah," she admitted, "that was me. I don't know what happened. I just got so scared, it flew out of me."

"Well, my name is Tasha and those boys are real bad news. They don't fuck with me, because they know my brother will kill 'em. There ain't much you can do about it, but try to avoid 'em. They aren't just fuckin' with ya; they would actually do the stuff they were threatening you with. They roam around here causing trouble for whoever is in their path. So don't take it personal. You live down at old lady Lea's house, don't you?"

"Yes, it was the only place I could find that I can afford. I just got a job at the dollar store on Broad Street."

Tasha laughed and Alessa felt mortified. The girl must have thought she was pathetic.

"Okay," she said, backing away, "well, maybe I'll see you around. Nice to meet you." Alessa retreated a few steps before realizing she hadn't introduced herself. She turned around again and said, "I'm Alessa, by the way."

As she walked away, Tasha yelled back, "Remember what I told you about those goons! Just stay away from 'em!"

Tasha felt sorry for the girl. She looked like she didn't have anyone in the world. And she was so fucking naïve! She wondered if Alessa would make it through the week in this neighborhood. People didn't live here without some kind of protection. She knew Alessa had no idea that she was living in a hell on earth.

Around dinnertime, Tasha's curiosity got the better of her and she walked down to old lady Lea's place, looking for Alessa. When she knocked on the front door, Lea opened it just a crack and said, "What do you want?"

"I am here to see Alessa. Can you get her for me or let me in?"

"Wait here. I don't want any trouble coming into my house."

Lea shut the door behind her and a couple of minutes later, Alessa came to the front door. She stepped out onto the broken porch and was surprised to see Tasha.

"Hey, what's up?" Tasha said. "I just stopped by to see if you wanted to go down to Kentucky Fried Chicken and get some dinner. I was on my way there and thought you might want to come."

Alessa almost wet herself in her excitement. "Okay, let me grab some money and I'll be right back down."

She reappeared within minutes and the two girls started walking down to the restaurant. Tasha talked about her family. Alessa discovered that Tasha's mother was white, while her father was black. The mix explained her beautiful complexion and fine features. Tasha told Alessa that her older brother, Harlin, was all white. Her mother had been married before to some Irish asshole and had lived in South Philly before he almost beat her to death. Then she had met Tasha's father and married him. Tasha was the only kid from that marriage. She also revealed that her brother was a badass motherfucker nobody in North Philly would ever dare mess with. Harlin and the gang he hung with were tough and didn't take shit from anybody.

When they got to Kentucky Fried Chicken, Tasha pulled out a big roll of cash to pay for her dinner. Alessa couldn't help but notice how much money she was carrying and blurted out, "Where did you get all that money?"

"I sell pot for Harlin," she replied nonchalantly, "and he takes good care of me. Some of this is from a couple of big sales I made before I got to your apartment and some of it is mine. I'm meeting Harlin after we're done eating to give him his money and get more dope. You want to come with me?"

Alessa had smoked dope once or twice at the Rope, but had never known anyone who sold it. "Sure," she said.

After dinner, they walked to a row home in the six-hundred block of Dauphin Street. Alessa observed that the front door and windows were barred and even the second floor windows had bars on them. The row home on the right was boarded up. The one on the left was rundown, but there were lights on inside. Tasha knocked and a man answered the door. He was muscular and nearly six feet four inches tall. Alessa couldn't stop staring at him. He had large green eyes, shaped like Tasha's, and light brown shoulder length hair. He had a strong face, with a well-defined chin and jaw. He flashed Tasha a broad smile, showing off his perfect teeth. For the first time since she had met Carl, all Alessa could think about was how much she wanted Tasha's brother to lean over and kiss her.

Tasha pointed to Alessa. "This is Alessa, a new friend of mine." Then gesturing toward her brother, she told Alessa, "This is my brother, Harlin."

"Is she cool?" Harlin asked, studying Alessa intently.

Alessa immediately wished she had taken the time to change into one of Rhonda's cooler tee shirts.

"Yeah, she's cool," Tasha assured her brother. "She's new around here. Living at old lady Lea's house."

Convinced Alessa was okay, Harlin opened the broken screen door and let them in.

Chapter Eleven

As Alessa followed Tasha into the house, she noticed a crowd of boys gathered in the living room. They were all drinking beer and smoking. Some were smoking cigarettes; others were pulling on bongs. Alessa felt intimidated by the group. The boys gawked at her, but seemed happy to see Tasha who handed her a beer before they sat down on the living room floor. There were no other girls around, but this didn't seem to bother Tasha. When she handed her new friend a joint, Alessa took a long drag on it, just the way Rhonda had taught her to, when they were going to the Rope. Alessa didn't really care for pot, but she smoked it anyway. She needed to dispel Harlin's doubts about her and if she didn't join in, she feared she might be asked to leave. Tasha stayed close to Alessa, sensing that she was not comfortable with Harlin and his tough friends. They were clearly people you didn't fuck with.

Before the girls left, Harlin handed his stepsister a bag containing smaller bags. Alessa could see they were bags of pot. In return, Tasha reached into her purse and handed him a wad of money.

Harlin smiled and said, "You are the best little sister. Keep up the good work, girl."

Tasha beamed as her brother hugged her goodbye. He didn't so much as look at Alessa as she left with Tasha.

Once outside, Tasha said, "I love Harlin. He is the greatest brother in the world. He makes me feel safe."

"I don't think he liked me going there with you," Alessa murmured. "Everyone seemed annoyed that you took me there."

"They are always like that around new people," Tasha reassured her. "Until they know they can trust you, they consider you the enemy. Don't worry about it. They knew you were with me anyway."

She walked Alessa back to her apartment. Alessa looked up at the house and said, "I would invite you up, but Lea said I couldn't have company."

"Yeah, she's an old bat. She's just afraid of us people from the street. We ain't all bad, though," Tasha said with a broad smile.

Alessa agreed and quickly went up the steps to the front door. Before going in, she turned to the other girl and said, "I had fun tonight. Thanks for stopping by and taking me along for dinner. Maybe we can hang out— if you want."

"Sure, we can hang out," Tasha said, smiling. "I'll see you around."

Alessa went over the events from the evening in her mind. She really liked Tasha and hoped they could become good friends, just like she and Rhonda had been. She was a little scared of Harlin and his friends, though. They weren't like the boys at the Rope. In fact, they weren't like boys at all; they were more like men. They were rough around the edges and the way they talked made her uncomfortable. They seemed like the type of guys who could kill you without second thoughts and forget about it in a minute. Harlin seemed a little less rough than the guys in his gang, but they all clearly looked up to him. When he talked, the others listened and when he said he wanted another beer, one of the guys always sprang up to get it for him.

The next day, Alessa woke up, took a shower and sat at her kitchen table until it was time to leave for her new job. When she got to the dollar store shortly before noon, she was greeted by two miserable cashiers. An older Hispanic woman came in exactly at noon and said, "You Alessa? You working with me today."

Alessa followed the woman around all day and learned how to use the cash register, restock shelves and greet customers. Not that anyone who worked there actually greeted customers, except for the Hispanic woman. By the end of the day, Alessa had learned her job. There wasn't really much to it and she was happy to have the training behind her.

When she stepped off the bus at nine-thirty that night, she saw Tasha standing on the opposite corner. There were a couple of teenage boys hanging around her. Alessa saw her take money from them and put it in her purse. When she saw Alessa, Tasha smiled and waved. Alessa went over to her.

"Hi Tasha," she said. "Just got back from work."

"Oh yeah, how was it?"

"Pretty simple, actually. Nothing much to it."

Tasha smiled and started walking Alessa home. "Do you want to go get some ice cream at the Dauphin Mini Mart?" she asked.

Alessa agreed and they walked the half block to the store. They bought their ice cream and were eating them outside the store, when Tasha asked her, "How old are you anyway?"

"I will be seventeen in three days."

"No shit? We need to celebrate. How about if I ask Harlin to give us a ride to Pulsations?"

"What's Pulsations?"

"It's this really cool nightclub. It has all these levels and different kinds of music. At midnight, this robot comes out of a spaceship from the ceiling and dances around. It's kind of corny, but so much fun. Harlin never goes there before ten o'clock. So that will give you time to get home from work and get dressed. Do you have ID?"

"It sounds great, but I actually don't have any ID. How old do you have to be to get in?"

"Twenty-one, but don't worry. I can hook you up with a fake ID."

The rest of the week was uneventful. Every night, when Alessa got off the city bus, Tasha was somewhere in sight. The two girls hung out and talked. They were really getting to know each other. Tasha finally asked her, "So where is your family? Why you here all alone anyway?"

Alessa had come to trust Tasha within a short period of time. After all, the other girl had kept no secrets from her; Alessa even knew that she sold pot to the kids on the street. She decided it would be safe to entrust her with her dirty secrets.

She related the whole sordid saga of her Uncle Danny, her mother and even Carl and the kids at the Rope. She told her about what had happened to Rhonda and how Zoe had helped her to escape before she was gang raped in her own home. Tasha listened intently, struggling to believe that this girl had put up with so much shit in her life. When Alessa had finished, Tasha reached out and gave her a hug.

"Girl," she said, "that is some fucked-up shit you been through! No wonder you're afraid of everything. I ain't never had to worry about those things 'cause I always had Harlin. My daddy is a good man too and my mama would have cut my uncle's dick off, if he ever touched me." Tasha went on, "Funny how you think that people are so very different from you, because they are a different color. Here I was, thinking you were here, because you were pregnant or something. So your parents have no idea where you are?"

Alessa explained, "No, it will be a week on Saturday that I've been gone. The only reason my mom would look for me is if Uncle Danny wants to move out. Then she would search far and wide to find me so she could pimp me back out to him. I hate her, Tasha. I know it's not good to hate your mother. I feel guilty about it, because I was raised to love and respect my parents, no matter what, but I just hate her!"

"Well, I don't believe any of that shit about having to love anyone," Tasha answered. "I don't blame you for hating her and your uncle. Hell, if that had happened to me, I would probably have found a way to kill both those motherfuckers! You have nothing to feel guilty about. You're here now and I'm glad. We need to think about something happier. Fuck your mother and her fucking family! On Saturday night, we gonna party and have a blast celebrating your birthday. We gonna need to do something about your appearance at the club, though. We'll work on that Friday night when you get home, okay?"

"Sounds great. Can you help me with my hair too? Rhonda used to help me. I never did any of it myself. So I'm not very good at hair or makeup." Alessa looked down at her own body and added, "Okay, I'm not that good at clothes either."

The girls belly-laughed as they both assessed Alessa's appearance.

On Friday night, when Alessa stepped off the city bus at nine-thirty, Tasha was waiting for her.

"Okay girl," she said, "it's time to give you a makeover."

They headed down Dauphin Street and made a right onto Fairhill. The row homes were much nicer on this street. They stopped in front of a row home that had grey stucco on the outside, with a red door and brass fixtures. There were bars on all the windows and four cement steps led up to the front door.

Alessa looked at Tasha and asked, "Whose house is this?"

"Mine. I live here with my parents. They've gone out to dinner tonight, but they won't care that you're over here. My mother would probably be thrilled to actually see another white girl here," she laughed.

When they went in, Alessa noticed that the furniture was worn, but well taken care of. The walls hadn't been painted in a long time and the green shag carpeting had lost all its shag. But overall, it was a huge step up from where she was living. Everything in the house was old, but it was clean and tidy.

Alessa followed her friend up to her bedroom on the second floor. Tasha pointed to the door next to hers and said, "That used to be Harlin's room. My mom turned it into her 'lady den', when he moved out. She keeps books and magazines in there. Her sewing machine is in there too. That's where she goes to get away from everything. Harlin painted it for her before he moved out and he also bought her the desk and the chair." Tasha motioned toward the furniture from the open doorway. Then she turned toward her own room. "This here, this is my room. I only really sleep here and spend most of my time outside the house."

"What grade are you in?" Alessa asked.

"I'm eighteen. Graduated high school last June. I ain't in school no more."

"So what are you going to do? I mean, since you are out of high school."

"I'm gonna keep selling weed for Harlin, until I save enough money to buy my own place. I ain't in no rush, though. My mom and dad don't give me any shit. I can come and go as I please. They know Harlin protects me out on the streets. So they don't worry none about that. Sometimes, they worry about me selling weed to the wrong person, but Harlin assured them I'd be fine."

Alessa, horrified, asked, "Your parents know that you and Harlin sell weed?"

"Yeah, girl. Ain't everybody's parents retarded like yours. They know what I do and I give them a little bit of money to help out around here. They say as long as I stay out of trouble, it ain't no issue for them."

Alessa tried to imagine having parents who actually believed in her. Clearly, the profession Tasha had picked for herself wasn't the most promising. All the more reason for Alessa to be impressed that her friend's parents supported her. It was amazing. Her own mother had beaten her for telling the truth about her uncle. And here was this world, where a daughter could tell her parents she was a pot pusher and the worst that happened was that they were concerned for her safety. It seemed a little unfair to Alessa that some people had families that were supportive, whereas she had come from one that had abused her in every way possible. She realized how fucked up her mother was; and even more fucked up was her nasty uncle.

Tasha sat Alessa down on a chair in front of a makeup mirror. Alessa couldn't believe all of the cosmetic products her friend had. She looked over them curiously. Tasha spun the chair around so that she couldn't stare into the mirror.

"Okay, now let's see," she said. "The first thing we need to do is even out your skin. Your complexion is great, but it ain't the same tone all over." She applied foundation and worked on Alessa's eyes next. She added a light, shimmering shadow and finished off with eyeliner and mascara. Finally, she applied a little blush on Alessa's cheekbones. Tasha took a step back and studied her. She seemed pleased. Then she picked up a pair of scissors.

Alessa cringed. "Are you going to cut my hair?" she cried out.

Tasha focused intently on her hair. "Well," she said, "I could just leave it looking like a rat's nest or I could help you work with those natural curls of yours. I ain't gonna take much off the length. I just want to give it a little shape and body."

Alessa smiled at her, silently hoping that Tasha didn't fuck it up. When she had finished cutting, Tasha picked up a spray bottle filled with water and wet Alessa's hair down. She pulled out her blow dryer and began using a small, round brush. She applied a little lipstick on her lips and stood back to observe the effect again.

When asked if she was ready for the big reveal, Alessa fidgeted with anticipation, nodding vigorously like a child. Tasha swung her around in her chair to face the mirror. Alessa stared at herself incredulously. The person she saw in the mirror was someone she couldn't recognize. Her large brown eyes looked dreamy and her lips were lightly covered with a pale pink shade of lipstick. The color was so close to her natural lips you could hardly tell she was wearing lipstick. Yet the shine made them look inviting. Her hair looked like silk and fell in soft curls around her face and down to her shoulders.

Alessa turned back to Tasha and hugged her hard. "I can't believe you did this. I can't believe it! You actually made me look good. Look at my hair! Oh my God! My hair has never looked like this!"

Tasha stood back, basking in the sheer pleasure of Alessa's happiness. She had felt sorry for her friend ever since she heard about her traumatic childhood. She knew it was the root cause of Alessa's lack of self-esteem and it was deeply gratifying to see her so happy now. Tasha knew that a little help would make Alessa hot and desirable. She felt content that she could give her this moment. She would teach her how to do it herself so she could continue to gain in confidence. Tasha liked Alessa a lot. The girl was down-to-earth and humble. She was the type of person who stayed your friend for life. Tasha even liked the fact that Alessa was naïve. It enabled her to introduce her to experiences she hadn't enjoyed before, just like the makeover that night.

"You are hot, girl!" Tasha said encouragingly. "Look at you! I'll show you how to do this yourself. It ain't hard at all. It only took me fifteen minutes."

"Thank you so much, Tasha."

Tasha was struck by Alessa's overwhelming and obviously sincere expression of gratitude. She wasn't used to people being that grateful to her. "Now, let's take a look at what you can wear tomorrow night," she said, opening the top drawer on her dresser. "You will have to wear your own jeans, because we ain't the same size. I got ass and you don't."

Alessa giggled as Tasha dug through her drawer and pulled out a black bra from her dresser. She told her to put it on and continued with her treasure hunt, until she had found a black netted shirt that was completely see-through. Alessa looked at her in surprise when she was asked to put it on.

"Just do it!" Tasha giggled.

Alessa put the shirt on and looked in the mirror. It was completely see-through, yes, but the bra underneath covered her breasts completely.

Tasha said, "That looks great. You got black shoes?"

"Yes, I do. I brought a pair of Rhonda's heels, just in case I needed them for work."

"Okay, wear those and your tightest pair of jeans. Here, wear this belt too."

Alessa was excited and couldn't wait to go out the following night. "All right, let's get you back to your apartment. Tomorrow night is a big night, birthday girl!"

Before they left Tasha's room, Alessa turned and hugged her again. "Thanks for all of this, really."

Both girls left the house smiling and feeling like they had established a much needed bond.

Chapter Twelve

When Alessa stepped off the city bus on Saturday night, Tasha, who was waiting for her, ran up to give her a hug. "Happy birthday, Alessa!" she said.

They walked the few blocks to Tasha's house. Up in her room, Tasha did Alessa's makeup and hair. Alessa changed into the clothes and shoes she had brought along in her duffle bag. When she was ready, Tasha quickly put on her own outfit, which was incredibly sexy. The v-neck of her shirt almost plunged down to her navel. The inner curves of her breasts peeked through and against her light brown skin shimmered, a beautiful silver necklace with a peace sign. The two girls appraised each other's appearance and decided it was time to go.

Shortly after ten p.m., they arrived at Harlin's house, where he and his friends were hanging out. When they entered the living room, Harlin glanced at Alessa, pausing for a second look. Alessa smiled openly. She knew he thought she looked good.

Tasha said, "You remember my friend, Alessa?"

"Yeah, I remember her," Harlin acknowledged. "She looks a little different tonight. She looks better, in fact. You do this work on her?"

Tasha put her arms around her brother's neck. "I sure did! I'm damn good at that shit, huh?"

"Yeah, you are. Maybe you should think about doing this shit for those movie stars."

Alessa noticed how close they were and detected the love Harlin felt for his sister in his hard eyes. How lucky Tasha was to have a brother like him, she thought.

Within minutes, they were in Harlin's van—a large black vehicle with chrome wheels and door handles—with five of his friends. When they got to Pulsations, Tasha took Alessa by the hand and headed toward the bar.

She ordered two beers and excitedly said, "Isn't this place cool? I love it here!"

Alessa was still taking in all the lights and sounds. The place dazzled. People were dancing everywhere. There were dancers in cages that hovered above the dance floor. When the bartender handed them their beers, Tasha grabbed her hand again and pushed her through the crowd onto the dance floor.

Alessa, who had always loved to dance, immediately started to move to the music. Soon she was swaying to the beat, as if the song had been choreographed with her in mind. Tasha was smiling at her, her eyes wide.

Alessa caught her look and stopped dancing. "What?" she asked. "Why are staring at me? Do I look stupid?" She suddenly felt very self-conscious.

Tasha shook her head. "There's something wrong with you, girl," she said. "No, you don't look stupid at all. You are an incredible dancer! Shit, I think every man within eyeshot was watching you."

"They were? You think I'm a good dancer?"

"Yes, they were," Tasha said firmly. "And I know you're a good dancer. Did you ever take lessons?"

"You're kidding me, right? No, I never took lessons. I barely had clothes that fit me and I wore shoes until my feet grew so big I thought my fuck-ing toes would break off. There certainly weren't any dance lessons. I always loved to listen to music. When I slept at Rhonda's house, we turned on music and danced in her living room. It's fun to dance, I love it."

Tasha and Alessa danced together all night. It was the best birthday celebration Alessa had ever had. In fact, it was the only one she could remember. Later in the evening, Tasha lifted her beer mug in a toast, "Here's to you on your birthday."

"And here's to you and Rhonda," Alessa responded.

The evening had been perfect and Alessa was happy to be alive. For once in her life, she was actually looking forward to the future, instead of regretting her past. As they left Pulsations and headed back to North Philadelphia, the two girls spoke excitedly about the evening, oblivious to Harlin and his friends who were busy making fun of their enthusiasm. Tasha just shot them looks and pointed her finger at them from time to time.

Finally, one of Harlin's buddies addressed Alessa. "Hey girl," he said, "you sure can shake that little ass of yours, can't you? Any time you want to shake that thing on me, I'd be happy to oblige."

Alessa's body suddenly stiffened.

Sitting next to her, Tasha felt the tension build up in her friend and struck out. "Why don't you shut the fuck up?" she spat out. "Her name is Alessa and she ain't nobody's bitch-whore. So don't be talking to her like she's one. You understand what the fuck I'm telling you?"

Harlin glanced over at his friend, a look of scorn in his eyes.

"Yeah, I got it," the boy said gruffly. "You don't have to get all crazy and shit. I was only messin' with her."

When they got back to Dauphin Street and climbed out of the van, Alessa thanked Tasha. Then she asked, "How come he got all nervous when you freaked out on him? He seems so tough."

Tasha said, "'Cause I don't cause no shit for anybody, but when I say something to one of Harlin's crew, he expects them to mind me. My brother knows I'm easygoing. If I have to call someone out, it must be important to me. When Harlin gave that guy that look, he knew he better not take that conversation any further or he would have to deal with my brother."

"Well, thank you. It was nice of you to stick up for me. Tonight was great. Thanks for everything."

"Tasha, I need to see you," Harlin called out.

His sister walked over to where he stood, leaving Alessa by herself.

"Tonight was great Harlin! Thanks," Tasha said to him

"Yeah, no problem," her brother responded. "What was up with you, freakin' out on my boy in the van? I know this girl is a friend of yours, but you haven't even known her for that long. Not long enough to side with her over one of my brothers."

Tasha took him by the hand and led him to some steps in front of an abandoned row home. She climbed onto the first step so that she was eye level with him. With his hand clasped in hers, she said, "Harlin, this girl means a lot to me. You know I ain't had any good friends ever. Alessa is different. She don't care where I come from or who my brother is. She likes me just for myself."

Harlin looked deep into Tasha's eyes, listening patiently to what she had to say.

"This girl has seen some bad shit, man," Tasha went on. "She ain't got no one. When I'm with her, I feel like I have a sister. I don't want no one disrespecting her. She is the kind of person you would want me to be friends with. So if you could tell your boys that she is off-limits, it would mean a lot to me. You know I don't ask you to tell your crew what to do. This is a favor I am asking of you now."

"Okay, baby," Harlin said. "If this girl means that much to you, I will make it clear to my crew that there ain't no fuckin' with her. I love you, girl. If you say she is important to you, I know she must be. Goodnight, babe. See you tomorrow."

They hugged tightly and Tasha held on to her brother for a few seconds longer than she normally would. Harlin wondered, as he walked away, just what made this girl so special. Now he was curious; what kind of bad shit had she seen?

When he caught up with his gang, Harlin told them, "Listen, no fuckin' with Tasha's friend. For some reason, this chick means a lot to her and we need to respect that. So I don't want any of you to say shit to her that we would say to other bitches. Everybody understand?"

The boys grumbled, but agreed to respect Tasha's wishes. After all, they all loved her and were protective of her. That was a rule of the club. Tasha was watched over by all of them and all the people they knew. No one fucked with Tasha, Queen of Dauphin Street, as they called her.

"What's so special about this little white girl anyway, Harlin?" one of his friends asked.

"I don't know, man. Tasha said she ain't got no one. No family or nothing. She said she's been through a lot of bad shit. We know we all seen bad shit. So Tasha wouldn't say that, if it wasn't something really bad. All I know is that little white girl can dance, my brothers! Did you all see her moving to that music?"

They all laughed and agreed that Alessa could move. On their way back to Harlin's house, the group passed Tag, the leader of the gang which had harassed Alessa on the bus. Harlin looked over at him and gave him a nod. Tag nodded back. Harlin could detect the fear in the boy's face. Satisfied that they were showing him due respect, Harlin kept walking. He knew these boys were trouble for the neighborhood. With nothing better to do, they were always fuckin' with the old people and the hookers on the street. Harlin also knew they were as ruthless as he and his crew could be. The difference between them was that Harlin was only ruthless with people who fucked with him or his own. Tag's gang of shitheads fucked with everyone just for fun. Harlin had set the tone with them early on. He had made it clear that they were never to fuck with any of his weed-selling territory, his gang and especially, his sister. The first time he had laid down the rules, Tag had tried to be a tough guy and asked him, "Who are you to tell me who I can and can't fuck with?"

Harlin had pulled out his .357 Magnum and shoved it into Tag's mouth. Then he had said, "Who the fuck am I? I am the grim, fucking reaper and I'll be here to collect your soul and send it to hell, you little punk motherfucker! You understand that I own this neighborhood and we'll get along fine. Get it?"

With the barrel of the gun rammed so high up in his mouth that it was practically touching the back of his throat, Tag had nodded vigorously. Meanwhile, Harlin's crew was eyeing the rest of boys who clearly understood that if they ignored Harlin's rules, there would be hell to pay. Everyone in the neighborhood was loyal to him. From that night on, the boys never got in the way of Harlin's business and they were all cool with each other. The boys were always up to no good, of course. They were nothing more than a pack of street thugs, with little to motivate them, other than making people's lives miserable.

Chapter Thirteen

A lessa's job at the Dollar Store was far from exciting. Brady, the manager, was a big asshole, just like the girls had warned. He would slither through the store, bossing them around, yelling that everything they were doing was wrong. He was a useless piece of shit and they all despised him. He would often tell Alessa, "Your tits are too small. Too bad you ain't got a pair of knockers like the other girls." She hated him, but knew he was harmless. He was just an obnoxious pig on a power trip, because his biggest accomplishment in life was becoming the manager at the Dollar Store.

Alessa knew that power changed people. It made them want to have total control over others. Brady was just like her Uncle Danny and even her mother, Caterina; they were each busy positioning themselves as a master puppeteer of those they perceived as weak. Alessa wondered what people like them got out of being cruel and manipulative. She told herself that someday, if she did come into a position of power, she would make sure she did not abuse it. On the contrary, she would use it to help people. Until that time came, though she doubted it ever would, she would just focus on the positive. The job at the Dollar Store was paying her rent and keeping her fed. For now, that would have to be good enough. She was proud that she was living on her own. And now, with Tasha as her friend, it seemed that she could even enjoy life a little too.

They hung out every night after Alessa finished her shift at the Dollar Store and they savored each other's company. In the months that had passed since Alessa first arrived in the neighborhood, Tasha had become her new family. She checked in with Zoe less frequently now, but was relieved to learn that there was no manhunt on to find her. Zoe had assured her that she was better off without her rotten family anyway.

Meanwhile, Zoe was still struggling to come to terms with her daughter's death. Even over the phone, Alessa could tell from her tone that her friend's mother was beginning to lose it. She had become a total recluse and had stopped "dating" altogether. Alessa still loved her and would never ever forget what she had done to help her in her hour of dire need. She felt guilty that Zoe had done all she could to help her move on, but was now in a situation where she couldn't help herself. Alessa felt impelled to do something for her and return the favor, but Zoe insisted that there was nothing the young girl could do.

"The only good thing to come out of Rhonda's death," she told her, "is that I was able to help free you of the chains that had bound you since you were a little girl. Let me take joy in that, Alessa. You have helped me by making me feel I have done something worthy for another person."

Alessa tried her best to avoid all the riffraff on the streets of North Philadelphia. She minded her own business and was careful not to make eye contact with anyone. Her senses were on red alert when she walked to and from the city bus stop. For the most part, she was left alone, aside from the occasional hooting and hollering that was directed at her, as she passed crowds of men or boys who always seemed to be drinking or smoking pot. Even Lea, Alessa discovered gradually, had a softer side to her personality that emerged in the girl's presence. Instead of the usual grunt with which she had acknowledged her new tenant earlier, the old lady actually greeted Alessa now when she ran into her. The other tenants at Lea's house were older and kept to themselves. Their aloofness filled Alessa with a sense of relief because of her persistent anxiety about people asking her more questions about herself than she could comfortably answer without giving her past away. Until she turned eighteen, she preferred to remain inconspicuous, to fly below the radar; she couldn't risk drawing attention to herself and ending up being sent back home.

Now that Lea knew neither Alessa nor her friend would cause any trouble, she even allowed Tasha to go up to her apartment. When Tasha first saw in what miserable conditions her friend was living, she felt sorrier for her than she ever had. At the same time, she developed the greatest respect for Alessa's ability to adapt herself to her circumstances and surroundings.

One night, while the two friends were having dinner, Tasha announced, "I'm leaving on a trip with my parents in a couple of days. We're going to

Atlanta to visit my aunt. I'll be gone for two weeks. Sure wish I could take you with me."

"That's okay," Alessa laughed. "I need all my hours at work, but I'll certainly miss you while you're gone."

The girls had been inseparable since Alessa's seventeenth birthday. They did everything together. Alessa even hung out with Tasha while she was selling weed on the street.

Once Tasha had left for Atlanta, Alessa realized how accustomed she had grown to having her around. One night after work, she stopped at the Dauphin Mini Mart to pick up some groceries. When she came out of the store, Tag and his boys were standing across the street. Alessa immediately stepped up her pace so she could get back to her apartment without any trouble. As she passed by an open lot between row homes, however, she caught a movement out of the corner of her eye. Before she knew it, the boys had grabbed her from behind and were dragging her to the trash-strewn lot. It was very dimly lit and not a soul could be seen in the vicinity. As she tried to anticipate the kind of torture that might be in store for her, Alessa's heart sank. Her stomach twisted with fear and revulsion as she remembered the boys telling her on the bus that if she puked the next time, they would make her eat her own vomit.

When they finally came to a stop, Alessa noticed they were now at the empty lot; there were six guys standing around her. They stared at her with contempt as she pleaded with them to let her go, offering all the money she had on her which was just 14 dollars. Tag made his way to the front of the group and stared down at her. There was no sign of a human being behind the dead brown eyes that took in the small world around him with a frighteningly vacant expression.

"Lift your skirt up, bitch!" he spat at her. "We want to pick up where we left off. I wanna see that sweet pussy we missed out on the last time."

Alessa began to cry, begging them, between sobs, not to hurt her. With one swift gesture of his head, two of Tag's boys seized her by the shoulders, wrestled her to the ground and pinned her down. Tag dropped to his knees, dragged up her denim skirt till it was bunched around her waist and ripped her panties off with one hand. As Alessa struggled to get free, he punched her in the left eye. She flinched from the blow, hitting her head hard against the ground and lost consciousness for what couldn't have been more than a minute. When she opened her eyes again, her shirt and her bra had been torn off her body. She lay there helplessly for a moment, naked and exposed for everyone to gape at. Then she began begging and pleading again to be left alone. The boys, however, seemed oblivious to her tearful pleas. She gasped in pain, as Tag mauled her breasts and shoved his fingers brutally between her legs. And it was only when he pulled his fingers out of her, thrust them into his mouth and sucked on them greedily that she realized to her horror what he was about to do.

"Now *that's* some sweet meat!" he said slowly and deliberately. "Just like I had imagined."

Tag motioned for his cronies to draw closer. One by one, they jammed their hands between her legs. Then their leader shoved his way to the front again and dropped his pants so that they lay around his ankles.

"Hold the bitch real good!" he ordered the boys. In moments, he had plunged all the way inside her, thrusting further and further into her with such unimaginable violence that Alessa feared he would snuff the very breath out of her. When he had finished, he turned to the heavy boy standing next to him and said, "You're next, brother."

The heavy boy dropped his pants, in turn, and said, "Sit the bitch up."

Alessa saw that his penis was peppered with open sores the size of a pencil eraser, oozing milky white fluid. The boy had herpes. She screamed in revulsion and began to squirm, struggling to free herself.

"Bitch," the boy bit out, "you gonna need to suck my dick, 'cause I don't want my brothers here gettin' none of this shit one of those nasty fuckin' whores gave me. That way, they can all get a good fuck in, when I'm done."

Alessa clenched her teeth and locked her lips shut, trying desperately to break free once again. Just as another boy was bending down to force her mouth open, she heard the roar of angry voices coming down the street. She wasn't sure if she believed in God anymore, but Alessa now closed her eyes and began to pray for help.

When she opened her eyes again, the first person she saw was Harlin. The rest of his gang was coming up quickly behind him. Harlin had his gun out, aiming it at her tormentors. Tag and his boys froze in their tracks and looked back at the other group. Harlin walked over to the boy who had his penis close to Alessa's face. Before he could react, Harlin's left hand had come up and the blade of the knife he was gripping had sliced through the boy's stomach. Then with a sharp motion, he pulled the blade upward right into his victim's chest. The boy collapsed on the ground in a heap of flesh, his still-pulsating guts spilling out of his stomach, the torn intestines unable to hold in his feces.

Harlin looked at Tag. "What's going on here, motherfucker?" he asked. "You assholes having fun?"

"Listen man, we don't fuck with any of your stuff," the other guy said defensively. "Me and my boys here are just lettin' off a little steam. What the fuck do you care? She ain't nothin' to you. I should fuckin' kill you for killing my boy here!"

"Oh yeah? Come on, you worthless piece of shit! Let me see you try!" With that, Harlin raised the gun in his right hand and placed its muzzle hard against Tag's temple. His gang of boys instantly took up position, their guns on the ready.

Tag threw his hands up in a gesture of surrender. "All right, man! I fuckin' get it, okay? Take that motherfucking gun away from my head!"

Harlin lowered the gun and grasped Tag by the collar. He pointed to Alessa. "You see that bitch there?" he said. "She's with me, motherfucker. If I ever see you or any of your crew near her again, I will hunt you down, one by one, and cut your fucking dicks off. You'll wish, then, that I had sliced you open quick, like I did your fat friend here. I'll make sure your death is a slow, painful one. Do you understand me?"

Tag pulled himself free of Harlin. "Yeah," he muttered, "I understand."

His boys hefted their dead comrade off the ground and carried him out toward the street.

Alessa was shaking so hard by now that her teeth chattered. Harlin looked down at her, then took off his shirt and wrapped it around her. He motioned to two of his friends who picked her up and carried her the few blocks to Harlin's house. Harlin instructed them to lay her on the mattress in the second bedroom. Alessa was still crying and trembling. She was so shaken, her mouth couldn't even form words; she just kept looking at all the boys with wide, terrified eyes.

A few minutes later, Harlin walked into the room with a blanket and told the others to go out into the living room and wait for him. He covered Alessa with the blanket and sat down on the mattress beside her. He talked to her softly, assuring her repeatedly that she was all right, that she was safe, until she had calmed down. Alessa didn't feel all right, but instinct told her she was safe with Harlin.

"What did they do to you, before we got there?" he asked gently.

Alessa answered in a quavering voice, "They all stuck their fingers in down there. Then Tag raped me. You walked up just as that fat boy was trying to force me to suck his dick. Harlin, he had herpes sores all over it!" She started to cry again.

Harlin reached out and hugged her comfortingly. "Those little pricks!" He growled. "Don't you worry. They'll pay for what they did. If I had known Tag raped you, I would have killed him on the spot. Just happened that we heard the commotion when we were walking down the street. One of my boys said he had seen you at the Mini Mart and noticed those assholes following you. I'm sorry we didn't get there sooner. Are you okay? You on the pill?"

"I'm okay now," Alessa responded. "And no, I'm not on the pill. I just finished my period."

Harlin had no idea what that meant, but took it as a sign that she didn't think she could get pregnant, although Alessa's point was that it increased the chances of pregnancy.

"You need a doctor or something?"

Alessa shook her head. There was no way she was going to a doctor or to the police. She wanted this horrible experience to just go away.

"Why is it men just want to fuck me?" she blurted out suddenly. "Do I have a sign on my head that says: 'Rape me'?"

Harlin looked at her in surprise. "What are you talking about?" he asked curiously. "You been raped before?"

Alessa nodded, acknowledging that she had.

"Nah," Harlin told her, "you ain't got no sign on your head that says, 'rape me'. You're just missing the sign on your head that says, 'don't fuck with me or I'll kill you.' We'll work on that." He smiled that brilliant, broad smile which warmed her in this darkest of moments.

"It's okay," he said soothingly. "You're safe now. You'll stay here with me for a while. At least, until Tasha gets home. Then you two can have that girl talk. I'm sure she can make you feel better."

The fear that had gripped Alessa began to lift as she lay back on the bare mattress. She shed silent tears as the reality of what she had just lived through sank in. She grasped Harlin's hand and said, "Thank you, Harlin. You saved my life tonight."

For the first time in his life, Harlin felt a tug at his heart for a woman other than his sister. He was new to the feeling and it took him by surprise.

He realized then that he liked Alessa. He was beginning to understand the special quality about her that appealed to his sister. He could see now that unlike other girls her age, Alessa took nothing in her life for granted. And her needs were minimal. All she wanted was to feel safe and cared for. He sat with her until her slow, steady breathing told him she was asleep. Then he walked out into his living room and looked at his crew.

"That motherfucker needs to pay," he told his boys. "He raped her. Any man who can't get sex without stealing it deserves to die."

Chapter Fourteen

The next morning, Alessa woke up tired. She had slept badly. All night, her dreams had kept drifting between the boys who had accosted her the previous night and her Uncle Danny. She was grateful she had two days off before returning to work.

When she walked out of the bedroom to use the bathroom, Harlin was standing at the sink, shaving. He wore nothing but a pair of sweat pants and Alessa noticed what a well-defined physique he had. His shoulders were broad and his torso narrowed at the waist. His stomach was well sculpted and his muscled arms rippled with strength.

He caught her staring at him and said, "How you doing this morning? Give me a minute to finish shaving and the bathroom will be yours."

"I'm doing okay," she replied. "I didn't sleep well and my body is sore."

Harlin looked at her, but didn't know what to say next. He was used to a world where he dealt with men who had been in battle and didn't talk about how they felt the next day. He really wished Tasha were home. "I called Tasha last night and told her what had happened," he said. "She's flying home tomorrow."

"Oh no, Harlin," Alessa protested. "She doesn't need to do that. This is her vacation and I'll be fine."

"Ain't no big deal," he answered. "She said the relatives were driving her fucking crazy. Besides, she was real upset to hear what had happened to you. I told her you'd be staying here with me, until she got home and she liked the idea. When you need to work again?"

"I don't have to be in until Monday afternoon."

Harlin's expression hardened. "You need to be working during the day. Coming home at night ain't a good idea for you. I'll make sure you get day work. One of my boys will drive you there and pick you up for a while, until we finish dealing with this shit."

Alessa's eyes widened. "What do you mean until you're finished dealing with it? Harlin, I just want this to go away. And I'm afraid if you keep going after them, they will come back and do it to me again."

Harlin put his hand on her shoulder and gave it a gentle squeeze. "You don't have anything to worry about," he reassured her. "You need to understand that this is bigger than you. In my neighborhood, men don't have sex without it being mutual. Last night didn't look too mutual to me and we need to deal with that. Otherwise, we'll have these punks thinking they can do whatever they want and get away with it. We do illegal shit and fuck people up who overstep their bounds, but we can't stand aside and let them start throwing down the women around here and raping them. You understand?"

Alessa nodded. When Harlin had left the bathroom to her, she stood for several minutes staring at her reflection in the mirror. She felt as if she were looking at a stranger. Less than twenty-four hours ago, she had, for the first time in her life, started feeling good about herself. Now, as she gazed at the dark circles under her eyes, with one eye nearly swollen shut from being punched, she was disheartened by the thought that life would, perhaps, never cease to be a struggle. Maybe, just maybe, she was meant to be unhappy? There must have been something she'd done to deserve such a shitty hand. She splashed some water on her face and turned to use the toilet. She wasn't wearing any panties, since they had been ripped off her and it was when she pulled up the large tee shirt she was wearing and sat on the toilet that she saw all the bruises and scratches between her thighs.

When she peed, the sensation was as if someone had thrown acid between her legs. She screamed involuntarily as her insides burned, bringing Harlin rushing into the bathroom. Rage inflamed him when he looked down and saw the carnage between her legs. His face turned red and his eyes burned with fury.

"I'm leaving," he said curtly. "When I come home later, I will walk you down to your apartment so you can get some clothes. Until I get back, you stay inside and don't let nobody come in."

"I just didn't expect it to burn this much,' Alessa said apologetically. "I'm okay, really. It just took me by surprise. That's all. I'm sorry for screaming out like that and being a pain in your ass." Alessa began to cry.

Harlin looked at the girl, sitting on the toilet and sobbing and felt bad for her.

"You ain't a pain in the ass," he told her. "How about you cook something good for me and my boys for dinner? That would be real nice. I got all kinds of shit in there to cook. My mom and Tasha are always bringing stuff over."

Alessa managed a slight smile. "Okay, I can do that."

Harlin left the house shortly after and headed down Dauphin Street in his black van. He was picking up his boys and they had two stops to make. The first was a visit to Tag, the neighborhood rapist; the second was the Dollar Store on Broad Street to discuss Alessa's new hours with her boss.

Harlin and his crew found Tag walking down North Orkney Street which was deserted at that hour. They pulled the van over and opened the side door, sucking their target into the van. Tag's eyes searched frantically for a way to escape, but he knew it was no use. He also knew if he put up a fight, he would piss Harlin's boys off even more and the beating he would get would be far worse.

"Hey man, what the fuck?" he said, trying to brazen it out. "I thought we settled this last night?"

Harlin looked at him. "Yeah bitch, that was before we knew you raped the girl."

Tag turned to one of Harlin's crew members. "Come on, man, help me out," he implored. "I didn't mean to rape her; I just got carried away is all."

The boy he had addressed glared at him as if he might snap his neck and said, "I ain't here to help you. You broke the code of Dauphin Street last night when you raped that girl. Now just shut the fuck up or I'll cut your fucking tongue out."

Harlin and his crew drove on for another thirty minutes before they reached an empty lot sheltered from the street by some abandoned and dilapidated buildings. Tag had no idea where they were, but felt broken glass crunching beneath his feet as they pushed him ahead of them into one of the rundown buildings. When they ordered him to take off his clothes, he groveled at their feet, begging for forgiveness.

Harlin walked up to him and grabbed him by the collar of his shirt. "Take off your fucking clothes or we can take them off for you, if that's what you'd like."

Tag began to cry as he stripped naked. When he was done, Harlin motioned to his boys. Two of them walked over and hogtied their victim's feet and hands together behind his back before laying him on his side. Tag shook with terror as his bare flesh met the cold cement floor. He knew his life was about to be snuffed out and he began to whimper, pleading for mercy.

Harlin walked over to him, a rag wrapped around his hand. He grasped Tag's penis with that hand, held it out straight in front of him and sawed his way through it with the large knife he was gripping in his other hand, till it was detached from his victim's body. Then he dangled it high above Tag's head for him to see. Screaming in pain, Tag started vomiting. "You won't be needin' this anymore," Harlin told him. Then he looked at two of his boys and said, "Let him bleed out; then burn the body."

As their van pulled away from the abandoned building, the glow of the fire was visible from outside. The crew had dowsed a blanket in gasoline, tossed it on top of Tag and lit a match.

"That was one ugly ass penis!" Harlin joked.

The boys in the van all broke into laughter as they headed to North Broad for a visit to the manager of the Dollar Store.

They walked boldly into the store and Harlin immediately asked for the manager. The girls at the register recognized him right away and started to get nervous, hoping there wouldn't be any shooting. One of the girls went into a back room and Brady came out almost immediately. He too knew who Harlin was. If you lived or worked anywhere in North Philadelphia, you had to live under a rock not to know who he was. Brady stepped up to Harlin and extended his hand.

"Hi," he said, "I'm Brady, the store manager."

Harlin ignored his hand and stared at him. "You got a girl named Alessa working here."

Brady quickly jumped in with, "Yeah, she's young and a little goofy. Do you want me to get you her address? I can go in the back and get it."

"No, motherfucker," Harlin told him, "I don't want you to give me her address. That girl is with me. If I ever find out you gave someone her address, I will kill you. Understand?"

Brady immediately regretted his attempt to suck up by making the offer and nodded vigorously in agreement. "Yeah, sure. I won't ever give anyone her address."

Harlin said, "She can't work that late shift no more. You're gonna need to give her hours during the day. I don't want her leaving here after five p.m. You make sure that starting on Monday, she is only working the day shift."

Behind Brady's broad smile, he was shaking with fear. "Absolutely, sir," he said submissively. "That's no problem. Alessa only works during the day from now on. No more night shifts. I completely understand."

"One other thing," Harlin said. "Don't ever let me hear that you've been disrespectful to her."

"I would never be disrespectful to her, sir," Brady assured him.

Harlin turned on his heel and, without casting another glance at Brady or the women working in the store, walked out, with his crew following close behind. As he got back into his van, he thought that Alessa could surely be doing something better than earning minimum wage at that dump. Shit, the girl could really dance! She oughta be at Double Visions, making some real money. Doubles, as they all called it, was a go-go bar. The girls there were hot and exotic and Alessa would fit right in. He would suggest it to Tasha when she got home the next day. As they drove back to Dauphin Street, Harlin convinced himself that it was a good profession for Alessa to get into. She could dance and make good money and he could provide her protection.

Chapter Fifteen

On Sunday morning, Tasha came barreling through her brother's front door. She looked at him anxiously and he nodded in the direction of his spare bedroom. She opened the door hesitantly and found Alessa in bed, lying on her back and staring vacantly at the ceiling.

"Sweetie, I'm here," Tasha whispered.

Alessa turned and looked at her, struggling to get her eyes to focus. But the moment her friend moved further into the room and came into view, Alessa started crying and reached out to her like a child in need of comfort. In a moment, Tasha was lying on the bed next to her, the two friends entwined like a pretzel. As Tasha held her tight, Alessa let the tears flow. They lay there together for a long time. Then Tasha pulled back so she could look at her.

"What happened?" she asked after a moment. "I want you to tell me everything those motherfuckers did to you."

As Alessa related the details of the incident, Tasha's expression changed from dismay to one of horror. By now, she knew all about Alessa's past with her uncle and Carl. She was aware that Alessa had fled her home for fear of being gang raped by her uncle's friends. And now, the very thing she had feared had come to haunt her here, on Daulphin Street. When Alessa hesitated for a moment while telling the story, Tasha could tell she was holding something back.

"Okay, girl," Tasha said. "What ain't you telling me? I can tell you're holding out. Come on now. You know you can trust me."

Alessa started to cry again. "Tasha, Harlin *killed* a man! He stuck a knife in him and split him from gut to heart! It was horrible! What if someone finds out it was Harlin? What if they think I started it all, that it was all my fault, and send me to prison? I know he was protecting me, but I saw him murder someone. I'm scared, Tasha!"

Tasha took Alessa's chin in her hand. "Listen, sweetie," she said gently. "You ain't got nothin' to worry 'bout. Here in the streets of North Philly, it's different from where you came from. Ain't nobody gonna tell the police that Harlin killed that fat motherfucker. Harlin told me what he did and it ain't no big deal. It ain't the first time he had to kill. You need to forget you ever seen anything. You understand?"

Alessa nodded, but her friend's assurance didn't help to ease her worry. Tasha helped her out of bed and led her to the bathroom. She helped her undress, turned on a hot shower and urged her inside.

"I want you get yourself washed up real good," she told her. "I will be back in a couple of minutes to check on you."

Tasha left to find her brother and ask him about the killing. Harlin didn't need to explain himself to her. She knew he needed to do what was right for everyone.

"Did she tell you that Tag raped her?" Harlin asked her.

Tasha shook her head.

"Well, I took care of that too. Ain't nothing left of him, but some ashes."

Tasha put her arms around her brother's neck.

"Thank you!" she said. "You're the best brother in the whole world!"

"You need to remind your little friend in there that she should keep her mouth shut about what happened that night," Harlin cautioned her. "She needs to understand that people who live in this neighborhood don't talk about the shit they see."

Tasha assured him that she had already explained it to Alessa and he had nothing to worry about. Satisfied with his sister's confidence in her friend, Harlin went back to weighing the weed he was placing in small bags.

Once Alessa finished showering, Tasha went into the bathroom to help with her hair. Then she noticed the bruises and scratches on her inner thighs. Alessa's eye wasn't looking too good either. She had come out with a nasty shiner. Tasha's blood began to boil at the thought of those bastards just grabbing what they wanted.

She helped Alessa dress, made her toast for breakfast and when she had eaten it, commanded, "Come on. We need to go down to the Dauphin

Mini Mart and get some things for this house. Harlin is out of orange juice and paper towels."

Alessa recoiled at the idea. "No, please!" she pleaded. "I don't want to go there. I'm afraid, Tasha. What if those boys are there? What if they hurt both of us this time?"

"Sweetie, you can't stay inside forever," she reasoned. "On these streets, news travels fast. So I'm sure most of the neighborhood knows that you were raped. To regain respect, you need to go back out and show them that you ain't afraid. If you don't, people will think that you let them win. What's worse, they will wonder why you are afraid to be out, with Harlin and his crew protecting you. That's what we do here. When bad shit happens, we just keep moving. Otherwise, we would never survive."

Alessa looked at her friend. She realized that Tasha couldn't bear to let anyone think ill of her brother. Harlin had saved her life. Recognizing that she was now part of something bigger than herself, Alessa agreed to go out, but only after Tasha had promised not to leave her side for even one second. An hour later, they were walking toward the mini mart. Suddenly, Alessa froze on the sidewalk. Tasha, who had been talking about her trip to Atlanta, stopped as well and looked at her.

"What's wrong, Alessa?" she asked, "why you stoppin'?" Then she followed Alessa's gaze to a spot across the street. Tag's gang was there. "Were they all there the other night?" she asked her.

"Yeah, all of them. Oh God, Tasha, what are we going to do? Let's go back."

Tasha looked at her like she was nuts. "We ain't going back nowhere!" she said firmly. Then with a swift jerk, Tasha snatched Alessa's hand, gripped it in her own and pulled her across the street toward the gang of boys.

When the two girls were standing in front of them, Tasha said, "I understand you motherfuckers messed with my girl. I also hear that Tag's been out of town ever since." She smiled tightly at them, her searing gaze taking in first one, then the others. "Maybe some more of you will be going out of town? You know, since you all had your hands in this 'sweet meat'."

The boys started shifting uncomfortably.

"Not too sure how this is going to work out for all of you," Tasha went on. "You know, she ain't just with me. She's with Harlin too. And you know how he gets when you mess with his shit."

One of the boys finally summoned up the courage to retort, "So what the fuck you want us to do? We didn't know she was with Harlin. And it ain't no big deal anyway. Ain't like we all got to fuck her. Fuck, girl, we just got a couple of fingers wet, before Harlin broke it all up!"

Tasha walked up close to the boy who had spoken to her and looked him in the eye. "Might not be a big deal to you, but it sure is to me. So I guess it wouldn't be no big deal, if someone stuck their fingers up your ass while you were being held down. I'll let Harlin know it ain't no big deal." Tasha turned and, taking Alessa by the hand, left the boys standing there with uncertainty, fear in their eyes. After Harlin's sister had dealt with them, none of them knew for certain if there would be a further price to pay for what they had done or if Tag's death had been revenge enough.

When they were far enough away from the boys, Alessa asked, "How do you know Tag is out of town? And what did you mean when you said that maybe they would go out of town too?"

"Listen, everything is taken care of," Tasha assured her. She added cryptically, "Harlin did what he needed to do and Tag won't be around to bother you no more. That's all I meant."

Alessa didn't press the point, but she had seen enough in the last few days to be convinced that Tag was dead. She had mixed feelings about it. The thought of Harlin killing her rapist nauseated her. At the same time, she was overwhelmed with relief. Guilt gnawed at her for not feeling devastated that a life had been taken on account of something that had happened to her. She was used to being exploited, not protected, and didn't quite know how to process the incidents that had overtaken her so rapidly.

When they got back to Harlin's house, Alessa went back into the spare bedroom. Tasha went to look for her brother and found him in the kitchen.

"Harlin," she said, "we ran into Tag's gang. I warned them to mind their own business."

"Yeah," her brother said, "stupid motherfuckers should know by now where they stand, but now they've been officially warned. How's she doing?"

"She's good. She ain't used to this. She'll be fine."

"I want to talk to you about her for a minute," Harlin said, leading his sister into his bedroom and shutting the door.

"Why all the secrecy? What's up?"

"I got her day hours at the Dollar Store—starting tomorrow," he informed her. "She won't be working nights no more."

Tasha smiled gratefully at her big brother.

"But I got to thinking," he went on. "That's a stupid ass job and it don't make no money."

Tasha thought for a minute that he was going to suggest that Alessa sell weed too, but she knew her friend wouldn't have the stomach for it.

"I was thinking she would be better off dancing at Doubles," he went on. "She'd make a lot more money and you have to admit the girl can dance. She's got the body for it too. I got to see it the other night, when I walked in on her in the bathroom after I heard her screaming."

Tasha considered Harlin's suggestion carefully. She didn't think it was a bad idea. The girls at Doubles were exotic dancers and performed topless, but they weren't allowed to dance completely in the nude. She knew a couple of girls who had danced there before and they hadn't been permitted to have sex with the clients either.

"See, I was thinking she could dance there and I could provide her protection," Harlin went on. "I would make sure she got dropped off and picked up so she wouldn't have to take public transportation. She could live here. And instead of paying old lady Lea three hundred a month, she could pay me fifty percent of what she earned at Doubles for rent and protection."

Tasha smiled at her brother. "I guess you want me to convince her that this is the right thing to do?"

Harlin pulled her into his strong arms. "Of course, baby. If you tell her its okay, she'll accept it."

"Okay, I don't think it's a bad idea either," Tasha admitted. "I'll talk to her, but I'm gonna wait a couple of weeks, until she recovers from the shit she's been through and calms down. In the meantime, she can live here with you so she feels safe. But we ain't officially moving her out of old lady Lea's until she agrees to it, okay?"

"Sure, Tasha. Whatever you think is right."

Chapter Sixteen

The weeks that followed were hard for Alessa. She kept getting lost in memories of that terrible night she was raped, the sequence of events revisiting her dreams every night. She longed for so much more than a life of unwanted sex and now, crime. One of Harlin's crew members, a boy called Jake, had begun driving her to work and back. And she couldn't help but notice the sudden change in Brady, the Dollar Store manager. Inexplicably, he was being very nice to her and was always considerate of her needs. It was clear, of course, that the other women employees were annoyed about having to share the late shift again. Despite the dirty looks they threw her and the whispered gossip about Harlin, from which she was pointedly excluded, Alessa confined herself to her work. She found herself bogged down by the monotony of filling shelves and sweeping floors.

She was still staying in Harlin's spare bedroom and over the last two weeks, Tasha had slept there with her every night. Alessa was beginning to feel normal again. Though a trace of guilt, the outcome of feeling partly responsible for the death of Tag and his gang member, still remained, she derived an odd sense of security from the thought of enjoying the protection of Harlin and his gang. Yet, it was from this very sense of security that feelings of doubt were born. How could she feel so safe amidst a flurry of crime and violence? Why did she feel more protected in the company of a murderer than with her own mother?

In another four months, she would be eighteen. Then she could finally do what she wanted to and live where she chose—legally.

One night, while they were lying in bed, Tasha rolled over on her side and looked at Alessa. "Listen," she said, "that Dollar Store job ain't doin' nothing for you. You know how you like to dance and all? Well, there is this place where girls get *paid* to dance. And they make a lot of money. A good dancer can make about 1,500 dollars a week—tax-free. I was talking to Harlin about it and he said if you wanted to dance there, you could live here with him and he would provide you protection—you know, make sure you get there and back so you ain't got to deal with public transportation."

Curious, Alessa asked, "What do you mean they get paid to dance? Are you saying that I would be a stripper?"

Tasha laughed. "Well, when you put it that way, you make it sound dirty. It ain't like that. I mean, you do have to strip, but they don't allow you to dance naked in this club. Only topless. And," she added quickly, "they don't allow their dancers to have sex with their customers. So you're not going to be under any pressure to do that. It's not like being a prostitute. You are just providing entertainment. You got talent and you might as well use it to make real money."

Alessa was silent for a long time. Finally she said, "Let me think about it.

Tasha smiled and wrapped her arms around her. "Sure, whatever you want. You think about it and let me know."

The girls continued to gossip until they had both fallen asleep.

When Alessa woke up in the morning, Tasha was already up and out of bed. She lay there for a while, considering the proposal her friend had made the night before. Alessa didn't really want to dance in a go-go bar. But if she could make 1,500 dollars a week, she calculated, it would come in useful for getting a plan together and moving on with her life. If she took up work at the club, she could study for her GED during the day and maybe even go to college and get a degree after that. Living with Harlin would allow her to save a lot of money with which she might even be able to buy a house of her own later. And maybe someday, she would actually meet a nice man, marry him and have his children. Everything seemed possible to her now. Although the thought of being a stripper was unappetizing, Alessa rationalized that at least she would be making good money doing something that wasn't nearly as revolting as the things she had been forced into doing as a kid. Maybe she could even buy a car and get some decent clothes. She could turn her life around and show her mother and her Uncle Danny that she was capable of rising above the role to which they had condemned her—that of a house whore.

When Tasha came back into the bedroom, Alessa smiled up at her. "I was thinking," she began, "that maybe I could use my dancing to make money. I want to go and see the place before I make a final decision, though."

"That's no problem," Tasha assured her. "The only other thing is that you'll have to pay Harlin half of what you earn to live here and have his protection."

Alessa's mouth dropped open. "But that could cost me 750 dollars a week—if I really do earn as much as you say I would," she protested. "That's a lot of money, Tasha!"

"I know, but you have to consider that it includes your rent and protection," she carefully reminded her. "Harlin will make sure you get rides to and from work. He will also make sure that no one messes with you. You know better than anyone that men can be pigs."

"I thought this place didn't expect the dancers to have sex with the men that went there," Alessa retorted.

"They don't, but you also need to be safe when you leave after work. Sometimes, men get really turned on and they take it for granted that the feeling is mutual. Well, Harlin will make sure that once you leave Doubles, nobody bothers you. When the gangs in the neighborhood find out you're dancing, they might think you're willing to sell yourself. Harlin will make sure that no one gets dancing and prostituting mixed up, especially here on the streets."

Alessa was clearly disappointed, now that she knew she would have to give up fifty percent of her earnings. The Dollar Store job was making her about 500 dollars a month, which meant that if she got to keep only 750 dollars a week from her income as a dancer, she would still be in a better place financially. It just might take her a little longer to save the money she had already spent in her head a few minutes earlier. Besides, she would be living with Harlin and that seemed to be working out. Alessa was starting to feel like part of a family at last. She had come to enjoy being with Harlin and his crew and they even called her by her name now. She figured she would give it a try, knowing if it didn't work out, she could just quit.

"Where is this place, Tasha?" she asked.

She explained to Alessa that it was in Horsham, near a military base. It was close by, but far enough away from this neighborhood to ensure there would be less riffraff there. Alessa liked the idea of it being outside the city of Philadelphia. People seemed a lot tougher in the city than they were in Plymouth Meeting. Maybe the people in Horsham would be more like what she was used to. Alessa still felt out of place whenever she ventured outside Harlin's house. She was afraid to make eye contact with people and they seemed less tolerant of just about everything. Alessa knew that this life, the life that had become hers, was enough to sustain her for now, but it would never be enough to fulfill her dreams.

The following night, Harlin and his crew took the girls to Doubles. As they walked in, Alessa observed that while there were girls dancing on the bar and on stage, the place had the ambiance of a regular bar. Men were sitting around, talking and drinking. The girls were up dancing and focusing their attention on the men who were giving them money. The staff behind the bar seemed friendly. It wasn't dirty or sleazy, like Alessa had feared it would be. She sat on one of the bar stools next to Tasha and they both ordered beers. The bartender carded the girls who immediately flashed their fake IDs. Harlin was off talking with some of the other men in the bar. Every now and then, Alessa noticed, he would stuff a bill in a dancer's thong.

They stayed for a couple of hours. Then they all piled into Harlin's van and headed back to North Philadelphia. Back at his house, Harlin told Alessa, "I was talking to the bar manager tonight. He was checking you out and promised to give you an audition. I told him I would take you back there tomorrow night." He handed Tasha 200 dollars and said, "Take her out tomorrow and buy her some costumes. Make sure you get her some really sexy stuff. I like those garter things that attach to stockings. Get stuff that matches and make sure it's unique. Jay, the bar manager, is real picky about the girls he hires."

For the first time since the subject had come up, something about the whole deal made Alessa feel cheap. Harlin was talking about her as if she weren't a living being standing right there in his presence. And when she heard him giving Tasha instructions about the kind of costumes she should buy, a stab of fear ripped through her gut. What if Harlin forced her to do things she didn't want to do? The reality of her new career, regardless of how much money she would make, was starting to sink in. She began to have doubts that she could actually get up on stage like the other girls for men to gawk at and pay her to put her ass in their faces. She did love to dance, but it hadn't escaped her that the dancers at Doubles had to make it a point to dance exclusively for the men's pleasure. Alessa had always danced for herself.

As Tasha accepted the money from Harlin, she was aware of how distant Alessa suddenly seemed. She suspected that her friend was probably overcome by doubt as to what she was about to do. Grasping her by the hand, Tasha said enthusiastically, "We are going shopping tomorrow and it's going to be so much fun. Just think how hot you're going to look in all the beautiful things we'll be buying you!"

She shot Harlin a look that told him he had said something he shouldn't have, but he wasn't sure what exactly that was. He wasn't used to women, other than his sister, being around. He was realizing, though, how sensitive Alessa was and it was beginning to wear on his nerves. He wanted her to do exactly what he had planned for her and stop her pouting. He had no intention of sugar coating anything. In fact, he didn't give a fuck.

Chapter Seventeen

The next morning, Tasha took Alessa to Frederick's of Hollywood to buy the things she needed for her audition that night. Tasha picked two outfits that she thought would blow them all away. The first was a white lace thong with a matching garter and white fishnet stockings. To offset all the white, she bought zebra print pasties. The second costume was a pair of black and silver striped panties that might as well have been a thong too. They sat low on Alessa's hips and were cut so high in the back that they exposed her ass. Tasha also bought the matching stockings that came up just over the knee and topped it off with silver and rhinestone studded pasties.

Both outfits were revealing enough to make Alessa a little uneasy, but she had a good time trying everything on. To soften the harsh reality underlying the purpose of the outfits, Tasha turned it into a game of dress up. Happy with their purchases, the girls headed to a trendy shoe store where Tasha bought her a pair of five-inch zebra print heels and a second pair of five-inch heels in silver, decorated with black studs. Alessa was laughing as she tried to walk in them. She felt like a small child, wobbling about, as it took its first steps in life. Tasha reminded her to practice walking in them once they got home.

Back at Harlin's, they rushed into the spare bedroom that was now Alessa's room. Alessa immediately tried on the zebra print outfit, her favorite. Tasha yelled out for Harlin and he came into the room and studied Alessa critically. Standing under his penetrating gaze in a costume that left little to the imagination, she grew more uncomfortable by the minute.

Harlin turned to Tasha and said, "Go wait in the living room."

By his tone, it was clear to his sister that this was an order, not a request. Alessa's heart started to pound as Tasha left the bedroom, throwing her a glance over her shoulder. Harlin shut the door behind her and sat down on the bed. "Come over here and stand in front of me," he ordered Alessa.

Oh God, she thought, *this can't be happening to me*! Had she been that stupid again? Alessa approached Harlin and stood two feet away, not daring to move a muscle.

"Come closer," he commanded. "I want you to stand right here." He pointed to the space between his legs as they hung over the edge of the bed. Alessa inched herself forward till she was standing close to his knees. Harlin suddenly lunged at her, grasped her by her bare ass with both hands and pulled her roughly toward him so that she was standing right between his legs, her knees grazing the side of the bed. His strong hands released her buttocks, only to cup both of her breasts. Then he slowly began exploring her body. She felt his hands sliding down to her waist and past her hips, until they were finally at her inner thighs. Alessa thought she would die when he instructed her to turn around, but she did as she was told. Harlin repeated the same kind of exploration, starting at her bare shoulders and moving down to her ass before finding his way to her inner thighs.

Then he stood up and said briskly, "I think you look okay. You'll need to practice, though. I'll send Tasha back in to fix your hair and put some makeup on your face. I want you out in the living room in fifteen minutes. You're going to dance for me and my boys."

Alessa felt as if someone had choked off her airway as she struggled to get air into her lungs. Tears welled up in her eyes.

Harlin noticed that at once. "Listen, none of that fucking bullshit!" he warned. "This is business and I need to make sure you'll be able to convince Jay to hire you tonight. I don't want any of that crying and looking all sad. I ain't got the time or the patience for it. You understand?" When Alessa didn't reply, he raised his voice and said sharply, "You understand?!"

"Yes, I got it," Alessa blurted out.

Harlin left the bedroom, satisfied that the girl was going to make him a lot of easy money. Hell, an extra 3,000 a month in his pocket just for driving her to work and back and letting her sleep in his spare bedroom! He was proud of his entrepreneurial capability. It wasn't that selling weed didn't make him good money, but this extra sum would help him expand into other things.

Once Tasha was back in the bedroom, she immediately asked her what had happened between Harlin and her. Alessa explained that he had just wanted to see how she looked. Tasha eyed her suspiciously.

"That's it?" she asked a little skeptically.

"Yeah, that's it. Now I need you to help me with my hair and makeup. Harlin wants me to practice dancing for him and his crew before we go back to see Jay tonight."

As usual, Tasha worked her magic on Alessa, giving her a dramatic hairdo that made her look exotic, without robbing her of her innocence. She applied more makeup on her than she normally did, using liberal amounts of blue eye shadow and bright red lipstick. When Tasha was finished, Alessa thought she looked good, but a bit trampy. Tasha explained that if she was going to dance at an exotic club, she needed an edgier look than she usually sported. To add the finishing touch, Tasha gave her a pair of hoop earrings to wear.

Taken aback by their size, Alessa remarked, "But these are huge! They're going to look stupid on me."

"Trust me," Tasha said confidently. "You need to wear big earrings. Everything you do in this job will have to be big. You need big hair, loud makeup, in-your-face jewelry and very high heels. The only thing that can't be big is your clothes."

Painfully aware that all she had on was a thong and pasties, Alessa followed her out into the living room wearing a terry cloth robe, which she clutched to herself for dear life. She had to resist the urge to turn around and run away, as the reality of what she was about to do hit her. Harlin's crew was present in full force; no one was about to miss the big moment.

Harlin looked up at his sister. "Tasha, baby," he said, "it's time for you to go. I can take it from here." When she protested, he silenced her with one gesture of his hand. "I said it's time to go," he repeated. "Everything will be fine. Trust me, it will be easier on everyone, especially Alessa, if you aren't around at her audition. I'll call you on our way back from Doubles and you can come back over then. Okay?"

Tasha reluctantly agreed. As she headed down Dauphin Street to sell weed for her brother, she wondered if she might have made a serious mistake in persuading Alessa to become a stripper.

Alone in a room full of staring men, Alessa began to feel dizzy with nervous anticipation. But before she knew it, there was music playing and

Harlin was instructing her to climb up on the coffee table in the center of the room. When she did so and stood there frozen, he ordered, "Dance!" Alessa started to sway her hips slowly and, with the men watching her intently, she began to feel the rhythm pulsing through her body.

"Take off that robe, girl," Harlin demanded. "Nobody wants to watch you swaying around in old lady shit."

Cringing with embarrassment, Alessa untied the sash around her waist and dropped the robe onto the floor.

At the sight of her nearly naked body, the men became instantly aroused. Some begged her for more. "Yeah, baby," they pleaded, "remove that stuff. Take off that thong."

Alessa looked at Harlin with pleading eyes. He shook his head, indicating that she was not to remove her thong. She continued to dance and was soon drifting into that mental state where, with her eyes closed, she could forget her surroundings and be completely at ease. It was as if the music possessed her. She was startled back to reality when she felt someone tug at the front of her thong. She opened her eyes swiftly and realized that one of Harlin's boys had slipped a dollar under the strap. She continued to move to the music and one by one, the guys approached her and slid money into her thong. Some of them took the liberty of running their hands down her breasts or across her flat stomach before they pulled open the thong to insert their dollar bills.

Suddenly, she found Harlin right next to her. "You need to bend over and touch your toes, baby. Put your ass and that pussy in their faces. Then you'll make some *real* money," he whispered.

Alessa carried out his instructions and the men groaned with excitement. But it was not enough for Harlin.

"I want you to lay on your back on the table and spread your arms and legs out sideways as far as they can go, like an X," he demanded.

Alessa obeyed and at the sight of her open crotch, the men who were facing her had to struggle to hold themselves back from pouncing on her.

Harlin was not done, however. "Now turn over onto your belly and raise that ass in the air," he ordered. "Shake it to the rhythm of the music and rotate yourself around the table so everyone gets some."

The men were now sliding money in between her thong and her vagina. She felt a couple of them exploiting the situation to plunge their fingers inside her. But with the memory of Harlin's displeasure over her tears serving as a warning, she tried not to react, desperately pretending to be quite oblivious to what was happening. She reminded herself over and over again that it was all a part of the business she was in. Harlin too had noticed what his crew was up to. But he convinced himself that if Alessa had decided to be in this profession, overtures of this kind had to be the outcome of a mutual understanding between stripper and client. Nobody was stealing anything from her. Besides, it was something she had to get used to.

When the music stopped, Alessa leaped off the table to snatch her robe up from the floor. But as she reached for it, Harlin grasped her by the arm. "No, it ain't over yet," he told her firmly. "Now we're all going to have a couple of beers and you are going to move around the room and let the guys get a good look at you. When you mingle with them, they'll be in the mood to give you more money when you're dancing."

Alessa moved through the room, feeling like a cheap whore, as she tried to make small talk with the boys. Some of them rubbed up against her as she passed; others touched her breasts or felt her ass. Finally, Harlin handed her a short silk robe and said, "We need to get going. Wear this robe instead. Used to belong to some girl I knew."

Alessa sat in the backseat of the van, sandwiched between two of Harlin's friends. One of them was rubbing her knee, while the other one squeezed the upper part of her inner thigh. Alessa prayed all the way to Doubles that she had made the right decision. Only a couple of weeks ago, these men were all protecting her; now they were treating her like their plaything. She couldn't describe how sleazy she felt. The closer they got to the club, the more convinced she was that she had made a terrible mistake. After what had just happened in Harlin's living room, she felt defenseless and vulnerable, prey to anything these boys might want to do to her. As they pulled into the club's parking lot, Alessa had no doubts at all that she was being taken to a new prison. She was about to embark on another dark and difficult journey.

Chapter Eighteen

lessa was directed to take a seat at the bar, as Harlin went off to find Jay. When he returned with the manager, Harlin motioned for her to follow them down a long hallway to the man's office. Once there, Jay turned to Harlin and said, "You stay out here. No need for you inside."

Harlin was visibly annoyed. He stood fuming at Jay's nerve in taking *his* property into the office, while telling him to stay outside, but he did not argue. When Alessa walked in, she was relieved to see another woman dressed in her kind of costume sitting in front of Jay's desk.

The manager took his position behind the desk and said, "This is Shiver. That's the name we use for her here, because the men say when she dances, it makes them shiver from head to toe. Shiver helps me with all the girls here. Keeps things in order and prevents the girls from trying to make money on the side doing the kind of shit I don't allow in my bar."

Alessa extended her hand and Shiver stood up and grasped it firmly. Pulling Alessa toward her, she wrapped her in a heartfelt hug. Responding to the warmth and friendliness of the embrace, Alessa felt herself melting into it. Shiver liked the young girl instinctively. She could tell by the response to her hug that the girl was nervous and instantly felt a stab of empathy for her.

"Okay," Jay said briskly, "take off that robe so we can see what you got underneath there."

Alessa complied. At the sight of her tight, young body, a smile spread across the manager's face. He instructed her to turn around and was pleased to see that she was well toned. Jay knew she wouldn't need any diets to keep herself in shape. And if she could dance, she would be a great addition to his lineup.

Turning on the music, he told Alessa to just relax and dance the way she wanted to. Her gaze flashed to Shiver, who gave her an encouraging look. A minute later, Alessa was moving to the music, caught up in its beat, as if there were no one else in the room. She threw in some of the moves Harlin had made her practice in his living room. She bent over and touched her toes, swaying her ass high in the air so that Jay could get an eyeful.

The manager and Shiver exchanged a look that confirmed the newcomer was a keeper. When the music stopped, Alessa appeared to emerge from a trance.

"Did I do okay?" she asked, as she caught Jay and Shiver smiling at her.

"Yeah, you did better than okay," the manager assured her. "I want to get you out there tonight. Shiver will teach you some moves that can help make you some more money. She will help you with everything you need. If our customers like you—which I'm pretty certain they will—I will need you to work at least five nights a week. You okay with that?"

Feeling quite at ease with the two of them by now, Alessa readily agreed. She already felt very comfortable with Shiver. Neither she nor Jay had done anything or made Alessa do anything to embarrass her or make her feel cheap. After Jay had left the girls on their own in his office, Shiver turned to Alessa.

"You're gonna like it here," she told her. "Jay is a really cool guy. He doesn't pull any shit with his girls. Just so you know, he won't tolerate you having sex with or giving sex to any of his customers. He will fire you immediately, if he finds out that you did. All you need to do here is strip, dance and socialize. The clientele is pretty decent. Of course you'll have some assholes trying to get you to do stuff, but just refuse them firmly."

Alessa was immensely relieved to have Shiver confirm that having sex with the customers was off-limits. Her sense of betrayal on being forced by Harlin to dance for his crew made her question his advice of everything he had told her so far about the profession.

Shiver led Alessa into the dressing room, where four other girls were getting their hair and makeup done. They all looked up as the two came in.

"This is Alessa," Shiver said, introducing her. "She doesn't have a stage name yet, but I'm taking suggestions, once you see what she's got. Alessa hasn't danced in a club before. So we need to watch out for her and make sure things go smoothly."

The other women were as welcoming as Shiver had been and Alessa started to feel things might work out. Shiver was quick to get her out on the stage. She assured her that the men would love her. The two of them practiced some moves on the pole in the dressing room. For the moment, her instructions to Alessa were to dance with the pole as though it were a lover. Most of the girls could hang on the pole and do other things that required practice.

"Over time, we'll all teach you new moves and erotic ways to dance. For now, just go out and do what you did in Jay's office. For a while, the men will like that you are new and trying to find your way." Shiver walked Alessa to the curtain behind the stage. "I picked a good song for you to start out with," she told her. "It has a great beat—not too slow and not too fast. It's perfect for your debut."

Shiver smiled warmly at the newcomer. She could see Alessa was becoming nervous again. Remembering how petrified she herself had been the first time she went out on stage, Shiver said, "Listen, you and I are going out there together. Once you get your rhythm, I'll go offstage and you can keep going, okay?"

Alessa immediately felt the tension drain out of her body. She felt much more relaxed, knowing she wouldn't be out there alone. She heard the music start and recognized the song: Def Leppard's "Pour Some Sugar on Me". She was relieved it was a song she knew. Shiver moved out from behind the curtain, with Alessa following close behind. Shiver danced over to the pole and motioned for her to go to the front of the stage, close to where the men were seated. Just as Shiver had predicted, the crowd immediately perked up when they noticed the newcomer.

Alessa moved to the music like she normally would without an all-male audience staring at her. Without warning, Shiver was behind her. Wrapping an arm around Alessa's waist, she whispered, "You want to get down on the stage and move around, honey."

The men had been steadily laying money on the stage while Alessa was dancing. When she got down on her hands and knees and swayed to the music, the money began pouring in so fast she was shocked. The men went crazy tucking bills into the side of her thong. When the song stopped, she rose to her feet with as much grace and dignity as she could muster under the circumstances and walked offstage. She was exhilarated by the feeling of having kept a roomful of men captivated while she danced.

As she was talking to Shiver, a tall man who clearly worked at the bar came over. Handing her a pile of money, he said, "This was for your dance."

Shiver laughed at Alessa's confusion. "That's the money the men laid on the bar," she explained. "After you finish your act, you need to delicately pick up all the money on the stage and take it with you."

Caught up in the pleasure of her performance, Alessa had forgotten all about the money the men had kept tossing onto the stage. When the two girls got back to the dressing room, she took all the bills out of her thong and added them to the pile the bouncer had handed her. She and Shiver counted the money. Alessa had made 88 dollars. She was beside herself with delight. She couldn't believe she made that much money in three minutes. She reached over and hugged Shiver.

"You and I should split this money," she suggested. "You danced with me."

"No, that's your money," Shiver told her. "I left the stage a minute after I led you on. That's just my way of saying, 'Welcome'. We're a family here. We all help each other and there is plenty of money to go around. We have generous clients."

Alessa hugged Shiver warmly, thankful she had met her and relieved that this place wasn't as bad as she had initially believed it to be.

"Okay," Shiver declared, "well, you're done for tonight. I'm sure Jay is happy with what he saw out there. The men were obviously impressed. They sure hooted and hollered enough! It means they liked you. You go home and rest up. Be back here tomorrow night at seven, okay?"

Alessa nodded, put her robe on and headed back out to the bar where Harlin was waiting. When he saw her, he smiled and asked, "How much you make?"

Alessa told him.

"That's real fucking good for one dance!" he declared. "You were great! You'll need some more pointers from me. Over time, I'll teach you what men are looking for."

In an instant, Alessa's mood was ruined. She didn't want Harlin telling her what to do. She had Shiver and the other girls now. They would help her with that. Pushing back the feeling of despondency that threatened to overtake her, she decided she'd just be happy with how the evening had turned out. She couldn't wait to tell Tasha everything when they got back to North Philly.

On the ride home, Harlin and his crew talked about Alessa and the other girls at the club. All of them seemed pleased by her performance. Once she had entered Harlin's house, he grabbed her by the arm and said, "I'm going to need half of that money you got now."

Alessa took the money from her small purse and handed him 44 dollars.

"At the end of your first full week," he added, "you're gonna need to pay me back the 200 dollars I spent on your costumes."

She promised to do so, annoyed and hurt that all he wanted to talk about was the money. Even though she knew by now that it was all about money for Harlin, she had mistakenly believed he might have come to care for her as a human being. Alessa realized that the sooner he was paid off, the better. For the first time since she had started living there, she felt a twinge of bitterness toward Harlin. He had a way of making her feel cheap and used and she didn't like it one bit.

Chapter Nineteen

———————◼———————

As the weeks and evenings passed, Alessa became more comfortable about dancing at the bar. She and Shiver had grown closer and were friends now. She understood why they called her Shiver. She was a beautiful woman. Her soft, square jaw outlined her strong face and the green eyes, framed by long, thick eyelashes, were stunning. Her wide mouth, with its plump, luscious lips, always shimmered just right under the stage lights. Shiver's nose was elegantly tapered along the bridge and had the perfect width at the nostrils. Her light brown hair gleamed with beautiful blonde highlights. Her long, lean body revealed her commitment to staying fit. Her stomach was taut with muscles and her long, shapely legs supported a high, round ass.

Although her beauty made her stand out in a room full of women, it wasn't until Shiver moved all that God had given her to the music's rhythm that her audience shivered. The first time Alessa watched this magnificent being dance, swaying to the beat in way that transformed eroticism into an art form, she had shivered herself. No wonder the men never got tired of Shiver. When she was offstage, she was sweet and warm and genuinely nice, never the least bit sleazy. This enhanced her sex appeal, while heightening the aura of confidence and innocence that surrounded her, so that she exuded all these qualities when she talked to the men at the club. Shiver taught Alessa how to do her hair and makeup, insisting that she unlearn all that she had picked up from Tasha.

"Less is more," she explained. "You have beautiful bone structure and small features. You need to enhance your natural beauty, instead of camouflaging it with all that makeup."

Alessa would arrive at the club early so that Shiver could take her shopping for stage costumes in her sleek Mercedes Benz. Alessa was building an exceptional wardrobe for her dance performances. The clients were happy to see the transformation she underwent as the weeks passed. Many of them wanted her to pay attention to them—both on and offstage. In her first several weeks, while on stage, Alessa was in her element when the music was playing, but she was awkward when it came to making her way around the bar and mingling with the clients. At first, Shiver stayed close to her while she socialized. As the weeks went by, however, she felt Alessa would do fine on her own.

After an exceptionally good evening at the bar, Alessa was socializing with the men, when one of them asked for a lap dance.

Startled, she replied, "No, I don't do that."

Harlin was within earshot and as she looked over at him, Alessa saw that his face had turned a bright, furious red. His jaw was clenched as he glared at her. No matter how far away she moved from him, Alessa could feel the intensity of his rage and disgust in his scorching gaze. She had never seen Harlin in such a fury. Her heart raced and her stomach churned, as though she were on a roller coaster.

An hour before her shift ended, Alessa went back to the dressing room to change into her jeans and tee shirt. She was so terrified by Harlin's reaction that she hadn't been able to focus on any of the customers. Shiver was in the dressing room, talking to one of the other dancers, when she noticed Alessa enter before her time was up.

"What's going on?" she inquired anxiously. "You still have another hour left on your shift. Has something happened? If one of our customers has been giving you a hard time, you just need to tell me who it is and he will be out of here in a minute. Jay doesn't tolerate his dancers being harassed."

"No, it's nothing like that," Alessa explained. "One of the men asked me for a lap dance. I told him I didn't do them. Harlin overheard me and I can tell he's really pissed. I've never seen him look so mad. He scared the shit out of me. I'm afraid of what he'll do to me, once he gets me in the car."

Shiver had been curious all along about Harlin's relationship with Alessa. Now she had the chance to ask about it.

"What is Harlin to you anyway?" she asked "He's always around with those creepy friends of his, watching everything you do. Is he your boyfriend?"

"No, he's my best friend's brother. He lets me live at his house and provides me protection."

Shiver laughed. "Protection from what?"

Feeling stupid now, Alessa mumbled, "You know, if any of the men that come in here follow me home after my shift. Harlin makes sure I don't have to ride the bus to and from work. He looks out for my safety in North Philly too."

Shiver was visibly disgusted by what she had just heard. "He sounds like an asshole to me," she quipped. "How much does this protection and living in his house cost you?"

Alessa plopped down on a chair. "I give him fifty percent of everything I earn."

"What!" Shiver yelled. "Are you fucking serious? That motherfucker is using you, Alessa! He is earning a lot of money for doing absolutely nothing!"

Alessa agreed with her. Weeks ago, she had caught on to what was happening. She didn't think it was fair that she should have to hand over half her earnings, but it was the deal she had made with Harlin. Shiver didn't have an inkling of the kind of power he held. She didn't know that Harlin could kill someone on a mere whim, without wasting much thought over it.

Shiver sensed the conversation was just making her feel more nervous than ever. Worry and fear were plastered large on Alessa's face. She was having a hard time focusing on what Shiver was telling her. *Poor kid*, Shiver thought to herself. She herself knew a lot about being on the streets. It wasn't like she had grown up in a perfect household and then decided to become a stripper. Shiver had begun dancing for survival. Now she danced because she enjoyed it and loved the money. It allowed her luxuries in life that she wouldn't be able to afford otherwise.

"Don't worry, Alessa," Shiver assured her. "Everything will work out. I promise. For now, keep giving the bastard half your money, but things will change soon. In the meantime, tell the prick that I am going to teach you how to perform a lap dance. You get paid a lot of money for lap dances and they are easy, not as scary as you think. I will teach you everything you need to know. Okay?"

Alessa reluctantly agreed, trusting Shiver not to make her do anything she wouldn't be comfortable with. She quickly changed and gave her a long hug.

"Thanks, Shiver," she said gratefully, "I don't know what I would have done without you."

"It's okay. I'm glad I can help. "When I started out myself, someone was there to help me. We're a family here, remember?"

Alessa smiled and headed toward the door.

"By the way," Shiver told her, "the girls voted on your stage name. It's Rana. It means beautiful and eye-catching. What do you think?"

"Yeah, Rana," Alessa said musingly, feeling the sound of it on her tongue, "I like it. But everyone who works here will still call me Alessa, right?"

Shiver smiled. "Of course, if that is what you want. You'll be Rana only when you're dancing."

When Alessa approached Harlin at the bar, she could tell that his fury hadn't lessened. He got up abruptly and impatiently walked out to his car, with Alessa and his crew hurrying to catch up. Getting behind the wheel, he glared at her and unleashed his fury.

"You fucking little bitch!" he snarled. "You don't turn down a lap dance. Do you know how much money you threw away tonight?"

Alessa was terrified of what he might do to her.

"I-I'm sorry Harlin," she stammered, "it's just that I've never done one and I don't know how to. I was scared. Shiver promised to teach me how to do one, though. Isn't that good?"

"Fuck Shiver!" Harlin replied through clenched teeth, "I don't give a shit what that bitch thinks. *I* will be teaching you how to perform a real, fucking lap dance! You hear me?" His eyes were wild and his words were cutting. "This is about making fucking money, bitch!" he screamed, his face inches from hers. "I thought we had an understanding. Maybe you're too stupid to get it!"

Alessa was totally silent as they drove back to North Philly. Her stomach burned as though she had swallowed acid. She couldn't figure out why Harlin had suddenly become so vicious. He had started out being a decent guy. Now he treated her like she was a piece of meat. Panic bubbled up in her chest when she heard him call Tasha.

"I don't want you coming over tonight," he ordered his sister. "I got some work to do with Alessa and she ain't gonna have time to hang out."

Alessa knew her friend was arguing about it, when Harlin said, "I ain't fucking playing! Tasha, you heard what I said. I will see you tomorrow." Then he snapped his phone shut.

Once they reached the house, he parked the van and ordered his gang to go home. They boys looked at him with knowing smirks, as they sauntered off. Then Harlin led Alessa up to the apartment and shut the door. Gripping her by the wrist, he said, "Go put on one of your costumes. Wear one with a thong—none of those short pants."

Filled with dread, Alessa went off to her room and began to change. Other than the time he had made her dance for his crew, before taking her to the club for her audition, she had never seen Harlin behave in this manner. It terrified her, particularly as she was alone with him in the apartment.

When she emerged from her room, he stared at her, then yelled, "Go put your fucking heels on, bitch! Don't you dare come out in half the fucking costume!"

Alessa went back in and obediently put on her high heels. When she returned to the living room, the lights had aleady been dimmed and there was soft, slow music playing. Her stomach began to turn at the realization that she was about to give a private show.

Harlin ordered Alessa to get up on the coffee table and start dancing. Trying to push down the nausea that was building inside her, she forced herself to relax and feel the music. Harlin sat on a sofa before her, reaching up and stroking her thighs whenever the mood seized him. After a minute or so of this, he rose abruptly to his feet, unzipped his jeans and tossed them down on the floor. Then he sat back on the sofa in his boxers.

Just as Alessa was beginning to feel relieved that he had, at least, kept his boxers on, Harlin ordered, "Now come on over here and straddle me on the couch."

His tone of voice told her clearly that she had better not disobey his command. Spreading her legs, she went on her knees on the couch so that she was straddling him. Harlin laid his head back on the sofa and put a hand on each of her hips.

"You need to fucking move around!" he barked at her, when she remained motionlessness, wondering what he wanted next.

As Alessa started swaying back and forth, Harlin grasped her around the hips and pulled her down on him so she was positioned on top of his erect penis. "Keep moving," he commanded. "I want you to do a slow grind." Then reaching up, he snatched the pasties off her breasts and tossed them aside. "Now start running your fingers through my hair and let them slide slowly down over my chest," he told her.

Alessa complied and felt his heart pounding under her fingers as they moved down his chest.

"That's right," he said, his voice growing languorous. "That feels good..." His hands crept to her inner thighs which he began caressing. Then without warning, his fingers slid inside her.

Alessa froze momentarily as she felt the intrusion.

"You don't stop until I tell you it's time to stop!" he snapped.

As Alessa continued to grind her hips, terrified of what he would do to her, if she paused, Harlin lifted his own hips slightly off the sofa, removed his boxers and flung them aside. Before she could react, he had stretched her thong taut so she was completely exposed to him and thrust himself into her. She felt as if his soul had left his body and he was no longer a human being, but a beast, as he gripped her cruelly by the hips and raised and lowered her on his penis. In between, he would maul her breasts and gasp at how good it felt. Alessa felt herself receding into the remote recesses of her quiet place until Harlin came, collapsed back on the couch and pushed her roughly off him onto the sofa.

When he opened his eyes again, it seemed to her as though he had regained consciousness. He was himself again. Then he looked over at her and said, "See, there's nothing to it. *That's* how you give a lap dance."

Wary though she was of the fury she might unleash, she couldn't help reminding him, "Jay would never allow that at his bar. The girls don't have sex with the clients. They aren't allowed to touch us either." She held back the stinging tears that seemed ready to burst from her eyes. "I thought you were against men stealing sex from women," she dared to point out. "You said it had to be consensual."

Harlin gave her a hard, assessing stare. "I didn't steal sex from you and it *was* consensual," he declared with complete confidence. "You are in the sex business now and that changes everything. As far as Jay goes, I don't give a fuck what he lets people do or not do at his bar. Listen carefully to what I'm telling you: you need to make as much money as possible and when you do lap dances, the clients need to be satisfied. Find a way to get them off while you're dancing. The lap dances are done in a private room. Make sure you give them their money's worth so they keep coming back for more. I will be working the bar to make sure you get plenty of business.

Just do what I tell you to and we'll make serious money. Hell, you are young, tight and white! That's *exactly* what men want. Now I'm going to bed and I suggest you do the same. By the way, we will be practicing your lap dance again tomorrow night, after we get home. And remember, until you get it right and are ready to start performing for those horny pricks at the bar, we will continue to practice!"

Alessa got off the sofa and headed for her bedroom. She started to take off the few scanty clothes she was still wearing. Before she had even changed into her pajamas, the tears started to flow. She replayed what had happened over and over again in her mind. She couldn't believe that Harlin had actually raped her. What was it with men that they felt they could treat her body with such utter disrespect and snatch sex from her whenever they so desired?

As she lay sleepless in bed, Alessa tried to sort through her emotions in search of an answer. She couldn't see a way out of the dangerous situation she found herself in. One thing she knew for sure: she hated Harlin more than ever and prayed that she would find a way to be rid of him. She cried herself to sleep, promising herself, before she drifted off, that things would get better. She didn't know how or when this would happen, but clung to the hope that a change would surely come.

Chapter Twenty

It was only nine in the morning when Tasha barged into Alessa's bedroom.

"What happened last night?" she demanded to know. "I could tell Harlin was mad. And he wouldn't let me come over. What did you do to make him furious?"

Startled awake, Alessa struggled to take in what her friend was saying. Having slept for only three hours, she tried to wipe the grogginess out of her eyes and sat up. "Harlin was mad because a guy asked me to give him a lap dance and I turned him down," she explained.

Tasha looked at her sympathetically.

"Apparently, men pay a lot of money for them and Harlin thought I should have said yes," Alessa explained further.

"So what made him so angry? Why didn't you just tell him that you weren't comfortable with the idea of performing lap dances?"

Knowing how devoted Tasha was to her brother, Alessa picked her words very carefully. "Well, I did, but he felt I should learn how to perform them. He sort of insisted. He said it was part of my job."

Tasha's face hardened. "Since when is it Harlin's place to tell you what you can and can't do? I'm going in there to talk to him."

Alarmed, Alessa seized her hand and held her back. "No," she said, "you don't need to. I appreciate your concern, but he's right. I talked to one of the girls and she said it wasn't a big deal. She said she would teach me how to perform lap dances. Harlin just wants me to make as much money as I can while I'm there."

Tasha hesitated. She had heard the rising panic in her friend's voice and realized that her brother must have done or said something to frighten her. She loved him, but she loved Alessa no less. She didn't want to pick a fight with Harlin, but she would, if she found out he had been bullying her.

She knew that Alessa couldn't stand up to someone like him. Hell, she couldn't stand up to anyone! Not because she was weak, but because she had never stood up to anyone in her life! Besides, Tasha thought, no one ever stood up to Harlin.

Later that afternoon, while Alessa was showering, Tasha found Harlin in the kitchen eating eggs and waffles. Just as he always did when he saw his sister, he flashed her his charming smile. This time, however, things were different. Tasha could tell he was hiding something. So instead of exchanging their usual hug, she gave him a cold, piercing stare. Harlin could tell she was fuming and wondered if that little bitch, Alessa, had told her about the previous night.

Tasha sat down at the table opposite Harlin. "Tonight," she began with grim determination, "when you drive Alessa down to Doubles, I want you to come back and talk with me. I can tell something is going on here and it ain't right. I don't know what it is, but you haven't been yourself for weeks."

"I can't make it tonight, baby," Harlin said placatingly. "I have things to do. I need to get some business for Alessa at the bar."

Tasha lashed out at him. "The way I see it, Alessa is doing just fine at the bar without you getting her more business. I don't know what you're expecting of her and that's what we're going to discuss tonight."

Harlin looked away. But his quick nod, even as he did so, indicated to Tasha that he would come back to the house to talk with her later that night.

Jake drove Alessa to the bar that night so that Harlin could meet with Tasha. When she arrived at the house, his crew quickly made themselves scarce, clearly under orders to go for a walk. When the two were finally alone, Tasha asked, "Okay, so what's going on? I could tell you were furious about something when you called me last night and told me not to come over. All Alessa will tell me is that you want her to do lap dances. I need to understand why that is any of your business. I promised her she wouldn't be forced to do anything that she didn't want to do. Now *you* seem to be making the decisions about what she should do at the bar."

"If she wants to dance at bars where she can really make money," Harlin answered, on the defensive now, "she needs to learn how to do a lap dance and stop being such a fucking prude! She's in the sex business now, Tasha. That's what this is about. If she's going to flaunt herself up on stage like she does, then she better deliver the goods. Get it?"

"Oh, I fucking get it!" Tasha exclaimed, her temper flaring. "You want Alessa to *whore* out for you. That's what you're telling me, right?"

Harlin thought hard before speaking. "C'mon, Tasha," he said, trying to sound breezily casual. "It's not like I'm telling her she needs to walk the streets. All I'm saying is that if she wants to move from Doubles to a bar that will let her make more money doing other things, she needs to get some practice beforehand."

Tasha was screaming at him now. "I told you this girl has been through some really bad shit in her life! She doesn't want to be a hooker, Harlin! Not on the streets or in a bar. When you suggested that she work at Doubles, you said it was just dancing. And now you want her to be your prostitute? What are you now, a fucking pimp?"

At that, Harlin sprang to his feet, towering over Tasha, but the menacing figure didn't so much as elicit a blink from his sister. In fact, she was so mad at him now that she wouldn't have cared if he were eight feet tall. Placing her hands firmly on her hips, she stared right back at him, not giving an inch.

Finally, he said, "This shit is beyond you, Tasha. This is between me and Alessa. We have a business deal. She agreed to the terms and now she needs to start fulfilling her part of the bargain. I'm not a fucking babysitter, you know! If that bitch wants to live here under my protection, she's gonna have to pay. And you need to step off and just let the two of us work this out. Alessa doesn't need you mothering her. She's a big girl who can make her own decisions."

"Fuck you, Harlin!" Tasha snarled. "You know she won't stand up to you. You'll get her to do whatever you want and she doesn't stand a chance of getting in a word about how things should be. So I'm *not* stepping off and I *won't* let you hurt her! You're just being a bully. Mom always said you were never intentionally mean to people, only to those who provoked you. What has Alessa done to provoke you? Or wait, that's right, this is just business! You get half of everything she earns. So the more she earns, the more money you make. I didn't think money was so important that you'd be willing to betray your family and hurt Alessa—just so you could turn a profit."

"When you turn a profit in the streets selling weed, you hurt people," Harlin countered. "You think when you sell weed to the teenagers around here, you ain't hurting them? You are, baby sister! But you're doing it so you can make money. You see, sometimes you need to just go with the flow. You make money and they get high. Ain't no different with Alessa. She and I both make money and the customer gets what he wants."

Tasha turned to leave, but stopped in the doorway. "The difference between you and me is that I would never force anyone to smoke weed. They do it without me ever suggesting it to them. You, on the other hand, are forcing Alessa into prostitution. I want you to think about what you are doing, because it's not something the Harlin I know would do."

Growing tired of the argument, Tasha's brother withdrew a small bag of white powder from his pocket. He put some on the table in front of him, chopped at it, rolled a bill up and snorted it.

Tasha looked on, aghast. Then she exploded. "What the fuck are you doing?" she exclaimed, outraged. "Since when have you been snorting that shit? You never did hard drugs, Harlin. What's going on?"

"It ain't no big deal," he said, looking up at her. "It's just a different high. That's all. I only do it once in a while. One of my boys turned me on to it and now that I have more cash flowing, I can afford to dabble in it a little. You want to try some?" Harlin held out the rolled up dollar bill.

Tasha stepped back, as though stung. "No!" she screamed, "I *don't* want to try some! Then her voice steadied. "Now I'm starting to see what this is all about. It all makes sense why you are acting so weird. You need to stop doing this shit now, before it's too late. Harlin, this isn't you! You've always been the strong one. This shit will screw up your head. Please promise me you'll stop! Please?"

Harlin laughed at her. "I'm fine. If you really want me to stop, kill the ragging, okay? I'm no different just because I'm doing a little dope."

Tasha left shortly afterward, telling him she would be back when Alessa got home from the bar. He looked at her scornfully.

"Alessa and I have business to discuss when she gets back here," he announced. "I can't have you here later in the evening, because it will only distract us from getting our jobs done. You stay home tonight and she will see you in the morning."

Tasha spun around and stared at her brother. "I don't think so," she said slowly. "With you putting that powder up your nose, it's more of a reason for me to be around. You better think long and hard about how you want this to play out, Harlin. You have a lot to lose and so does our family."

Chapter Twenty-One

In the weeks that followed, Harlin's addiction to cocaine grew alarmingly. He was using so much now that it was costing him all the money that Alessa brought in. As a result, his demands on her increased by leaps and bounds. He continued to "teach" her how to do lap dances and the pressure on her to get into prostitution at the bar was unrelenting. He did not hesitate to demean and degrade her at every opportunity. He declared her useless, a failure, so dumb she couldn't even follow simple instructions on how to perform a lap dance. Even his crew noticed the distinct change in him and became guarded of his erratic behavior.

Harlin finally decided to take matters into his own hands. If Alessa wasn't going to do things his way, he would force her hand and arrange everything himself. And so he did on Saturday night at Doubles. Alessa had just finished her last set on stage and changed into a new outfit, before heading out to mingle with some of her regulars at the bar, when Harlin stopped her.

"I have five guys lined up for a lap dance," he told her. "They expect to get what they pay for. When you get in that room with them, you will do what I taught you. If you don't, there will be a price to pay when we get back home. Be sure you don't end up embarrassing me."

Alessa's eyes immediately welled up with tears. His words stung, reminding her of why she had ended up on Dauphin Street in the first place. She had run away from the prospect of servicing her Uncle Danny's friends. And here she stood, before a man whom she had once idolized for saving her life. He had now been reduced to a pimp, searching for an easy way to score enough cash for a hit of crack.

Harlin gripped her viciously by the arm and brought his face so close that his nose rubbed up against hers. "What did I tell you about crying?"

he hissed. "Pull yourself together and get in there and do what I said. Right now!"

Alessa was tempted to complain to Jay or Shiver, but resisted the impulse. She was terrified of what Harlin would do to her later. He was a loose cannon and no one, not even his crew, knew when he was going to detonate. Everyone he knew had started shying away from him and she was aware that he was becoming more desperate for money to support his habit.

When she went back into the room where lap dances were performed, Alessa was shaking. The first client was already waiting there. He was a tall, handsome man with broad shoulders. The muscles on his arms rippled and as he sat on the sofa, she noticed he had unzipped his pants. Alessa turned on the music and began the dance moves Shiver had taught her. The man watching her started panting, but was careful not to be too openly aggressive with her. She continued with the dance, grinding herself on his lap. Then just as Harlin had done, the man wrenched her thong aside and pressed himself inside of her. At the same time, he slapped her ass with one hand and caressed one of her breasts with the other. All through the thirty minutes he spent with her before he finally came, he would stop her from time to time so that he could maintain his erection for as long as possible. When he finally finished, the client looked up at her and said, *"That* was good! Are you here tomorrow?"

Feeling defeated and miserable, Alessa told him she would.

Just before he left the room, he turned to her and said, "That guy of yours is going to be good for your business. He sure was right about you. That was worth the fifty bucks I paid him!"

Stunned, she gasped, "You paid him fifty bucks!"

The man nodded and with a big smile, left the room. Alessa returned to the bar. Within minutes, another client had come up to her for a lap dance. This man was short and forty pounds overweight. Tattoos crawled over his flabby arms and his teeth were yellow with decay from the overuse of tobacco. The stench of stale whiskey on his breath was so overpowering, she feared she might get drunk on it, if she had to kiss him. His fingernails were encrusted with dirt and a pungent odor hung about him as she began to perform her lap dance. The extra weight on his belly made it impossible for him to get his penis inside her. She was secretly relieved at this, until he told her to turn around and face away from him. It was a blessing, however, not to have to look at his disgusting face anymore as she continued to dance in his lap. He began to grunt and groan and the most revolting noises escaped from his twisted lips. Alessa had to resist the urge to scratch his eyes out, as he pulled her down on him and she felt him enter her. The fat fuck had turned her around so that his penis could penetrate her without his blubbery stomach getting in the way. Suddenly, he sounded like he might explode. When he came, it sounded to her ears like a freight train was rushing past. Alessa couldn't wait to get away from him. All she wanted to do was shrivel up and die.

The man smiled his yellow tobacco smile at her. "Baby, that was hot!" he declared. "I like that sugar pussy you got there. Did it turn you on too?"

Alessa looked at him, shocked, but remembered Harlin's warning. "Yeah, sure," she answered mechanically, "it was a real turn on."

He winked at her and left the room.

Alessa serviced three more men that night. She was numb and exhausted by the time she went back to the dressing room to change out of her costume and into regular clothes before going home.

Shiver noticed that Alessa looked tired. "You doing okay?" she asked, concerned. "You had a lot of lap dances tonight."

Alessa said, "Yeah, I'm fine. Like you said, the lap dances are pretty easy. I'm just tired. I haven't been sleeping well lately."

Shiver took Alessa at her word. "Well, you go home and rest up. Drink warm milk before you go to bed. That should help you sleep better."

It's going to take a lot more than warm milk to help me sleep, Alessa thought to herself. She smiled weakly and went off to find Harlin, the big asshole, in the bar.

Chapter Twenty-Two

To Alessa, Doubles seemed like a prison now, a prison where she was forced to fuck every sleazy bastard Harlin could find. Worst of all, though, was the fear that Jay would catch on. The number of lap dances she was doing now on a single shift far exceeded that taken on by the other girls. When she talked to Harlin about her share of the money, he told her curtly that she would be getting only fifteen bucks.

"I have to put a lot of work into getting these men lined up." he told her with a brazenness that astonished her. "That's worth at least seventy percent of the takings. As for you, all you do is show up."

Knowing she could never win with Harlin, Alessa let it go. Having escaped from Uncle Danny's clutches, she was back to feeling like a prisoner again. It was just like being at home once more with her uncle, only worse, because now she got paid to be sexually abused. Without her even realizing it, Harlin had transformed Alessa into a prostitute, bit by bit. She wanted to run away again, but wasn't sure how to break free from Harlin's grip. Besides, even if she could escape, was there any place left in the world that was safe for her to run to?

The morning after a long night at the bar, Alessa walked into the bathroom, still half-asleep. Pushing open the door, she came upon Harlin sitting on the edge of the bathroom tub, a belt fastened around the top of his arm, with one end clenched between his teeth to hold it tightly in place. His other hand was inserting the needle of a syringe, filled with his heavenly fluid, into his arm. Startled, she stood there watching him for a moment, wondering if she was still asleep and dreaming. He looked up at her and grunted for her to get out. She ran back into the hallway, stricken with fear. She realized then that she had to do something drastic to get out of his house and his life. She also knew that the fact that she supplied the money to support his habit would make it that much more difficult for her to escape.

Things at the bar had changed. Rumors were flying around about Alessa's lap dances and she could tell that both Jay and Shiver were on to what she was doing. Shiver suspected the truth: that Harlin was making her have sex with the men. And Jay, as she knew, had zero tolerance for employees having sex with customers.

On a busy Friday night, Alessa had just begun to mingle with the clients in the bar after her dancing was over. Harlin had already lined up more men for the lap dances than Alessa could handle. When the first guy, now a regular customer, approached her, she led him to the room where the performances took place. She had danced for no more than ten minutes when the man shoved his penis into her. At that very moment, the door flew open and there stood Jay.

He was angry and outraged that she had jeopardized the reputation of his bar and disgusted that she had turned out to be nothing but a whore. He ordered her to gather her costumes and leave.

"Don't ever set foot in this bar again!" he told her.

A flood of tears began to roll down her flushed cheeks, as Alessa walked back to the dressing room to collect her belongings. She noticed Jay out on the floor, standing close to Harlin and motioning to his bouncers to escort him to the door. By the time she reached the dressing room, Alessa was crying so hard she had to gasp for air. The other girls were trying to comfort her, as Shiver came busting through the dressing room door minutes later.

"Why, Alessa?" she asked. "Why would you do this? You knew the rules. Besides, you're made for better things than that. You don't have to sell these pigs sex."

Alessa looked into her eyes and said, "I'm in big trouble, Shiver. Harlin is going to kill me. He's shooting cocaine and he made me do this for the money he needs. I don't know what I'm going to do. I don't know how to escape him now. He'll just keep on making me dance at the bars where the girls are expected to do more for their clients."

Shiver understood Alessa's plight. She too had been in the same predicament when she was younger. Unfortunately, Alessa would need to figure things out for herself. Shiver didn't want any trouble at this stage of her life. She had escaped her own "Harlin" when she was in her early twenties.

She tried her best to muster up an encouraging smile and said to her, "You need to be strong. Find a way to move on. You need to be very careful, though, because once they're shooting that shit, they become very unpredictable. He is going to panic tonight, because he knows that the money he was making off you is gone—here at this bar, anyway."

Alessa's bloodshot eyes widened with fear.

"Listen, Alessa," Shiver went on. "Be prepared. Harlin is going to turn you out on the streets, until he can get you into another go-go bar. The first time he puts you out there, you need to keep going. Don't stop and don't look back. Just keep going."

Alessa understood exactly what she meant. She had done it before, when she left her own home. Now there was more uncertainty in store for her.

The two women embraced for a long time. When they parted, Shiver said, "I love you." She knew she wouldn't see Alessa ever again and hoped she would follow her advice. She knew everything would be harder for Alessa. She needed to start over. This meant facing the unknown, having nowhere to go and not knowing whom to trust.

For Alessa, the ride home with Harlin was filled with apprehension. Normally, she would be embarrassed that he yelled at her in front of his crew, but tonight, she was glad for their company. She was afraid that Harlin might actually kill her in his fury. He blamed her for everything. He told her she was a stupid loser and she would need to make it up to him. The next part she had already anticipated, because Shiver had warned her.

"Your ass will be out on Dauphin Street tomorrow night, you get it?" he seethed. "Now you've made my job harder, because I got to keep you safe on the streets. You're a little bitch for what you did to me tonight! And that little prick, Jay, is a fucking asshole! He will pay for treating me that way."

Ten minutes into the car ride, Alessa mentally shut off Harlin's abuses. She was already planning her escape. She had managed to save 4,000 dollars of her dance money. That gave her enough to leave the following night and start over again. She realized she hadn't talked to Zoe in months and silently scolded herself for being so self-centered.

When they got back to Harlin's, she immediately went into her bedroom and continued to plan her exit. About an hour later, Tasha came in and sat on the bed. She looked at Alessa and said, "I heard what happened.

I figured he was making you do those things. I'm sorry, Alessa. I did not want this to happen."

Alessa sat down on the bed next to Tasha and put her arm around her. "It's not your fault," she said soothingly. "No one is to blame, but Harlin. He is shooting the cocaine now."

Tasha stood up quickly. "What? Are you sure?"

Alessa told her about what she saw in the bathroom. She also told Tasha everything, starting from the first lap dance Harlin had made her perform, to the scumbags at the bar and their antics and how Harlin had handled all the "business". Tasha listened, appalled to discover the truth about her brother, but not entirely surprised. She was aware of the big changes that had taken place in him over the last several months.

Alessa then told her about Harlin's plan to turn her out on the streets the following night.

"He told me tonight on the ride home," she said. "I can't do it, Tasha. I need to move on. Please don't tell him or he will kill me. You understand, don't you?"

Tasha hugged her. "Yes, I do."

Her confirmation that Harlin could, indeed, kill her, if things didn't go his way, sent a chill up Alessa's spine. She confided in Tasha about her plan to leave the next night, when she knew Harlin wouldn't see her. Tasha agreed to help divert his attention to give her enough time to make her escape.

Alessa packed a small duffle bag of clothes and threw it outside her bedroom window. As Tasha was leaving, she picked up the bag, planning to bring it back to her the following night. Before Alessa went to sleep, she pulled a shoebox, where she kept her money, from under the bed. She opened it, only to find it empty. As she stared at its bare cardboard lining, her heart sank. That motherfucker had stolen all of her money!

She took out her purse to count how much she had made that night. She had just under 200 dollars from dancing and another 150 that she had stashed away for emergencies. She knew that 350 dollars wasn't much, but it was enough to get her out of North Philly. She had learned a lot since she first arrived here. She was no longer scared of the streets or the people in them. She had learned that most people were harmless, that they were more unfortunate than dangerous. Alessa had seen much during her short stay and knew she would find a way to move on.

Chapter Twenty-Three

The next morning, Harlin barged into Alessa's bedroom without knocking and declared, "Tonight when we go out, I want you wearing something real sexy. I already have some guys lined up. These are people I can trust. So I ain't worried you're gonna get hurt."

Alessa pretended to pay attention to him, but nothing he said mattered any longer. With the help of his own sister, she would be long gone. She stared silently at him as he droned on. But with every word that emerged from his pie hole, her mind was screaming: *fuck you, fuck you, fuck you*!

Tasha came over at dinnertime and the two girls went out for a quick bite. They went over their plan again. Tasha told her that a cab would be waiting for her. She should get in and take it to Broad Street, where another cab would be waiting to take her to the corner of Juniper and Arch Streets in Philadelphia. There she would find a homeless shelter that took in women and children only. Tasha assured her it would be a safe place to stay for a couple of days. Alessa was immensely grateful to her for all the help that she provided. The two would miss each other a lot once they parted, but they realized it wouldn't be safe for them to be in touch, because if Harlin found out they had worked together to thwart his plans, he would kill them both.

As promised, Harlin yelled for Alessa to come out at nine o'clock that evening. When she stepped into the living room, he looked her over carefully. She was wearing a red midriff top with black shorts that sat on her hip bones. At Harlin's command, she turned around. The shorts revealed the cheeks of her ass. Her five-inch black patent leather boots rose to a point just above her knees. Harlin nodded with approval.

"Let's get going," he said. "I have your first client set for nine-thirty, but I want you out there for others to have a long, hard look at you. Once you're done with the first guy, they'll be rushing to line up for their turn."

133

Alessa nodded, confirming that she had understood his point. When they got out on the street, Harlin told her exactly where to stand. "When the first guy shows up, you take him up that alley," he directed, pointing to one midway down the block.

Alessa got out of the car and stood on the sidewalk. Before driving off, Harlin told her he was going to score some weed and would be back. He assured her there was no need to worry about her first customer, since he knew him well.

Once he had pulled out and disappeared down the street, Alessa headed toward the location where Tasha had told her the first cab would be waiting. When she got there, Tasha was standing by the cab, waiting anxiously for her. Tears streamed down Tasha's cheeks as she handed Alessa her duffle bag. They embraced in silence, too overwhelmed by the moment of parting to speak.

Alessa got in the cab and rolled down the window. "Tasha," she murmured tearfully, "I love you. I will never forget you."

As the cab pulled away, she realized that despite the fact that Harlin had turned out to be another nightmare, she would always remain connected to his sister.

Reaching Broad Street, the driver pulled up behind a second cab. Alessa got out and climbed into the other cab. This time, the driver took her to the corner of Juniper and Arch Streets. She paid the driver and stepped out into the cool night air. She looked around at the buildings and absorbed the impressions the people walking by on the streets made on her. Everyone here looked normal. She headed up Arch Street, just as Tasha had directed her to, and noticed a large brick building decorated with a bright floral mural on its side. It wasn't until she reached its front door that she discovered that the beautiful mural belonged to her final destination: the Eliza Shirley Shelter. Like many of the buildings in the area, its windows were guarded by thick iron bars, but at least it looked safe.

Alessa climbed the steps, then murmured a quick prayer, before walking in. She hoped she had done the right thing by coming here. She pressed a small button to the right of the door, heard a buzzer go off inside and waited anxiously for something to happen. Finally, after what seemed like five minutes, she heard the door's inside lock click open. She pushed through and headed up the stairs. There she found a small, stout woman sitting behind a gray metal desk. Alessa's eyes met hers. The woman's serene expression exuded a deeply reassuring quality as she approached her visitor and introduced herself as Sam, the night manager.

"Short for Samantha," she explained. "And how are you tonight, honey?" she went on. "You doing all right?"

Dressed the way she was, Alessa was immediately taken aback by the woman's nonjudgmental attitude. Sam hadn't even noticed or seemed not to care that she looked like a prostitute. Had Alessa been wearing a Chanel suit, she would have treated her in the same manner. She relaxed immediately as the tension of her escape from Harlin seeped out of her.

"My name is Alessa," she told Sam. "I don't have anywhere to stay tonight and was wondering, hoping, that I might be able to stay here."

Sam's smile faded. She took Alessa's hand gently in hers and said, "I'd love to help you out, but we can't take anyone in after ten p.m. It's already eleven o'clock. I feel like breaking the rules for you, but I can't. But listen, I want you to come back here tomorrow morning at eight. The day manager, Ebby, will be here. Tell her I told you to come back, okay?"

Visibly disappointed and worried about where she would go that late at night, Alessa had little choice but to sheepishly agree. She turned to Sam. "I would like to change out of these clothes. Is there a bathroom I can use? I don't want to be out on the streets tonight dressed like this... Please?"

Sam had worked at the Eliza Shirley Shelter for almost twenty years. She was well aware of the kind of hardships people like Alessa had endured. Reaching over, she gave her a hug.

"Of course," she said. "Let's go to the ladies' shower room. You can take a quick, hot shower and change out of your clothes."

Alessa followed Sam down a long hallway and into the shower room. It was well lit and clean. Sam handed her a towel and pointed her toward the shower.

"I'll stay out here on the bench. I can't leave anyone who isn't a resident unattended," she explained apologetically.

Alessa was relieved that Sam would be nearby as she showered in this unfamiliar place. As she allowed the water to stream down her body, panic gripped her again. *Where would she stay for the night*, she asked herself. With only 350 dollars, she needed to be careful about how she would spend her money.

Anxiety continued to gnaw at her, as she dried herself with a towel and put on a warm baggy jogging suit and sneakers. She thanked Sam for her kindness and the two headed back to the front entrance. Just before Alessa left, Sam put her hands on her shoulders.

"Remember," she reminded her, "eight, tomorrow morning. Ebby will be waiting for you. I'll make sure of it. Be safe tonight. And you be careful where you sleep. Don't eat or drink anything that someone might try to offer you. Eight, tomorrow morning, you hear?"

Alessa gave her a small smile and headed down the front steps. Once back on the sidewalk, she reminded herself it was almost midnight. She only had eight more hours to go, until she could come right back to the shelter. As she headed down Arch Street in search of a safe place to camp out, Alessa noticed the fenced-in parking lot right next to the shelter. With her duffle bag on her back, she climbed over the fence and made her way in. Rows of mostly white vans were parked inside the lot. Alessa headed to the far corner of the building where she would be concealed by the vans. That way, she could stay out of sight for the night.

Alessa threw her duffle bag into the corner of the brick building and sat down on the pavement. Its hard, cold surface sent a shiver through her body and she pulled her knees up to her chin and huddled for warmth. As alone and scared as she was, she knew she was in a better place. Being out in the cold in this parking lot, she felt, was certainly an improvement on how she had lived over the last nine months. Once her body had grown numb from the cold ground beneath her, she found herself retreating to her mental space. Given the life she had lived from childhood, she feared that after she died, her place would be in hell. She tried to focus on what her life would be like in six months' time, but couldn't seem to visualize it. All she could think of was this moment and those she had left behind.

The sound of passing cars comforted her as she huddled against the corner of the building. It was a reminder that there were other people on earth and that perhaps, she wasn't as alone as she felt. She listened, as the city continued to move even in the dark of night. She heard students, not much older than her, hustling through the cold night air, giggling with glee on their way home from a party. Two homeless men passed by, stopping only to argue over the last swig from a bottle of liquor. The city was alive, but Alessa felt dead.

Then without warning, a thought struck her and she found herself paralyzed with hopelessness. She realized that if she were to drop dead then and there, no one would miss her. The harsh reality of her situation overwhelmed her and fear seized her in its tentacles. She did the only thing she could in the circumstances; she blocked out her thoughts and focused on the darkness so that she could sleep.

By six in the morning, an exhausted Alessa had drifted in and out of several short naps. The sun was starting to rise and with it, she told herself, would come a new life. She was going to do whatever it took to have a better life. By six-thirty, Alessa had picked up her duffle bag and climbed back over the fence onto the pavement. She spotted a small café down the block and went in to get breakfast. She figured that on a new day, with the promise of a new life stretching before her, she could at least treat herself to a real breakfast.

The aroma of bacon and freshly brewed coffee greeted her as she pushed open the café door. She ordered a lavish breakfast and silently told herself, before she took her first bite of pancake, "Today, I will start my life over. And tomorrow, I will build on today and carry on in the same way every day thereafter."

At eight a.m. sharp, Alessa buzzed her way back inside the Eliza Shirley Shelter. A tall woman with soft, wavy black hair approached her with a big smile. "Let me guess: you're Alessa. Right?"

Alessa smiled broadly. "Yes, I am. I guess Sam told you I was coming?"

"Of course! I'm Ebby and I am the day manager here. I am also a therapist for the young women who come to stay here. How about some breakfast?"

"No, thank you. I've already eaten," Alessa said politely.

Ebby could see the girl was tired and figured she hadn't slept well the night before. "Did you stay out on the streets last night?" she asked.

Alessa answered somewhat bashfully. "Yes, I did. It was a long night and I didn't get much sleep. I was kind of scared something might happen, if I fell asleep."

"Well, come on, then," Ebby said. "I'll let you lie down for a couple of hours. When you wake up, we can talk. I will get all the information I need from you then. Okay?"

Alessa nodded, unable to prevent the tears from welling up in her eyes. "I'm sorry," she apologized, "I've never been in a shelter before. I'm not sure what will happen or how this will help me."

Ebby put her arm around her. "First, you sleep," she suggested gently. "And then we will talk all about the options open to you."

Ebby led her into a sparsely furnished office. In the corner sat a cot. She pointed to it and said, "Now go and sleep. I will be back in a couple of hours. And Alessa, it's okay to let yourself relax. It's perfectly safe here."

Chapter Twenty-Four

Ebby woke Alessa up at noon. When she saw the time, Alessa was shocked. She couldn't believe she had slept for so long.

"Oh my God, that was the best sleep I've had in a year!" she blurted out. "It felt like I was in a coma. I didn't wake up and I didn't have any dreams either. I feel like a new person."

Ebby smiled down at her. "You *are* a new person," she told her. Today, you will begin to chart the course of your future and we are here to help you along the way."

Alessa closed her eyes and smiled. She secretly prayed that Ebby was right. She really wanted to believe her, more than she'd ever wanted anything in her life. She followed her into a small office. They both sat down on a sofa set against a pale yellow wall, with the sunlight pouring in through the beautiful old window. "Tell me about yourself, Alessa," Ebby urged.

No one had ever asked her to do that before. What was there to say?

Alessa began cautiously. "Well, about nine months ago, I left home. I was living in North Philadelphia for a while. Then I decided to move back into the city. I came here, hoping you could help me get a job and get me on my feet. Actually, I'm not even sure if you do help people to get jobs. My friend told me that this was a homeless shelter and that I should come here."

"That's exactly what we do here and I'm glad your friend told you about us. I suspect you're about eighteen or so. Is that right?"

"Yes, I'm eighteen," Alessa lied.

"Okay. Well, can you tell me why you left home so young? Did your parents throw you out?" Ebby could tell Alessa was uneasy by the way she squirmed in her seat and avoided eye contact. She decided she would have to put her fears to rest. "Maybe I should tell you a little bit about us first," Ebby began. "We will never judge you. We are only here to help. Young women come here all the time, women who have been battered by their partners, women who have been raped. Some have lived on the streets since they were very young and others are just hitting hard times. We even have those who got pregnant and their parents threw them out of the house, leaving them nowhere to go. Have you ever been pregnant, Alessa?"

"No, thank God! Not yet. I don't want to get pregnant, until I have a husband and a home."

Ebby rubbed her forehead. "Alessa, you can trust me. There isn't too much I haven't heard. I have been working here a long time. Is there someone you are running from? If so, I will need to know, so we can keep an eye out, not just for your safety, but for the safety of the others who are staying here."

Alessa knew that if Harlin came here and did anything like she had witnessed him doing in the past, she would never be able to live with herself. "Well," she ventured, "there is this guy who I'm sort of running from. I really don't think he'll come here, because everything he does is in North Philly."

"Okay," Ebby said. "Now we're getting somewhere. What does he look like?"

Alessa gave her Harlin's name and a description of what he looked like. Ebby asked, "Could he be violent?"

From Alessa's body language, it was clear that she wouldn't be getting any more information. She had to earn her trust first. Sam had filled Ebby in on how Alessa was dressed the previous night. She figured this Harlin character was her pimp. They had seen this many times. Young girls hooked on drugs and becoming prostitutes to make money to feed their drug habit. Ebby had to wonder about this, though, as the girl seemed completely sober. Maybe something else was going on with Alessa? Ebby knew she'd find out soon.

In her line of work, there were two things that helped her to help others: trust and respect. Ebby suspected there was a lot more to Alessa's story than she was willing to divulge. Despite the girl's aloof, defensive façade, she liked her. There was an air of vulnerability about her that made Ebby curious to know more. She took Alessa around the rest of the facility and soon afterward, the two sat down in the small cafeteria to have lunch together. They spoke easily and found they shared a similar sense of humor.

Alessa could be amusing and theatrical when she spoke. Her vocabulary was quite limited and her sentences were peppered with profanities. Ebby was no prude. Though she didn't resort to that kind of language herself, she heard it all the time from the people who lived there. Alessa liked this woman, but was still intimidated by her. She was afraid Ebby might share her secrets with others. Besides, she secretly feared that she was judging her. How could someone like Ebby, who read books all the time and used words that Alessa hadn't even heard before, not judge her?

They were drinking iced tea back in Ebby's office when she asked Alessa, "So why did you leave home so young?"

Alessa hesitated. She wanted to take a leap of faith and tell her everything, but the thought that Ebby might call the police held her back. After all, she had run away from home when she was a minor.

"You know, Alessa, you're eighteen years old," Ebby said encouragingly. "Unless you killed someone, no one can hurt or blame you for telling me the truth."

Alessa hesitated a moment, "Okay," she conceded, "but I want you to know that I'm really nervous about telling you everything."

Ebby nodded in understanding. "You should only tell me as much as you're comfortable with, Alessa. You don't have to tell me anything you feel I shouldn't know."

Alessa took a deep breath and began describing her childhood and her relationship with her mother and her Uncle Danny. It was almost as if she were talking about someone else's life. Ebby listened intently. Even as she was relating the incidents from her childhood, Alessa hoped she wasn't giving too much away. She was terrified that Ebby would think badly of her, but couldn't stop the flow of words that poured from her lips. With great difficulty, she described the first time with her uncle, the anal and oral sex and the climax of events that forced her to run away from home. She told Ebby what Carl had done to her at the Rope.

Ebby had seen and heard much during her days here, but never had the incidents been described in such detail and in such explicit language. Alessa held nothing back. She described, bit by bit, the tragedy of her youth. Ebby's stomach turned sour and she reached for a bottle of Tums. When Alessa came to the bit about Rhonda, Ebby gasped in horror, her hand shooting up to her own mouth in a reflexive gesture. Alessa explained how Zoe had helped her and how she had ended up in North Philly.

Ebby's mind started fast-forwarding to Alessa's current situation, trying to imagine what might have happened to bring her here. She figured the girl would tell her she had started prostituting to survive. So she was stunned when she heard about the rape in the alley, her stint at the go-go bar, the antics of Harlin and his crew and the lap dances he had "taught" her. She listened in horror as Alessa told her of the many men Harlin had forced her to "service", as she put it, at the bar. Ebby tried keeping her feelings to herself, but her furrowed forehead and open mouth gave her away. Alessa felt like she had told her way too much.

Finally, she described how Jay had caught her having sex with one of the bar patrons and fired her. She did not spare Ebby the details of what Harlin had planned for her just the previous night, before she fled from his clutches and showed up at the shelter. In her anxiety to establish that despite all that had happened to her, she was a normal human being, capable of normal human feelings, Alessa also told Ebby about her relationships with Tasha and Shiver, about how much she loved them and how acutely she would miss them. She desperately needed to convince Ebby that she wasn't a bad person.

What struck Ebby most forcefully was the way Alessa described some of the most traumatic events of her life as if they were nothing out of the ordinary. It was precisely for this reason that she had entered into this line of work. She was here for people like Alessa.

Chapter Twenty-Five

Back in North Philly, Harlin had become an angry lunatic over finding Alessa. He had bought a bag of meth to keep himself awake as his crew searched high and low for her since the night she had escaped. Knowing he would be off his rocker over Alessa's disappearance, Tasha went over to her brother's house early the next morning and found him pacing in the kitchen. She stopped in the doorway and stared at him, appalled by his appearance. His pupils were dilated, the veins on his forehead were popping out and he was grinding his teeth.

"What the fuck are you looking at?" he snapped when he caught her staring. "Where did that fucking little bitch go? Do you know where she went? When I find her, she is going to be really sorry! Fucking cunt! All that I've done for her and she runs off like the little whore that she is!"

Tasha let her jaw drop in fake surprise. "Are you telling me she isn't here, Harlin?" she inquired. "What the fuck did you let happen to her?" To calm her brother down and stop him from searching for Alessa, she was trying hard to create the impression that her friend had not really run away, but met with some mishap.

"How the fuck do I know what happened to her?" Harlin screamed. "I turned her out last night. I had set her up with a guy I knew and when he showed up, the little bitch wasn't there! She is probably hiding somewhere. Maybe back at old lady Lea's house. Yeah, that's probably where she went. Stupid whore! Thinking I won't figure it out."

Worried that Harlin might hurt Lea in his quest to find Alessa, Tasha said hurriedly, "Of course she wouldn't go back there, Harlin! What the hell would she do there? I think someone hurt her, Harlin. Alessa would never run. She would be too afraid that you'd find her. Besides, maybe it's better that she's gone. You need to stop all these drugs. You look like a fucking train wreck!"

Harlin whipped around and glared at her. "You know something! I can tell. I know you and you know something. You better fucking tell me where she is! How could you turn on me for her, of all people? What the fuck are you thinking?"

The way he was looking at her terrified Tasha, but she managed to recover quickly.

"How dare you accuse me of turning on you!" she counter-attacked. "You, of all people, should know I would never betray you. No one loves you more than I do. I can't believe you're blaming me for this!"

Tasha managed to dredge up some tears to lend conviction to her act. It wasn't all that hard, because she was scared shitless that he would find out the truth. She had no regrets whatsoever about having helped Alessa escape. In fact, looking at Harlin now, she realized she had done the right thing. Maybe for the first time in her life, she told herself, she had done the right thing.

Chapter Twenty-Six

Alessa spent the rest of the day with Ebby and the shelter's other staff members. They were easy to get along with and she enjoyed being in Ebby's company. She was such a patient and sympathetic listener that Alessa was impelled to tell her more about herself. It was as if for the first time, she had discovered her voice. She had something to say and there was a person who seemed really interested in every detail. It was clear that Alessa still felt lost and lonely, but at the shelter, she experienced a brief sense of well-being. Having been stripped of her sense of self for as long as she could remember, however, she no longer had any idea of who she was. She had come to believe that she was a weak and worthless person.

Alessa was assigned a room where she slept with three other homeless women. Two of them were drug addicts and the third was a raging alcoholic. They were all waiting for a place in rehab. It wasn't, by any means, the first rehab for any of them, but at least, they had a plan and a place to go to, once room was available. Alessa, however, had no clue as to what was coming next in her own life and the uncertainty made her worry a great deal. She knew the shelter had a lot of resources and wondered if they would help her find a job and an apartment. She might even be able to get her GED, as she had planned earlier. As she drifted off to sleep on her first night at the shelter, Alessa's exhilaration over the change that was taking place in her life briefly overcame her uncertainties.

She fell asleep and dreamed that she was sitting in the living room of the house where she had grown up. Everyone around her, even her mother, Caterina, was happy. Alessa could see everyone talking to each other amicably and behaving as a family should. She could hear her sister, Rosabella, laughing and her beautiful hair drifting across the small of her back. Her Uncle Danny was there. He was the man she had known before he moved into their home, the uncle she had once loved.

When she woke up the next morning and realized it was all a dream, Alessa experienced an overwhelming sense of isolation. She washed her face and made her way down to the cafeteria for breakfast. She noticed Ebby sitting at a corner table with other staff members, but went over to an unoccupied table and sat down.

Ebby joined her immediately. "Why are you sitting here all by yourself? Is there a problem with your roommates?" she inquired.

"No, not at all," Alessa was quick to reply. "I feel like being on my own. Besides, I just don't have much in common with them. They all have some kind of addiction. I heard them talking about how they would steal things from people and stores to pay for their high. None of them know I was a prostitute. It just makes me feel uncomfortable. I don't want them to ask me any questions. I'm sure if they knew the stuff I did, they would be completely grossed out by me."

"I'm sure if they knew what you were *forced* to do, they wouldn't give a crap," Ebby said firmly. "All they really care about right now is getting placed in rehab. Everyone knows they have hard work ahead of them, if they're to kick their habits. Besides, why would you care if they did think ill of you? What happened to you is *your* life. That doesn't make you a bad person. Unfortunate, that you have such a rotten family, but that isn't your fault."

"Really?" Alessa said, surprised, crinkling her face. "Well, I was thinking about it last night. Ebby, I have probably fucked eighty different men at the go-go bar in just six months! I was doing about four guys a night. That's disgusting!"

"No, it's not," Ebby said in a comforting voice, "it's just the facts of your past. It's all behind you now."

Alessa thought Ebby had gone mad. "What are you talking about?" she said. "In case you didn't hear me right, I have pretty much been a whore since I was seven years old. Look at me, Ebby. I'm a fucking mess! I have no job, no place to live. And who knows what filthy diseases I might have picked up from all those men!"

Ebby refrained from comment. She listened for a while more, then said, "Things happen and people do what they need to do to live."

Alessa was flabbergasted. She had come to expect so little from the world. She felt that as long as Ebby didn't plan on having sex with her or forcing her to have sex with others, she might just be an angel God had sent to save her sorry ass.

Meanwhile, Ebby was pondering over Alessa's concern about picking up diseases from all the men she had been with. "I want you to consider getting some medical attention. We can help you with this. We have a very nice gynecologist you can go to. You should also get some blood work and a general checkup done. I can schedule it for you. Does that sound okay?"

"Might as well. I'd rather know now than later."

Ebby liked her matter-of-fact attitude. She had discovered that while Alessa was apprehensive about her future, she wasn't afraid of the truth. Alessa had never spared a thought for the risks of disease until that moment. She wondered now how she had lived through the past year without worrying about such things. She must have been walking around in a fog. How could she have been so naive?

Chapter Twenty-Seven

Meanwhile, in North Philly, Harlin was falling apart. Not so much because Alessa was gone or because he missed her, but because the money she had earned for him was no longer there. He had had his crew canvassing the neighborhood in search of her since she had disappeared. The longer she was missing, the more her absence fed his rage. He gloated over all the ways he would teach her the lesson of her life, when he found her. He would make her regret she had ever been born. He knew Tasha was in on it and intended to get the truth out of her. He didn't care if she was his sister. No one double-crossed Harlin, not even Tasha.

Now that Alessa wasn't around, Tasha visited her brother far less frequently. When she looked in on him, she could see he was becoming desperate for income to support his drug habit. Two of his three large television sets were gone, along with some of the paintings he had bought over the years. She assumed he was selling his belongings for cash to buy dope. He was also beginning to pressure her to sell more weed. The quantity she'd been selling for years and which he had considered enough to meet his needs was insignificant to him now. She tried to talk to him about his addiction in an attempt to make him want to get help, but this only enraged him further.

Tasha also knew that he was on edge from his drug use and his obsession about finding Alessa. He could very easily become violent. She had told her parents about what was going on with Harlin before she went to his house on a Friday morning so that they would be there shortly after she arrived.

"Hi Harlin," she said. "You doing okay?"

He scowled at her. "I will be doing better when you tell me where she is. Don't even try to lie to me, Tasha. I know that you helped her. Otherwise, you would be a crazed bitch by now, wanting to know what had happened to her. You better tell me now. The sooner you tell me, the easier it will be."

"I don't know where she is," Tasha said, trying to control the tremor in her voice. "And what do you mean by 'the easier it will be'? Are you threatening me?"

"Nah, course not!" Harlin said nonchalantly. "I don't need to threaten my baby sister. Tasha, I don't care who you are. If you fuck me over, I will always make it right. You know how I operate and you know what I am capable of doing. So the way I figure it is, if you don't tell me where she is, you will have your sweet ass out on the street tonight making me money. I'll have clients set up for you by noon. The decision is yours. Either I turn you out on the streets tonight or you tell me where she is and this all goes away. What's it gonna be?"

For the first time in her life, Tasha began to panic. She knew Harlin all too well and understood perfectly that he would do exactly as he had threatened. Until this moment, she had never been as terrified of him. Tasha tried to buy time. She knew her parents would be there any minute. She didn't want to tell her brother where Alessa was, without warning her first to give her time to move.

"Harlin, why are you treating me like this?" Tasha began, forcing out some tears. "Don't you love me anymore? How could you even think of sending me out on the street to sell sex? I have nothing if I don't have you, Harlin."

Harlin stepped up close to her. "You're so right!" he said. "You don't have nothing without me. So you tell me where she is or *you* will be out making me the money she owes me."

Just then, the front door was flung open and Harlin's parents stepped into his living room. Tasha breathed a silent sigh of relief. Harlin's parents were shocked at his appearance. When they confronted him on his drug use, he turned belligerent.

"So what?" he said defiantly. "What the fuck do you want from me? If you don't like it, get the fuck out of my house!"

Harlin's mother rose to her feet and slapped him across the face. She turned to her husband and gripped Tasha by the arm. "You can see us when you decide to make your life right," she told her son. "Until then, you are not to come near us. Do you understand me?"

Harlin gave her a wicked smile. "Sure, Mother, whatever you say." Then he looked at Tasha and said, "You know the deal."

As Harlin's parents and sister left his house, they were all visibly shaken. Their mother turned to Tasha and asked, "What did he mean by 'you know the deal'?"

Tasha's eyes darted away from her mother. "Nothing, Mom," was her evasive reply. "He's just talking shit, because he's all fucked up on dope. I have no idea what he meant. Let's just go home."

Tasha knew she needed a plan and quick. She would call Alessa at the shelter, when she got back to her house. She needed to find a way to protect both of them now, even as she mourned the loss of the brother she had once loved deeply.

Chapter Twenty-Eight

During the same two weeks that Tasha was racking her brains to find a way out of the trap her brother had set for her, Alessa was living the closest to a normal life she had ever known at Eliza Shirley. There were always people around. The staff was friendly and helpful. Her roommates were nothing to write home about, but for the most part, they minded their own business. Although they wanted to know about her past, Alessa did everything she could to avoid giving them any information. All they got out of her was that she had left her home in Plymouth Meeting and magically appeared here at the shelter. Behind her back, Alessa's roommates gossiped about how she must be some spoiled brat who had had a tiff with Mommy and Daddy and gone running.

Alessa took long walks in the city with Ebby. She had completely changed her appearance. She had cut her hair short and dyed it blonde. She had bought a cheap pair of sunglasses from a local store and never went out without wearing them. Sometimes, she would wear a baseball cap that Ebby had given her. In spite of that, she lived in constant fear that Harlin would find her or that one of his crew would recognize her.

Ebby tried to allay her anxieties by reminding her that two whole weeks had passed since she left North Philly, but Alessa knew better. She knew that when Harlin was mad, he got revenge. Ebby assured her that a detailed description of him had already been given to the police. Alessa tried to relax, but was certain Harlin would find her. In therapy, Ebby tried coaxing her to get in touch with her sister, Rosabella. Based on what Alessa had told her, she understood that Rosabella had never caused her sister any harm. Alessa believed that out of all her family, Rosabella alone may have been aware of what had happened to her and how Caterina and Danny had both used her.

Although Alessa thought about calling Rosabella, she was apprehensive of being rejected by her. While she would have loved to have at least one family member in her life as part of her support system, she was terrified that it would give the others the license to come rushing back into her life too. Not that any of them had ever searched for her. When she last talked to Zoe nine months earlier, she had learned that no further inquiries had been made regarding her whereabouts. Alessa was glad the pricks had gone back to their fucked-up lives and left her alone. She hated all of them, but she especially despised Caterina and Uncle Danny. She would never forgive either for the life they had condemned her to.

While at the shelter, Alessa started classes to prepare for her GED test. She knew education would be the first step to a better life. Her roommates teased her that GED stood for "Good Evening, Dummy." She thought that was clever of them and giggled.

All these years, the people in Alessa's life had always sprung surprises on her, forcing her into situations that were hurtful to her. Ebby was a surprise too, but a pleasant one. She had come to love her in a way that was different from the way she loved Rhonda and Tasha. The girls had both protected her, but Ebby was teaching her to move forward.

Ebby never judged or made fun of anyone. She taught Alessa how to be kind to herself and to look deep inside to find her inner strength. Alessa, of course, still wasn't sure if she had any. Within a few short weeks, however, she knew she had a chance for a new life.

Ebby had told her, "Not everyone can turn their life around. It takes a lot of resilience to take your life back into your hands and many people give up. You managed to deal with the ugliest circumstances, without making your life any worse than it already was. That takes a lot of courage and inner strength. Why do you think you were able to survive the way you did, Alessa?"

"I don't know, Ebby," she replied. "I guess I've never seen it as survival. It was just my life. Most kids are raised on Cheerios, but I was raised on sex." Alessa blushed. "I really don't know. I always wanted to be something more so that I could get away from all that fucked-up shit. I'm not sure why bad shit follows me, though. It's not like I go looking for it."

"No, of course you don't look for it. For some reason, people take advantage of you. We need to fix that part of you so it doesn't happen again. We need you to give out signals that you are NOT to be messed with and that you command respect. I believe you will achieve that kind of freedom in your life. You are certainly capable of anything. So now we just need to get you focused on moving forward."

Alessa loved her sessions with Ebby. Time spent with her always made her feel as if there were no limits to what she could be or do. She confessed to her that when they weren't together, her inner hope and confidence seemed to recede.

Ebby tilted her head to the side and said, "You know, there is nothing I can say that will make you any stronger than you already are. You need to find the place inside yourself to hold onto your confidence. There's no magic by which I can give you confidence and strength. If you have it when you're with me, then it is yours and you need to acknowledge that as the truth. If you give me credit for how you feel, you're just denying yourself once again of the power that you hold. Give yourself credit and stop second-guessing everything. The sooner you learn to be kind to yourself, the sooner you will heal and move on with the life you want. It's time to stop letting other people run your life and control how you feel."

Two weeks had passed since Alessa escaped Harlin's iron rule. She remained on alert, fearing that any moment, he would come looking for her. But she was starting to see that she could have so much more than she had ever had before.

She was in her room, studying for the GED, when one of the staff members entered. She told her there was a telephone call for her. Alessa's heart began to pump wildly in her chest. The only person who knew she was there was Tasha.

Alessa practically ran to get the phone."Hello?"

"Alessa," Tasha said urgently, "you need to move. Harlin is turning me out on the streets tonight, if I don't tell him where you are. You need to leave from there right now! Your life depends on moving fast. I'm sorry, sweetie. I love you."

Before Alessa could respond, the phone went dead.

Chapter Twenty-Nine

Alessa darted off like a rocket to find Ebby. One look at her and Ebby could tell the girl was terror-stricken. She rushed over to her and asked breathlessly, "What's wrong?"

Alessa told her about Tasha's phone call. "Ebby, you have no idea what he will do to me! No one gets one over on Harlin. I need to leave this place *now*. Otherwise, he will find me and kill me or worse, take me back to North Philly. Oh Ebby, I can't go back there again!" she wailed, flinging herself into Ebby's arms.

Ebby assessed the situation quickly. She didn't want to lose Alessa to the streets again, but she would also have to consider the safety of the other women in the shelter. She led Alessa to her office and asked one of the staff members to have the shelter director come and see her. "Tell him it's an emergency," she said urgently.

Ebby sat Alessa down on her small sofa and seated herself beside her. The girl clung to her and cried, her mind racing ahead to consider what her next step should be. Perhaps she could move to another shelter in the city?

Jon, the director, came into Ebby's office within minutes. A handsome black man, he was six feet two inches tall and had the physique of a body builder. "What's going on?" he asked in a voice that rang with authority and commanded immediate respect.

As Ebby explained the situation to him, there was an extra edge to the concern in her voice which did not escape him. The next moment, he had picked up the phone and dialed the Philadelphia Police department. They had experience dealing with this kind of situation in shelters all over the city. In the past, pimps and abusive partners had gone looking for the women who had fled to the shelter for safety. Jon stepped out of Ebby's office for a few minutes and returned with one of the staff members who led Alessa to the office across the hall.

When they were alone, Jon turned to Ebby again. "What's going on?" he inquired. "We've been through this a hundred times, but I've never seen you this shaken."

Ebby explained the nature of the relationship between Harlin and Alessa. "It goes beyond him pimping her out, Jon, this man sounds like the Godfather of North Philly," she said. "Alessa has seen him kill a man. From what she told me, this Harlin character opened a guy up with a knife from stomach to sternum. He was apparently protecting Alessa, after he caught another man raping her. However, since then, he has been earning a pile by forcing her to have sex with other men. It's a real knight in shining armor tale."

Jon grunted his acknowledgement of the situation just as someone knocked on the office door. The Philadelphia Police had arrived within minutes. The two of them told the officers about Harlin, without divulging all the details that Alessa had shared. The policemen knew the routine. They could gauge from Jon's expression that this asshole, Harlin, could become a real problem for Alessa and everyone else at the shelter. Just to be on the safe side, they posted two men inside the shelter lobby.

The officer-in-charge turned to Ebby. "Ma'am," he told her crisply, "she has to be moved out of here today. We can help with transportation, but you'll have to find somewhere else for her to go. We wouldn't recommend moving her to another shelter in the city, because that will be the first place the guy goes looking."

After the police had left, apart from the two officers staked out in the lobby, Ebby brought Alessa back into her office and sat her down. Alessa had calmed down, knowing the police were in the building. Ebby explained to her that she would have to leave the shelter, both for her own safety and for that of the others who lived and worked there. Alessa frantically searched her mind for a response, but could find none.

"You're not in this alone, Alessa," Ebby reassured her. "I'm going to help you, but you need to be strong. You were strong enough to leave Harlin. And now you have to be stronger still. I'll be honest with you: this is not going to be easy. I'm in this with you, though. I will do everything I can to help you, okay?"

Alessa nodded.

"Do you think you might be able to stay with your sister, Rosabella, for a couple of weeks?"

Unsure of everything now, Alessa said, "I don't know, Ebby. I haven't talked to her in almost two years. My family doesn't even know if I'm dead or alive."

"Well, I think it may be worth a try," Ebby decided, leading the girl to her desk. "Do you think you could call her?"

Very reluctantly, Alessa agreed and gave her her sister's full name and last known address. Ebby dialed Information and got Rosabella's telephone number from the operator. Then she looked at Alessa and asked, "Are you ready?"

Alessa nodded. Ebby dialed the number she had been given and handed the receiver to her.

Rosabella answered on the third ring. "Hello?"

"Hi Rosabella, it's Alessa. How are you?"

It took a few seconds for this information to sink in. "How am I?" Rosabella responded. "I'm fine. Alessa, where the hell are you? I thought you were dead. Uncle Danny told everyone that some creep had come and picked you up the night you left. He said you had told him that you hated us all and if he tried to stop you, the dude you were with would kill him. Mom acted real upset at first and everyone felt sorry for her. The way she presented it, it was all about her. She played the grieving mother to perfection. She got a lot of attention for a while and you know how she thrives on attention. Anyway, at that point, the family and the neighbors were bringing in food and shit."

Alessa was silent as she listened to Rosabella. She had been right all along; they had never really made a serious effort to look for her. And her Uncle Danny had gone out of his way to make it her fault. Sick old bastard, she thought.

"Rosabella," she finally said, after her sister had finished speaking, "none of that is true. None of those things ever happened. I left, because I couldn't live there anymore. Uncle Danny wasn't very nice to me and once Rhonda died, I was like a prisoner in the house."

By her sister's tone, Rosabella suspected there was more to the story. Their mother was not only a liar, but someone who lived in denial, the queen of her own fantasy world, believing only what suited her. Rosabella *never* had any respect for their mother, but she had not thought to share her feelings with her younger sister. "Where are you?" she asked her now.

"I'm in the city. I came here after I left home. I was living in North Philadelphia, until a couple of weeks ago. Rosabella, I'm in trouble. There's this guy looking for me and I need a place to stay where he won't find me. He's very dangerous. I ran from him when he turned me out on the street to prostitute for him. He does a lot of drugs, and Rosabella, I watched him kill a man. Do you think I could come and stay with you for a couple of weeks?"

Rosabella hesitated. "Alessa," she said gently, "I would love to help you out. Really, I would. But since you left, I've had a baby and I'm living with my boyfriend now. He was okay, at first. But he's turned out to be a big asshole. I have to ask his permission for anything I do. I could ask him about your coming to stay, but if it pisses him off—and everything seems to these days—he'll just beat the hell out of me."

"Oh my God, Rosabella!" Alessa cried out, alarmed. "Why are you staying with someone like that?"

Rosabella was sobbing now. "Where am I gonna go?" she mumbled between tears. "Our parents are useless and everyone else we know thinks we're just white trash. It's not like I have a lot of options. Besides, he's okay as long as I don't piss him off. How did our lives get so fucked-up?"

"Because our parents abandoned us a long time ago," Alessa replied sadly. "They focused on their own survival at the cost of their children. Mom is a selfish fucking bitch!" She took a deep breath before asking, "What about Anna or Anthony? Where are they?"

"Anna met some guy, got married and moved to Arizona," Rosabella told her. "I talk to her about once a month. She seems happy, but she did admit that her husband drank a lot. She doesn't have any kids yet. Anthony moved out and is living with a girl he met at a bar. They seem content, but he works long, crazy hours. So I rarely get to talk to him. Being the only boy in the family, he didn't have as difficult of a time growing up as we did. Mom always favored him over us girls. You know that whole 'my Italian son' bullshit. When I see him, which isn't often, he always slips me some money to buy stuff for the baby."

"Do I have a niece or nephew?" Alessa asked her.

"You have a niece. We named her Eva; it means the 'breath of life'."

It was only natural that Rosabella should choose a name based on its meaning, Alessa thought. From the remote recesses of memory, she dredged up the meaning of her own name: "defender of mankind". Not that she felt like a defender of anything at all, but she did cherish the fact that her grandmother had chosen the name because she had seen at least some good in her. Maybe someday, she would be able to live up to her name, but today was not the day. Today, all she wanted was to run and hide. Get as far away from Harlin as humanly possible. "Listen, Rosabella," she said, "I have to go now."

"But where will you go?" Rosabella screeched into the phone. "How will I know you're okay? Who is this guy anyway?"

Alessa expelled a long sigh. "I'll be fine," she reassured her sister. "Please don't worry about me. I will tell you everything once I get settled. I'll call you then."

"Do you promise to call me, Alessa?" Rosabella's voice sounded desperate.

"Yes, I will. You take care of yourself and Eva. Be safe and don't let that asshole beat on you."

Alessa hung up the phone, having concluded that Rosabella's life wasn't much rosier than her own pathetic one. At least, her sister hadn't been forced to fuck her own uncle or strange men to make money.

Ebby had been overhearing Alessa's side of the conversation and didn't need to be told that sending her to her sister's place to stay for a while wasn't an option. Alessa seemed stoic as she told Ebby she would leave the shelter and figure out a solution. She was beginning to withdraw, once again, to her quiet place, an alternative universe within her mind, from which she drew her strength.

Ebby watched her disengage, and took her by the shoulders and shook her gently. "No," she said firmly. "That's not how it's going to be. Go pack your belongings and meet me out in the lobby in half an hour."

Alessa stared at her, as if she were talking to her in another language. But she obeyed.

Thirty minutes later, she was back in the lobby.

Ebby was waiting for her. "Come on," she told Alessa, "we are leaving through the back entrance."

Stepping out into the sunlight, Alessa saw a black sedan waiting for them. Ebby guided her to the car and they both got in.

Ebby turned to Alessa. "The Philadelphia Police department arranged for this car to get us out of here," she explained. "That way, if anyone is watching, he won't know you're in here."

Alessa looked scared and confused. "Where are you taking me?" she asked in alarm.

Ebby put her hand comfortingly over Alessa's. "To my house," she answered.

Chapter Thirty

Alessa couldn't believe her ears. Ebby was actually taking her home with her! Of course, Alessa admired her very much and knew that Ebby was fond of her too, but allowing a shelter resident into her own home was something else. She wondered why Ebby gave a damn about her. After all, she was used to spending every day of the week with homeless people, coming across drug addicts, alcoholics, prostitutes and single mothers in her line of work. It just didn't make sense to Alessa.

She quietly reflected on the matter for a moment before speaking. "Ebby," she said, "the first day I arrived at the shelter, I realized that no one in the world would miss me if I died. I want to be the kind of person people will miss, when I'm gone."

Ebby smiled. "That's certainly a worthy goal, Alessa, but no one is dying today." She was silent for a while, before she spoke up again. "You know, Alessa," she said, "it sounds like your sister, Rosabella, would have helped you if she could. I hope you have realized this. She just isn't in a position to do so at this point in her life. She needs a lot of help herself. But I think it's important for you to recognize that you have connected with a member of your family who genuinely cares for you. There is at least one of them out there who wants you to be a part of their life. You see that, don't you?"

Alessa nodded. "My mother fucked us up so much," she said. "She is such a manipulative bitch! She raised us as if we were nothing more than meal tickets, whether it was collecting food stamps on our behalf or selling me to Uncle Danny. I think when she gave birth to us, she was just too ignorant to understand what having children meant. You know, the commitment, time and love that need to be devoted to a child. What I can't forgive, however, is my mother's failure to protect me from her brother, even after I told her what was happening."

"Well, you don't need her right now," Ebby reminded her. "Nor do you need to dwell on her." Then to lighten the mood, she added, "Consider her nothing more than the host that carried you into the world. Now it's up to you to make something of your life."

Both lapsed into silence for the rest of the ride to Ebby's home in Folsom, Pennsylvania. The car pulled up on the side of a small, one-story home. A rustic bay window overlooked the front of the house and the front door was flanked on either side by small patches of garden, where flowering shrubs grew in profusion. Alessa was somewhat surprised to discover how tiny Ebby's home was, certainly no larger than an apartment. But as she entered, the place looked warm and inviting. A fireplace opened into the small living room on one side and into the kitchen on the other. Alessa just loved the fireplace. Ebby showed her the guest bedroom. Then they went into her kitchen for iced tea.

They sat there for hours and talked. As Alessa disclosed more details of the experiences she had lived through with her awful mother, Uncle Danny and Harlin, it confirmed Ebby's belief that the girl was far more vulnerable than she let on. Alessa had cultivated an overconfident façade that was part of the hard, protective shell she used as a shield against the world. But behind it was a tender young girl who would sometimes break down and let her pain show.

At five o'clock that evening, Ebby's husband, Ryan, came home from work. It had never struck Alessa that Ebby could be married. She wondered now if she had children as well. As Ebby introduced her guest to her husband, Alessa noticed how Ryan's brow furrowed and his jaw clenched. She excused herself and went to her room to rest before dinner, snuggling up under the handmade quilt that covered the guest bed. Alessa's instinct told her that she wouldn't be able to stay at Ebby's for more than a couple of days and should mentally prepare herself for what came next. While worrying about all the uncertainty she faced, she fell asleep.

At six-thirty p.m., Ebby came in to wake her up. Dinner with the couple was wonderful, although Ebby did all of the talking.

After dinner, the three of them sat in the living room.

"So what are your plans for the immediate future, Alessa?" Ryan asked her.

Events had overtaken her so swiftly that Alessa hadn't really had the time to deliberate on her next move. So she talked to Ebby's husband about what she thought would be the right thing to do under the circumstances.

"Well," she began, "I was thinking that if everything goes well and Harlin stops looking for me, I could go back into the city and stay at a different shelter. I was reading some pamphlets at the shelter and found out that the Philadelphia Housing Authority has apartments that people can live in. I don't know the details as yet, but I was wondering if I could live there for a while. After I get my GED and a job, I can probably afford to move out and rent an apartment on my own."

"Well, that certainly sounds like a good use of my tax dollars!" Ryan barked. He was watching Alessa, waiting to see her reaction.

Alessa realized, to her dismay, that he was being sarcastic. After all she had been through, she couldn't take this lying down. "Why are looking at me like I'm guilty of something?" she shot back. "What the fuck am I supposed to do? It's the only plan I have right now, okay?"

There was irritation in Ryan's voice as he countered, "I wasn't making fun of you. I was just stating my opinion. It's not easy for someone like me to have to pay for everyone else to live their lives the way they want to, but you wouldn't know about that, would you?"

Alessa exploded. "Actually," she retorted, spitting out the words, "I *do* know what it's like. I had to fuck my uncle so my family could pay the bills!"

At that, Ryan rolled his eyes. "On that note, I'm off to bed," he announced. He shot Ebby a look of annoyance on his way to the bedroom, but she seemed totally unaffected by his antics.

"Well," she said to Alessa when her husband was out of earshot, "Ryan has managed to rub you the wrong way. I'm sorry he was so rude to you."

Alessa looked remorseful. "I'm sorry too, Ebby," she replied softly. "I was really rude to him wasn't I? But I couldn't help losing my temper. He made me feel like a piece of trash. I'm so tired of taking shit from people!"

"Ryan just doesn't understand, Alessa." Ebby said in his defense. "He can't figure out what motivates me to work at the shelter. And he certainly will never understand what it's like to live the kind of life you have so far. He just can't relate to it, which annoys and frustrates him. I wish I could tell you that he'll come around eventually, but that's not a promise I can make on his behalf. I'm still holding out hope that someday, he will have more empathy for other people."

"I don't understand what you mean," Alessa said, bewildered. "Why would he need to come around? What does he think of people like me?"

Ebby was forthright. "Ryan believes that people willingly get themselves into bad situations, not that he doesn't have sympathy for a helpless victim of sexual abuse. In fact, he condemns your uncle's behavior. But he isn't entirely convinced you were forced into prostitution at the go-go bar. On the contrary, he thinks that by working at the go-go bar in the first place, you allowed yourself to be exploited. I would do anything not to hurt your feelings or to cause you more pain, but I feel you should know that as you go ahead with your life, you will come across both supportive people and those who think you deserved what you got."

Alessa hurried to justify all she had done, but Ebby stopped her.

"There is no need to justify yourself to anyone, Alessa," she told her firmly. "I'm just trying to prepare you for what you might have to face in the future. Certain people will regard you in a negative light. If you allow their views to influence your own opinion of who you are, you will always live on the defensive and never allow yourself to realize your full potential. Better to have learned the truth here and now, where it's safe, rather than in an alien and hostile environment. Do you understand what I'm trying to say?"

"Yeah, I get it," Alessa replied. "I guess some people are just pricks. They can't see past their own noses to have any concern for how other people have to live. Whatever! I think you're great, Ebby, but your husband is a jerk off."

Ebby laughed until her belly hurt.

Chapter Thirty-One

The next morning, the phone rang at Ebby's house. She rushed to answer it. It was the shelter. Alessa listened to Ebby's side of the conversation and realized that something serious had happened. She heard her ask if Sam, the day manager, was doing okay and what hospital she was in. She asked about the other residents before hanging up the phone.

"Well, that was Jon," she told Alessa. "Apparently, Harlin showed up at the shelter yesterday afternoon, while the two police officers that were guarding the shelter went to grab a bite to eat just down the block. Harlin was pretty wild. When he confronted Sam and she kept denying you were there, he stabbed her in the right shoulder. Fortunately, Harlin was still there, when the two police officers got back. One of the officers had to fire on him when he pulled out a gun. Harlin was shot in the left thigh. Both he and Sam are in the hospital."

Alessa stared at Ebby in disbelief. "How is Sam doing?" she asked, concerned. "Oh my God, Ebby, can I go and see her? This is all my fault! If I hadn't gone to the shelter, she wouldn't have gotten stabbed."

Ebby assured her that Sam was fine. Jon had said she was in stable condition. While the knife wound was deep and had torn through nerves and muscle, she was not in any imminent danger.

"You won't be able to visit her, though," Ebby told her, "because Harlin is in the same hospital, until they move him out to a prison to await trial for assault with a deadly weapon. We don't know if any of his gang will be around looking for you and we can't take the risk. If they find out you had been at the shelter, they may head there for revenge. Sam never let on that she knew you or that you were ever at the shelter. It would be safer for everyone concerned, if you didn't visit her. I'm getting dressed to go to the hospital now. I will let Sam know you were asking about her."

Consumed by guilt, Alessa hung her head and headed back into her bedroom. She felt dreadful about the whole incident. Then her thoughts went to Tasha and she began wondering what might have happened to her. She must have told Harlin of her whereabouts. Otherwise, he wouldn't have known where to look for her. Alessa didn't bear Tasha any grudges for betraying her location to her brother. She had lived with Harlin long enough to be convinced that he would destroy anyone who failed to comply with his demands, even Tasha.

While Ebby was out at the hospital visiting Sam, Alessa called Information and got Tasha's home phone number. She dialed it and nervously waited for someone to answer. Finally, after four rings, Tasha's mother picked up the phone. Alessa asked for Tasha.

When she heard her friend's voice on the phone, Alessa choked up for a moment. Then she managed to say, "Tasha, it's Alessa. How are you? Is everything okay?"

"Yeah girl, I'm doing fine," she assured her. "Harlin ain't doing so good, though. He got shot in the leg and now he's gonna have to stand trial for assault with a deadly weapon on some woman who works at the shelter. My mom and dad are a mess about what happened to him. Were you there when it happened?"

"No, I wasn't," Alessa replied, "after you called, the staff got me out of there pretty quick. They were worried Harlin would go looking for me. Right now, until I figure out what to do next, I'm staying for a couple of days at the house of one of the therapists."

"Listen," Tasha said, "don't call me for a while, okay? Just 'cause Harlin is going to be locked up don't mean his boys will be. They will be trying to hunt you down. They're all crazy right now, with Harlin gone and him getting shot and all. It's better if you just hang low and do what you need to do. It ain't that I don't love you and I really miss you too, but this is just a fucked-up time for me and my family. Even though Harlin is alive, we're all mourning his loss. He just ain't the same person no more. Maybe jail will help clean him up, but my mom and dad are worried it'll just make him worse. He's been treating my parents real bad too. Like I said, it's all fucked up. I have to go. You take care of yourself, okay?"

Disappointed that Tasha wouldn't be able to talk with her anymore, Alessa sighed. "Okay, Tasha," she said morosely. "Thanks for warning me yesterday. I hope everything works out for you and your family. 'Bye."

Ebby came home with heartening news: Sam was doing well and in good spirits. "They have her pretty hyped-up on painkillers. So she doesn't really care about anything right now."

"Can I go back to the shelter now?" Alessa asked forgetting everything Tasha had just warned about Harlin's gang looking for her, "I mean, if Harlin is in prison, I think it should be safe, right?"

Ebby shook her head. "No, Alessa," she said, "it would be too dangerous, both for you and for everyone else at the shelter. We're going to have to figure out something else. Maybe there's another relative or friend you can stay with in the long run? Otherwise, we may have to get you to a shelter outside the city. Let's look into it and see what options you have, okay?"

The next day, Alessa devoted all her time to finding a place to live. She felt edgy and displaced. Ebby was at the shelter, working during the day. By the time she got home for dinner that night, Alessa was happy to talk with her. Ryan was proving to be the arrogant son of a bitch the girl had suspected him to be from the time she met him. He constantly corrected the way she spoke and criticized her clothes as too revealing, suggesting she should dress more modestly. At night, Alessa could hear him arguing furiously with Ebby about allowing her to stay there.

"I don't understand, Ebby," she would overhear Ryan say. "Why do you have to bring this trash into our home? When the hell is she going to leave? She just about had Sam killed by her pimp, for God's sake! It's insane for you to let her stay here with us."

Ebby's reply was calm, but assertive. "Ryan, you know this is the work I do. I'm sorry that she had to come here, but only because you have such a problem with it. I do not have a problem with it. I can only hope that someday, you will realize just how fortunate you were to have lived such a normal life. Not everyone is that lucky, Ryan. Where is your compassion?"

"My compassion is for my family, for you and your well-being, not for some hooker you took in off the street. How do we even know she won't rob us? What if she has some foul disease?"

Ebby's voice began to falter as she said, "Listen, Ryan, I need a couple more days. Once we get a place for her to stay, she'll move on and you won't have to deal with it anymore. You know that won't change a thing about how I feel toward that poor girl. Ryan, she is different from the others I've worked with over the years. There is something special and very tragic about her and the awful hand life has dealt her. Don't you have any empathy for her at all?"

"Actually, I don't," Ryan said brusquely. "I feel sorry about what happened to her when she was a child. It must have been a truly horrible time for her. But now she's a grown woman and she hasn't made any significant effort to turn her life around. Why do you always get drawn to the underdogs? Just once, I'd like to see you engage with someone of your own caliber and class, Ebby."

After that, there was silence. Alessa heard the bathroom door slam shut and figured that Ebby had stormed away, needing time alone to cool off. Sitting in a chair by the bedroom window, she regretted causing trouble between Ebby and her husband. She knew she would have to move on the next day. Alessa decided she would get in touch with some shelters in Norristown, back out near Plymouth Meeting, and get the hell out of Ebby's home before she ruined her life too.

Chapter Thirty-Two

The next morning, Alessa announced she was going to contact some of the shelters out in Norristown and see what was available. From her matter-of-fact manner and her sudden haste in searching for available accommodation, Ebby could tell something was wrong. She hoped Alessa hadn't overheard her heated argument with Ryan the night before, but suspected she had. She handed Alessa a pamphlet for shelters in Montgomery County run by the Salvation Army.

"Thanks, Ebby," Alessa said gratefully. "I'm sure I can find a shelter and will probably be able to leave your place today."

Ebby was overwhelmed by sadness as she left for work that morning. She knew Alessa wouldn't be there when she returned home.

By noon, Alessa had called the few shelters listed on the pamphlet and learned that they were full. The shelters in the city were now out of bounds for her, because her staying in any one of them might put the lives of the residents and the staff in jeopardy.

She called Ebby at the Eliza Shirley Shelter. "I found a shelter in Norristown that has room for me," she lied. "I'm taking a bus there at one-thirty this afternoon. I'll call you, once I get settled."

When asked for detailed information about the place, Alessa picked a name from the pamphlet she had been given and read out the particulars. Happy that Alessa had found a safe haven and a little relieved as well that Ryan would now calm down, Ebby prayed the girl would remain safe and asked her to call as soon as she could. She added that she would like to continue being her therapist, even if it meant talking with her over the phone until it was safe for Alessa to visit her again.

Alessa agreed to that and promised to call later. She thanked Ebby for everything she had done for her. "You're the kind of woman I hope to be when I grow up," she told her with feeling. "What I love most about you

171

is that you never treated me like I was a piece of shit. You always made me feel like a normal person. That means everything to me."

"You *are* a normal person, Alessa," Ebby assured her. "You're a normal person who endured and overcame abnormal conditions. Call me when you've settled in."

By one-thirty that afternoon, Alessa was at the bus stop. She was about to head back to the city of Philadelphia, she wasn't going to Norristown like she had told Ebby. As she stepped onto the bus that would take her to the Thirtieth Street Train Station, she had no idea where she would eventually end up. Her plan was to get to the station before deciding on another destination. Maybe, she thought, she could live somewhere that was warm all year.

Once inside the station, Alessa observed all the activity and chaos around her. Everyone there seemed to have a direction to follow, a destination to head for. Alessa kept sitting on one of the benches inside the enormous station, oblivious to the passing time. Before she knew it, hours had gone by.

Hungry, she found her way to a McDonald's and ordered a burger and fries. Then she returned to the bench where she'd been sitting earlier and finished her dinner. As the station emptied of its busy commuters, Alessa noticed the scattering of people who, like her, hadn't moved at all. The later it grew, the fewer the number of people loitering about in the station. Alessa understood that the people who had remained behind like her had nowhere to go; they were probably homeless too. She felt relieved she wasn't alone, but as the hustle and bustle of the day died away, she felt a darkness descend on her like a shroud.

By eleven p.m., security guards were making their rounds, rousing those left on the benches and sending them back into the street. Alessa followed the small stream of homeless people trooping out of the station. Once outdoors, they all dispersed, heading in different directions. Alessa stood there, paralyzed, not knowing where to go. The dread settling in the pit of her stomach was so acute that tears began to roll down her face. Through her blurred vision, she saw a teenage girl approach her quickly.

"Hey, you all right?" the girl asked, concerned.

For a fleeting moment, Alessa was unsure as to whether she should trust her. Then feeling she had nothing to lose, she dove in. "Well,

I'm...I'm...I don't have anywhere to sleep tonight and I'm just not sure where to go," she blurted out.

The teen extended her hand. "I'm Sara. It's going to be okay. There's a group of us that stick together. None of us have anywhere to go either. We stay under a bridge a couple of blocks from here. You can come with me, if you want to."

Chapter Thirty-Three

—————————————◼—————————————

Alessa cast all her reservations aside and drew closer. "I'm Alessa," she said. "Thank God, you're here! Yes, if I could stay with you tonight, that would be great."

As the two of them walked the few blocks to the bridge, Sara gave her an overview of the group she would be staying with. All of them had been homeless for a while, starting from six months to several years. They stayed together in a group, because it provided greater protection against other homeless people and street gangs. They didn't tolerate stealing from members of the group, but stealing from others was acceptable.

Sara also revealed that all the kids had been either sexually or physically abused by someone in their family. Every one of them had fled their homes to live on the streets. She herself had been raped by her brother when she was twelve. When she confided in her mother, she had been beaten so brutally she couldn't walk for weeks. After the bruises healed and she was able to walk again, Sara had left home. She had been on the streets for six years. She was eighteen now, but to Alessa, she seemed mature beyond her years.

When asked for her own story, Alessa turned defensive. "I really don't want to get into it right now," she told her. "Maybe later."

Sara accepted the answer with poise. By the time they had reached the group of teens under the bridge, the two girls felt connected. Sara introduced Alessa to the others. The one who stood out the most in the group was an eight-year-old girl they called Lucy. Sara explained how they had found the child roaming the streets. Lucy was being harassed by some drunken teenagers, when the group walked up and snagged her away. She had been with them ever since. They weren't sure of her whole story, but knew her parents had abandoned her. Alessa listened, feeling scared for the young child she was meeting for the first time. All of the other teenagers seemed to have accepted Lucy as one of them.

Alessa sat on an old tire which served as a chair for the group. Lucy immediately approached her and asked, "Are you also here because your mommy and daddy don't love you?"

Alessa stared into the child's sad young eyes. "Yes, Lucy," she answered, "but you know what? You are pretty lucky to have all these other people here who love you."

The child smiled and sat down next to her. "I have a blanket that we can share tonight, if you want to sleep near me," she offered hopefully.

"That's very generous of you, Lucy," Alessa told her. "I would be honored if you shared your blanket with me."

The two of them found a small patch of grass and lay down side by side. Alessa covered Lucy and herself with the blanket and the child snuggled up close against her. Her heart went out to the little girl by her side and she put her arms around her. Soon, the two were sleeping peacefully.

As morning broke, Lucy started to stir. Alessa sat up.

"Did you sleep okay, Lucy?" she asked.

The child nodded with enthusiasm and rushed off behind a pillar at the foot of the bridge to pee. Alessa followed slowly and did the same.

When they joined the group again, Sara told Alessa, "The group voted for you to stay with us, if you want to. Just remember that we have rules everyone here obeys. I've already told you about the first one: no stealing from any member of the group. The second rule is that we don't use any drugs, other than weed and alcohol. So if you're using other stuff, it's not gonna work here. The third rule is, we share whatever we steal or make from begging."

Listening to her, Alessa began to understand that they were no different from any other family. The only difference was that they had no one, but each other. For the first time in her life, she had found herself with a group of people whose sole purpose in life was to take care of each other.

"The fourth rule," Sarah went on, "is that everyone looks out for Lucy. She's the baby of our family and while she's a lot more street smart than she used to be when we found her six months ago, she is still very naïve. We keep a close eye on her. The newcomer to the group always has responsibility for Lucy's day-to-day whereabouts. That means, she stays with you all the time. Okay?"

Alessa quickly agreed to all the conditions. Not only did she want to remain in this group, she also felt a natural urge to protect and take care of

Lucy. In the child, she saw herself as she used to be when she was just eight years old. She didn't know the little girl's story yet, but figured she would find out over time. Sara told Alessa that the group would give her a day or two to settle in. But then, she would have to contribute.

"If you find food or make some money begging and buy food with it, you're supposed to bring it back for us to share. The other thing is, we're always looking for clothes, blankets, pillows—shit like that—mostly, from dumpsters and people's trash. If you bring that stuff in, you'll be contributing too. The boys do most of the stealing, but I'm pretty good at it too."

"When the weather is nice, like it is now, we wash ourselves here, in the Schuylkill River. You have to be careful, though, and only wash in shallow water. In the winter, we mostly use different bathrooms at the train station and at fast-food joints. It can get really cold sleeping outside in the winter. So sometimes, we head over to one of the churches in the city. Sometimes, they let us stay inside without asking us a bunch of questions. Most of the group isn't eighteen yet. So we're always careful about that kind of shit."

Alessa was intrigued by this little community. Who would have known there were kids just like her, surviving by taking care of each other?

When all the teenagers had left for the day, leaving her alone with Lucy, Alessa began looking around at her new home. It was dark when she had gotten there the night before, but now, in the sunlight, she could see where she was really staying. The main area where the teens lived was sort of like a living room, to Alessa's way of thinking. There was a dirt floor, with a stone ring in the center, where they lit a fire. It gave them warmth and was used for cooking. Resting close to the circle were a few old pots and one pan that had been washed. Old tires and broken tree logs served as seats; a few cinder blocks were used as tables to hold their food and beer. The roof was nothing more than the natural covering offered by a large tree whose widespread branches extended thirty feet out on either side. The branches were high in the air, with so many layers rising into the sky that Alessa could see why they hadn't bothered to try and build a roof. Beyond the main dirt area, there were patches of grass and some smaller trees. Here, she noticed sleeping bags, blankets and pillows, rolled and folded just so. These were their bedrooms. It was all very basic. Yet, as she sat there with Lucy, she realized how lucky they were to have found each other.

Alessa was startled from her thoughts when she heard Lucy say, "Alessa, I'm hungry. Can we eat breakfast?"

She looked around her, but couldn't see any food anywhere. "I don't see any food here, Lucy," she remarked. "Maybe we should go get something?"

The child took her by the hand and led her over to a box behind the big tree that provided shade and shelter for their main living area. Lucy pulled back a ripped old sheet and opened the box. Inside was half a loaf of bread, a box of Captain Crunch, an unsealed pack of graham crackers and three brown bananas. Alessa handed Lucy a slice of bread and an old banana. The child ate them without a fuss. Munching away, she gabbed to Alessa about where they would spend their day.

"I think we should go over to the dumpsters on South Street. The restaurant people put the food left over from the night before in the back near their dumpsters. They're all pretty nice people. They know we come and take whatever food other people don't want. We ain't picky. That's what Sara says. She told me we are all happy we have each other and we need to do what we can, so we can all eat."

"Is that so?" Alessa asked. "Well, that sounds just about right. Sara is a very smart girl. Do you like living here with all these people, Lucy?"

The little girl averted her gaze and stared at the dirt floor, her excitement from a minute ago seeming to have suddenly ebbed away. "Well," she said, "I was all alone before they found me and let me live with them. They are all really nice to me. They call me the baby of the family and that pisses me off, because I'm eight years old. I'm not a baby anymore. But I like living here with them. Will you stay here with us too?"

"Yes, Lucy, I'm going to stay here," Alessa replied. "At least for a while, until I figure out what's next. Until then, you and I are stuck together like glue, okay?"

Lucy's smile spread across her dirty face. "Yeah, that would be okay."

Chapter Thirty-Four

After breakfast, Alessa took Lucy over to the river and washed her face and hands, using an old tee shirt she had in her duffle bag. Then the child led her out of her new home and toward South Street. Lucy was right; there was food left out by the dumpsters of various restaurants. Alessa was careful as they sifted through the food, knowing it had been left out all night and could have been contaminated by animals or just spoiled from not being refrigerated. They paused at Jim's Steaks, looking in the window to watch the men making steak sandwiches for people waiting in line to get them.

The two gathered all the salvageable food they could find and brought it back to their home. Lucy was quiet through most of the day. Alessa just kept gabbing and told her all about Ebby.

"Can we go and visit Ebby?" Lucy asked enthusiastically.

Alessa knew that was too risky. "No, not just yet," she answered, "but I told Ebby I would call her. Let's take a walk up to a pay phone so we can call her now. I promised I would and she'll worry if she doesn't hear from me."

Excited by the prospect of calling Alessa's friend, the child jumped up and grasped her hand. "Okay, let's go!" she declared breezily.

They found a pay phone three blocks away. Alessa pulled out Ebby's business card and dialed the number to the shelter.

"Hi Ebby, it's me," she said when the phone was answered. "I was just calling to check in and let you know I'm okay."

Ebby's voice betrayed her excitement when she realized who was on the other end.

"Alessa! I'm so happy to hear from you. How is it there? Are you doing okay?"

"Yes, I'm fine," she replied.

There was something different in Alessa's voice that Ebby caught immediately. She knew that either something was wrong or the girl was lying.

"What's all that noise in the background?" she asked her, puzzled. "It sounds like cars."

Alessa recovered quickly. "Yeah, it is cars," she replied. "I took a walk into downtown Norristown."

"Can I talk to Ebby?" Lucy suddenly piped up.

"Who's that?" Ebby asked suspiciously.

"Her name is Lucy and she is staying at the shelter," Alessa lied glibly. "I was telling her all about you and she wants to say hello."

Ebby was confused. Normally, a shelter wouldn't allow underage children to go out without their parents. "Where are her parents?" she inquired.

Alessa lied again. "Oh, they both had job interviews the shelter had set up. So I said I would keep her with me for the day."

Ebby thought it rather strange, but accepted the answer. "Well, put her on," she said.

Lucy got on the phone and chirped, "Hi Ebby. I'm Lucy and Alessa told me all about you. You're like her mom. I wish my mom had been as nice as you. Alessa said she got to sleep over at your house. Maybe I can sleep over too sometime?"

Ebby laughed. "Sure, sweetheart! Maybe someday, you and Alessa can come over and we'll have a sleepover party."

Lucy was excited at the idea. "Alessa has to take care of me now," she babbled, "because she's the newest one in the family. I don't mind, though, because I like her best. She talks to me about different things and we have fun together. Last night, I shared my blanket with her and today, we went out to get food together. Everyone else is nice to me too, but Alessa tells me stories about different people that she knows. She told me lots of stuff about you."

Ebby listened intently, starting to realize that her instincts were right. She knew Alessa was hiding something from her.

"Well, it was nice talking to you, Lucy," she said. "Can you put Alessa back on the phone?"

Lucy said goodbye to her, promising they would call again.

When Alessa got back on the phone, Ebby asked, "What did Lucy mean when she said you were the newest member of the family and that you had to take care of her? What's going on, Alessa?"

Alessa didn't know how to tell Ebby the truth. She wanted to be honest with her, but was embarrassed to admit that she was now homeless and living under a bridge in the city. "Oh, that's just something the teenagers made up at the shelter," she replied after the slightest hesitation. "The newcomer gets to hang out with Lucy. It just means that if her parents have interviews or job training, she stays with me."

"Really?" Ebby said mystified. "That sounds odd to do at a shelter. You know the staff takes care of the children here, when their mom has other obligations. Are you sure everything is all right? "

Alessa assured her it was and got off the phone in a hurry, explaining that they needed to get back to the shelter before someone started to worry. "I'll call you later in the week, Ebby," she promised. "Okay?"

The moment they hung up the phone, Ebby reached for the brochure to get the number of the shelter where Alessa was supposedly staying. She felt a bit guilty about calling them, but her gut told her Alessa wasn't being totally truthful with her. Since the girl was intrinsically honest, deception didn't come naturally to her and it was easy to detect from her tone that she was lying.

When the receptionist at the shelter in Norristown answered the phone, Ebby asked to speak to the day manager. After a few moments, a friendly man answered and introduced himself. Ebby explained she was the day manager at Eliza Shirley and she was calling to confirm the identity of one of their residents.

The man hesitated. "I would love to help you out," he said sincerely, "but you know how it works. I can't give you any information about the people who are staying here. I have no way of confirming your identity. It's standard procedure to protect all the residents who live here. I'm sure you understand."

Ebby thanked him and silently chastised herself for even expecting to be given the confidential information she sought. She was disheartened at being back where she started, but did feel somewhat reassured that the man had refused to divulge any information about the residents. Alessa would be safe for now.

Chapter Thirty-Five

Weeks had passed and it was early fall. Alessa had noticed how cold it was getting at night. She and Lucy huddled together under a blanket, stealing body heat from each other to keep themselves warm. Alessa wondered how they would possibly make it through the winter, if they had to remain outdoors day and night in this weather. Lucy had not yet spent a winter with the group and Alessa was concerned about how she would survive the cold. The two of them were inseparable. Even when a new teenage girl joined the group, Alessa insisted that Lucy stay with her. She was like her own child now and Alessa had grown very protective of her, although the group of teens *was* like a family.

Alessa kept her own story close to the chest, not wanting to share her deep, dark secrets with everyone. She had told the group that her parents just hadn't wanted her anymore and had told her to move out. She was just another throwaway child.

One morning as the two went to their usual spot to pee, Lucy cried out that her pee was burning her.

"It will be okay, Lucy," Alessa reassured her. "We'll get you some cranberry juice today and it will be all yours. No one else can share it. That will stop the burning. You probably just have a small infection."

Lucy's gaze dropped to the ground. "It burns the way it used to after my dad had put his penis in me," she whispered.

Alessa had guessed something unpleasant must have happened to the child, but was shocked, nevertheless, to hear her put it in words. "Did you tell your mommy?" she asked her.

Lucy looked at her, undecided, wondering if she could trust her or not. Tears started to roll down her cheeks.

Alessa took her in her arms and soothed her. "It's okay," she reassured her, "you can tell me. I had really bad stuff happen to me too, when I was your age."

Lucy looked surprised. "Really? Well, I couldn't tell my mom because she already knew. She was always there when he did it to me. She would stick her fingers in down there and then tell my dad that I was ready for him. While Daddy was putting his penis in me, she would watch and put her fingers in her own, you know, down there."

White-hot rage flared up within Alessa. She wanted to rip Lucy's parents to shreds, to take them apart, limb by limb. She couldn't believe how fucked-up people were. She willed herself to calm down and asked the child, "How long did they do this to you?"

Lucy seemed to shrink back in embarrassment. "I don't know," she mumbled. "I guess when I started kindergarten. Then they got caught sniffing some white stuff by this guy I never met. We had to run away from the apartment where we were living, because they said the man would hurt us, if he found us. We moved into a place with only one room. Then one day, we went to eat at McDonald's. My parents told me to wait there while they went to the bathroom. I sat there until it got dark outside, but they never came back. I started walking down the street to look for them and then these weird boys began bothering me. I was really, really scared. That's when my new family found me. They thought I was just lost, but when I told them how my mom and dad had left me at McDonald's and never came back for me, the group brought me back here. For a long time, the boys from the group would take me back to that McDonald's every day to see if my mom and dad had come looking for me, but they never did."

Both girls were crying by now and clung tightly to each other. Alessa remembered the terrified seven-year-old she had been when her Uncle Danny had raped her. She knew that Lucy was confused and it would be many years before she fully understood the meaning of what had really happened to her.

"I will never leave you," she assured the child. "We will always be together. Okay, Lucy?"

The little girl looked up at her. "I was afraid if I told you what had happened to me, you wouldn't like me anymore. You don't hate me, though, do you? How come?"

"Because the only people not to like are your mom and your dad," Alessa explained, choosing her words carefully. "What they did to you was wrong and they should be very ashamed of themselves. They are bad people and you're a good girl. None of this was your fault. You've been very brave. Do you know that?"

Lucy and she were kindred spirits and Alessa vowed to herself she would take care of her as if she were her own. With the child having unburdened herself, the two had drawn closer. Given her own horrific childhood experience, Alessa was more capable than most of helping Lucy cope with what had happened to her. They talked often about what her parents had done to her. And they always chose to stay together. Alessa and Lucy picked through dumpsters during the day, looking for useful items or food the group could use. At night they sat and talked with the others by the small fire they would light inside the ring of rocks. They were all one big family.

They did not, however, neglect to call Ebby at least twice a week.

Finally, Lucy said one day, "I want to dial the phone to call Ebby."

Alessa inserted the money in the pay phone and handed the child the number. That was their new thing now; Lucy would always dial the number and talk to Ebby first.

Ebby had not given up probing. She continued to ask Alessa what was going on, but she stuck to her story about staying in the shelter in Norristown and helping to take care of Lucy. Though she had never met the child in person, Ebby had also grown attached to her. She could tell that Alessa was evolving as a person and, she believed, for the better. Her relationship with Lucy seemed to be helping her deal with her own past. Little by little, Alessa's confidence in herself was beginning to bloom.

Chapter Thirty-Six

By Halloween, the weather had turned much colder. The nights, especially, were becoming harder to get through. Alessa hated being so cold in winter. The group had even spent a couple of nights in a local church, when it rained. And as they made do with public restrooms, washing up as best they could, Alessa longed for a hot shower, real soap and shampoo, toilet paper, flushing toilets and clean clothes that weren't tattered beyond repair. These were the necessities she missed most in her state of homelessness.

On Halloween, Lucy begged Alessa to take her trick or treating. Her pleading finally succeeded in making the group of teens cave in.

"But what will I wear for a costume?" Lucy asked.

One of the boys suggested she could go as a bum. They could put mud on her face to give her an authentic look. Lucy was really excited by the idea, though secretly, she would rather have been a princess.

"Besides," one of the girls added, "at least we can all share the candy."

That night, Alessa, Lucy and one of the older boys headed out to a neighborhood in South Philly. As they went from house to house, families gushed over how cute Lucy was. And the little girl certainly was adorable, with her large blue eyes and curly blonde hair that was so pale it almost verged on white. What didn't strike the families they visited was that Lucy wasn't wearing a costume at all. She was in regular clothes, with just a little smudge of dirt on her face to give her the urchin look.

Alessa wished it were Halloween every day, because people were treating them like normal human beings for a change. On other days, they were considered objects of dismal pity. Their appearance alone advertised their homelessness in unequivocal terms. Alessa had noticed how women would sometimes take their children by the hand and lead them away from her, when she was out with Lucy. She had come to conclude that the worst thing about being homeless was the reaction of other people. They all wore the same expression of relief that they weren't in her shoes.

When they returned from trick or treating, all the teens gathered around Lucy as she sorted through her candy. She told them they could have whatever they wanted and they each took their turn, picking candy and thanking the child for sharing her goodies. All of them loved her and knew how hard being homeless was on her. It was just as well that she was still too young to really understand the hopelessness of their lives.

By mid-November, sleeping outdoors was no longer feasible. None of the group could stand the bitter cold anymore and this was promising to be an unusually severe winter. They gathered by the fire, one night, and decided they would all beg on the streets during the following week to earn enough money to buy train tickets to Florida. Alessa agreed to help all she could, but had no intention of moving to Florida herself. She had also decided she would keep Lucy with her and was determined to find a way to make enough money that would enable her to rent a room for the duration of winter. She still had 170 dollars left over from the money she had earned as a lap dancer, holding onto it as if it were the most sacred thing in the world. She had spent it sparingly on essentials like tampons and things that Lucy needed, at times. By the end of the next week—Thanksgiving week—the teens had begged and stolen enough money to pay for one-way tickets to Florida.

They were quite upset when Alessa told them that she and Lucy were staying back in Philadelphia. They had lived together as a family for so many months, they couldn't imagine leaving any member behind. Alessa convinced them that she and Lucy would find a shelter in the city. The oldest of the boys handed her 50 dollars. It was the cash equivalent of part of the price of two train tickets that Alessa and Lucy would no longer have any use for. Alessa thanked them all for their support and generosity. Two days later, the group departed, leaving blankets and pillows behind for the two girls to share, until they could find a shelter.

Alessa and Lucy spent their first night alone, wrapped in all the blankets that had been left behind, but they were so worn and thin with use, it didn't seem to make much of a difference. The next morning, Alessa packed the little clothing they had into her duffle bag and told Lucy they were going to find somewhere else to stay. Not knowing where to go, she headed into the heart of Center City, with the child in tow.

Chapter Thirty-Seven

In search of a short-term shelter for the homeless, Alessa and Lucy headed down Market Street. While the child chattered away, believing this journey into the unknown to be an exciting adventure, Alessa was overwhelmed by doubt. With a deeper insight into the kind of uncertainty that was in store for them, she was terrified, even as she feigned enthusiasm. She didn't know where to go or whom to turn to for help. They spent the day begging for spare change. When dusk descended, Alessa led Lucy to a local church where she knew they might be able to get beds for the night.

They stood in line for three hours with the rest of the crowd, until the church doors opened. The homeless people waiting along with them were a jumble of old and young, men and women, and included almost every nationality under the sun. That night, they slept in cots. The room was spacious, reminding Alessa of her high school gym, and accommodated 200 cots, each equipped with sheets and a wool blanket. After Alessa and Lucy had claimed their cots, they made their way to the food line, where they were given beef stew, string beans and bread. Both were so delighted to have a hot meal in a heated place that they didn't notice how soggy and tasteless the stew was. After their meal, they found the ladies' room and joined the other homeless women and children in cleaning themselves at the sinks, showers being an unavailable luxury in an emergency shelter.

When they returned to their cots, their coats were missing. All that remained were the old, tattered tee shirts they had left, along with the coats, on each cot to stake their claim. Alessa panicked. Taking Lucy by the hand, she went off to find one of the volunteers.

The tall, thin, dark-eyed woman with a long face who listened to their complaint said, "Oh my! I'm so sorry to hear you lost your coats. This often happens with so many of you in need. You should never leave your coats or anything of value unattended. We have a stock of extra clothing for emergencies. Let me check and see what we can find for you."

The two of them headed back to their cots. Alessa could not forgive herself for being stupid enough to leave their coats unattended. Having spent months on the streets, she should have known it would happen. While most homeless people were kind, there were others who were cruel and would do anything at all to meet their needs. In the world of the homeless, you kept an eye on your belongings at all times. Alessa hoped the volunteer would be able to find them decent coats, before they left the church in the morning.

A couple of hours later, the woman appeared carrying two coats. Alessa's heart sank when she realized they were men's coats. They were so large she knew the cold air would blow right through them. But they had little choice. They would have to make do with them. Alessa took the coats from the woman and thanked her politely.

The two of them slept that night with their coats on, fearful that these too would be stolen if they weren't careful. The night was long and unsettling, filled with the noise of children crying, adults snoring and people yelling out in their sleep.

In the morning, Alessa and Lucy carried all of their belongings with them, as they stood in line to get breakfast. They had to be out of the shelter by ten a.m. and couldn't go back in, until it opened again at five p.m.

They spent the day wandering around the city. They begged for money and huddled together in doorways of buildings until they were chased away. They spent two dollars of their day's earnings on cups of hot chocolate at McDonald's. They stayed inside the restaurant for as long as they could, each sipping her cup of gold as slowly as possible without arousing suspicion.

Back out on the street, the sky was cloudy. The wind whipped through the gaps between large buildings, chilling them to the bone. That afternoon, on their way back to the shelter, they paused outside a pizzeria long enough to look in through the window and observe people eating and chatting and laughing.

Alessa hugged Lucy close, trying to keep the wind from ripping the flesh off her bones. A couple came out of the pizzeria and glanced over at them. The man and the woman appeared to be in their late twenties. They walked past the girls, but stopped abruptly at a point just a few feet beyond. The woman turned back and approached Alessa and Lucy. In her hands was a pizza box containing the slices left over from their dinner. She handed it to Alessa and said, "You know, we've already eaten and there were some slices we couldn't finish. Would you like them?"

"Yes, we would like them," Alessa replied, embarrassed, taking the box from the woman. "Thank you."

The two girls sat on the cold pavement, managing to forget everything for the ten minutes it took them to gobble down the slices and appease their hunger. Then they made their way back to the church by two p.m. to stand in line for the next three hours so they could get a cot again that night. When they were allowed inside, Alessa told Lucy to go get their food while she stayed with their belongings. She didn't want to risk being robbed again. By the time Lucy came back, Alessa had seen enough of her surroundings to decide they would have to find another place to stay.

The next morning she told Lucy they couldn't stay at that shelter anymore, she asked, "Why? What's wrong with this place?"

It wasn't safe there, is all Alessa had told her. She chose not to divulge the details of the scene she had witnessed inside the church while Lucy was getting their dinner. One homeless man had robbed another of his gloves by threatening him with a knife. Alessa couldn't get the scene out of her mind and barely slept that night, worried for Lucy's safety.

As they left the shelter, Alessa realized they would have to find another group of teens they could bond with; it was the only way to remain safe, when homeless.

The two of them made their way into West Philly. Alessa had heard of the several abandoned houses there, where homeless people were squatting for the winter. She banked on the hope that they would find a compatible group to settle in with.

Chapter Thirty-Eight

During their explorations, the girls came across several boarded-up properties in a rundown West Philly neighborhood. As dusk fell, Alessa picked the house that had the greatest number of boards still covering the windows. The front of the house was overgrown with wild ivy and the steps to the porch were blocked by overgrown bushes. The paint on the porch had flaked and the white stucco was covered with grime and graffiti. On the small lawn lay a ripped mattress, with a hole burned into the center. A sheet of plywood hung in place of the front door to deter intruders. The girls walked around to the back of the property and entered through the back door, where the plywood had been pulled down and was leaning up against the doorway to prevent the cold air from blowing through. Alessa pulled the plywood over, allowing Lucy to slip in, and quickly followed her.

The girls found themselves in a kitchen. The wall cabinets had been stripped of their doors and a rusted sink stood in one corner. As Alessa and Lucy picked their way carefully through the debris on the floor, they noticed that the walls, once plaster, were stripped down to expose the wood support structure. When they reached the living area, they heard voices floating down from upstairs. But before they could approach the staircase and go up to investigate, the girls' attention was drawn to several homeless people lying here and there on the cold floor. Most of them were covered with blankets so you could barely tell there was anyone underneath. The two kept walking until they had reached the foot of the stairs. Lucy hesitated, clinging to Alessa's side. Just then, a man came down the stairs, drinking a quart of beer.

"Get the fuck outta the way, will ya?" was all he said, pushing past them.

The girls climbed to the second floor. Upstairs, there were more people, most of them partying, some of them openly shooting drugs. Alessa pretended she belonged there. They looked into each of the bedrooms, trying to find an empty one; they were let down, but not really surprised, to find none. Finally, they settled on the bedroom with the least number of people inside and walked in. The other homeless teens in the room, along with the twenty something's, sized them up shrewdly. Alessa quickly moved Lucy into a corner of the room and told her to sit down.

Alessa sat shielding the child and buried their measly belongings in her lap. It was cold in the house, but within its walls, they were protected from the harsh wind. Lucy was asleep in minutes, but Alessa was too on edge to relax. No one had uttered a word to them since they arrived. She sensed they were not welcome.

About half an hour later, a young black woman approached Alessa. "What the fuck you doing here with that kid?" she barked. "This here is our room and you're sleeping in our spot."

Surprised by the intensity of the attack, Alessa said, "Listen, my kid here needs to sleep. Just let us stay here tonight and tomorrow, we'll find another spot that doesn't belong to you, okay?"

She wanted to let Lucy sleep on, but the other girl took exception to her response and snarled, "I told you, bitch—move your fucking ass out of my spot! This ain't your fucking house! You just got here. So take your shit and your brat there and move your ass before you get hurt!"

Unwilling to further endanger Lucy and herself, Alessa rose to her feet, snatched up her duffle bag with one hand and cradled Lucy in her other arm. She led her over to the opposite corner and made her lie down again. Alessa looked around the room, waiting for someone else to object. But no one seemed to notice them at all, except for the young woman who had just threatened her.

Alessa managed to catch catnaps throughout the night, too wary of her new surroundings to let down her guard.

In the morning, it was Lucy who woke up first. Her stirrings startled Alessa awake and instinctively, she checked to see if the child was all right.

Lucy was smiling at her. "Good morning," she said brightly, "I'm hungry."

Alessa stretched. "Me too. Let's go out and get something to eat."

She looked over at the young woman who'd given her a hard time the night before. Now she lay in the opposite corner, clinging to her shopping bags filled with her belongings. The morning light left Alessa with no illusions about the sordidness of her surroundings. There was trash everywhere. Graffiti scrawled across the walls. In the bedroom where they'd slept, remnants of old wallpaper—red, with gold velvet flowers—recalled a grander, long-forgotten past.

The girls went downstairs, only to find more people scattered everywhere. Some of the homeless slept huddled in small groups. Two people, obviously suffering from various degrees of mental illness, moved clumsily, talking incessantly to themselves. Alessa prayed that one of the smaller groups would accept her and Lucy into their fold.

Stepping out of the house, she told Lucy that they would have to find food, just as they had when they lived under the bridge. She explained that if they brought food in, they would, perhaps, be allowed to join one of the small groups they had seen as they left the house. Lucy approved of the idea and promised Alessa she would put on her best little 'poor girl' face, the way Sara had taught her to, to make people feel sorry for her and give her food and money. The two girls worked the streets for nearly six hours. When they were done, they had enough food to fill a grocery bag.

By the time they returned to the house peppered with squatters, it was early evening and a party was in full swing. Alessa and Lucy went straight up to the spot where they had slept the night before. The young black woman was there now. There was a guy with her and they were smoking pot.

The moment the black girl saw them walk in, she yelled out, "There's the bitches I was telling you about! Got some fuckin' nerve, thinkin' they gonna come in here and try to take over *my* spot!"

Alessa walked over to her and said, "I'm sorry about last night. We didn't know that was your spot. I promise we won't do that again. I'm Alessa and this is Lucy."

The black girl scowled at them.

Alessa persisted. "What are your names?"

The guy spoke up first. "I'm Rock and this is Crystal."

Crystal shouted, "Don't be telling people my name, motherfucker! I can speak for myself!"

Alessa took a step closer. "Well, nice to meet you," she said pleasantly. "Lucy and I are going to sleep over in that corner. Is that okay?"

"This ain't no place for a kid," Crystal blurted out. "We party up in here. Maybe you should find somewhere else to stay."

Lucy spoke up. "I'm not afraid," she said bravely. "Alessa and I have been on the streets for a long time. We know how to take care of each other."

Crystal dismissed them with a wave of her hand and looked away, but a smile trembled at the corners of her mouth at the child's tenacity.

Chapter Thirty-Nine

———————— ■ ————————

Alessa and Lucy moved to their corner of the room and started pulling food from the bag. The others looked on as the girls ate, their pot-induced appetite increasing by the sight of food.

Crystal walked over to them and demanded, "You gonna share any of that?"

Alessa reached into the bag and gave her a half-eaten deli sandwich they had fished out of the dumpster behind a restaurant. Crystal took it without thanking them and turned back to Rock.

"Come on, Rock," she said, "lets go score some beer."

As the couple descended the stairs, others in the room were moving toward Alessa and Lucy to see if they could get some food for themselves.

After three days in the abandoned house, the girls were beginning to settle in. They were surrounded by thugs and drug addicts, but for the most part, no one bothered them. At night, to keep Lucy warm, Alessa would let her sleep with her small freezing cold hands resting against her back. By day, the girls worked the streets. They had earned 40 dollars from begging. Every night, when they returned to their new home, they brought back food other people had thrown away.

On their fourth night there, Crystal and Rock came into the room as they sat eating. Approaching them in a belligerent manner, Crystal barked, "Whatcha got for me to eat?"

Desperately wanting to make a connection, Alessa told her what was left in the bag. Crystal and Rock took a half-eaten chicken and a loaf of stale bread. Then they retreated to their own corner without uttering another word to the two girls.

The next day, while looking for food, Lucy asked, "Alessa, why do we keep giving Crystal and Rock food? They're never nice to us and they don't bring anything back to share with us."

Feeling a little foolish, Alessa replied, "I'm hoping they will eventually become our friends and we can hang out with them. I mean, they don't seem so bad, right? At least, they don't bother us. And Crystal hasn't been that mean to us since we started sharing our food."

"But that's not how it works!" the child retorted, agitated. *"Everybody should contribute, not just us!"*

"I know, Lucy, I know," was all Alessa could say in response.

That night, it started snowing hard. The weather was calling for ten inches. Lucy and Alessa had done all that they could to find extra food to keep them going for a couple of days, in case they were snowed in. Back at the house, there were more people than usual this time. The house regulars complained it was because of the storm. The girls nestled into their corner and ate their dinner.

Before they were done, four girls entered the bedroom. Alessa hadn't seen them before. Dressed in black, they all appeared hard as nails. Tattoos snaked over every visible inch of their bodies and their faces and ears were decorated with multiple piercings.

The newcomers immediately walked over to Alessa and Lucy and stood over them. The girl who looked the meanest was missing several teeth and was about fifty pounds overweight. She wore a fake black leather jacket and her hair was cut close to her head. Large, flashy rings adorned her fingers.

She kicked Alessa's shin and commanded, "Give us your food, motherfucker!"

Annoyed at the intrusion into what they considered their home now, she said, "Go find your own food. This is ours. We walked the city all day to get this."

The girl burst out laughing and appeared to turn away, but without warning, she whipped back quickly and snatched the bag of food from Alessa.

When Alessa stood up, a reflexive gesture of self-defense, rather than a threatening one, the girl pushed her back to the floor. The others in the room watched the scene unfold. It was common for homeless people to fight over food and liquor, but many of them felt sorry for Alessa and Lucy now, because the girls had shared their food with others. Still, none of them uttered a word in their support. Crystal watched as well. She didn't like Alessa, but she didn't hate her anymore either. Alessa and Lucy had turned out to be harmless and they did know how to find food.

The four girls proceeded to drink and smoke pot with the others. They made their way around the house. Everyone knew they were what the homeless called "DBs" or "destitute bullies". The homeless had nothing, but the DBs took out the anger they felt over their lost lives on all the other homeless people. DBs were the worst of their kind on the streets. When they didn't get their way, they usually resorted to violence. Alessa had heard about them and knew these girls were part of this sick crowd. Realizing that they could seriously hurt her or Lucy, she retreated into her corner and tried to get the child as warm as she could that night. Crystal had watched Alessa's interaction with the DBs and was impressed that she had portrayed no fear of this gruesome bunch.

By morning, there were twelve inches of snow on the ground. Lucy was hungry when she woke up, but there was no food left from the night before. She was also eager to go out and play in the snow, but Alessa couldn't let her get her only warm clothes wet. All of the homeless stayed inside the "Abandominium," their name for the abandoned home they shared. For most of the people there, the snowfall was like a signal for an instant party. They drank and smoked all day long. Some of the older people gave Alessa and Lucy small portions of food they had stashed away, which was enough to keep them going until the streets cleared and they could get out and scout for food in dumpsters.

Chapter Forty

———————■———————

Lucy had been whining most of the day. Alessa assumed it was because she had been prevented from going out and playing in the snow. But as the evening wore on, she started coughing. Soon, she was burning up and shaking violently from fever induced chills. Crystal watched as Alessa tried everything to keep the child warm. Finally, she walked over and handed her a couple of blankets. Another regular at the Abandominium gave her an aspirin, which Lucy was able to swallow only after several attempts.

During the rest of the evening, the group went out of its way to help the child. The men and women there covered her with their coats and melted snow to make sure she had enough fluid to drink. The next morning, the fever hadn't broken.

Crystal approached Alessa. "Listen," she said urgently, "I know this doctor a couple of blocks away, who will give you antibiotic samples. Maybe you could take your kid there to get some?"

Alessa was grateful for any help she could get. "Yes!" she agreed. "Will you take us there?"

Wrapping Lucy in several blankets, she followed Crystal out of the house, carrying the child.

When they got to the doctor's office a few blocks away, Crystal led them inside.

The receptionist looked up from her computer. "Uh oh! What did you do now, Crystal?" she asked.

No sooner were the words out of her mouth than she noticed the small bundle of torn, dirty blankets that Alessa was holding in her arms. She called for the nurse and within minutes, the three of them had been whisked into one of the examining rooms.

The doctor Crystal had mentioned entered the room, introduced herself and directed Alessa to remove all the blankets. The woman felt a rush of pity when she saw the small, filthy child, weak and burning with fever. She conducted a thorough examination of Lucy before turning to Alessa.

"Well, it looks like Lucy has the 'flu," she announced. "She will need some medication and complete bed rest. She needs lots of fluid too." Then the doctor addressed Crystal. "I have some medication samples I can give her, but she needs to be in a warm, dry place for at least the next three days."

Clearly annoyed, Crystal said, "What the fuck are you lookin' at me for, Doc? She ain't my kid."

"I'm looking at you because I know how resourceful you are. And I think these two can use a little help. So like I said, the child needs to be in a warm, dry place for at least three days."

Crystal stomped her foot like a child. "Yeah, fine," she grumbled. "We'll work it out."

The doctor turned to the nurse and asked her to get three blankets. Moments later, she returned with three clean pink ones. The doctor wrapped Lucy in them and gave the old blankets to Crystal.

"Okay, now Lucy, you should be feeling better soon," she told her patient. Then she turned to Alessa. "I want to see her back here in three days."

Alessa was relieved to know it was only the flu, but she was beside herself with anxiety as she wondered how she would keep Lucy in a dry, warm place for three days. She assured the doctor she would pay her back for the office visit, but the woman shooed her off.

"I don't want you to worry about money," she told her. "If you or your daughter are sick, you come back to see me. Okay?"

They left the office together and back on the street, Crystal asked, "You got any money saved? "

Alessa told her that she had 100 dollars.

"Well," Crystal mused. "I know this motel not far from here. They charge 50 dollars a night. Sometimes, my johns would take me there. We'd fuck and they'd let me stay there overnight. Anyway, you can go there, I guess."

Alessa was happy that Crystal had thawed enough to want to help, but she still didn't have enough money to pay for the motel for three nights.

The two girls walked the five blocks to the motel, with Lucy in Alessa's arms. When they arrived, Crystal walked into the office and told them she needed a room for two days.

The man behind the counter scanned the three girls. Alessa was carrying Lucy wrapped in the blankets.

"Listen," he snapped, "I won't have any of that child porn here, you understand me?"

Alessa felt the blood rush to her face, a combination of embarrassment that someone could actually think that of her and anger, because the prick had just accused her of being a pedophile.

She spoke up and her voice was soft, but with a hint of steel. "No sir," she said, "we don't do shit like that. My sister is sick and the doctor said she needs to rest up for a few days."

The man pushed the room key toward Crystal and said, "That'll be a 100 dollars."

Alessa handed Lucy to Crystal. Then she unzipped her coat and went through multiple layers of clothing. She opened the safety pin attached to the shirt against her body and removed a small cloth bag that contained the only money she had. She handed the man 100 dollars and picked up the key from the counter.

Seeming to soften just enough so that he appeared halfway human, he said, "Here, it looks like you'll need this." He pushed a large plastic bag in Alessa's direction. It contained miniature versions of soap, shampoo, conditioner and toothpaste.

Alessa picked the bag off the counter, turned on her heel and left. The hotel's exterior looked like it had withstood an earthquake. The stucco was cracked and missing in places, exposing the cinderblocks. There were seedy looking vehicles parked at many of the doors, including a couple of old Cadillac's and rusted out pickup trucks. One car had so much duct tape on it, it seemed as though it was the only thing holding the vehicle together.

The parking lot was covered with snow and Alessa figured it would probably stay that way until it melted on its own. She walked up to her motel room and unlocked the door. The heater in the room had been turned down low and she immediately turned the fan on full blast. There were two double beds in the room. The walls were cinderblock, painted a very pale blue, and the rug was brown. The furniture was old and mismatched. The chairs had fake wood seats and thin chrome legs. The folding table pretended to be a desk. Suspended from fake gold chains, tacky lighting fixtures hung over it and the broken nightstands.

Alessa pulled the covers down on the first bed and carried out a quick inspection. It seemed clean enough, though she did notice long black hairs on the pillows and knew at once that these weren't fresh sheets. That didn't matter, though, after sleeping in a dilapidated, abandoned home with no plumbing or any other amenity. Compared to that, this place felt like the Ritz. She had Crystal put Lucy down on the bed and the two covered her with the blankets. Alessa gave her a dose of her prescribed medication, then went into the bathroom and filled the tub with warm water.

Once that was done, Alessa carried Lucy into the bathroom, undressed her and placed her in the tub. Even through her fever and sickness, Lucy managed to relax when she felt the warm water flow over her body. It was as if she were thawing out for the first time in weeks. When Alessa had finished washing her, she wrapped her in the hotel towels that were scratchy and tissue paper thin, but felt like a sheet of the richest cotton to Lucy who hadn't had a real towel on her body in months. Alessa dressed the little girl in an old sweat suit and put her back into bed.

All this while, Crystal had been lying on the other bed, watching television. This was something she hadn't done in a long, long time and she was transfixed with the Price Is Right. But she peeled her eyes off the screen for a quick minute to ask, "How about if I go to the mini mart at the end of the block and get some juice for her to drink?"

Relieved to have Crystal there with them, she readily agreed and thanked her. While she was gone, Alessa treated herself to a hot shower, washing away months of filth and grime.

When Crystal returned with the juice, Alessa immediately poured some and helped Lucy to sit up so she could drink it. She turned to Crystal.

"You know, if you want to take a shower, you can," she offered.

The girl's face lit up and for the first time since they had met, Alessa saw her smile. She was missing many teeth on both sides of her mouth, but she still had a nice smile.

When Crystal emerged from the bathroom twenty-five minutes later, wrapped in a towel, she looked completely different. They all looked different with the dirt washed away and their hair clean and combed.

"Thanks, that felt real nice," Crystal said. "Ain't nothing like washing the funk from your body." She laughed. "I might be able to pick up some johns while I'm still clean."

Pensive for a moment, Alessa said, "You know, if you want to stay here with us for a couple of days, you can. I mean, we have two beds. I can sleep here with Lucy and you can have the other bed."

"You fuckin' with me?" Crystal snapped. "Don't fuck with me 'cause I don't like being disappointed!"

Alessa put her hand to her forehead, as if to indicate that Crystal was giving her a headache. "No, I'm not fucking with you," she said wearily. "I said you could stay."

Confident that Alessa was being sincere, Crystal relaxed. "Yeah," she said, "that would be great! I'll see to it I get the extra fifty bucks for the last night and a little to spare, so we can eat."

Alessa knew that Crystal was going to hook herself while she was at the motel and all cleaned up. They both knew how to make money when they really needed to. Alessa had given hooking some thought too; she knew that she could sell herself for the three days she was here and have enough money to extend their stay. She tucked the thought of prostituting herself in the back of her mind, knowing she could pull it out and act on it, if needed.

Alessa got into bed next to Lucy. For the next two hours, they watched television in silence. For dinner the first night in the motel, Crystal went out and bought them a bucket of Kentucky Fried Chicken. She and Alessa ate well that night, while Lucy only managed to nibble on a chicken leg.

Chapter Forty-One

The next morning, Crystal went out for a while. When she returned early in the afternoon, she announced that she had paid the motel for another two days stay.

"Wow!" Alessa marveled, "you made 100 dollars today? I'm impressed!"

Crystal sat down on the edge of her bed. "Yeah," she said, "thank God for horny men! I got me twenty-five bucks a guy today."

Alessa knew that if Crystal could get twenty-five a client, she might be able to get fifty. She was relieved to get two more days at the motel. The longer they stayed, the greater the chance of Lucy recuperating and regaining her strength. Over the first thirty-six hours of their stay, the child had, in fact, become more alert and aware of her surroundings and her appetite was improving by the day.

On the third day of their stay, Alessa motioned Crystal into the bathroom while Lucy was asleep and shut the bathroom door behind them.

"Here's the deal," she said. "I just can't take Lucy back to that house where we were staying. She needs to live like a normal kid. I don't think her tiny body can take much more of this shit. I need to go out for the day and make some money. In fact, if I can make enough, I'll extend our stay here for a couple more days until I can find somewhere for Lucy and me to go."

Crystal remembered a time when she had nurtured hopes for her own children. It was, in fact, her desire for them to live like normal kids that had finally given her the strength to entrust their care to her boyfriend's parents. She hadn't seen them in six years. Her own drug addiction prevented her from doing all that Alessa planned for Lucy now.

"Okay, I can stay with her while you're out," Crystal agreed. "But you do know what you're doing, right? I mean, even under all that dirt, you never did look like the type of girl who would fuck someone for money."

Alessa's face suddenly wore a distant expression, as though a window had just slammed shut. "Things aren't always what they seem," she said noncommittally. "I've done a lot of things I'm not proud of, but at least this time, I'll be doing it for a good reason."

Chapter Forty-Two

———————◼———————

Alessa showered and fixed herself up as best she could. She put on a pair of tight jeans she had washed in the tub the day before and a low-necked tee shirt that had belonged to her from the time she lived on Dauphin Street. Then before leaving for the day, she leaned over and gave Lucy a hug.

"I'll be back later, Luce," she announced. "I'm going to see if I can get some work."

Still weak and listless from her illness, Lucy murmured, "Okay, see you later. Alessa, will you bring me some ice cream when you come back?"

"Sure, I'll bring ice cream back for you."

Alessa steeled herself for what might be in store, before opening the door and stepping out into the cold darkness that lay beyond the threshold. Luckily, she didn't have to go too far to turn tricks. Several of the men noticed her standing out in the motel's parking lot and invited her in. Others spotted her from the street when she stood out on the sidewalk, a block down from the motel. As she engaged in different sexual acts with each of the men that day, Alessa mentally distanced herself from what she was doing. Her sole aim was to get Lucy and herself off the streets. She couldn't risk the child falling ill again and was well aware that staying in the house of squatters was neither a healthy alternative nor a safe one for either of them. There was always the threat of violence and rape.

Alessa had to compromise on her price on that first day and had given each of her customers an hour for 35 dollars. She had "done" five men and made 175 dollars. She paid for two more days at the motel and spent another 25 dollars on food which she brought back to the room. Counting the two days Crystal had paid for and the two she had just paid for herself, they could now stay four more days at the motel. In those four days, Alessa figured she could save enough money to make her next move. If she could sell herself to five men a day, she calculated, she and Lucy would be set to move on.

In the weeks that had just gone by, Alessa had talked to other homeless people she'd met on the streets. Many of them had suggested she try getting accommodations at a hostel, if she wanted to live indoors during the winter. It cost money, of course, but the cost would be minimal. Alessa had scoped out the information in a telephone book and knew there was a hostel on Spruce Street. She had called them that afternoon and made a reservation for Lucy and herself four days later.

The woman on the phone had made it clear to Alessa that it would cost her 250 dollars a month. "That's one hundred and fifty for you and one hundred for your little sister."

Alessa didn't really know what to expect of the place. Nor did she care. All she knew was that young people lived there or stayed there for a while. They had showers and towels, the prospect of which thrilled her to no end. The woman cautioned her that the residents there were mainly older teens and young adults. So Alessa would have to keep her little sister with her at all times, because while they allowed children, they usually didn't have any staying there.

Over the next four days, Alessa had sex with twenty men. She could have accommodated more, had she succeeded in finding buyers. She was determined to earn and save as much cash as possible in the short time that was available to her.

Crystal was in awe of Alessa's stamina. On the third day, she remarked, "Girl, I ain't never met nobody that can find people to fuck like you do."

Alessa laughed and shared some of her experiences at Doubles with her. She confided how Harlin had forced her to have sex with the clients when she took them back for a lap dance.

Crystal listened intently. When Alessa had finished her account, she said, "Well, I guess it's a good thing you learnt how to do all those things. You've made yourself a lot of money in these past few days. It doesn't bother me none—fuckin' for money."

On their last day at the motel, Alessa had their checkout time extended so as to be able to hook for as long as possible before moving to the hostel. When she returned to their room that afternoon, Lucy was herself again and Crystal was lying on the bed watching television. The child had already packed their belongings and when it was time to leave, Alessa and Crystal turned to face each other.

"Well, okay," Alessa said, holding out her arms to hug Crystal.

Crystal quickly hugged them both without saying a word and moved to the door. Just before she closed it on her way out, she said, "You two take care of each other, you hear?"

Alessa and Lucy left the motel and headed to their new home. When they arrived at the Loftstel on Spruce Street in University City, they found themselves surrounded by college students. They seemed to be everywhere. But considering how close they were to the University of Pennsylvania, it was only to be expected. The hostel was a large twin home located in a neighborhood that looked no different from any other residential area. In fact, the place looked great. Far better than the apartment building in North Philly where Alessa had lived, before moving in with Harlin.

Chapter Forty-Three

―――――――――――■――――――――――

When Alessa and Lucy entered the Loftstel, they were hit by a blast of warm air, a sensation they both welcomed after the chilling cold outside which was nearly unbearable. Alessa went through the formalities of checking them in. The woman at the reception desk told them they would be staying in Room 2B on the second floor.

The girls went up to their room, carrying the clothes they had brought with them. Once inside, they took in their new home quickly. Bunk beds were fitted along three of the four walls. Two of the beds sat with bare mattresses, the sheets folded neatly and placed at the foot, ready for their occupants. Alessa chose the top bunk for herself and left the lower one for Lucy. Lucy argued that she wanted the top bunk, but Alessa refused, fearing she'd roll over and fall out during the night. Alessa compromised by promising Lucy that she could share her top bunk with her for fifteen minutes every night before going to sleep.

Having settled in, the first thing they did was head for the common showers with the towels they had been handed and the shampoo and soap Alessa had bought from a Five and Dime store on the way to the hostel. Both girls got into the open showers and reveled in the feel of hot water on their bodies. The motel shower had certainly been better than nothing, but there was hardly any water pressure and the water never got really hot. Alessa washed Lucy's hair before she washed her own and both scrubbed their bodies with soapy washcloths till they were done. Then they looked at each other, exhausted by their efforts and satisfied by the outcome. Alessa dressed Lucy and herself in the cleanest clothing they had and headed down to the laundry to wash all the clothes they owned.

Feeling good from the hot shower, the girls ventured down to the common kitchen area. They couldn't believe their eyes when they saw how well equipped it was. There was a stove, a refrigerator and a microwave.

The hostel provided all the facilities and the utensils to cook with. But the residents had to buy the food themselves. Alessa had enough money to buy food that would keep them going for a couple of weeks, but she would need to find work so that she could pay the rent. The two of them made a list of the food items they would bring back to the hostel so they could cook meals together.

Just off the kitchen was a dining area where a group of older teens were sitting having a meal. They greeted the girls and invited them to join them for lunch. Alessa explained they had just gotten there and hadn't yet bought any groceries. The teens insisted they had more than enough for them. Alessa and Lucy noticed the peanut butter and jelly sandwiches they were making and joined them happily. They both ate like savages as the group watched them with curiosity.

Alessa looked up from her sandwich and noticed how they were all staring at the two of them. She wiped her mouth with her napkin and put down the remaining morsel of her sandwich. "I'm sorry," she admitted a little shamefully. "We're eating like pigs. We've been traveling for a couple of days and haven't really eaten much on the way. We're both starving."

Lucy couldn't care less what they thought. She finished the last remnants of her sandwich, licked her fingers clean and asked, "Can I have another one?"

The teens laughed, telling the girls to go ahead and prepare another sandwich for themselves.

After lunch, they thanked the group and found their way outside. As they strolled along the streets of Philadelphia, Alessa worried about her next step, listening half-heartedly to Lucy chattering away about how nice the people were at the hostel. Later that night, after the child was asleep, Alessa thought hard about her next decision. She knew she could dance at one of the go-go clubs in the city. That wouldn't be an issue. She knew she was very good at it and remembered how much money it had made her at Doubles. She could work retail, but realized she would make just enough money to get by. And that wouldn't be enough. If she were to give Lucy and herself any kind of life, she needed to earn a substantial amount. It boiled down to two options: selling sex or dancing at a club. Alessa decided that without someone like Harlin involved, dancing would be very lucrative for her. She was convinced she didn't want to work as a prostitute. She'd only done it the last four days to get them off the streets.

She made the decision to go back to dancing—this time, on her own terms. After she had saved enough money, she would look to buy her own house. Uppermost in her mind was her desperation to keep Lucy off the streets. There was only one problem: she would have to leave her on her own when she went off to the club at night. She decided to talk to her roommates and try to persuade them to take turns in keeping an eye on the child. She would say she was stocking shelves at a grocery store in the evenings. With her plan all chalked out, she told herself: *fuck anybody that ain't me*! That would be her new attitude from now on. She was past being everyone else's bitch. She was going to make things better for herself and for Lucy and dared anyone to get in her way.

The next morning, Lucy and Alessa went to the pay phone in the hostel for their weekly call to Ebby. Lucy dialed the number and excitedly told Ebby about all the new teenagers they had met the day before. Ebby listened carefully. She had long since concluded that Alessa had been keeping the truth from her. She suspected they were living on the streets. After all, months had passed and she knew from experience that shelters for the homeless typically never allowed people to stay on for an indefinite period. There was one other thing that disturbed her: Lucy never talked about her parents.

When Alessa got on the phone, Ebby said, "I haven't heard from you in a while. What's going on? Where are you? Alessa, I know you're determined to take care of yourself without depending on others, but it's time you stopped lying to me. I need to know the truth."

Alessa caved in. She spared Ebby nothing, recounting the details of her life under the bridge, in the abandoned house, in the motel they had moved to, after Lucy fell ill, and now at the hostel where they were staying at present. Ebby heaved a sigh of relief, but scolded Alessa for lying to her. Alessa was apologetic, but explained how she had been determined to figure out her situation on her own and resolve her issues by herself.

Then she asked, "Ebby, have you heard anything from the police about Harlin? I was too afraid to ask you about him all these months, but now I need to know."

"I have," Ebby replied. "Harlin was convicted of assault with a deadly weapon two months ago. He was sentenced to five years in prison and will be eligible for parole in three years."

Alessa let out a quick shout of relief. "Thank you, God!"

Ebby laughed.

Alessa's concern over Harlin had to do with her decision to dance again at a go-go club. She knew that he, along with his crew, frequented those clubs. And now that he was no longer welcome at Doubles, there was a very good chance of him prowling the other joints and finding her.

"So what will you do now to pay rent at the hostel?" Ebby asked.

"I managed to get a job stocking shelves at night at a grocery store," Alessa promptly answered. "I'll make enough to keep us here, until I can save money and move on."

"And what about Lucy?" Ebby persisted. "Where are her parents?"

Alessa's response was abrupt, "She doesn't have any, Ebby. She's just got me. I am her only family now. She's happy and so am I. So don't worry, okay?"

Ebby said she wouldn't, but couldn't help cautioning her. "Alessa," she said, "you still need to be careful. You do realize that you have no legal right to keep Lucy with you? I am going to work on some things from my end and see if we can get her into school."

"Thanks, Ebby. That would be great. She's really smart and I think she would love going back to school. I'll call you again tomorrow. Bye."

Knowing that Alessa was talking about her, Lucy had perked up. "Am I going to school?" she asked. "I really want to go to school, Alessa. Can I go, please? Please?"

Alessa smiled as she took the child in her arms. "Ebby is going to see if she can help us get you back into school," she said. "We need to be careful, though. We have to make sure that no one separates us. We're family, but other people might not see it that way. I'm sure Ebby can help, but we'll have to be patient."

Chapter Forty-Four

The next evening, after Lucy had fallen asleep, Alessa left the hostel and headed to a go-go club in the city. She had already talked to their roommates at the hostel who were eager to help her by minding Lucy. When she reached the club and asked for the manager, the bartender eyed her guardedly, "Wait here," he directed. "I'll go get him."

As Alessa waited she took in the sights of the club. It was a much larger place than Doubles, but that was not the only difference. The girls who worked there were different too, but in a way that made her heart sink. They were downright sleazy and the customers—men of all ages, most of them piss drunk. As the girls danced on stage, their clients kept reaching out to touch them. Most of the dancers were topless and a few were even stark naked. It was no wonder there wasn't a vacant seat in the area offering a ringside view of them. As at Doubles, the girls who weren't dancing were busy mingling with the customers. Alessa noticed some of them leading customers through a door next to the stage and guessed the lap dance rooms lay beyond.

The bartender eventually returned and asked Alessa to have a seat at the bar. Ten minutes later, a short man with blonde hair emerged through a door behind the bar. He was nicely tanned with ocean-blue eyes. Alessa thought he was built well and his clothes were expensive. He was actually very good-looking. Had he been taller, he would have been perfect, she decided.

The man approached her and held out his hand. "Hi, I'm Parker," he said. "What can I do for you?"

Alessa didn't feel nervous at all. She had watched the girls dancing and knew she was way better at it than any of them. "I'm Alessa," she told him. "My stage name is Rana. I'm looking for a job dancing. I have experience. Do you need anyone?"

Parker studied her from head to toe. She was decent-looking enough, he thought. She needed a little makeup and would have to do something with that rat-nest of hair on her head, but what the hell!

"Oh yeah," he replied. "Well, why don't you change into your costume and I'll take a look at what you got to offer?"

Alessa had forgotten all about a costume. She didn't have any money to buy one anyway. "Well, I sort of had to get out of Dodge, if you know what I mean, from my last gig. I didn't take any costumes with me. So I don't have any to dance in."

"Yeah, I know what you mean," Parker said. "This is a tough business. Okay, well, you're wearing underwear, right?"

Alessa nodded.

"Let's go in the back and I'll take a look at what you can do."

Alessa followed Parker into his office. When he closed the door, she realized it was going to be just the two of them. He sat down on a small sofa, turned on the music and said, "Okay, let's see it."

Alessa began to dance and was instantly swept away by the music. It came as naturally to her as riding a bike did to others. She kicked off her shoes and slowly removed her shirt. Next, she bent over, her ass in his face, and slowly slid her jeans off. She turned around and continued to dance for him. She was moving perfectly to the rhythm of the music.

After a few moments, Parker said, "That's good, honey, but you need to take all your clothes off for me."

Alessa had never danced completely naked. She had never danced topless either. She had at least worn pasties. She felt a little jittery as she unhooked her bra and dropped it to the floor. Her nipples were hard. When Parker's gaze shot to them, he let out a small sound. It didn't go unnoticed.

Then Parker said, "Come on, your panties too. But first stick your hands down them and play with yourself a little, before you take them off."

You sick motherfucker, Alessa thought to herself, but she really needed the work. Obediently, she slid her hand into her panties and pretended as if she were masturbating.

"Yeah, baby," Parker said. "Come on, slide them off now."

Alessa slowly slid her panties down and stepped out of them. Now that she was fully naked and alone with this man she'd just met, she felt terribly awkward and it showed in her dance moves. Parker assured her she was doing a "good, fucking job" and reminded her to keep moving. Alessa continued to dance and soon slipped back into a frame of mind where she was able to block out the rest of the world.

But Parker wasn't done with her yet. "Turn around and slide your hands down your legs until you touch your toes."

Alessa turned her back to him and slowly began sliding her hands down her legs until she was fully extended and touching her toes. As she looked back at Parker through the gap between her legs, she caught him unzipping his pants. She realized she was now fully exposed to him even as he urged her to "swing your hips and stay in that position".

After a short while, Alessa stood upright again and faced Parker. Another song had started playing by then.

"Yeah, baby, that was good," he said with approval. "Now let's see how you do with lap dances. My clients love to get them here."

Alessa reached for her panties, but Parker stopped her.

"No panties," he told her firmly. "The girls here don't wear panties when they give lap dances. Just bring yourself over here the way you are."

Alessa complied, stepping up onto the sofa and straddling him. She did her usual lap dance routine in this position, but didn't actually ever lower her body onto his lap. He was looking up at her as he reached up and caressed her breasts. By now, Alessa had no doubts at all that he was a slimy pig. But she had no illusions either about how this worked. She needed a job bad, she reminded herself through gritted teeth, and it wasn't like she hadn't fucked what seemed like a million men before.

Parker slid his hands slowly down her flat stomach first, then ran them over her hips and caressingly over her ass. Then without warning, he grabbed both cheeks and grunted. He dropped his hands to her inner thighs and ran them up lingeringly until his fingers had slipped inside her.

"Does that feel good, baby?" he asked.

Alessa closed her eyes and responded, "Yeah, that feels good."

Parker continued to finger her. Then he pulled back and jerked himself off with her still straddling him.

Alessa thought, *well, this sure is different*. When he came, she quickly rushed over and put her clothes back on. She looked him in the eye and inquired, "Well?"

"Yeah. Tomorrow night, be here at seven-thirty."

"I need 100 dollars to buy a couple of costumes," Alessa demanded.

Parker pulled the money from his pocket and handed it to her. As she was leaving the room, he said with a grin, "Girl, you're going to make a lot of money here."

Alessa looked at him with disgust and replied, "I'm counting on it. By the way, that is the first and last time you will ever stick anything that belongs to you inside me. Don't ever do that again."

Parker looked at her. "I needed to try it out and make sure it's okay," he explained.

As she closed the door behind her on the way out, he heard her say, "Whatever, motherfucker."

Alessa knew how to play the game. She didn't like it one bit, but it was all she knew how to do. She was grateful to have a job, but in her new maturity, she wasn't about to let Parker think she was his new toy. He had got a taste and now he needed to stand clear.

The next few days fell into place just as Alessa had hoped. Ebby had managed to get Lucy into the Penn Alexander School without too much trouble. The little girl was now nine years old and should have been in fourth grade, but she had been out of school for the past year. So Ebby put her into third grade to start. Lucy didn't know any better and was just thrilled to be going back to school again.

Chapter Forty-Five

Alessa began dancing at the club. She had made up her mind that she would go for the big money and dance naked. The men loved her and within days, she was making the kind of money she hadn't dreamed of. After she had been dancing for a week, Alessa took Lucy out early one evening to buy her clothes. She knew that eventually, the kids at school would give the girl a hard time about how shabby her clothes were and decided that this was the moment to get her some new things before the "new girl" effect wore off. Lucy was happy and content.

With every passing week, Alessa's savings began to grow rapidly. She was making nearly 1,500 dollars a week. Working five nights a week, she was averaging 300 a night—more, if she had a steady flow of lap dances. She was frugal with her money and only bought essential items they couldn't do without. Alessa took public transportation to avoid the cost of cabs. Only on the nights she left the club really late would she splurge on a cab, more out of concern for her safety than for reasons of convenience. Alessa and Lucy talked with Ebby three times a week now; both of them seemed well on their way to recovery, healing from the traumas of the past.

By springtime of the following year, Alessa had saved close to 20,000 dollars. This time, she was smarter about handling her money. She had rented a safety deposit box at a local bank where she kept all of her cash. She and Lucy were living comfortably on 500 a week and the rest was put into savings. Both of them were happy living at the hostel. While residents kept coming and going, the girls had no problem making new friends.

On the weekends, the two would go into the city and window shop. They would buy soft pretzels to hand out to homeless people. Sometimes, they would go to the Salvation Army and buy cheap clothes and shoes, to give away to those among the homeless who needed them badly. Both girls remembered how hard it was when they themselves had been homeless and invisible to all the human beings around them. Alessa had established a rapport with the homeless children and adults. They could relate to her, because she too had been homeless once and was just getting on her feet. They respected and admired her for wanting to leave the streets, because many of them, especially the older ones, had lost the will to try and no longer minded being homeless. The younger ones, though, the children and the teenagers, often felt there was more to life than pulling food from garbage cans and begging for quarters. Alessa spent her days volunteering at homeless shelters, when she wasn't studying for her GED. Every week she called her sister, Rosabella, planning for the day she would take the train out to Norristown with Lucy, so she could meet her niece, Eva.

In early June, Alessa arranged for Lucy and herself to have lunch with Ebby in the city on a Saturday afternoon. They had been talking on the phone for nearly a year, but hadn't seen each other in all that time. At Ebby's suggestion, they met at the White Dog Café in University City, a quaint little restaurant that was very popular with the locals. Alessa and Lucy arrived first, barely able to contain their excitement at the prospect of seeing Ebby.

The moment she walked in through the door, Alessa rushed to greet her. They hugged for a long time, before Lucy interrupted them.

"What about me?" she protested. "Ebby, aren't you glad to see me too?"

Ebby leaned down and lifted the child into her arms, "Of course I'm happy to see you, sweetie!" she said affectionately. "Who in their right mind wouldn't be happy to see you?"

Lucy beamed with delight as the other two exchanged a playful glance. Ebby was trying to assess both girls without making it apparent. They looked healthy and were dressed decently. She could see Alessa was happier than she had been just a year ago.

Once they were seated at their table, they all ordered burgers and talked excitedly. Alessa told Ebby she was taking the test for her GED the following week. Lucy raved about her teachers and her friends at school.

Ebby asked Alessa how much longer they intended to stay at the hostel and was told of their plans of moving out at the end of the summer, before Lucy started fourth grade.

The little girl perked up and asked, "Alessa, does this mean I won't see my friends anymore?"

Alessa comfortingly covered the child's hand with hers. "No, Lucy," she assured her. "We're going to stay in the area so you can still go to the same school."

Satisfied with the answer, Lucy asked if she could get ice cream for dessert. They were all enjoying their time together. As they were finishing dessert, Alessa turned to Ebby.

"I'm nineteen years old now," she declared. "I want to adopt Lucy and I need you to help me do it. What do you think?"

Ebby stiffened. "Alessa," she said carefully, "sometimes, these things get complicated. Lucy's parents aren't around and the courts could legitimately want to put her into foster care. However, you might have a chance, given the fact that she has been with you for a year now and you have a stable job at the grocery store. There is an attorney who volunteers at the shelter. I could make a few inquiries without divulging too much information."

Alessa froze. She hadn't told Ebby she was dancing at a go-go club again. She didn't want disclose any information that might jeopardize her chances of keeping Lucy with her. She turned to the child and asked her to go to the bathroom and wash up before they left. Lucy readily complied. As soon as she had left the table, Alessa looked intently at Ebby. It was obvious to her that what Alessa was about to say was important.

"Ebby, I've been lying to you," Alessa confessed.

"Oh my, what now?"

Alessa looked somber. "I don't have a job at a grocery store," she told her. "I have been stripping at a go-go club since early December. I make an incredible amount of money and I don't have sex with anyone. I strip; the men get off on it. Some of them touch a little, but nothing hardcore. I want to adopt Lucy, but what if they find out that I am dancing for a living?"

Ebby frowned. "First off, I'm not happy that you lied to me *yet again*. Second, I am very concerned about you stripping. I really wanted to see you doing something that didn't involve allowing yourself to be exploited all over again. Third, I don't think a court in the land will let you adopt Lucy while you're stripping. Let's face it: you don't even show any money on the books, right?"

Alessa nodded.

"And fourth, I don't want you to ever lie to me again. I am your friend and I love you. I will never judge you for the choices you make. My suggestion to you would be to just keep Lucy with you and not do anything that would draw attention to the relationship."

Alessa was clearly disappointed, but appreciated Ebby's honesty. It would keep her out of trouble. At that precise moment, Lucy returned to the table, cleaned up and ready to go. They could see she was tired. It had been a long lunch with a lot of excitement.

Once outside, the three of them embraced for a long time.

Alessa said, "Maybe we can meet for lunch once a month. Do you think that would work?"

"Of course that would work," Ebby replied. "I couldn't keep myself away from little Miss Lucy over here, even if I tried!"

Lucy threw her arms around Ebby and whispered in her ear, "I love you, Ebby, and Alessa loves you too. You're our family."

The moment brought tears to Ebby's eyes and Alessa just looked on with joy in her heart. Her child—which is how she saw Lucy now—and her only real friend loved each other.

Chapter Forty-Six

----------◼----------

When the Fourth of July holiday came around, Alessa and Lucy were living comfortably. Alessa had passed her GED and applied for grant money to attend the Philadelphia Community College. After months of working with the homeless on the streets and in shelters, Alessa knew she wanted to go into counseling. She was good at it, especially when it involved teens and children. She related to what they were going through and encouraged them individually to be strong and resilient. Her work with each of them was limited, though, since she was only a volunteer.

On July 4th, Alessa took Lucy to Penn's Landing to watch the fireworks on the waterfront. There were thousands of people there. Most were drunk by the time they arrived, at seven p.m., but Alessa kept Lucy clear of those who were openly too drunk to be near. Alessa was no stranger to drunks and drug addicts. She wasn't afraid for herself. She just wanted to protect Lucy. She had seen way too many perverts at the club and some of them had really given her the willies. She knew there was evil in the world and that also included the world in which Lucy lived. She found a spot where a family was standing and planted Lucy and herself next to them. She figured staying close to a family would keep them safe from all the rowdy partygoers.

Lucy and Alessa stood on Columbus Boulevard and enjoyed the beautiful fireworks display. Both the girls felt exhilarated and hopeful, as they watched the burst of color against the night sky. The show didn't get over until well after ten p.m. and Alessa decided it would be best for them to take a cab back to the hostel instead of riding the bus. The crowd began to thin out and Alessa noticed that those who remained were still partying and having a good time. She saw a pay phone in the strip mall across the street and took Lucy by the hand to lead her there.

Just as they were crossing Columbus Boulevard, they noticed a young man sitting up the road, barely in sight. From what Alessa could see, he was doubled over and rocking back and forth. With Lucy at her side, Alessa walked past the strip mall and over to the young man who was sitting under an overpass. The street was dark. As she approached, Alessa called out to him.

"Are you okay?" she asked anxiously.

"No, I need help!" the young man cried out.

Used to the streets and to people who called them their home, Alessa hurried over to him and bent down to look at his face. Within seconds, three other young men had surrounded them. Seeing them up close, it was clear to her that these were not homeless men. She knew at once that she had made a huge mistake.

One of the men seized Lucy and eyed her with longing. Another twisted Alessa's arm behind her back as the young man on the curb jumped up, a smirk on his face. They were all very drunk and the stink of alcohol seeped out of every part of their being. Alessa could feel the adrenaline pumping through her body as she frantically tried to think of a way to get Lucy out of there.

The young man holding the child said, "I don't know about you assholes, but I'm gonna get me some virgin lovin' tonight."

Alessa felt her heart flutter in her chest. With more aggression in her voice than she intended to display, she said, "Oh no, motherfucker! That virgin is my kid and she doesn't know shit about how to make a man feel good. Here's what we're gonna do: you're gonna let her go and I'm gonna make it worth it for all of you. I have more experience and know what I'm doing. You don't need to take a crying kid, 'cause that's all she's going to do, just cry and scream. Me, on the other hand, I'll have you crying and screaming, once you lose those pants."

The young men eyed her with curiosity. Then one of them asked, "Oh yeah? Whatcha gonna do for us?"

With more courage than she actually felt, Alessa replied, "Whatever I need to do to make you feel better than you ever have! But you need to let my kid go first."

She looked at Lucy who was crying, her face stricken with pure terror, and said, "Sweetheart, I want you to go back to that restaurant we just passed, the Ruby Buffet. Buy yourself a soda and wait there until I come and get you."

The child nodded and Alessa told the men to give her a couple of dollars for a soda.

As one of the men handed her three dollars, he looked Alessa in the eye. "This better be worth it, bitch," he warned, "and if your kid tells anyone we're here, we'll slit your fucking throat!"

Alessa looked at Lucy calmly and said in a steady voice, "I want you to go have a soda. Drink it slowly, don't tell anyone that I'm here and don't leave there, until I come to get you. Do you understand me?"

The child was crying, but she nodded vigorously and ran off toward the strip mall.

The four men led Alessa deep into the underpass. The first man demanded a blow job. The second wanted to have anal sex with her, as did the third. The last man, the one who did all the talking for the group, wanted regular sex, but he wanted it rough.

When his turn came, Alessa was already fully naked and lying on her stomach. He started by slapping her hard on her ass. Then he turned her over on her back and told her to jerk him off. When he was hard as a rock, he straddled her, his feet planted close to her shoulders, and ordered her to lick his balls. Finally, he lowered himself onto her bare stomach and gripped her breasts hard. He pinched her nipples so viciously that she couldn't stop herself from reaching up involuntarily to push his hands away.

"Oh, you don't like that, do you bitch?" he snarled in ridicule. Then he slapped her hard across the face. "You don't like that either, you little cunt!" he sneered.

He motioned to his buddies who each grabbed one of Alessa's legs and spread them wide. His entry was so brutal that she screamed out in agony. In response, he punched her in the ribs and went back to thrusting himself into her. One of the men holding her legs reached in, while his friend was on top of her, and sliced her thigh with a large knife he was holding. She flinched backward in pain and shock. The man having sex with her paused momentarily, yanked her head up by her hair, and slammed it back into the ground.

"What did I tell you, bitch?" he growled. "You're a real fucking killjoy! How the fuck am I supposed to come, with you moving all over the place and yelling out like that? If I want that, I'll go get that kid of yours."

He noticed Alessa's eyes widen with fear and knew, at that moment, that he was in complete control. When he finally came inside her, he began to pound his fists into her body and her face. The other men joined in by kicking her legs, sides, head and arms. Alessa found herself drifting in and out of consciousness. She was being beaten so badly that her body had gone numb. She had stopped feeling anything at all. And after a while, she could barely hear or understand what they were yelling at her with each blow they delivered. Before losing consciousness, Alessa believed she was going to die. They were going to beat her to death and she asked God to keep Lucy safe.

It was eleven thirty p.m. when the waitress at the Ruby Buffet asked Lucy if she was there by herself. "We're getting ready to close, honey," she told her. "Is there someone you can call?"

She took the child over to the phone and she dialed Ebby's number. When the night manager came on the line, Lucy told her who she was and said she needed to talk to Ebby. It was an emergency. The night manager, like the rest of the shelter staff, knew about Alessa and Lucy from the many stories Ebby had shared with them. He took the phone number of the restaurant and promised to have Ebby call right back.

A few minutes later, the phone rang and the waitress picked it up. "Yeah, she's here," she said to Ebby. "The kid is all by herself and we need to close. Here, you can talk to her," she said, handing the receiver to Lucy.

Lucy broke down and started to sob as soon as she heard Ebby's voice.

Trying to conceal the panic in her own voice, Ebby asked, "Where's Alessa?"

"With some men down the road. They wanted me to stay too, but Alessa made them give me three dollars to come to the restaurant and have a soda," Lucy answered, disclosing the information with obvious reluctance, as Alessa's instructions played in her mind.

Ebby asked the child to describe her exact location and promised to be with her in less than thirty minutes. Then she asked for the waitress to be put back on the phone.

"Hello?" the woman said.

Ebby concocted a story about Lucy being her granddaughter and how she had been separated from her mother during the fireworks. Then she asked, "I know you're trying to close, but can you just stay with her, until I get there?"

The waitress looked at the child who was plagued with fear. She had also overheard her saying that her mom was with some guys down the street.

"Yeah, sure," she assured Ebby before hanging up the phone.

The waitress walked over to the counter, poured Lucy another soda and sat down in a booth with her arm around the small child to wait for her ride to come.

Chapter Forty-Seven

E bby lost no time. She called a detective she knew at the Philadelphia Police Department. They had become friendly over the years, while dealing with various domestic and drug-related issues faced by the residents at the shelter. She admitted to him that she didn't know much, but suspected foul play. She told him where she was headed and asked if he'd meet her there. When Ebby arrived at the Ruby Buffet, her detective friend and his partner were already sitting in their car in front of the restaurant. She immediately thanked them for coming.

When Lucy saw Ebby enter the restaurant, she sprang to her feet, rushed over to her and clasped her in both arms, as though she would never let her go. The child sobbed and poured out her story, as Ebby held her and tried to make sense of the nearly incoherent words. The detectives grasped as much of the story as they needed for their investigation and headed down Columbus Boulevard to the underpass. With Lucy having told them there were at least four men involved, they had radioed for backup, just in case. Moving deep into the underpass, they came upon a lifeless form, lying face down in the dirt, naked. At first, they feared she was dead. That she was badly bruised and bleeding was apparent even in the darkness that hung like heavy curtains around her body. One of the detectives leaned down and felt for a pulse.

"It's very faint," he announced to his partner, "but there is a pulse. Call for an ambulance."

While one officer stood over Alessa, another covered as much of her as he could with his jacket. They didn't want to move her for fear of aggravating the damage already done to her broken body. When the ambulance arrived, the paramedics gently turned Alessa onto her back to place her on the gurney. The sight of her battered face drew a collective gasp of horror from the men. She had been beaten so brutally, you could barely tell she had any features left. Her face, in fact, her entire head, was bruised and bloodied and swollen so badly that it looked like a perfectly round ball. The men suspected that she might have suffered severe head trauma. They quickly loaded her into the ambulance and took her to the Hospital of the University of Pennsylvania, not far from the hostel where she and Lucy were staying.

The emergency room doctor and nurses converged on Alessa as they brought her through the doors. The ambulance staff had alerted them they were bringing in a young woman who had been severely beaten around her head and body. The attending doctor suspected multiple fractures and possible internal hemorrhaging.

When Ebby and Lucy arrived at the hospital and rushed through the emergency room doors, the nurse at the front desk asked them to have a seat and called back to the ER to let them know "the poor girl's family had arrived". Ebby drew Lucy onto her lap and held her tight as they waited. When the ER doctor came out, he told Ebby that Alessa had been badly beaten. An arm, a femur and several ribs had been fractured. There was bruising all over her body, including her genitals. His greatest concern, however, was the injuries to her head. Alessa was getting a CAT scan, as they spoke, and he would know more in the next hour or so.

"We are doing everything we can to help," he assured Ebby. "Her pulse was very weak when she arrived."

Ebby already knew from the paramedics that Alessa had lost a lot of blood from the deep cuts that covered her body and the doctor's prognosis filled her with alarm. Sick with grief over what had happened to her, she was relieved that the exhausted Lucy had fallen asleep in the ER and would surely stay asleep for the rest of the night. Ebby's mind spun with endless questions as she prayed that Alessa would survive this ordeal and come through. She begged God to give her some coverage from heaven or just leave her the hell alone and let the girl get on with her life. For the first time in her life, Ebby was angry at God. Where was he and why had he neglected this child? How much shit did Alessa have to take before she caught a fucking break? Ebby was livid at the rotten bastards who had hurt her. She cursed all the pricks who had abused her in the past. She was even angry at herself for failing to protect Alessa.

It was hours before the emergency room doctor came out. He told Ebby that Alessa did have some minor head injuries, but nothing she wouldn't overcome. They had set her broken leg and arm and she was sleeping peacefully and comfortably with the meds they had given her. She hadn't regained consciousness since she arrived, but given the degree of trauma she had suffered, that was par for the course.

The ER doctor planned to admit her to the surgical intensive care unit so that they could keep a close eye on her. He still wasn't satisfied with her vital signs and they had to give her a blood transfusion. He suggested Ebby go home and rest, but she refused. So he took her in to see Alessa. Ebby gazed at the girl, shocked. Her injuries were so extensive that she was virtually unrecognizable. She knew there was no way she could allow Lucy to see Alessa in this condition. The nurses promised to watch the child to allow Ebby to catch some much needed sleep.

Ebby sat in the chair next to Alessa's bed and rested her head on the edge of the mattress. She woke up several hours later. It took her a minute to orient herself. Then her eyes went directly to Alessa. She was satisfied that her young friend was still sleeping peacefully and was moving carefully off the bed so as not to awaken her, when she noticed one of Alessa's eyelids fluttering. Ebby spoke to her in a soothing voice, told her where she was and assured her that Lucy was okay. Alessa acknowledged her words with the slightest nod of her head and struggled to speak.

Ebby knew exactly what was bothering her. "Alessa," she reassured her, "they never got near Lucy. She is fine. In fact, she was the one who called me from the restaurant. I won't let her see you just yet, but you needn't worry. Lucy will be staying with me, until you get better."

She saw Alessa's body relax and in minutes, she was asleep again.

Chapter Forty-Eight

E bby found Lucy awake and talking to the nurses. When the child caught sight of Ebby, she ran to her and threw her arms around her. "How's Alessa?" she cried. "Is she dead?"

Ebby scooped her up in her arms. "She's going to be fine," she reassured the little girl. "But she is very sick right now. It's going to take a long time for her to feel better. You'll be sleeping at my house with me, until she does. Okay?"

Despite her relief that Alessa would live, Lucy's small, thin body was still shaking as she clung tighter to Ebby. "This is all my fault, Ebby," she mumbled.

"No." Ebby stated firmly. "No, this isn't your fault. It was those terrible men who did this to her. Besides, Alessa would be upset if she knew you thought that, Lucy."

The child was sobbing now. "Ebby, they wanted me," she blurted out through her tears, "but Alessa talked them into letting me go. That's why I was safe at the restaurant where you found me. I know I'm only nine, but I know what happened. If she had let them take me instead of her, she wouldn't be in the hospital now."

"How did it all start?" Ebby inquired.

Lucy explained to her how the guy sitting on the curb had called out for help and they had walked over to see what was wrong. Without warning, the others had appeared from nowhere, surrounding them. She repeated everything Alessa had said to them and that when she left for the restaurant she thought Alessa was in trouble. "I didn't know what to do, Ebby," Lucy said remorsefully. "I always listen to Alessa. She's the one who takes care of me and I let her get hurt!"

Ebby took the child home shortly afterward and introduced her to her husband, Ryan. She had called him during the night to tell him that Alessa was in big trouble.

"Ebby," Ryan had said to her on the phone, making no effort to hide his disapproval, "this is the kind of stuff you're going to have to deal with, when you make these people your friends."

"Listen, Ryan," his wife had retorted, "don't you ever say that again. 'These people,' as you put it, are just as normal and vulnerable as we are. I am bringing Lucy home to stay with us for a while. She is only nine years old. So don't start with your shit. I am Alessa's friend and I need to do this for her. What's more, I expect you to help me. Do you understand?"

It was the first time in their married life that Ebby had used harsh words with her husband. While he neither liked what she told him nor agreed with any of it, he knew his wife was dead serious.

When they got to her house, Ebby showed Lucy her bedroom and went off to fix her lunch. The two of them, joined by Ryan, ate the meal together. Ryan seemed to be making an effort with the child, which Ebby really appreciated.

After lunch, Ebby left Lucy with her husband and went back to the hospital. Arriving at the SICU, she checked in at the nurse's station to get an update on Alessa. The nurse gave her more information than she had received the night before. Alessa was being watched for an acute "subdural hematoma".

Ebby's mouth dropped open. "What's a subdural hematoma?"

The nurse placed a comforting hand on her shoulder. "I'm sorry. It means that her brain was bruised. The good news is that the hematoma is small. When they are small, the body usually just heals itself. We will monitor her carefully until we see substantial progress."

Ebby couldn't hold back her tears as she asked, "Will she be okay? I mean, will this cause permanent damage?"

The nurse shook her head. "We won't know if there is any damage until she is fully awake. Right now, the doctor is keeping her heavily sedated and giving her fluids to allow her brain and body to recover."

Ebby thanked her and went to the bay where Alessa had been kept, pulled over a chair and sat next to her. She talked to her in a soft murmur and reassured her again that Lucy was fine, but there was neither response nor movement. Alessa just lay there motionless.

Later that day, Ebby reminded herself to put on a happy face as she went home to Lucy. She told her that Alessa was still asleep, but getting better every minute. This was not entirely untrue. Alessa's vital signs were encouraging and according to the doctors, the blood transfusion had helped her. Ebby could read the anxiety on Lucy's face and consoled her as best she could. The child wanted to go see Alessa, but Ebby knew it was still too soon. The swelling on her face had subsided a little in the last twenty-four hours, but until Alessa regained consciousness, Ebby wasn't about to take Lucy in to see her. After all, Alessa was all the child had.

By the next morning, when Ebby arrived at the SICU, the nurses told her that Alessa had just been moved out to a regular room. She had apparently done well over the last forty-eight hours and her condition had stabilized, to the relief of the doctors on duty. One of the nurses gave Ebby Alessa's new room number and she hurried down to the elevator to go find her.

When she walked into Alessa's room, she felt immensely grateful to find the girl awake. Ebby knew she was going to be fine. She approached the bed and bent over to kiss her on the forehead.

"How are you feeling, sweetie?" she asked tenderly.

Though still a bit confused, Alessa responded, "I'm doing okay now. Where is Lucy? Is she okay?"

Ebby moved closer, so her face was inches from Alessa's, and whispered, "Yes, Lucy is absolutely fine. She is staying with Ryan and me. I guess you don't remember me telling you this earlier?"

"No, I don't remember much after I passed out."

"Do you remember what happened to you?"

Alessa looked away. "I remember," she whispered. "How could I forget? What's wrong with me anyway? How long do I have to stay here?"

Just then, the nurse came into the room and inquired, "Well, how are you feeling, young lady? You take a licking and keep on ticking, I see. Your blood tests look good and the swellings are continuing to subside, but don't be in such a rush to leave us. You have a little ways to go still. How's your pain?"

"My leg is throbbing and I have a really bad headache, but I'm okay."

The nurse observed Alessa for a few moments. "I'm going to give you something for the pain," she said briskly. "You have some broken bones, but they will heal just fine, if you stick with me."

Alessa smiled at her weakly and asked for a mirror. "I want to see my face," she explained. "My lips feel like they're huge and I can't open my eyelids all the way."

To stall her, the nurse said quickly, "I'll tell you what. Let's get some pain medication in you and we'll see if we can find you a mirror later."

She had no intention of allowing Alessa to look at herself in a mirror. She knew from experience that it would be the worst thing to do at that moment. The staff would keep stalling her for another two or three days until the swelling was dramatically reduced.

Ebby followed the nurse into the hallway. "How is she really?" she asked nervously.

"Honestly, she's lucky to be alive," she stated grimly. "They really worked her over. She'll be fine, but we want to keep mirrors away from her for the next couple of days until she starts looking more normal. If she finds out how she's looking now, it will only demoralize her. Do you know if the cops managed to catch those bastards?"

"No, they haven't found them yet," Ebby said, disheartened. "Her younger sister got a look at their faces and gave a description to the cops, but nothing has turned up so far."

The nurse gave Ebby a reassuring look. "The doctors were able to get sperm from her vagina and her anus," she confided. "The poor thing was really ripped to shreds. If they find these guys, they can identify them through their DNA."

Ebby thanked the nurse, well aware that Alessa would have no interest in pursuing these men. Her only concern was Lucy. She wouldn't jeopardize her chances of keeping the child just to get even.

When Ebby went home that night, she told Lucy all about Alessa's recovery. The child was delighted to hear she was awake and asked her when she could go to the hospital to see her.

"In a couple more days, Lucy," Ebby told her. "Alessa needs time to get better. She has been asking about you, though. She says to send her love and tell you everything is fine."

Disappointed that she couldn't go and see Alessa right away, Lucy was, nonetheless, relieved to hear she was doing better now.

Two days later, Ebby drove Lucy down to the hospital so they could visit Alessa together. To prepare her for the initial shock, Ebby had carefully explained to Lucy, "Alessa is bruised and has a broken leg and arm.

It looks a lot worse than it actually is," she told her, "but once the bones are healed, she will be just fine."

When Lucy entered the room and saw Alessa, she burst into tears. Alessa looked over at her and squealed, "Lucy, the love of my life! Come over here and give me a hug!"

The little girl rushed to her and hugged her gingerly. As glad as she was to finally see and touch Alessa, Lucy couldn't stop her tears from flowing. Even at the tender age of nine, she knew how close she had come to losing the only person she really loved.

"So, I hear you've been sleeping at Ebby's," Alessa said fondly. "I see how it is now; you're having sleepover parties without me," she teased.

This brought a grin to Lucy's face. "It's been fun, but I wish you were there with us," she said.

The three of them talked for the next hour, until Ebby noticed Alessa fighting pain and sleep and announced that it was time for them to go. Having been allowed a glimpse of the old Alessa that told her she was going to be okay, Lucy was quite content and promised her that she would be back to visit again.

As they were riding home, the child asked, "How come if Alessa broke her leg, she doesn't have a cast on it?"

Ebby smiled. "The doctors put a metal rod in her leg. That's what they do when you break your thigh bone."

Lucy grimaced at the thought, imagining a metal rod in her own leg.

"Will she be able to walk with the rod?" she asked anxiously.

"Yes," Ebby reassured her, "eventually, she will. It will take her several weeks to start walking again and maybe two to three months, before she is back to normal."

Lucy looked bewildered. "Wow, that's a long time!" she exclaimed in awe. "How will Alessa work at the grocery store at night if she can't walk?"

"She won't be able to work until she is completely recovered."

This reminded Ebby that she needed to make some phone calls the next day and see if she could get the girls housing and public assistance until Alessa was well enough to fend for herself and look after Lucy. She knew how greatly Alessa treasured her independence and wouldn't relinquish it even while she healed.

The following morning, Ebby began looking into housing options and decided to pull a few strings by getting in touch with a friend at the

Philadelphia Housing Authority. She fed her a story about Alessa being a disabled and displaced nineteen-year-old who was solely responsible for her little sister. She explained that the girl would be released from the hospital within seven days and they needed a place to stay immediately.

Ebby was thrilled when her friend called back and confirmed that she had been able to put them in a two-bedroom unit at the Courtyard Apartments that provided housing for seniors and families. Based on the information Ebby had provided her, her friend had decided the older residents would be supportive and good for the morale of the young girls. This would also be a safer place for the two of them, until they got back on their feet.

Chapter Forty-Nine

The Courtyard Apartments were located in a residential neighborhood on Fourth Street, which seemed ideal. A week later, with Alessa on crutches and Lucy by her side, the two moved into their new apartment. Ebby had explained to Alessa before they arrived that the apartment was paid for by the federal government and they would receive food stamps as well.

Alessa was pleased with the new apartment. It was small, but well lit, with white walls and beige furniture. Ebby had got her the furniture from a yard sale and while it was moderately worn, it was still in good condition. Each of the bedrooms came with a bed, linens, a closet and a dresser. All the items had been bought at a yard sale from a couple who were about to divorce and go their separate ways. Lucy was thrilled to finally have her own space, a room that was all hers.

Ebby and Alessa sat on the sofa together, while Lucy unpacked her things. Turning to her, Ebby said, "I know you are dealing with a lot right now. We have been focusing on your physical health so far, but I'm just as concerned about your state of mind. We haven't talked at all about the rape that night. I'm worried that you are holding everything in. I would like to talk about it, if it's okay with you."

Alessa stared blankly at Ebby for a long time. She had complete trust in her and knew no one had ever understood her the way she did.

"Ebby, it was awful!" she finally confessed. "I know I'm no fucking virgin, but this was different. The attack was so violent! I felt completely humiliated, as though my entire being had been violated. It wasn't the sex itself, you know. I mean, it was terrible, but it didn't even matter. It was how vicious they were to me, as though they had nothing but hatred for me and were bent on destroying me. I gave them what they wanted. So why did they have to hurt me?"

"I have no way of knowing why anyone would want to do this to you," Ebby said sadly, trying to console Alessa. "Maybe the boys were drunk or high on something. Maybe they are just rotten to the core. But I do know that even if they are never caught, they will suffer a lifetime of misery. No one who treats another human being the way they treated you can ever be at peace."

"Why do you think being beaten bothers me more than being raped by them?"

Ebby moved closer to Alessa and put an arm around her. "I'm not sure," she said gently. "It could be because you've been raped so many times that—awful as it sounds—you've come to accept it as nothing out of the ordinary. On the other hand, you've never been beaten like that before. Men have violated you, but they never tried to break your spirit like these men did. It's something you've never experienced...maybe that's why the beating traumatized you more than the rape."

"I made a decision while I was in the hospital," Alessa said quietly. "I'm not going to dance anymore. I want to get out of the sex business altogether. I'm tired of it, Ebby. It's just that I don't know what else I can do to make enough money to turn my life around. I have almost 30,000 dollars in cash in my safety deposit box. I was going to buy a place for us, while I worked on getting a college degree, but now I can't figure out what to do."

Ebby could feel her hopelessness. She considered Alessa capable of so much more than just devoting her life to stripping for a pack of horny bastards.

"Well," she told her, "what you're going to do is focus on your recovery, getting yourself into college and choosing a career that will not only prepare you to earn a living, but also give you joy."

When Ebby talked to her in that confident manner, she made Alessa's own goals seem clear and well defined. She made her believe that she had options. The young woman approved of the plan Ebby had decided on for her and promised to call the Philadelphia Community College the next morning. With renewed hope, Alessa went into her new bedroom to unpack her things, just as Lucy came bouncing into the living room, bubbling with excitement.

"Alessa, we have our own bathroom!" she squealed. "And did you see all the stuff Ebby bought for us? We have real comforters on our beds and towels to shower with and everything!"

Alessa took delight in the child's enthusiasm and thought to herself, *Ebby's right. I can make a life for Lucy and myself.* Maybe God was actually cutting them a break. And about time too!

By early evening, Ebby was ready to go home to Ryan. She promised to be back the next day to take Alessa to her physical therapy session. The three of them embraced and after Ebby had left, Alessa and Lucy sat on the sofa and watched television. They had never done that before, at least not in privacy and not in their own space. Both enjoyed every minute they shared. It felt as if they were really a family, a normal family just doing a normal thing.

Later that evening, once Lucy was asleep, Alessa reluctantly let her mind wander to the rape. Secretly, she felt shattered and raw from the whole experience. She knew as long as she had a plan and set goals for herself, she would never have to look back. Once she was well enough to get around on her own, she would even get back to visiting and helping the homeless, just like she had before the incident on July 4th.

Chapter Fifty

————————◼————————

When Alessa arrived at the physical therapist's office, she was pleasantly surprised to see how nice everyone was to her. They all made her feel welcome. After filling out some papers, she was shown to a small room where her therapist would meet her. The woman at the front desk informed Alessa that he was the best therapist they had and if she followed his advice, she would be back on her feet in no time.

Alessa had been waiting for a few minutes when a tall man with blue eyes and light brown hair entered. He extended his long arm and took her hand in his.

"You must be Alessa," he said. "I'm Remo and I will be working with you to get you moving and feeling better than you ever did."

Alessa liked him immediately. There was an air about him of confidence and compassion. Remo watched her as she pushed through her pain and tried her best to acquire movement in her legs. His heart went out to her. She was an attractive girl, built beautifully, but her eyes were far older than the rest of her. He was intrigued and impressed by her drive and determination. Even though she told him that the very thought of therapy intimidated her, once Alessa started she gave it her all.

Alessa too was pleasantly surprised by her impression of Remo. She felt safe with him. She knew instinctively that he would be supportive and that she could count on him to help her recover. As the hours wore on, they talked effortlessly and shared details about their lives during their therapy session. They were going to spend a lot of time together over the next three months and so, Alessa figured she'd better settle in and get acquainted with him.

Remo had been born in the city and raised by his foster parents, Patrick and Hannah. He regularly volunteered at homeless shelters, providing light physical therapy to some of their residents. He and Alessa had a similar

245

sense of humor and neither of them had ever been in a serious relationship. Like her, he was aiming for a better life and had decided to go to college to become a physical therapist. His childhood had been normal and his foster parents had eventually adopted him. He loved them both dearly and had dinner with them at least once a week. He lived alone and liked to do just about everything. He even cooked for himself.

Though Remo had disclosed a great deal about himself, Alessa found herself at a loss for words when asked about her own background.

She hesitated before saying, "Well, my childhood wasn't exactly great. It was really hard, actually, and I'd rather not talk about it."

She was petrified he would be repulsed if he knew the truth and she didn't want to start off on the wrong foot with him. Remo was wise for his years and figured Alessa would eventually tell him her story, but was content to have her focus on her recovery for now. Often, he had to spend time getting many of his patients psyched up to work hard on their therapy, but with Alessa, that was not necessary. Without any prompting from him, she would launch herself into her therapy, gritting her teeth to get her through the pain. He had discovered what a strong person she was and by the end of their first session, was glad she had been assigned to him.

Remo hadn't been told much about Alessa's history, other than that she had been victim to some kind of an incident a couple of weeks ago that had injured her badly. He figured it couldn't be domestic violence, since she had already told him about never having been in a serious relationship. Remo was respectful of people's privacy and knew if she wanted to tell him more, she would, over time.

Alessa shared more of her life, as their sessions went on. She told Remo that she and her little sister, Lucy, lived together at the Courtyard Apartments. Remo knew that was public housing, but didn't let on that he knew.

"It's public housing," she told him. "We'll only be there long enough for me to get a degree and find a good paying job. I applied for financial aid and I am trying to go to Philadelphia Community College."

Remo was impressed and curious about her now. She was young, raising her sister on her own and had aspirations that would, if fulfilled, allow her to flee a life dependent on welfare. After a week of therapy, the two had become good friends. They talked about everything—except Alessa's past.

Ebby had begun to notice that the girl was now paying a great deal of attention to her appearance before going to her therapy sessions. She would fuss over her hair until it was just right and even bought herself a couple of new outfits which she wore to her sessions.

Two weeks later, Ebby was driving Alessa to her therapy session. They had stopped at a red light, when she looked over at Alessa with a smirk.

"What? What are you smirking at?" Alessa asked her, a grin breaking through.

"Oh, I don't know. Looks to me like you might have a crush on Remo. After all, new outfits, hair and makeup!" Ebby teased.

Alessa pretended to be shocked. "Oh, I do not! What's wrong with wanting to look good?"

Ebby patted her hand. "Absolutely nothing, sweetie. Just wanted to point out that it isn't going unnoticed, either by me or by him, I'm sure."

Alessa looked worried. "Yeah, maybe so," she mused worriedly, "but I haven't told him about my past and he thinks Lucy is my sister. Once he finds out about everything, he won't care how good I look."

Ebby shook her head. "Don't be so sure about that," she told her. "I met him too, you know. This one is different I think maybe he's one of the few good guys left. So you better snatch him up while you can."

"Yeah, right. Whatever you say, Ebby. You're so delusional. Men like Remo don't want to be with a woman like me. I swear, sometimes you are so clueless! Don't you know I'm destined to attract every asshole in Pennsylvania?" Alessa grinned, turning the whole thing into a joke.

Ebby became serious. "No, Alessa," she said. "You aren't destined to be with an asshole. You have traveled a rocky road so far and you deserve better. You're unique and I think you're very courageous. Once you believe in yourself, so will others. It's called confidence."

She drove the rest of the way in silence. Alessa did not speak either. Ebby pulled up in front of Remo's office.

"Go get 'em, tiger," she growled.

Alessa laughed at Ebby's optimism about her future and her conviction that she was something more than she believed herself to be.

Chapter Fifty-One

As the months passed, Alessa became stronger and more mobile. She and Remo were very comfortable together, not just as therapist and patient, but as friends too. Often, after her therapy sessions with Remo were over, Alessa and Lucy would go with him and check on the homeless and volunteer time at shelters throughout Philadelphia. Lucy and Remo got along well and enjoyed each other's company, especially when they were planning a silly prank on Alessa. Ebby was pleased for both girls. She could tell Remo was good for them and they enjoyed being together. Ebby often thought what a close knit family the three of them would make.

As time wore on and the therapy sessions were nearing their end, Alessa realized how hard it would be for her, once she and Remo went their separate ways. She had got so used to his company. They had spent a lot of time together and while they would still carry on with their volunteer work, they would see each other a lot less now. They had shared much about their lives and Remo, along with Ebby, had encouraged Alessa to go to college. He had cheered her on, telling her she was smart enough to do anything she wanted to.

In her three months of therapy, Alessa had received financial aid for community college and started her first real college class. At first, she was apprehensive, aware that she had to pick up the skill of acquiring knowledge, something her childhood hadn't taught her. However, with Remo and Ebby to support her, Alessa had found her groove in college and she was beginning to take it all in stride. Lucy, for her part, was thrilled that Alessa had gone back to school. She told everyone they knew—and these were mostly homeless people—that Alessa was going to college.

By the time Alessa had completed her therapy, she was walking almost as normally as she had before the incident. At her last session, Remo asked her to dinner to celebrate. She was thrilled and promptly accepted the invitation. On the same day, Remo and the other therapists threw a small party, with balloons and a cake. They even invited Ebby and Lucy. Alessa was moved to tears and thanked them all for their kindness and their help with her recovery. They all admired her for being brave and capable of moving past whatever had happened to her just three short months earlier.

As Alessa was leaving, she turned to Remo and said, "I never could have done this without your help. You are an amazing therapist and I want to thank you for everything."

In response, he reached out and gave her a hug. "You really worked hard, which made it easy for me to look like a rock star. Now go home and rest. We have a date tonight, remember? I'll pick you up at seven. Wear something nice, because I've made a reservation at a restaurant I think you'll love."

Alessa smiled and gave him one last hug. She turned to Ebby and Lucy who were watching them with expressions of pure happiness on their faces. Remo walked over and picked the child up in his strong arms.

"Okay," he boomed, "make sure Alessa is ready and on time tonight. I'll see you on Saturday, when we go to the shelter."

Lucy happily agreed to be Alessa's "boss" and make sure she followed his instructions. She just loved it when Remo put her in charge of things. It made her feel needed.

As Alessa, Ebby and Lucy drove back to their apartment, Ebby asked, "You do have something to wear tonight, right?"

"Yes," Alessa said happily. "It just so happens that I bought a little black dress a couple of weeks ago. I bought the whole outfit and shoes to match for 32 dollars at the thrift store near our apartment. The stuff doesn't look used at all."

Ebby was humbled by how accepting Alessa was. It didn't matter to her that she would have to make do with a secondhand dress and shoes. That was the thing about her that moved Ebby to tears; she had never pretended to be someone other than the person she really was and she wasn't afraid to let people know that she was content with the small, simple things in life.

Back at the apartment, Ebby prepared to babysit Lucy, while Alessa went out with Remo. Lucy turned on the television while the other two went to the kitchen for a glass of iced tea. Alessa looked anxious as they sat at the kitchen table.

"What's wrong?" Ebby asked, perturbed. "Why do you look so upset?"

"Remo described tonight as a 'date'. I've never been on a real date before. I'm not sure what I'm supposed to do. What if I do all the wrong things?"

"Alessa, pull yourself together," Ebby said firmly. "You have spent a lot of time with Remo over the last three months in therapy and doing volunteer work. You don't need to worry about tonight. Just be yourself."

Ebby knew Alessa and Remo were drawn to each other. It was obvious to anyone who saw them together. They would always stand a little closer than necessary and their eye contact lingered for just a moment too long. It was no big secret they were attracted to each other.

"But Ebby," Alessa persisted, "he doesn't know anything about my past. Do you really think a guy like Remo is going to say that it's no big deal that I was an exotic dancer? I mean, let's be honest. I fucked men for money. That means I was a prostitute. This whole thing is just ridiculous!"

Then Ebby said something that surprised Alessa. "Just tell him the whole truth. He will either accept it or run as fast as he can. It's his choice whether he wishes to win or lose. If he stays, he will win big. But if he runs, he will spend the rest of his life comparing every woman he meets to you. The important thing in life is not where you came from, but where you are going. You're going places, Alessa."

As always, Ebby had this knack of making her feel better about herself. With renewed confidence, Alessa said, "You're right. You're always right."

At six-thirty p.m., Alessa emerged from her bedroom in her newly acquired secondhand dress and shoes. Ebby thought she looked beautiful. The black dress fit her perfectly. It showed off her flawless figure in a way that made her look sophisticated. Alessa had drawn her hair back and fastened it with a clip so that her natural curls flowed down her back. She looked young and vibrant. The night was hers and her life was just beginning.

When Remo knocked on the apartment door, Lucy darted forward to open it. He looked handsome in black pants and an ocean-blue shirt that further highlighted the blue of his eyes, if that were at all possible. When he saw Alessa, he had to catch his breath for a moment, before recovering sufficiently to tell her she looked great. Alessa hugged Lucy and Ebby and took Remo's arm, heading out of the apartment into the warm night air. With her new optimism, she felt anything was possible. She had paid her dues and now it was time for her life to become her own. Tonight would determine if Remo was in it for the long haul. She planned to tell him everything. Or a lot of it anyway, because if he couldn't accept who she had been in the life she was about to leave behind, she didn't want to get romantically involved with him and include him in her future.

Chapter Fifty-Two

Remo took Alessa to the Moshulu, a boat restaurant on the Delaware River at Penn's Landing. She couldn't get over how beautiful the place was, with its rich upscale wood furniture and classy clientele. For a moment, Alessa felt awkward and inadequate in her secondhand dress.

Sensing her nervousness, Remo leaned toward her and murmured, "You are the most beautiful woman in here tonight."

Alessa smiled brilliantly at him, thankful to be standing next to this man who had become such a good friend and—hopefully, if there was a God—her boyfriend. After a short wait, they were seated at a table next to a window that looked out over the river. The ambiance was just right. They both ordered surf and turf for the special occasion and just enjoyed being with each other. The evening would have been perfect, but for the nagging question that still troubled Alessa: should she tell Remo about her past or not?

After dinner, the two of them strolled along Penn's Landing, talking and laughing. They had paused to gaze at the river when Remo took her gently by the shoulders, turned her to face him and kissed her softly. The moment his lips touched hers, Alessa felt as though her body was going to completely melt away. She'd never wanted to kiss anyone the way she wanted to kiss Remo. Afterward, they walked slowly back to his car. Once they were seated in it, he asked if she would like to go back to his apartment for a glass of wine. Not wanting the evening to come to an end, Alessa agreed without hesitation.

Remo lived in a one-bedroom apartment on Walnut Street in Rittenhouse Square. It was simple, yet classy, in a masculine sort of way. Walls, upholstery and accent pieces in warm shades of blue, green and beige created an understated effect that was soothing. After he had given her a quick tour of his apartment, the two of them went into the small living room and sat on the large brown sofa that was so soft and comfortable it made Alessa feel as though she were sitting on an enormous pillow.

Remo poured them each a glass of wine. As he handed it to her, he quipped, "I'm a criminal now, giving alcohol to a nineteen-year-old."

Alessa laughed. "Listen," she said, "if I can raise a kid and live through therapy with someone as tough as you, I deserve a glass of wine."

Remo looked at her playfully. "Oh really, now you're saying I was tough? Well, if I was, it was only because you needed me to be tough."

They both laughed and Remo leaned over and kissed her again. She felt just like she had when he'd kissed her not even an hour ago. She wanted the feeling to last forever, afraid that if they stopped, she might never get it back again. As they pulled away from each other, she gave him a slight push and put her hand flat against his chest, as if to hold him back.

"What is it? I thought you were attracted to me. Am I wrong?" he asked, surprised.

"No, you're not," she said. "Of course I'm attracted to you. It's just that you don't know anything about me or my past. I don't want to take this too far, before you know the truth about me. It would not only be wrong to do, it would hurt us both."

"Okay, so tell me about your past," Remo said.

Alessa told him her story about the rapes and the beating that had brought them together in the first place. She didn't spare him a single detail, right from how the boys had targeted Lucy and, that she had to talk them into taking her instead. She explained that she had just assumed they would move on, if she gave them what they wanted. She had never expected to be beaten that way. However, if she had it to do all over again, she would. She would do anything to keep Lucy safe.

"I knew you were beaten," Remo said quietly. "We had heard that much, but none of us knew the whole story. My God, Alessa, this is just awful! Lucy is lucky to have a sister like you. She might have been killed, if they had gotten their hands on her. You took that all on yourself. I don't know if I've ever seen a love more pure than what you feel for Lucy."

Alessa was grateful for his kind words, but couldn't help wondering if he now felt differently about her. Remo urged her to tell him the rest of her story. Alessa took a deep breath. Then she began telling him about her lost childhood, her sordid experiences as an exotic dancer, and the many, many men who had paid her for sex. She described the nature of her relationship with Harlin and finally, her life as a homeless teen and how she had met Lucy. She gave him every detail of the events that had overtaken her over the years and the emotions they had aroused in her, as each chapter of her life unfolded before him. There was nothing Alessa wanted to hold back from him. She knew that if he decided to move on after hearing her out, she would be hurt, but not devastated. The time to tell him was now.

When she finished, her eyes met Remo's. He was looking at her, stunned. She assumed their relationship was over, even before it had started, but felt she had done the right thing, despite the acute embarrassment it had caused her.

But it was Alessa's turn to be surprised when Remo told her gently, "I didn't think I could be more impressed than I already was by your desire to make a better life for yourself and Lucy. But this, Alessa! This is just unbelievable! You have been through so much! No child should ever be treated the way you were. I don't blame you for running away from your home. Do you know how brave and strong you are? I mean, here you are, having survived the most traumatic childhood and events that are no less horrific, and you still look at life with such abiding hope."

"You think I'm brave?" Alessa said uncertainly, "I thought you might think I'm a slut, but not brave, by any means!"

Remo gently took her in his arms. "Alessa," he said tenderly, "you did what you needed to do to come out the other side alive. All your past experiences have gone into making you who you are today. I think you are a warm and loving person, capable of doing anything you set your mind on. I'm going to be completely honest with you; what you have just told me is a lot to take in, but it doesn't change how I feel about you. If anything at all, it just confirms that you have an immeasurable reserve of strength. The fact that you have been taking care of Lucy, as if she were your own, is so incredibly heartwarming."

Then Remo bent down and pressed his lips against hers in a long, slow kiss. Alessa thought she would faint from the emotions that overwhelmed her. She had never felt like this with a man before. She had never even wanted a man before now. In the frame of mind she found herself in now, the whole evening seemed surreal to her. It was perfect and so were the people in her life: Remo and Lucy. Her life was starting to belong to her again and this new feeling was something she never wanted to lose.

They didn't make love that night, even though they felt so close after having shared so much with each other and were aware of the powerful emotions playing within them.

When Remo took Alessa home, it was well past three in the morning. He stood at her door and kissed her, then just held her for several more minutes. By the way he was embracing her, she assumed that this was the last she would see of him. He was offering one final goodbye.

As she turned and unlocked her door, Remo bent down and whispered in her ear, "I'm a really good cook. Are you and Lucy free for dinner tomorrow night?"

Ecstatic, Alessa couldn't help, but squeal, "We would love to come for dinner! Are you sure? Look, I laid a lot of shit on you. Shit that most people wouldn't be able to handle. I'm no saint. Please don't do this just to be nice."

"Who 'da fuck you callin' nice?" Remo joked in his fake South Philly accent. "I ain't no nice guy!" Then he grew serious. "Alessa, your past is horrible. I mean, truly horrible. I've never known anyone who has had to live through what you did. But only an idiot would think it was your fault. You did what you needed to do to get to this point in your life. Period. End of story. Besides," he added, ending on a light note, "I don't do sympathy dinners."

Alessa laughed. "You're a very special person, you know? I'm glad that I told you everything. I feel so much better now that you know. Goodnight. Lucy and I will see you tomorrow."

When she entered her apartment, Ebby looked up from the book she was reading. "Well," she inquired, "I assume everything went off well?"

Alessa performed a few dance steps for her. "Yeah, it did. I told him everything, Ebby. Then he asked me if he could cook dinner for Lucy and me tomorrow night." Alessa was jumping up and down and clapping her hands together. "Oh my God, Ebby, he's such a good kisser!" she said breathlessly, reliving the moment. I've never kissed anyone before because I genuinely felt something for the guy. I can't believe how awesome the real thing can be! By the way, I got to see his apartment too. It's really nice." Then she noticed Ebby's furrowed brow and said, "We didn't fuck, if that's what you're worrying about. God, Ebby, you have such a dirty mind!"

Ebby looked at her young friend gravely. "I'm very relieved you didn't *make love* to him. This isn't a man you're going to *fuck*, Alessa. This is someone special, maybe even your first real love."

Alessa sat down on the sofa close to Ebby, so close, in fact, that she was practically sitting on top of her. "Yeah, that's right," she said, "we didn't *make love* or fuck like rabbits." Then she started tickling Ebby.

"You are exhausting, Alessa," she said with mock-seriousness. "Remind me to teach you some manners next week."

They both giggled. Neither had ever had a friend whom they loved more than they did each other.

Chapter Fifty-Three

The next couple of weeks were like a dream. Alessa couldn't believe how much she had missed by never dating anyone seriously before. If Alessa and Remo weren't together—which they were at least five nights a week—they were talking to each other on the phone for hours. They discussed her past more than anything else. Remo asked a lot of questions. Not because he was looking to unearth more secrets that she might have kept from him, but because her life had been so bizarre and strewn with difficulties that it made him curious as to how she had made it through at all. He couldn't quite wrap his mind around all of the details yet. Although two whole years older than her, he felt as if she were far more mature than he and others his age could ever be.

One Saturday night, Remo took her to the Irish Pub in the city to meet his friends. Alessa was nervous about the impression she would create. The two of them entered the bar and following Remo's gesture, they began making their way to the table where his friends sat waiting, along with the girlfriends a few of them had brought along. As the two of them approached the table, she found herself stiffening with tension. For there, among Remo's friends, was a man she recognized as a client from the go-go club in the city. She didn't know much about him, except that he had been a frequent visitor, and she recalled performing several lap dances for him. She could see from the knowing look he gave her that he had recognized her immediately. Sensing her sudden withdrawal, Remo looked at Alessa. He knew his friend frequented the go-go clubs and had, before long, figured out that he might have been a customer at the one where Alessa had worked.

Remo excused himself and Alessa for a moment and led her to the bar. He ordered a soda for her and a beer for himself.

"What's going on, Alessa?" he asked. "You know my friend from the go-go club, right?"

Alessa was mortified beyond belief. It had not occurred to her that she might run into former clients when she was with Remo. "Yeah, I do" she confessed. "I feel really awkward. He used to pay me to perform a lot of lap dances for him."

"Okay. Did you ever have sex with him?"

The very fact that she was being asked this question, by her boyfriend, made Alessa feel like a worm, "No, never," she answered quietly, "just lap dances. But he has seen me naked. The last club I worked at, I had to dance in the nude."

Remo's response surprised her. "Well, good," he said matter-of-factly. "Then he knows how lucky I am to have a woman as hot as you. I hope he's jealous. Just relax, okay? Honestly, I don't give a fuck what anyone thinks and neither should you."

Alessa rose on tiptoe and planted a wet kiss on his cheek. "It amazes me how all of this doesn't get to you. Don't you feel ashamed of me?"

Remo looked taken aback. "Ashamed?" he asked. "Ashamed that you danced naked somewhere? Why would I feel ashamed? Listen, until other people walk in your shoes and live your life, they can't know or understand anything about you. So just relax."

When they went back to the group, they quickly joined in the conversation. The girlfriends noticed that Alessa was different. She was quiet and didn't wear particularly stylish clothes. She was attractive in a unique way, but it was the way she connected with all the men that annoyed them the most. It was as if she fit right into their world effortlessly. Remo seemed extremely pleased with his catch and set the girls wondering why he had picked Alessa over all the others he had dated.

After catching up with his friends, the two of them eventually left the bar and went back to Remo's apartment to hang out. They had known each other for four months since Alessa started her therapy, but had been dating seriously for almost a month. Remo started kissing her on the sofa. Before they knew it, they had stripped down to their underwear and moved into his bedroom. It was clear they both knew what they wanted from each other.

Yet, Remo asked Alessa, "Are you okay with this? I don't want to move too quickly for you."

She merely smiled and kissed him back passionately. When he unhooked her bra and saw her bare, perfectly round breasts, he could barely control himself. But he took it slowly, aware that Alessa had never had sex with a man that involved passion or her own pleasure. He was sensitive to her feelings as he slid her panties down and dropped them off the side of the bed. Then he ran his hand down her breast, softly over her belly and finally slipped his fingers between her legs. Alessa let out a silky soft purr and Remo took it as confirmation that he should go ahead.

They continued to passionately explore each other's bodies, each finding pleasure in giving the other pleasure.

Remo looked at Alessa and asked, "You okay?"

Her dazed response was, "Yeah, I've never felt like this before. Don't stop. Please."

As Remo entered her for the first time, she felt sensations and emotions coursing through her body she had never experienced before with other men. It was as wonderful as it was exciting. They were completely caught up in each other. When they finally came, they lay back on the bed, spent.

"I've never had an orgasm with a man before," Alessa confessed.

Remo propped himself up on his elbow. "Are you serious? You've never had an orgasm?"

Alessa smiled. "No, I said I never had one with a man before."

For the first time since he had known her, Remo looked concerned. "Are you telling me you're gay?"

Alessa laughed out loud. "No, I'm not gay, but I've only had one orgasm in my life. My best friend in high school gave it to me. I told her I'd never had one and she, you know, did whatever, until I did. It was purely educational and nothing like what I just experienced with you."

Remo smiled. "I guess that's not a bad friend to have. When will I meet her?"

Alessa's eyes clouded. "Rhonda died when we were teenagers. Remember, I told you how her mother, Zoe, helped me? Rhonda was shot dead by the wife of one of her mother's boyfriends."

Remo scooped Alessa into his arms, "I do remember. I just don't remember the orgasm story, but it's certainly interesting."

They held each other tight and an hour later, they made love again. This time, it was just as good, if not better than the first time.

The next morning, Remo drove her to Ebby's house to pick up Lucy who had stayed there the previous night. The little girl came running out into the kitchen to give them both suffocating hugs.

"How come you guys didn't take me with you last night?" she inquired crossly. "I had fun here with Ebby, but she could have come too. Ryan probably wouldn't have come, because he likes to stay home and watch television."

"We went somewhere young kids aren't allowed to go," Alessa explained, "but I think it's time for Remo to cook for us again. What do you think, Lucy?"

Remo grabbed hold of the child and started to tickle her. She giggled uncontrollably, but when he stopped, she shrieked, "Tickle me again, Remo!"

Ebby looked on, hoping that these three perfect human beings would, one day, become a single family unit.

Chapter Fifty-Four

Everything began to fall into place for the threesome. Alessa and Remo were deeply in love and Lucy was just like their natural-born child. Alessa continued with her college education. On weekends, they spent time together, walking the city streets, talking to homeless people and helping them in little ways. Sometimes, it was just lending someone a shoulder to cry on; at others, it meant buying people a soda or a cup of coffee. The three of them loved helping people in need. Now that Remo was better acquainted with life on the streets by listening to Alessa and Lucy's account of their own experiences, he had become more deeply involved than ever in helping the homeless in as many ways as he could.

Alessa had her own special rapport with the homeless. It was clear to all that she was genuine and spontaneous in her encounters with every one of them and they loved her very much and looked up to her. She was particularly effective with young teenage girls, building a relationship with each one of them by sharing her own story. Disarmed by her honesty, they put their wariness aside and opened up to her, connecting with her instantly. When Remo witnessed the closeness she shared with these people who had, not so long ago, been virtual strangers, he felt lucky to have Alessa in his life. He marveled at the way she did it all so naturally; without ever being condescending to them or believing she was doing them a favor.

"I'm just like them," she would often tell him. "They are just people with a story, looking for a happy ending. I know what it's like to be there and how it feels to be so alone, even when you're with other homeless people. It's a struggle every day to remember you are a person, a human being. You have to keep reminding yourself that you deserve a better life. People who lead regular lives see you on the streets and pretend you don't exist. They probably fear that if they see or acknowledge you, they will attract the bad luck which put you on the streets in the first place. After a while, you actually begin to feel you've become invisible. Then you have to remind yourself that you're just homeless. It's very humbling to have been homeless, Remo. My own experience makes it impossible for me to be judgmental about others."

Lucy and Alessa often talked to Remo about their own misfortune in having been homeless. They described where they had lived and slept. Lucy would tell him about how she had learned to beg and pick through garbage for food and household items they needed. She took great pride in relating these stories, because to her way of thinking, it had to do with skills she had acquired that Remo hadn't, because he had never been homeless. She felt that in some ways, she knew more than he, an adult, did. Remo encouraged her to confide in him and couldn't help admiring the two girls who had learned to be so resourceful while living on the streets. They all felt fortunate to have found each other and Lucy, especially, believed herself to be the luckiest girl in the world, protected and loved as she was by both the adults.

One night, after a long, hard day, Remo and Alessa had just finished dinner at his apartment and were relaxing on his sofa, chatting the way they usually did.

"You do realize we're coming up on our first anniversary, don't you?" he reminded her. "I was thinking we should do something special to celebrate."

"Oh really, like what?" Alessa asked excitedly.

"I was thinking I would get a two-bedroom apartment near here, so Lucy and you could move in with me."

Alessa hadn't expected him to make such an offer. After all, she was still going to school and wasn't making her own money yet and Lucy was only nine years old. It was a lot for him to take on. Until now, they had just been playing house, so to speak.

Trying to rein in her happiness, she said, "Remo, there is nothing I would love more, but you realize that Lucy is still quite young and I'm only nineteen. It's a big commitment for you and I don't expect you to do this for us."

Remo wrestled her lovingly off the sofa and onto the floor. "I know what I'm doing," he said confidently. "Look, we practically live together now. We do everything, but sleep under the same roof. I want to be with you and you know how much I love Lucy. Don't be such a downer. Come on, Alessa, let's give it whirl. I can cook, you know."

Alessa laughed. "So now you think you can bribe me with cooking? Well, okay, that works. Lucy will be out-of-her-mind giddy when I tell her. All right, fine. When does your chariot pick us up, with all of our shit?"

The moment Alessa got home she called Ebby to give her the news. Ebby was truly happy for all of them. She had, in fact, known this was coming. Remo had called Ebby earlier and felt her out on the idea before springing it on Alessa. He had been nervous about scaring her off and had wanted some reassurance from Ebby that it would work.

Ebby now said, "I think it's wonderful, Alessa. The three of you are very happy together and God knows you all deserve to be happy. Enjoy the moment and try to hold the feeling you have now in your heart so that you can keep it forever."

During the month that followed Alessa, Lucy and Remo were busy looking for an apartment that would be just right for them. While he made a decent living as a physical therapist, Remo wasn't wealthy and Alessa confessed how guilty she felt about not contributing financially. She knew that once she left public housing, she would lose her food stamps as well. She told Remo about the 30,000 dollars she had in a safety deposit box, but he insisted she keep that money. Someday, it would come in handy when either she or the three of them were planning to buy a house.

"You danced your ass off, literally, to save that money," Remo reminded her. "So some day, you can have a home of your own. The money stays put, until you're ready to do just that. We'll manage fine with the money I earn, until you get your degree and start your new career."

After a month of searching and looking at apartments all over the city, a two-bedroom opened up in Remo's building. The three of them went off to see it immediately. Remo filled out the application form and wrote a deposit check. The woman who had shown them the apartment told them they could have it right away. Since Remo had lived in the same building for years, she wasn't worried about waiting for the application to be processed. Lucy talked incessantly about how Remo would paint her new room purple and how much bigger their new apartment was, compared to the one they were living in now.

It was a peaceful and happy time for the three of them. Alessa often reflected back on her life, unable to convince herself that it was finally coming together in such an incredibly smooth way, unhindered by obstacles. She believed in fate and tried to glean and cherish the positive elements in every adverse situation she had been thrown into in the past. She told herself that if all those terrible things hadn't happened to her, she wouldn't have had Remo and Lucy in her life today. The way she saw it, they were all meant to happen to bring this precious moment into her life.

"Sure," she told God, one night, "it didn't have to be a complete fucking disaster from the moment I was born. And I could have done without all the unwanted sex, but thanks, anyway, for giving me Remo and Lucy. I would say you've redeemed yourself with me. Please keep the good shit coming my way and send the bad shit to the bad people. Now there's an idea. Amen."

Alessa's education was coming along well. She had decided, long before Remo asked her to move in with him, that she would get a four-year degree in psychology. She wanted to use it to help homeless people and abandoned or lost children living on the streets. She wanted, more than ever, to be an advocate for others, just like Ebby had been for her. She understood the importance of helping someone pick up the pieces of their life from the gutter. Lucy was doing very well in school. She was a bright child and a unique one. Her experiences had made her more compassionate and understanding of her peers than most other ten-year-olds would have been. Her teachers and classmates loved her. Back to school night was always a treat for Alessa, because everyone told her how lucky she was to have a sister like Lucy. Of course, no one needed to remind her about this. She knew just how fortunate she was to be given the privilege of loving a child like Lucy.

Chapter Fifty-Five

By the following weekend, both Remo and Alessa had packed up their belongings and vacated their apartments; they were moving into their new one. Remo had kept his promise and painted Lucy's room purple. The child was ecstatic when it was complete. The walls were a pale lilac, set off by a white ceiling over which Alessa had stenciled stars with bright yellow paint. She had also gone out and bought matching bedding for Lucy, using the money they had made selling the furniture from their old apartment. She had, in fact, tried returning this money to Ebby, since it was she who had originally paid for it all, but Ebby insisted they use it for their new place.

Remo was beyond happy watching the two women he loved the most in the world find such joy in the mundane things of life that their deprived past would never allow them to take for granted again. He felt fortunate to be part of such a special family and wanted nothing more than to ensure that the happiness they exuded would remain with them forever. Of course, living together as a family demanded its own form of adjustment where the two adults were concerned. Alessa and Remo, who were accustomed to privacy in his apartment, now needed to be more discreet in the expression of their passion for each other. But the apartment was the home they had longed for and they all began to settle in within a couple of weeks.

Just when things were getting to normal, Remo told Alessa over dinner that he wanted Lucy and her to meet his parents.

Alessa cringed at the thought. It wasn't that she didn't want to meet them. After all, Remo had told her so much about them over the last year. He had described them as loving and supportive. They lived in Chester County and he didn't see them as much as he would have liked to, but he talked with them every week. Alessa knew he had never taken a girlfriend home to meet them, because he had never really been serious about anyone until he met her.

Remo had caught the change in her mood the moment he mentioned his parents.

"What's the problem?" he asked. "Too much, too fast? If you don't want to meet them now, it's okay. But at some point, I'll want them to get to know you."

"It's not that, Remo," Alessa replied. "I'm just not the type of girl you take home to meet Mom and Dad. I'm afraid they will think I'm not good enough for you. They sound like great people, but what if they hate me? I don't want to disappoint them or you."

Remo smiled. "I think if you can manage not to say 'fuck' for an evening, they will just love you."

They both laughed, aware that Alessa's vocabulary included every vulgar word that had ever been invented.

"What will we tell them about Lucy?" she asked apprehensively. "I mean, I would hate to lie to them."

Remo moved closer to her. "We can tell them the truth. That you found Lucy on the street and took her in as your own child. No one in their right mind would ever judge you harshly for being a compassionate person."

After much angst over the whole idea, Alessa finally agreed. Lucy, who was sitting at the table listening to the whole conversation, felt overprotective about Alessa.

"Remo," she declared, "if your mom and dad don't like Alessa, I won't like them either, okay?"

Remo laughed. "It's a deal. I'll tell you what: if my parents don't like Alessa, I won't like them either. Does that work for you?"

Satisfied with his answer, Lucy went back to eating her dinner.

Later that evening, while Alessa was getting her tucked into bed, Lucy piped up, "Alessa, no matter what Remo's parents think, I will love you more than anyone else in the whole world. If they don't love you too, then I think they are just stupid. Okay?"

Touched, Alessa hugged her close. "Lucy, if you love me, then that's all I really need," she said. "Remo is right, though. I'm sure we will all get along just fine."

Secretly, Alessa was surprised by how protective Lucy was of her. She had always known the little girl loved her, but hadn't realized that a ten-year-old could be so protective of anyone. Alessa was certain that Lucy would grow up to be a wonderful person, with a great deal to offer others. She was grateful to be loved by two of the most wonderful people in the world—three, if you included Ebby. She understood how far she had come in the last three years. Maybe God does love me, she mused.

The next morning, Remo called his parents about going over to their place for dinner the following weekend. He told Alessa how excited his mom and dad were about meeting Lucy and her. The two of them looked at Remo as he tried to alleviate Alessa's tension over meeting his parents for the first time.

"Good!" Lucy blurted out. "They *should* be excited. My Alessa is better than anyone I know. That includes all of my teachers too." Then she turned to Alessa. "What are we going to wear?"

Alessa hadn't thought about that. Neither of them owned really stylish clothes. Nor could they afford to go out and buy any for that one evening.

"We'll find something in our closets, okay?" she reassured the little girl.

Lucy nodded, but looked at Remo for approval.

"You two are always gorgeous," he said fondly in response. "There's nothing to worry about. Jeans are fine."

All through the following week, Alessa fretted over the dinner with Remo's parents. On Saturday morning, she and Lucy spent some time picking out their outfits. Lucy was going to wear a dress they had bought at the Salvation Army for Easter. It had a lot of purple in it—Lucy's favorite color. Her white shoes were scuffed. She set off to the living room to find Remo so she could ask him to help her clean them up. Alessa picked a pair of jeans she had taken from Rhonda's clothes when she left Plymouth Meeting and a white blouse with small green and yellow flowers. It was the most conservative outfit she owned. Unfortunately, she only had her old sneakers to wear, but they would have to do.

Remo purposely dressed down, so that the two of them could outshine him. He had spent years as a bachelor and had plenty of clothes to wear, but didn't want to make Alessa more nervous than she already was.

At five-thirty p.m., they left the apartment to drive out to Kennett Square, where Remo's parents lived. An hour later, their car was making its way up a long driveway that led to a beautiful two-story house with a stone façade. The surrounding garden was artistically landscaped, with well-trimmed trees and bushes and vibrant flowers creating a rainbow of hues just outside the front door.

Alessa turned and looked at Remo as he parked the car.

"You never told me your parents were wealthy," she said, her apprehensions growing by the minute.

"You never asked," he replied. "Besides, they aren't filthy rich, Alessa. They worked for everything they have and live comfortably. My parents started out with nothing. My mom is an interior decorator who made a name for herself early on in her career. Now she only deals with high-end clients. My father was going to law school when they first got married, while my mother worked. When my dad graduated, he got a job at a prestigious firm in Philadelphia. He was made a partner in less than eight years, which is a really rapid rise in the legal profession. Eventually, Dad and another attorney left that firm and opened their own business. It has been really successful."

This, Alessa realized to her growing dismay, was nothing like the story of her own parents who had lived on welfare and handouts. She thought back to the house she had grown up in, complete with a rec room, as her mother had called it, filled with cigar smoke. They had made do with worn old furniture. They had a patchy lawn that got mown once every two weeks. When things had broken in her house, they had stayed that way. Caterina would glue, paste or staple things back together to make them semi-functional. They had slept on hand-me-down beds donated by relatives who were better off than them. She and Rosabella had shared a toothbrush for years and years. In Alessa's world, Remo's parents were filthy rich.

They all got out of the car and stood looking at the house.

"Wow, this house is great, Remo!" Lucy exclaimed. "I'm going to live in a house like this when I grow up."

Remo admired her attitude, her confidence and her self-esteem. "That you will. You'll have everything you want, Lucy."

Chapter Fifty-Six

The house was filled with wonderful aromas wafting out from the kitchen. The foyer was spacious, with a black and white marble floor and a sweeping stairway that gracefully curved its way up to the bedrooms above. To her left, Alessa could see a room fully furnished in oak, with well-stocked bookshelves covering an entire wall. She felt inadequate and completely out of place. About to head to the kitchen, they met Remo's mother coming through the doorway.

"Remo!" she said cheerfully, "how are you, son? I've missed you so much!"

Mother and son hugged, before she turned to look at Alessa and Lucy.

Alessa extended her hand. "Hi, I'm Alessa and this is Lucy."

Remo's mother was tall and thin. She had blond hair and green eyes that glittered like emeralds.

She shook Alessa's hand and said, "I'm Hannah. Nice to meet you, Alessa. Remo has told us a lot about you. We've been bugging him for ages to bring you over so we could meet and we were starting to think you didn't really exist. We thought he had just made you up to stop us from asking him when he was going to meet a nice girl and settle down."

Alessa smiled. "No, I'm real," she said. *You probably wouldn't think I was a nice girl, though*, she thought.

Hannah immediately turned to Lucy. "Hi Lucy, we've heard a lot about you too."

Brimming with pride, the child replied, "Did Remo tell you he painted my room purple? It's so cool! Alessa and me, we bought all this stuff that matches and Alessa painted stars on my ceiling too!"

Hannah was pleasantly surprised by how outgoing the child was. "Come on," she said, taking her by the hand. "Let's go to the kitchen to meet Remo's dad."

Lucy fell in step with her and Remo put his arm around Alessa and followed them into the kitchen.

"Hi Dad," he said.

Remo's father rose from the kitchen table and walked over to them. "Son, how are you?" he asked. "You're certainly looking well. This must be the woman who's keeping you in line!" He turned to Alessa with a warm smile.

"I'm Alessa and this is Lucy," she said by way of introduction. "We're so glad to meet you."

Patrick was smiling at the duo. "I'm Patrick, but I guess you know that already. Nice to meet you too!" he said in response. "Why don't you come in and make yourselves comfortable? Would you two young ladies like a glass of pink lemonade?"

Alessa and Lucy both accepted the offer. They both *loved* pink lemonade. As Remo and his father fell into conversation, Alessa made her way over to the stove where Hannah was cooking.

"Is there something I can help you with?" she asked.

Remo's mother accepted the offer willingly. "If you could clean the lettuce for our salad, that would help a bunch," she said.

Thank God, thought Alessa, *something I actually know how to do!* The two women chatted as they worked in the kitchen. The conversation was pleasant and superficial, dwelling on the things people yammer about when they meet for the first time.

During dinner, Hannah said, "So tell me how you two met. We weren't able to get much out of Remo. He can be really closemouthed when he doesn't like us asking him too many questions."

Alessa looked at Remo for reassurance. Then she took a deep breath and said, "Remo was my physical therapist. I broke my femur and arm and he helped put me back together again."

"Oh, my! That's awful!" Hannah exclaimed, shocked. "How did that happen?"

Alessa thought, *fuck, fuck, fuck*, and congratulated herself for not saying it out loud. Lucy was staring at her, waiting for the words that would follow, tense at how uncomfortable the situation was making her.

Alessa's expression grew solemn. "I was mugged by four men near Penn's Landing. I tried to fight them, so they got pretty angry with me."

Hannah's mouth dropped open. "You were mugged and beaten? Is that what you're saying?"

Remo could see his mother was beginning to freak out. Questions were bubbling on her tongue. It was time to step in.

"Yes, Mom," he confirmed, "that's what she's saying. It was pretty brutal and Alessa has managed to put it behind her. So how about changing the subject?"

Embarrassed by her involuntary outburst, Hannah said hastily, "Of course we can. Now how are you and Lucy related?"

Alessa swallowed hard. "Well, we aren't related by blood. Lucy was abandoned by her biological parents. We met shortly after they left her and have been together ever since. Now we think of ourselves as sisters."

Hannah's eyes widened with alarm. She shot Remo a fiery look. There were a million questions she wanted to ask, but Patrick was giving her that look which screamed: *Don't push it, Hannah. Our son loves them.*

Remo took charge of the conversation from that point onward. He talked about his patients and Alessa getting her degree in psychology. Patrick thought Alessa was terrific. She was funny and he could tell she was warmhearted too. She only seemed to tense up when Hannah tried to pry into her past. But overall, he thought Alessa and Lucy were delightful. Hannah wasn't as convinced. She could tell there was a lot they didn't know about the young woman. She also suspected that her son didn't want them to find out.

As the evening wound down and Remo was hugging his mother goodbye, she whispered in his ear, "We need to talk, son. I have many unanswered questions." She looked at him pleadingly as he stared at her.

Remo knew how much his parents loved him. He owed them some truth, so that at the very least, his mother would stop worrying. He knew, however, that the truth might upset her even more. Remo decided he would talk to his father first and feed him the truth in small doses. Patrick was much more open-minded than his mother, when it came to what Remo wanted in life.

Hugging his father, he said, "I'll call you tomorrow, Dad."

Patrick knew exactly what his son meant. "Okay, son. I'm looking forward to your call."

Lucy hugged Hannah and Patrick goodbye and Alessa shook their hands.

When they got into the car, Remo looked at Alessa and said, "Well, what do you think?"

"I think they're both great," she told him. "But you know they have a lot of questions about me, especially your mom. This is exactly what I had feared. I didn't want to cause any trouble between you and your parents."

"Nah, I think it was fine," he said, trying to ease her fears. "I'm sure they have some questions. Hell, you're the first woman I've ever brought home. So they would have questions, no matter who you were. There is nothing to worry about, Alessa. I can tell they loved you."

Lucy piped up from the backseat, "I like your dad better than your mom. I think he's nicer, but your mom sure makes good apple cake. The best I've ever had!"

Alessa turned to the child in the backseat and smiled. "And probably the only apple cake you've ever had?"

Lucy giggled. "Yeah, that too!"

Chapter Fifty-Seven

———◼———

Remo called his father the next day to answer some of the questions that discretion and courtesy had prevented his parents from posing at their dinner. He knew he would have to give Patrick enough information about Alessa to placate his mother or she would be relentless in her quest to find out more.

"Hi Dad, it's me," he said. "I know you guys have a lot of questions about Alessa and Lucy. Mom even whispered the warning, as I was leaving your place, that she would need answers."

Patrick knew this wasn't going to be easy on his son. He suspected there was a story behind the girls.

"Son," he said gently, "you know we're just worried about you and yes, we do have some questions. I mean, we didn't really understand how Alessa and Lucy had met. Nor are we quite clear in our minds about how Alessa was mugged and beaten. Are you sure you can handle this?"

"I'm fine, Dad. I'm going to tell you the story, but I really need you to keep some of it to yourself. I love these two and I don't want Mom to make this difficult for all of us. I know she only wants what's best for me, but you both need to have faith in my judgment. Okay?"

"Sure, son," Patrick agreed. "Tell me what's going on."

Remo took a deep breath. "First," he began, "Alessa was mugged and beaten by four men, just like she told you, but she was also brutally raped. We met when she came in as a patient for physical therapy. We spent a lot of time together and over the months, we got to know each other. It was a mutual thing."

"Jesus Christ!" Patrick whispered. "She was raped by four men? Are you sure she is capable of making the right decision about living with you? I mean, did she see a therapist after it happened? Rape can really screw up a woman. Stripped of everything she knows and cherishes, a lot of times, the experience leaves her hollow from within, like an empty shell."

Remo expected this response. His father was right and he needed to reassure him this hadn't been the case with Alessa.

"Dad," he went on, "there's a lot more to her story. Alessa was sexually abused by her uncle from the time she was seven years old. He continually raped her until she ran away from home at the age of sixteen. She fell in with the wrong crowd and was dancing at strip clubs, where there was more abuse. To cut a long story short, she wound up living on the streets to escape all this bullshit and that's where she met Lucy. Lucy was also raped by her father and molested by her mother. They've been together for two years now and Alessa has raised Lucy as if she were her own. There, now you have the bigger picture."

There was silence on the phone for what seemed an eternity.

Then Patrick said, "You've got to be fucking kidding me! These girls have been through hell. Your mother would have a fucking stroke, if she knew about this!"

Remo laughed. He had never heard his father use profanity before and it both shocked and amused him now. "Well, that's why God made husbands," he countered. "To bear the brunt of the shit their wives can't deal with. But seriously, Dad, you have to believe me when I say that Alessa has come through all of this and remained a good and decent human being. She isn't fucked up. I mean, she has her issues—we all do—but it's not like she's in meltdown. Actually, she is the strongest person I've ever met and I love her, Dad."

All Patrick said was, "If you love her, then she must be worth loving."

"Thanks, Dad," Remo said gratefully. "You know I love you and Mom. It's important to me that you can look beyond the shell and take the time to see what's really inside. Both of you always taught me to be open to anything. It's because of you that I am lucky enough to have these two girls in my life today. You've raised me well. Now go treat yourself to a beer."

Patrick laughed. "Thanks, son. I think I'll need a couple of beers to digest what you just told me. But don't worry. I'll handle your mother. I'll give her an abbreviated version of what I've learned, excluding the go-go clubs and that bit about Alessa and Lucy living on the streets."

They talked some more and right before they hung up the phone, Patrick said, "Remo?"

"Yeah, Dad?"

"Can you live without her?"

"I wouldn't want to, Dad," he answered promptly.

"Okay, then, that's good enough for me. For the record, I did think both of them were great."

Relieved to have his father on his side, "They are. See you soon."

Just as Patrick had promised his son, he gave Hannah only enough information to quell her suspicions about Alessa. They were planning their annual 4th of July party at their house and had, as usual, invited all their neighbors and friends to join them. Remo, Alessa and Lucy were invited as well. Remo filled them in about the 4th of July party which, he explained, was a big event for his parents. There would be dancing, singing and even fireworks. All the regulars looked forward to it every year.

Alessa bought Lucy a pair of white pants with a red tank top and a sleeveless blue sweater. The child felt quite the patriot as she came into the living room, all ready to go to the party. They arrived an hour earlier than the guests to help Hannah and Patrick with their preparations. Lucy helped Hannah put food into bowls and Alessa found herself cleaning the lettuce—again. As she leaned over the sink to wash twelve heads of lettuce, she made a mental note about learning to cook a dish. The whole salad thing was a real, fucking drag!

When the guests began arriving, Remo introduced them to Alessa, one by one. All of them were curious about the girl who had managed to inspire deep enough feelings in the incurable bachelor for him to finally want to settle down. They were just as curious about her sister.

About an hour into the party, a middle aged couple showed up. When the man saw Alessa, he froze in his tracks.

"What's wrong?" she heard his wife ask.

Alessa turned to see what was going on. Then like a kid in a game of hide and seek, she suddenly ducked behind one of the thick pillars on the massive porch.

Remo, who had followed the developments, caught up with her. "Whatever just happened, Alessa, you need to relax," he told her softly. "You look like you've just seen a ghost. Someone you know, no doubt."

Shaken, Alessa looked back at him. "Oh God! Yeah, I know him," she admitted. "I'll tell you later."

She pretended, as best she could, that nothing was wrong. Later in the evening, when they were getting dessert ready, Remo came in to steal Alessa from his mother.

"Okay, what's the deal?" he asked, when he got her alone. "When my parents' next door neighbor walked in, he almost shit in his pants and you looked like you wanted to run and hide."

"Oh fuck, Remo! This is embarrassing," Alessa said, trying to stall.

"Don't be embarrassed. You know how I feel about these things. I don't give a fuck."

Alessa laughed. "Not embarrassing for me," she explained. "I meant, embarrassing for him. I know him from the strip club. He used to pay me for lap dances, but he was really freaky. When we went into the room, he would take off all his clothes, put an adult diaper on, hold a rattle and have me give him a lap dance. He would insist that I repeat, 'What a bad, bad boy you are!' He would act like a scolded child and we would just repeat the routine over and over. I didn't have too many clients who were really freaky, but he was definitely one of them."

She and Remo burst out laughing at the same time. Alessa was amused by the memory of the man's fetish; Remo found the visual conjured up by her account hilarious.

"Remo, it didn't occur to me that I would ever meet the men I had once danced for at the club," she confessed. "It's just like the time I saw your friend at the Irish Pub. There are so many men I've danced for and in front of; I could be running into them at any time, like I did here, at your parents' party."

"Yep, shit happens," Remo said understandingly. "Let's go back out to the party. They're getting ready to set off the fireworks."

Alessa, Remo and Lucy sat on a blanket spread over the grass and watched the fireworks. They were beautiful without being lavish. As the girls watched, their minds went back to the same occasion a year back, when Alessa had been raped and beaten.

Lucy snuggled up closer to the older girl. "You remember, right?" she whispered.

"Yeah, it's hard not to," Alessa admitted. "Things are different now, though."

"I know," Lucy said. "I love you, Alessa."

"I love you too, Lucy."

Chapter Fifty-Eight

The next morning, Patrick called the apartment. Alessa answered the phone.

"Hi Alessa, this is Patrick. Did you have a good time yesterday?"

"I had a great time," she replied, with more enthusiasm than she had felt about the occasion.

"Good. Glad to hear it. Is Remo around?"

A few seconds later, Remo was on the phone. "Hey Dad, what's up?" he asked.

Exercising as much tact as he was capable of, Patrick told him how his neighbor had issued a veiled warning about Alessa. "He doesn't think she is the right girl for you," he went on. "Said he could see something wasn't right about her."

Laughing, Remo confided in his father, sharing the story he had heard about the man from Alessa the night before.

"Okay, I see," Patrick said matter-of-factly. "Now that makes more sense. But son, you do realize that this is the kind of stuff you will need to deal with, if you live with Alessa. You need to be sure you can handle her past. If you can't, then living with her wouldn't be fair to either of you and especially not to Lucy, who would be caught in the crossfire."

Remo sighed. "I know. The truth is, Dad, I don't have an issue with her past. I dated a lot of girls who did the same thing as Alessa. They just didn't do it for money. They did it because they wanted to. I love Alessa. She is my soul mate. I just feel whole, when I am with her."

Alessa, who had overheard Remo's side of the conversation, figured the neighbor had said something derogatory about her to Patrick. Remo hung up the phone and walked across the kitchen to take her in his arms. Within seconds, Lucy had walked in on them.

Remo yelled instantly, "Group hug!"

Lucy lunged into the two of them and the three clung to each other in the middle of the kitchen floor for several minutes.

While they were all laughing and embracing, the phone rang again. Remo reached over and picked it up. His expression turned serious as he turned to Alessa.

"It's your sister, Rosabella," he said. "She's crying."

He led Lucy out of the kitchen to give Alessa her privacy as she took the phone. Hearing Rosabella sob, she figured her sister's boyfriend had been beating her again.

"Alessa," Rosabella said in a muffled voice, "Dad died. He had a heart attack last night and they rushed him to the hospital. He died about forty-five minutes ago."

Alessa stood holding the phone, not sure what she should say. She didn't feel tearful or even sad. She felt nothing at all. She found herself consumed by guilt, however, for being unable to share her sister's grief. She pulled herself together and consoled Rosabella, assuming that at least she was doing her sisterly duty.

Then her older sibling asked, "Can you come to Mom's house tomorrow? We will all be there. There's no way I can get through this without you there, Alessa."

Alessa reluctantly agreed, but regretted it immediately. As she hung up the phone, Remo came back into the kitchen with Lucy.

"What's going on?" he asked.

Alessa was trembling like she had been standing naked in the cold for a while. "Rosabella called to tell me my father had just died."

"Oh Alessa, I'm so sorry," Remo said, rushing over to console her.

Alessa looked at him expressionlessly. "Yeah, I appreciate that and all, but the thing is, I just let Rosabella talk me into going to my mother's house tomorrow. What the fuck was I thinking?"

"Don't worry, Alessa," Lucy chimed in bravely, "You don't have to go alone. I'll go with you."

"Me too," Remo jumped in quickly.

"I haven't seen my family in four years," Alessa explained. "My mother, that fucking whore, will be there and so will my Uncle Danny. How the hell can I go back there? I promised Rosabella I'd show up, but I don't want to go at all. I left that family behind a long time ago."

"Well, look," Remo suggested, "we don't have to stay long. Lucy and I will protect you, right, Luce?"

Lucy quickly agreed. "It'll be fine, Alessa," she assured her. "You'll see."

The next day, they piled into the car and headed to Plymouth Meeting. They had to pick up Rosabella and her daughter, Eva, on the way. Alessa had never met her niece in person and the excitement of seeing her for the first time was the only bright spot in her day.

When they stopped at Rosabella's she flung open the door, put her arms around Alessa, and held her tight. Alessa loved her sister. Having talked to her on the phone over the past year, she knew her more intimately now than she had during the first sixteen years of her life that they had spent together in the same house.

As they headed for the home Alessa had grown up in, her anxiety levels rose alarmingly. Rosabella had informed their mother that her younger sister would be accompanying her, but confessed to Alessa on the way that this news had elicited no response at all from Caterina.

When they reached the house, Rosabella led the way in, carrying Eva in her arms. Remo and Lucy flanked Alessa on either side. Both of them felt like warriors going into battle to protect their queen. Back in the house she had fled from so many years ago, Alessa immediately felt she didn't belong. The memory of all the agonies she had suffered during her traumatic childhood came flooding back to haunt her now. The helplessness and the sense of shame she had lived with overtook her, as she looked around the house that hadn't changed since she had left it four years ago.

Alessa followed her sister into the kitchen and stopped abruptly. Standing directly in front of her was her mother. When their eyes met, Alessa involuntarily moved closer, imagining for a fleeting moment that Caterina would actually come forward and embrace her. She stopped short, however, as her mother's expression changed to one of sheer disgust.

Caterina's viciousness oozed from her, as she said, "Oh, so now you decide to come back! *After* he's dead and gone. Where the hell have you been, girl?"

Alessa's initial instinct was to ram her fist down her mother's throat and stop the flow of cruel words. In that moment, she realized that her relationship with her mother had changed forever. Things were different now. She was no longer the girl that Caterina could shit all over. Alessa had grown up. She was braver and bolder now and from her new perspective, her mother was no longer the big, bad wolf. On the contrary, Caterina seemed puny and insignificant, a pathetic creature who had acquired all her power through a game of guilt and manipulation. It was all so clear to Alessa now. For the first time in her life, she understood that her mother hadn't been strong enough to save her from her uncle. She just didn't have the resilience or the will power to survive on her own. How could she have protected anyone else? Having discovered how weak Caterina really was, Alessa had no intention now of giving her the chance to bully her again.

"I've been off making a life for myself," she said evenly, in response to her mother's query. "For the first time, I'm actually living."

Caterina grunted at her, then stared at Remo and Lucy. "And who are they? What did you do? Find yourself a man that already had a kid? Christ, you really are stupid, a complete idiot!"

Alessa looked at her mother long and hard. Then she said, "They are my family. They are people who love me—unlike you."

"You ungrateful little bitch!" her mother sneered. "Do you know how much I had to sacrifice for you? For all you damn kids?"

Alessa's lips curled in a nasty, mocking smile. *"Really?"* she said, infusing the word with as much sarcasm as she could. "How about all the 'sacrifices' *I* had to make for *you*? You pimped me out to your own brother. You are a horrible woman and I have nothing but hate for you."

Remo and Lucy quickly gripped Alessa by the arm and led her outside into the sunlight. As they left the kitchen, they heard Caterina yell, "That's right! Run, you stupid bitch!"

Out on the porch, Alessa began to regain her composure. She hadn't said all the things she had wanted to, but she didn't know if this was the right time for it or if there would ever be another opportunity in the future. Rosabella came out to see if her sister was okay. Everyone had heard the exchange between Alessa and their mother and tension ran high in the house.

Just then, Alessa's oldest sister, Anna, and her brother, Anthony, came out of the house and saw her. Both came forward and wrapped her in warm, welcoming hugs. Alessa introduced them to Remo and Lucy. As she listened to them talking about their father, she felt they were speaking of a stranger she'd never known. He had remained a complete mystery to her, because apart from just being there, he had done so little.

Alessa's siblings asked her the usual questions about where she was living and what she was doing. No one brought up the subject of her running away from home or not hearing from her in four years. It was business as usual, Alessa thought. Her family had lived in constant denial of reality. A poor family, lost and unsure of how to get back home, they had all just tried to live up to other people's expectations of them, pretending, both to themselves and to the world, that they were more than they really were. In their pretend world, there was a rose garden and a white picket fence and everything was normal.

By now, Lucy was clutching Alessa's hand and wasn't about to let it go. The little girl felt protective about her again and afraid for her, because she could sense the isolation in which Alessa had grown up. Lucy's mind wandered back to the tragedy of her own life, as Caterina's older offspring pretended that nothing had happened in the house between their mother and Alessa just minutes ago.

Caterina came to the door to announce that lunch was ready. As Alessa's siblings started to go back in, Remo said, "We can leave now, if you want. You came and you tried. Maybe we should just go."

Rosabella overheard him. "No, please stay," she implored them. "For the first time in my life, I got to see someone stand up to our mother. I need you to stay, at least for lunch. Please?"

Alessa shot Remo and Lucy a brave look and said, "We'll leave right after lunch."

As they ate the sandwiches Caterina had prepared, Alessa could sense her mother looking at her curiously. She realized that Caterina didn't know her anymore and was trying to figure out what her next step should be. Ah, Alessa thought, I backed the bitch into a corner! This was something none of her children had done to her before. She paused for a moment to enjoy a silent celebration.

After lunch, Alessa told Remo they would be leaving right after she used the bathroom. Lucy followed her and sat in the rec room, so she could use the bathroom too. Alessa came out in a moment and urged the child to hurry so they could leave. Waiting in the hall for Lucy, she couldn't help but contemplate with some curiosity the closed door of the room across the hall that had once been her bedroom. It was in that very room that her nightmare had started. She approached it with some trepidation and slowly pushed open the door. It didn't appear very different from the way she remembered it. The fact that it was unchanged probably had more to do with Caterina's sheer laziness than with her desire to preserve the memories of a daughter who had disappeared, leaving no trace of her whereabouts.

Alessa stepped into her old bedroom, wondering how it would feel to have good memories of her childhood instead of the ones that had haunted her for so long. But try as she might, she could not obliterate the pain and humiliation of the repeated rapes she had endured in this very room. She walked over to her beat-up dresser. There, on top, was a picture of herself and Rhonda, her only high school friend. She smiled at the picture, remembering what a good friend Rhonda had been to her.

Suddenly, she felt a hand on her ass. Another had crept up to her left breast. Startled back to reality, she turned to see her Uncle Danny standing there. He was looking at her with a strange mixture of longing and contempt. It was the creepiest look she'd ever seen on a human face.

She quickly jerked herself away from him, but he would not let go.

"Don't worry," he said. "I locked the door. No one will bother us."

Terror engulfed her. Alessa's blood was pulsing through her veins like a high-speed train, as she pushed him away.

He smiled as he came at her again. "Oh, you like it rough now, do you?" he sneered. "Okay, I can do rough."

He slapped her across the face, sending her crashing back onto the floor. He was on top of her in a moment, pushing her skirt up. She was struggling and thrashing under him to get him off her, when she heard a knock on the door.

"Alessa, are you okay?" It was Lucy. She had seen the older man go into the bedroom and shut the door. Before Alessa could yell out, she heard Lucy scream in a shrill voice, "Remo!"

Uncle Danny got up off Alessa, made for the door and unlocked it. He looked down at Lucy who was standing right outside and said in a caressing voice, "Well, aren't you a beauty! I bet all the men want some of you."

Alessa ran over to the child and wrapped her arms protectively around her. "You dirty motherfucker!" she snarled. "You ruined my life. You took everything from me. You will live in the fires of hell some day! You are a rotten, dirty old man and I hope you die a painful death. God, how I hate you!"

By now, Remo too was standing behind Lucy. He was glaring at Alessa's uncle with a hatred he had never felt for anyone before.

Rosabella came into the hallway and asked, "What the fuck is going on?" She looked at Uncle Danny. "You leave her the fuck alone!" she warned, gesturing toward Alessa, "If you touch her, I'll kill you."

"I don't know what the hell you're talking about," the man retorted. "You better shut your dirty mouth or I'll tell your mother what you just said to me."

Rosabella stepped up close to her uncle. "I don't fucking care what you tell her!" she bit out. "She's just as evil as you are for allowing Alessa to be victimized. So fuck her too!"

Uncle Danny's face twisted into an ugly expression. Cocking his head in Alessa's direction, he declared, "I didn't rape her. *She* raped me."

Remo rolled up his fist and struck Danny on the chin, knocking him back into the room. Then he took Alessa and Lucy by the hand and led them back into the rec room. "We need to get the fuck out of here," he said urgently. "These people are fucking nuts!"

Caterina came bolting into the rec room. "What the hell happened?" she demanded to know. "What is all the commotion about?"

Emotionally exhausted by now, Alessa said listlessly, "Your brother just tried to rape me again. You know, that sex thing that you insisted was affection when I was a kid? Remember, you didn't believe me at the time?"

Caterina's mouth hung open. She was unable to utter a single word, as Remo, Lucy, Alessa and Rosabella looked on. Finally, she said, half to herself, "I was a good mother and I took care of my children. I sacrificed my career and stayed home so I could be here for you all the time. I could have gotten a job, but chose to be here for all of you. Do you think that was easy for me? I had to raise four kids on welfare. I want to see you raise four kids on the measly amount of money they give you."

Alessa said calmly, "You were here in this house all the time, but you were never home. I expected you to help me, to protect me, but you didn't. You just never came home to us. You were simply physically present in the house and you were useless. It was always about what *you* wanted and needed. You would have sacrificed anything not to go out and get a real job. You sacrificed *me*. I told you what Uncle Danny was doing to me, but you chose not to believe me. You sacrificed me, so you could continue to pay the bills by taking his money month after month. So, *Mother,* you either ignored what that old motherfucker was doing to me or you are just the stupidest woman on earth. Which is it?"

Caterina was silent.

Alessa stared at her mother for a long time. Then she turned to Remo and Lucy, put her hands on her hips and said, "Okay, now, let's go home. I've said all that I needed to."

Chapter Fifty-Nine

On their way back to the car, Remo could clearly see that the face off with her mother, followed by the encounter with Uncle Danny, had left Alessa flustered and furious.

"You okay?" he asked gently.

"I'd forgotten how much I hated Uncle Danny," she said with a deep sigh. "I thought there wasn't much left to learn about him, but when the motherfucker actually touched me, I wanted to rip his heart out! Same with that bitch who pretends to be my mother. I'm glad I came back, though, to see her. I got to defend myself the way I couldn't all these years and I feel good about that."

Lucy chimed in from the backseat, "Alessa, we don't ever have to see them again. I hate your uncle and I hope he dies!"

"Me too!" Alessa agreed.

Remo placed his hand over hers and gave her a look of such profound reassurance it made her feel instantly safe. He flashed her his brilliant smile, then yelled out to the child in the backseat, "What do you say, Luce, shall we get some ice cream?"

"Yeah, baby!" Lucy bellowed in response.

Remo took them to Dairy Queen. While he and Alessa sat at a picnic table, Lucy was busy running around with other kids she had met just minutes earlier.

"How are you feeling?" Remo asked Alessa. "I mean, I know this is a lot for you to swallow and I can see you're stressed out."

Alessa started to cry. "I just don't want to feel like this now," she wept. "All these years have been so hard for me and now things were finally falling into place. I was starting to feel normal. I feel that by going back to visit my old home, I've just opened the door to these demons and am letting them walk back into my life. For the first time in over a year, I feel

I'm back where I began, with no control over anything that's happening to me."

Remo stood up and took her gently in his arms. "You haven't lost control of anything, Alessa," he murmured. "You mustn't let people make you feel like shit. No one is in control of you, except yourself. You're not that child anymore who got used and abused; you have complete control over your life now. Besides, you got your chance to tell them both exactly how you felt about them."

Alessa put her arms around his neck. "You're right," she agreed. "How did I manage to live without you all these years?"

"That's what all my girlfriends ask," Remo quipped with a smile. "I don't know how any of them manage without me."

Alessa pretended to punch him in the stomach. "Oh yeah?" she said playfully. "Is that what all your girlfriends ask? Who are these girlfriends you're talking about?"

Remo kissed Alessa on the neck. "You're the only girl for me. I'm the envy of every man alive."

Alessa waved at Lucy who was playing with the kids. "Whatever," she said, taking Remo's hand as they headed over to tell Lucy it was time to leave.

On their way back home, Lucy asked, "Your Uncle Danny lives in that house with your mom?"

Alessa threw her a look over her shoulder. "Yeah, the big fucking asshole!"

The following weekend, the three of them met Alessa's siblings at Capone's restaurant and enjoyed themselves so much it was hard to believe they had just buried their father a week earlier.

Rosabella said, "Mom was upset that she wasn't invited here tonight. We figured you wouldn't want to see her again after what happened last week."

Alessa shrugged. "She may be your mother," she said calmly, "but she isn't mine anymore. She stopped being my mother, when she deliberately turned a blind eye to what her brother was doing to me."

Anna seemed to suddenly come alive. She was eight years older than Alessa and while she had heard bits and pieces of the accusations made by their youngest sibling a week ago, she wasn't aware of what had happened to her as a child.

"What does that mean?" she now asked.

Alessa put it bluntly. "Uncle Danny began raping me from the time I was seven. When I told *your* mother, she refused to believe me. That's why I had to leave home."

Stunned, Anna didn't know how to respond, while Anthony pretended to be deaf.

"I had no idea," Anna said, after she had composed herself. "How the fuck did this happen? We all lived under the same roof. How could this have continued to happen for years without any of us coming to know?"

Anthony looked over at Alessa. "Are you sure?" he said, looking a bit skeptical.

"I don't know, Anthony," she replied, trying in vain to keep her voice even. "Your uncle stuck his dick into my vagina when I was seven years old. Is that rape or not? *You* tell me. What the fuck do you mean, am I sure?"

Regretting his callous response, Anthony tried to appease his sister. "Calm down. I was just asking a question. You know sometimes things happen and people blow them out of proportion. It's a shock hearing all this and I just wanted to be sure. Uncle Danny was good to everyone. When we were kids, we wouldn't have had anything, if it weren't for him. He was the one who gave Mom money to run the house and pay the mortgage on it. It's just hard for me to believe he would do something so nasty."

Alessa forced herself to be calm, because she wanted to sound far more confident than she felt. "He didn't buy all those things for us and give all that money to 'dear old Mom' for nothing. He was getting something in return and *I* was that something. I don't really care if you believe me or not, Anthony. I don't care if none of you believe me. I know what happened. I know what he did. And I know that the woman who was supposed to protect me allowed it to happen so she could 'make ends meet'."

A heavy silence fell over the table.

Finally, Rosabella spoke up. "Let's just drop it for now," she suggested tactfully. "This isn't going anywhere or making anything better. But for the record, I believe you, Alessa."

Lucy sat up in her chair and said boldly, "I believe you too."

The rest of the dinner was tense, as Remo tried to carry the conversation with non-family-related topics. He had the gift of the gab and it helped them all to get through a very awkward evening.

As they were leaving, Alessa hugged each of her siblings. When it was Anthony's turn, he said to her quietly, "It's just hard to believe this about him. He's always been so good to us."

Not wanting to cause another scene, Alessa held her rage in check. Without uttering another word to him, she turned to give Anna a hug. Her oldest sister held her tightly. "We'll see you soon, right?" she asked hopefully.

Alessa nodded. "Yeah, sure."

As they headed back to the city, Remo said, "I can understand why you left home, Alessa. I couldn't believe my ears when I heard your own brother doubting your word. I've never seen anything like that in my life!"

Alessa leaned back into the seat of the car. "Welcome to my world," she said, half in jest, "the world of denial. But you know, it's not like I expected to get much support from them. I mean, sure, it really pissed me off, but I learned not to expect much from them a long time ago. I just want to go home now, Remo. That's all."

Lying awake in bed that night, Alessa thought back to her experience with her uncle a week ago, to the familiar feeling of loathing that his touch had aroused in her. The look on his face was, however, quite different from the one she had been used to seeing when she lived in her parents' house. His expression seemed to suggest that he was caught between twin desires: to kill her or to fuck her. Maybe, he wanted both. Then Alessa thought of her mother and wondered what she had ever done as a child to make her become so vile. Maybe Caterina was in love with Uncle Danny and, therefore, jealous of her? Her thoughts, restless, morbid and extreme, twisted and turned that night in a way so sick, they made her feel disoriented and lost. Grappling with them for hours, she just couldn't lay them to rest. Finally, at two in the morning, she got out of bed and called Ebby.

When Ebby answered the phone, her voice was groggy with sleep. But the moment she recognized Alessa's voice, she panicked. "What is it, Alessa?" she asked, alarmed. "What's happened? Are you and Lucy okay? Where's Remo?"

Alessa laughed, warmed by the thought that even if her mother didn't love her, there were other people who cared. "Everyone is fine, Ebby," she reassured her. "I had an awful evening that wound me up tight. And since I wasn't able to sleep, I thought maybe you'd be up and I could talk to you. I'm sorry I woke you up. I'll let you go so you can go back to bed."

"You're kidding me, right?" Ebby said, feigning indignation. "You wake me up, then want to go? I actually just got to sleep about a half an hour ago. You know me; I do my finest work in the middle of the night."

Alessa laughed. Then she related the details of the evening she had spent with her siblings. Ebby was already aware of the previous week's fiasco with Caterina and Danny. She listened patiently without interrupting Alessa even once.

Then she said, "Alessa, your mother and your uncle have given you enough grief. If your own family doesn't believe you, well, that's just too bad. It sounds like Rosabella has some sense, though. Maybe, even Anna does. As for your brother, well, people just say the wrong thing sometimes. Especially when they have to face ugly truths that are beyond their imagination. There's a chance he's feeling guilty, because he didn't protect you from Danny. Or maybe, he still has such a high opinion of your uncle that he's struggling to come to terms with the idea that Danny could have done something so barbaric. You may never get to know what kind of dilemma Anthony is going through, but you shouldn't ever let it affect how you feel about yourself. *You* know what happened to you. Just because someone else isn't convinced about it doesn't change the truth."

"I know, Ebby," Alessa said sadly. "I knew they would be shocked, but I thought they would at least believe me."

Ebby sighed deeply. "You're a smart and capable woman, Alessa. I'm not sure why you continue to expect certain responses from people when your instinct tells you otherwise. As for your uncle, he will burn in hell with the other maggots of the earth. Your mom...well, we've discussed this. I would say she isn't quite right in the head or just plain evil or maybe, just stupid, like you said. As for your siblings, it's up to them to come to terms with it on their own. They are either with you or they're not. There is no middle of the road on this one, Alessa. Accept this and move on. You have a good life now. Don't slide backward. Keep your eyes focused on the road ahead."

Alessa thanked Ebby for being such a patient listener and giving such sound advice. Until she met her family again, Alessa had been, over the past year, resolving her issues, coming to terms with what had happened to her and preparing to put it all behind her. But their incredulous reaction to her story had set her back, making her feel as if she were to blame for everything that had happened to her. She had begun to question her own perspective, her take on the past. Had she provoked her Uncle Danny into raping her? She had loved him so much, maybe, too much, and maybe, just maybe, she had brought it all on herself? She couldn't discount the wisdom of what Ebby had said, however. Alessa knew she must never look back. Looking back would simply lead her to believe that God was punishing her for all the sleazy things she had done over the last four years. After all, what was she, but a whore? Nothing Ebby or Remo could say would ever change that fact.

Chapter Sixty

In the weeks following Alessa's run in with her family, she spent more time on the weekends in homeless shelters. Remo and Lucy were always with her. The residents at the shelters had remarked a noticeable change in Alessa. She was quieter than usual and her characteristic enthusiasm was absent.

On a Saturday afternoon, one of the teenage boys she had been working with for sometime approached Alessa in the park. He had been on the streets since he was thirteen. In the three years he had been homeless, Alessa, he felt, was the only person who understood him. The boy had been offering sex for just enough money to buy himself meals. Since he was gay, the other homeless teens assumed he was making money doing something he enjoyed. Alessa, however, understood the sacrifices he was making to keep himself alive.

"Alessa," he now told her, "I don't know what's wrong, but you ain't been acting like yourself. If you need to talk to someone, I'm here to listen."

For a change, Alessa was eager to share her feelings with someone other than Ebby or Remo.

When she finished relating what had happened with her family, he said, "See, that's the shit that makes you so special. People fuck you over and you keep on barreling along like an eighteen-wheeler on an open highway. I don't know why you feel bad. Sounds like you said all the shit you needed to say. You've faced your monster and you're still here. Get over it."

After he left, Alessa mulled over his words. Thinking how right his advice was, simple though it sounded, she laughed to herself. The boy was dead on with his opinion. She had to get over it. She had faced her monster and was still alive. *So I was raped when I was a kid*, she thought to herself. *Maybe that's why I'm stronger. Get over it.* She knew the people on the streets didn't judge her for having been a stripper and a prostitute. In fact, they loved her all the more, because she had used what God had given her to make a living and wasn't embarrassed to tell people about it.

After her conversation with the boy, Alessa found herself feeling more positive. She did not reject the idea that maybe, God had allowed this to happen to her so she could help others. Maybe he had wanted her to find Lucy. Maybe God had needed her to suffer so she could understand the suffering of others and help them heal. She realized her line of thinking was a bit theatrical, the kind of stuff you saw in the movies, but it was certainly better than assuming she deserved to be punished for her past.

In bed that night, Alessa told Remo, "When I get my degree and a job, I'm going to open a shelter for the homeless. You know, a safe house for young girls or young mothers with kids."

Remo rolled over and scooped her up in his arms. "That sounds like a good idea," he murmured. "We don't have to wait until you get your degree, though. You could use the money you saved from your dancing for a down payment on a house and we can use my salary to pay the mortgage."

Alessa hesitated. "Really?" she said, somewhat skeptical. "How will you pay a mortgage on your salary alone?"

Remo smiled. "We'll work it out. We don't have to figure it all out now."

Alessa stared at him, wondering if he had gone mad. "Remo," she said, "I get what you're saying, but we can't just do this without knowing how we'll pay for everything."

"Alessa, you just need to jump in, sometimes, and believe," he told her. "You need to believe like a child."

Her expression darkened, as she wrestled with a concept that was so alien to her. "I don't know what that looks like, Remo," she said wistfully. "I never got to be a child."

Remo realized his mistake and was furious with himself for his insensitivity. She was so strong now he'd forgotten that Alessa never had a normal childhood. She had never dreamed about her future.

"When I was a child," Alessa said miserably, "all I focused on was how awful I felt. I dreaded every single day, never believing that better times would come, that the future could hold something positive for me."

Remo felt her anguish and his heart went out to her at the thought of how much she had lost. "Well," he said gently, "most kids live with the excitement of getting a new baseball glove or going to Disney World. Kids don't think about how good stuff happens. They just know good things will come."

Alessa smiled. "That sounds like a wonderful place to be," she said wonderingly. "Teach me how, Remo."

"First, you have to believe. You need to just expect good things to happen and they will. You are where you are today, because you just expected it to happen, right? You wanted a better life and believed you would have one. That's what I'm talking about."

Alessa burrowed herself into his bare chest. It meant everything to her that Remo loved her enough to invest in her dream. She struggled with herself, hesitating to believe it would be so simple. Then she thought about all the things that had brought her to this moment. *Maybe*, she thought, *I do know how to believe like a child, after all.*

Chapter Sixty-One

The very next morning, Alessa and Remo shared their plan with Lucy. It thrilled them to see how excited she was over it. The little girl loved the homeless people they visited. She knew them all, feeling as though she had family all over the city. And now she would get a chance to do something important for them. Brimming with enthusiasm and eager now to find a house that would serve as a shelter, Lucy hounded the two of them to start searching.

"You know," Remo remarked, "most ten-year-old girls want to go clothes shopping, but not you. You're more excited about buying a place to help your friends out than getting stuff for yourself. How did you get to be so special?"

Lucy jumped on top of Remo who was sitting on the sofa. "From you and Alessa," she giggled. Then her young face turned serious. "And because I know what it's like to be homeless. It really sucks, Remo. It really, really sucks! You never know if you're going to have food or will have to go hungry and some people are mean to you, just because you're not as lucky as they are. They look at you funny and it makes you feel like something is wrong with you."

Remo got up from the sofa and pulled out the telephone book. "Let's see here. Yeah, there it is." He picked up the phone and dialed the number.

Alessa and Lucy just looked on and listened to his side of the exchange.

"Hello, my name is Remo," he said into the phone, "I'm looking for a realtor who can help me find a multi-family property. Yes, I can. Well, I live right down the block from your office. Yep, we can meet you in thirty minutes. Great, I appreciate your help. See you soon. Bye."

Remo turned to the two women in his life. "Okay," he said decisively, "the realtor can see us in thirty minutes. Let's do it!"

They all cheered and went to their rooms to get ready for the appointment.

A fifteen-minute discussion with the realtor and they were off to see row homes scattered throughout the city. They visited several, one after another, and by the time they retreated to their apartment, it was one confusing blur. The three agreed during further debate that they hadn't found the right place just yet. They told the agent to line up more for the next day and the threesome sat down to dinner. Alessa had started trying her hand at cooking in order to contribute her bit to the household. With Remo paying all the bills, she felt she needed to do something more constructive than just going to school. The thought of opening a shelter for the homeless gave Alessa renewed hope and Remo was happy to see her in better spirits.

By the next day, they'd found the perfect place. The fourth row home they visited was the one they set their hearts on the moment they entered it. It was a three-story building. A large two-bedroom apartment occupied the top floor. It had been recently renovated, with hardwood floors throughout. Lucy went crazy at the thought that if they did buy it, she would have her own bathroom. Alessa and Remo loved the master bedroom too. There was also a large, open kitchen and a cozy living room. What the three of them loved the most, though, was the space on the first and second floors. There were three two-bedroom apartments on each floor and while they were much smaller than the one on the top floor, they would comfortably house four to six people.

Before they left, Remo made the realtor a fair offer.

Back at home, they talked endlessly about all the things they could do and the people they would be able to help. An hour later, the telephone rang and Remo answered it. Alessa and Lucy clung to each other tensely, watching the expression on his face for a sign that their offer had been accepted. Knowing quite well that the girls were waiting for some indication from him that the house was now theirs to live in, Remo mischievously kept them in suspense by maintaining a poker face.

Then he hung up, turned to them and announced matter-of-factly, "Pack your shit. We got it."

The girls shrieked with delight and ran to hug him. Knowing from personal experience what a blessing the shelter would be for some of the homeless people who had become their friends, Alessa and Lucy could hardly contain their excitement and their joy.

The next two months flew by, as they prepared to move into their new home. Their next big responsibility involved the selection of the people who would live there. So many of the homeless needed housing and the house they had bought could only accommodate thirty-six residents. Alessa decided they would give priority to women and children. Six in each apartment would be tight, but she knew it was a better option than the streets or the "typical" homeless shelters that existed in the city. The three agreed not to discuss the matter with their homeless friends until they had figured out who would live in their shelter. They came up with three criteria to help them in their decision. The residents would have to be women under the age of twenty-one. Once they moved in, they would either have to work or go to school. And they could only live there until they were twenty-one. Alessa felt this was the only fair way to decide. The idea was to get younger people off the streets and back into school or working, so they could support themselves. This new home, as she visualized it, would be a place to rest, between heaven and hell. She couldn't give them everything and she couldn't help everyone, but she could make a difference—thirty-six people at a time.

When the day of settlement on the new home arrived, they were all excited. After closing, they quickly drove to the property and buzzed through the house.

"This is the greatest fucking moment of my life!" Alessa exclaimed to Remo. Her excitement was that of a child's on Christmas morning who had come downstairs to see what Santa had left her. "Next to finding you and Lucy, of course," she added. "Now, let's go upstairs and see our new digs."

Chapter Sixty-Two

Over the next month, when Alessa wasn't in school, she would be painting and fixing the place up in a mad rush to get it ready for the people it was meant for. Remo and Lucy fell in line like two soldiers, as Alessa barked orders at them. The three of them had a great time working on this project together.

Ebby came to see the house and was proud of them all. In a quiet moment, she sat with Alessa and said, "You have really made a good life for yourself. You should be proud. You probably never realized how much you've accomplished. No matter how hard your life has been—and it was really hard—you never let self-pity get you down. You are someone most people would envy, Alessa."

Alessa laughed at her and said, "Oh no, you wouldn't envy me, if you saw some of the guys I had to fuck."

Ebby wrinkled her nose, as if she had just smelled shit. "When are you going to clean out your potty mouth?" she inquired, mockingly.

Alessa put her arm around her. "Never," she said, smiling. "It's in my DNA. You should know that by now. It might do you some good if you dropped the F-bomb every now and then."

As the two women settled back, they shared great energy and a feeling of closeness and contentment. Alessa had loved all the friends she had made along the way, including Rhonda and Tasha, but her relationship with Ebby was different. This was one woman who had given her the sense of inner peace she needed to motivate her into being a better person. It was the same with Remo and Lucy. They continued to nourish her spirit with the hope that she could achieve more than she had ever imagined.

When the house was ready to be occupied, Alessa made a list of the homeless teenagers she thought they should invite in first. It was a harrowing task, because there were so many of them who needed help to get off the streets. When she showed Remo and Lucy the list, they agreed with all, but a few. Lucy was adamant about including one eighteen-year-old girl they knew, who had been beaten so brutally and regularly by her parents since she was a small child that her arms and legs were permanently scarred. The girl had related how her father would make her get under the shower so she would be wet before he beat her with his belt. The scars from her wounds would serve as an eternal reminder of the hell she'd escaped. Alessa gave in, because Lucy's reasoning was compelling. She knew she would have to take some other poor soul off the list to give this teen a place. It was a bitter sweet process.

The decision to help a selected few, while others remained on the streets, was hard. Alessa persuaded herself that it was better to help some than none at all, but it didn't make the process any easier. Remo chose not to intervene, as Alessa and Lucy prepared the list. He knew many of them, but didn't know all their stories or what had driven them to homelessness. Alessa knew everything there was to know about each girl. They opened up to her and she was the one they often went to, when they needed to cry or scream or laugh about their lives.

Alessa was relentless in her pursuit to make a difference in the hell she had escaped. Remo told her he didn't understand how she could keep going back to her past. In her place, he would have wanted to push those memories into the far recesses of his mind. Alessa explained that her experiences on being treated like an invisible being when she was homeless drove her to help those condemned to the streets to make their presence felt, to be seen. That was the key to Alessa's impact on them. When they were with her, they were seen. For some, that was the difference between hope and hopelessness.

Once the residents' list was settled, the three of them set out to talk with each of girls they had chosen. Meeting them, one by one, they explained what they were offering: the right to live in their row home for free, but on the condition that they worked or went to school. Those who worked could keep their earnings, as long as they could prove that they were saving at least fifty percent of what they earned. It took them the whole weekend to talk to the thirty six teenagers that would be the first residents. The girls all accepted the terms and conditions, which didn't surprise Alessa, since she had picked those with the most passionate desire to make a better life for themselves and, for some, their children.

On Sunday night, the three of them were eating dinner and talking excitedly about the upcoming week.

Suddenly, Alessa blurted out, "Oh my God!"

Remo and Lucy both looked at her, startled.

"It just came to me," Alessa said. "We need a name for our new home. We can call it the Outside Inn."

Lucy immediately sprang up from her chair. "I *love* that name, Alessa," she said enthusiastically. "Remo, can we get a sign to put on the house?"

"You bet we can!" he replied. Then he turned to Alessa "It's the perfect name for our new home. God, I love you, Alessa."

Lucy piped up, "Me too. I love you too!"

Alessa felt content as she finished her dinner. She couldn't have thought of a better way to end the weekend.

Remo had a sign made of wood that he hung over the threshold of the porch. It read: "Outside Inn." Over the next week, each of the selected teenagers and children arrived, some with nothing more than the clothes on their back. Remo beamed, realizing how lucky he was to be a part of this moment. Alessa couldn't have been happier. At the end of the first week, Ebby came over to meet the new residents. They all greeted her with smiles. Alessa had told them so much about her that by the time she arrived to meet them, it was as if they had known Ebby for a long time. And they trusted her, because Alessa did. Alessa, of course, was blind to how powerful her influence was on them.

Ebby had, in the meantime, worked with her contacts all over the city to furnish the apartments with used furniture. She even reached out to a friend in the hotel business who managed to get them beds and linens. None of the furniture was new or represented the latest in designs, but it was functional and made each of the apartments feel homey and lived in. Alessa and Remo had persuaded local grocers and store owners at the Italian Market on Ninth Street in South Philadelphia to donate day-old food that would normally be thrown away. This provided all six apartments with food in their refrigerators. Each group of six residents had the responsibility of cooking their own meals and cleaning their apartment. The whole house worked together to keep an eye on the children.

At ten that evening, Ebby and Alessa walked up to the top-floor apartment of the Outside Inn. Remo and Lucy were on the sofa watching a sitcom.

Remo looked up. "Long day. We're beat."

"It was long, but worth every minute," Alessa concluded.

Ebby stepped into the room and went over to Lucy to give her hugs and kisses. The child was always happy to see her.

"Hey Ebby, come into my bedroom," she invited. "Alessa bought me a goldfish. This is the *first* time in my whole life that I have a pet!"

Ebby laughed. "Yes, a goldfish is certainly worth waiting a whole lifetime for, even though for you, it's ten years. Hardly an old lady yet! Let's go see your new pet. Have you given it a name?"

Lucy proudly announced, "Yeah, I named her Ebster."

Ebby put her arm around her. "You named your first pet after me?"

In a very serious voice, Lucy explained, "Well, you're the one who helped Alessa and me. And now we are helping other kids."

Ebby hugged her. "Well, thanks, Lucy. I'm honored."

In the living room, Remo looked at Alessa with concern.

"What's wrong, Remo?" she asked.

Remo hesitated, feeling embarrassed and a little selfish. "Nothing is really *wrong*," he said. "I guess I'm just a little worried at the thought of not being able to spend enough time together. I mean, I never really thought about all these other people living with us."

Alessa slid across the sofa and sat on his lap. "Listen," she said, "they're all getting settled. In the next few days, they will get into their groove and our life will be back to normal."

Remo eyed her up. "Really?"

Alessa kissed the tip of his nose. "I promise."

Chapter Sixty-Three

————————————— ■ —————————————

True to Alessa's word, within a week, things were falling into place nicely. The older teens were taking care of the younger ones. Those who had found jobs, with Ebby's help, would buy food and bring it back to the apartments for the others who were going to school. That's the way it worked when you lived on the streets; everyone brought what they could to the table for the bigger group to share. It was no different at the Outside Inn.

In the meantime, Remo had been instrumental in arranging for donations of food and clothing from various businesses around the city. In his line of work, he met people from all walks of life and told everyone about the shelter on the chance that they would be interested in helping the residents in one way or another. Remo and Alessa had applied for subsidies to help pay for the utilities and it was quite amazing to what extent the various businesses were willing to help them. The Outside Inn was humming with happy teenagers, all eager to start a new life.

One evening, while Alessa was studying for an exam, Remo snuck into Lucy's room. Looking up from the book she was reading, she could tell that he had a secret he wanted to share and smiled at him. The two of them shared a special bond. Both loved Alessa and felt she had saved them, although she herself was convinced that it was Remo and Lucy who had saved her.

"You know Alessa's going to be twenty-one in a couple of weeks, don't you?" Remo asked her now. "I thought we could plan a surprise party for her in the backyard. We know thirty-six people who would be very keen to attend it—well, thirty-nine, if we include you, me and Ebby."

Lucy could hardly contain her excitement. "This is the greatest idea ever!" she squealed, then lowered her voice conspiratorially. "We can get balloons and buy a cake."

Remo chuckled. "Exactly what I was thinking," he said. "I can grill hot dogs and hamburgers."

Lucy kept her voice just above a whisper as she said, "Okay, I'll call Ebby. She'll help us."

Remo's expression softened as he said, "I was thinking of asking Alessa to marry me, but I wanted to check with you first to see what you thought of it."

Lucy gingerly slid into Remo's arms. "I think that's an even better idea than the party," she said. "You better tell Ebby, though. She's like her mom, you know."

Remo smiled. "Yes, I know. I was planning on calling her tomorrow from work, but only after making sure you were okay with it."

Just then, a horrifying thought popped into Lucy's head. "If you and Alessa have kids, will you still want me?" she asked, in a feeble voice.

Remo held her tight. "Of course we'll want you," he said, giving her a reassuring squeeze. "We will always want you. You are our daughter, Luce, the love of our lives. And no one, not even the kids we might eventually have, can ever take your place."

Appeased, Lucy went off to call Ebby about the party, promising not to disclose the secret about Remo's impending proposal.

Ebby was excited by the idea of the surprise party and ready to help in any way she could. It was decided that she would pick Lucy up from school the next day and take her to a local ice cream parlor, where they would plan the party.

Lucy shared their plans with Remo.

"How about if I show up tomorrow too, so I can ask Ebby what she thinks of my idea of proposing to Alessa?" he suggested.

Thrilled beyond belief, Lucy exclaimed, "Oh my God! I'm so excited! This is going to be so much fun!"

Remo watched in wonder as she expressed her joy over all the pleasant surprises they were planning for Alessa. He knew that no child could ever replace this one. Not for him and never for Alessa. There was a bond between the two girls that went far beyond a normal mother-daughter relationship. He felt like the luckiest man in the world.

The next day, he met Ebby and Lucy at the ice cream parlor as planned. The little girl was already digging into her vanilla ice cream with rainbow jimmies, when he arrived. Both Ebby and Lucy smiled at him as he approached the table, but noticed that he was looking a little nervous. He gave them each a warm hug and sat down.

Lucy pushed her bowl of ice cream toward him and asked, "You want some?"

"No Luce, I'm good. But thanks," he replied, pushing the bowl back in her direction.

Lucy and Ebby reviewed their plans for the cake and all the decorations they would buy. They were going to talk to a couple of girls at the Outside Inn to see if they could get Alessa out of the house for a few hours.

When they were finished, Remo said, "You two have everything figured out. Ebby, I wanted to give Alessa another surprise that I need to talk to you about."

"Sure," Ebby said. "What do you have in mind?"

Remo fidgeted in his seat like a two-year-old, nervous about Ebby's reaction. "I want to ask Alessa to marry me."

As the words sank in, Ebby's whole face glowed with a radiant smile. "I think that would be the perfect gift for Alessa!" she gushed.

"You're okay with it, then?" Remo inquired, still looking tense.

"Of course I'm okay with you marrying Alessa!" she laughed. "I appreciate your asking me about it first. However, it's really up to Alessa."

"I know, but what you think of the idea will be important to Alessa," he reminded her.

Ebby turned to Lucy. "So, Little Miss Thing, you knew all about this and didn't tell me?"

Lucy smiled a mischievous smile, outlined with a generous layer of ice cream. "It was Remo's secret and I promised him I wouldn't tell anyone about it."

Ebby laughed. "Well, good for you, Lucy! When did you get all grown-up?"

Lucy said in a voice that was dead serious, "Ebby, I'm going to be eleven, you know. I'm not a baby anymore."

At that, the adults laughed hysterically, with Lucy joining in. While Lucy was finishing her ice cream, Ebby's thoughts drifted off to Alessa. So much good had happened to her since they first met. She was genuinely happy for her and pleased to see that a once-broken person was on her feet and turning her life around, while helping others to do the same.

Good for Alessa! Ebby thought.

Chapter Sixty-Four

————————————■————————————

 It was mid-July and the heat was oppressive in the city, as Ebby, Remo and Lucy planned Alessa's party. Since Alessa's birthday fell mid-week that year, the party was scheduled for the Saturday night after. Her actual birthday was on a Wednesday and Remo and Lucy decided to mark the occasion by cooking dinner at home and sharing a small cake between the three of them. Lucy bought Alessa a new shirt, while Remo gave her a pair of shoes she had admired at a local store. Alessa enjoyed the small celebration and thanked them both for the dinner and the gifts. Ebby called her that night to wish her a happy birthday and apologized for not being able to drop in to see her.

With the weekend approaching, party related activities were in full gear. As planned earlier, a couple of the girls now living in the house took Alessa out on some pretext, giving Remo and Lucy the freedom to rush around and get things set up before they returned at six p.m. Ebby showed up to help right after Alessa had left. Remo had taken the liberty of inviting Alessa's brother and her two sisters to the party. Anthony was not going to be able to make it and since Anna lived in Arizona she had to decline. But Rosabella and Eva would be there and had planned to sleep over so they didn't have to drive back to Plymouth Meeting after the party.

By the time Alessa got back to the house, all was quiet. Lucy came sauntering down from the third floor and announced casually, "Remo is barbecuing for us. We're having hot dogs and hamburgers. He's out in the backyard setting up the grill and everything."

Happy to be freed from the mundane task of cooking dinner, Alessa gladly followed Lucy out the back door and was startled to hear people yell out in chorus, "Surprise!"

For a moment, she had no idea what was going on. Then she noticed the balloons and realized a birthday party had been organized for her.

She snatched Lucy up in her arms and hugged her, thanking her for being so sweet.

"Remo and Ebby did most of work," Lucy told her. "We've been planning for weeks!"

Alessa made her way through the crowd, hugging people as she went along, until she had finally reached Remo and Ebby. She put an arm around each of them and the three clung to each other in a close, loving embrace. Lucy, of course, had no intentions of being left out. Not long after, she nudged her way in and made herself an important part of the group hug.

Remo freed himself, turned and handed Alessa a glass. "Your first legal beer," he announced.

Alessa snatched it right out of his hand. "That's right," she said perkily. "I'm legal now. So watch out!"

The night wore on and everyone was having fun, when Lucy and Ebby brought out the birthday cake. As they all sang for the birthday girl, Alessa felt as if she were having an out-of-body experience. It was as if she were watching the scene happen, with someone else at its center. She had an overwhelming urge to giggle, as the joy of the moment washed over her. She had just blown out the candles on the cake, when Remo took her hand and knelt down next to her. For a moment, Alessa wondered if he had lost his mind or drunk too much. She started laughing at him, thinking that perhaps it was a huge joke. She panicked for a moment as his expression turned serious.

Before she had time to make sense of it all, Remo held out a ring and asked, "Alessa, will you marry me?"

Everyone had lapsed into silence. Even the background music seemed to have muted itself. Alessa's gaze went to Remo. It moved to Lucy and finally rested on Ebby. Then it returned to the beautiful ring in Remo's hand. Looking into his eyes, she declared, "Of course I will! I can't fucking believe this!"

All of the teenagers cheered. As she and Remo embraced, Alessa looked over at Rosabella. Her sister's smile told her that she loved her and was happy for her.

But before Alessa could make her way over to hug Rosabella, Remo said, "Wait! I have one more surprise." He got back down on one knee, but this time, in front of Lucy. "Luce," he said solemnly, "will you accept this ring as a token of our life together. You, me and Alessa?"

In his hand was a small gold ring with a beautiful blue sapphire—Lucy's birthstone—in the center. Lucy and Alessa both burst into tears. The child threw herself into Remo's arms and they clung to each other for what seemed an eternity, as everyone looked on happily.

Then Lucy took the ring from him and said, "I love you."

She turned to Alessa and threw her arms around her waist. The two clung to each other tightly, sharing a feeling of belonging. That night, after Lucy was in bed, Alessa kissed Remo passionately. She thanked him for her party and told him how excited she was about marrying him. She had one more thing to say to him and was worried for a moment that he might take it the wrong way. "Remo, I need to be sure of one thing," she began tentatively.

Remo let out an exaggerated sigh, "Now what?"

"You need to know that I will always love Lucy more than anyone else in the world," she told him. "She is my kindred spirit. It's important to me that you always love her most in the world too, even more than you love me."

Remo was amused by Alessa's seriousness. He knew how paranoid she was about ensuring the child's well-being. She always protected Lucy in the way she herself had secretly wished to be protected as a child.

Now he turned serious. "Of course I will. You know I love her."

"No. Not just love her," Alessa urged, "but love her more than anyone else in the world—always. This means, if you ever have to make a choice between Lucy and me, you will choose her."

Remo loved them both. He knew how special Lucy was. "Okay, it's a deal," he said in surrender.

Alessa relaxed as she slid up against him. She grabbed his ass mischievously. "You know something? That also means I will always choose her over you."

Remo playfully pushed her away. "Yes, Alessa, I know. Now can we get back to what we were doing?"

"By the way," she went on, "the ring you gave Lucy was about the coolest thing I've ever seen in my life. She really loves you."

Faking impatience with her, Remo said, "Yeah, I know. Thanks. Now, less talk and more action!" With that, he unzipped her jeans and slid his hand inside.

Chapter Sixty-Five

———————◼———————

"**I** need to call my parents today and tell them we're getting married," Remo announced the next morning at breakfast.

Alessa was shocked. "You mean, you didn't tell them before you asked me? What if they're mad at us?"

"No, I didn't tell them and they won't be mad. They know how I feel about you and I'm pretty sure they won't be all that surprised."

Lucy looked up from peeling a banana, "Don't forget to tell them how you asked me to be a part of your life. Tell them about the ring you gave me," she added.

Alessa realized how simple it all was for Lucy. She was so open and honest with them. It was hard to believe she would be eleven soon. Three years had passed by so quickly. Alessa felt as though they had been together all their lives, not just three short years from the time they had met. She reiterated the child's request. "Yeah, don't forget to tell them about Lucy."

"I won't," Remo moaned. "You two give me no credit at all."

While he was confident of his father's approval, Remo anticipated that his mother would be none too pleased by his decision to marry Alessa. And it was not simply because it was Alessa he was marrying. His mother would be pissed off that he had already proposed without keeping his parents updated on the developments in his personal life. She would treat it like a nasty surprise. Hannah hadn't changed her opinion of Alessa over the last year. In fact, she had become more deep-rooted in her view that she was the wrong woman for him. Intuitively, Remo knew that his mother was having a harder time letting him go than in accepting Alessa. He realized that she kept looking for reasons to justify her dislike of Alessa.

He called his father first.

Patrick was excited by the news and understood how much Alessa meant to his son. Then he asked, "Are you going to call your mother?"

"Do I have a choice?"

Patrick laughed. "No, not really."

Remo hesitated. "Any words of wisdom you could bestow upon me, old man?"

"Make it quick and painless," he sighed in response. "If you drag it out too long, you'll merely succeed in building up her anxiety and make her reaction to the news that much worse."

Remo hung up the phone and took a deep breath before dialing his mother.

Hannah brightened when she heard her son's voice. "Remo!" she exclaimed. "Hi son. How are you?"

"I'm good, Mom. I wanted to tell you that Alessa and I are getting married. I asked her last night and she said yes." There, he had put it all out on the table.

After an uncomfortably long silence, his mother said, "Well, if you think that's best. It's your life. I always thought you'd find someone who was more your type."

Annoyed, Remo asked, "Really? What's my type, Mom?"

"You know, someone with a better background and upbringing," she answered in a tight voice. "I mean, Alessa is a nice girl, but she's never going to set the world on fire."

With the disappointment palpable in his voice, Remo said, "Mom, Alessa is exactly my type. When you say, 'Set the world on fire,' I know you're talking about earning a lot of money. While Alessa may never earn a million dollars a year, she does things for people that you can't put a price on. She sets the world on fire with the goodness in her heart. I want you to be happy for me. This is a great time in my life and I need your support."

Hannah softened. "Okay. I can do that. Shall I call her to discuss wedding arrangements? Did you pick a date?"

Now desperate to get off the phone, Remo answered, "No we haven't picked a date yet. Why don't I have Alessa call you once we do pick one? In the meantime, do you think you could call her and congratulate her? She's not stupid, Mom. It's obvious how you feel about her."

Hannah surrendered. "Okay, fine. I will call her later today. I just hope you're making the right decision."

As promised, Hannah called Alessa later that afternoon. "Hello Alessa, this is Hannah," she said.

Alessa's palms instantly broke out in a sweat. "Hi Hannah. Remo isn't here right now. Do you want him to call you when he gets home?"

Hannah's voice was devoid of emotion. "No. Actually, I was calling to congratulate you on your engagement to my son. I wanted to let you know that once you two pick a date, you and I can start planning the wedding. Have you told your mother yet?"

Alessa told her she hadn't and offered no explanations.

Unable to keep calm, Hannah allowed her animosity to spill out. "Why haven't you told your mother? The first thing most girls do in a situation like this is call their mother to let them know."

Alessa tried to defend herself without being rude. "Hannah, it's complicated," she explained politely. "I would discuss this with you right now, but I have to run or I'll be late for class. Thanks for calling."

After Alessa hung up the phone, she felt annoyed at Hannah for judging her so harshly. She was also self-conscious and embarrassed about not sharing the kind of relationship with Caterina that most daughters took for granted. Alessa wasn't one who needed everyone to like her, but she just couldn't understand why Hannah went out of her way to dislike her. *Fuck it*, she thought, *I'll talk to Remo about it later.*

But try as she might, she couldn't dismiss Hannah from her mind and was bothered all day long over their phone conversation. It gnawed at her like a deep, persistent pain. That night, she told Remo about her conversation with his mother. She could see he was hurt, but wasn't sure if it was because his mother was a bitch or because she herself couldn't just go with the flow.

Finally, he said, "Look, we're all going to be family now and you two will need to learn how to get along. I know my mother isn't easy to deal with when it comes to me. You need to understand that she's just being protective, like you are with Lucy."

Alessa lost her temper. "Yeah, I get that," she said angrily, "but I've done nothing to make her feel defensive about you. She treats me like a piece of shit, because she thinks you're too good for me. You know it and so do I. Let's stop the bullshit and just get it out there. Truthfully, Remo, I don't give a fuck what your mom thinks about me. I just don't want you to expect me to pretend that everything is rosy."

Remo stood up and began pacing the living room. "Okay, fine. If you want to hate my mother, then hate my mother! What can I say?"

Alessa stomped out of the room, but not before saying, "For your information, it's the other way around. I don't hate your mother; she hates me."

An hour later, Remo went back into the bedroom. He sat down next to Alessa and said, "Here's the deal. I love my mom. She was a good mother and has done a lot for me. She will never change her mind about you. Honestly, I don't think it's you. It would have been the same with any woman I decided to marry. She feels like she's losing me. I'm not going to try to change her mind. If she can't see how great you are, then that's her loss. Either way, I need us all to get along. I'm asking you to be the bigger person here. I'm asking you to just kill her with kindness."

"Okay," Alessa said. "I'll try my best. I'll swallow all the shit she dishes out to me, but remember: I'm doing it entirely for you, because you asked and not for any other reason."

Remo reached out, lifted her dress and laid her back on the bed. Alessa let herself melt into him. She enjoyed making love to him, craved it, even. Because of the love they shared, their sex life was intense. Alessa's past sexual experience also helped to keep things exciting. When Remo teased her that no one gave head better than she did, she would retort, "I was a young learner, remember? At least one good thing came from it."

Alessa wasn't afraid to experiment with sex. She was often the aggressor. Not that Remo ever complained. What man in his right mind and with a set of balls would complain? Alessa loved the way he touched her. She felt suspended in midair and her skin was covered in goose bumps, as she felt the warmth of his tongue against her flesh and his strong fingers that could be so gentle find their way inside her. Remo was an extremely evolved sexual being and she reciprocated his passion.

Chapter Sixty-Six

T he following Saturday night, Remo and Alessa drove out to see Remo's parents, with Lucy in tow, supposedly to celebrate their engagement. Patrick and Hannah were excited for their son. In fact, Remo's father was excited for them all. Hannah, though, while excited about the wedding, was not necessarily enthused by her son's choice of bride. When she shared her cynical opinion of Alessa with her husband, he had warned her that if she continued down this path, she would lose her son forever. Hannah didn't care what Patrick thought. She was convinced that Alessa was not the right girl for Remo. She suspected that by latching onto her son, the girl had found herself a knight in shining armor. Alessa, she feared, came with too much baggage and their relationship would be harmful for Remo in the long run. The thought of the young woman giving her a grandchild made her cringe with distaste.

Hannah carelessly chose to overlook the fact that Remo had never really been happy until he met Alessa. If she had been honest with herself, Hannah would have acknowledged that Alessa had brought something different, something better into Remo's life.

She and Patrick were in the kitchen when the three of them arrived. Hannah rushed over to give Remo a hug. She turned to Lucy next, as the child held up her hand to show off the ring Remo had given her. Finally, she turned to Alessa. Alessa put on her brightest smile and humbly greeted Hannah who said, "Let me see the ring," Hannah said rather assertively.

She was surprised at the size and clarity of the diamond and knew that Remo had paid a lot of money for the ring, a fact that annoyed her deeply. She was against her son spending his hard earned money on a girl who didn't deserve him in the first place.

She asked Alessa, "How big is the diamond?"

Alessa was quite ignorant of and oblivious to these details. She turned to look at Remo in bewilderment.

"It's a carat," he said nonchalantly.

Hannah turned to him. "Well, it's just beautiful. The clarity of the diamond is terrific. You must have paid a lot of money for it. Do you think that was really necessary?"

Remo stiffened from the blow. "It doesn't matter how much money it cost, Mom," he said, trying to sound unruffled. "The jeweler said it was a pretty clear diamond and the price was reasonable."

As Patrick watched the exchange, tension tightened his gut. He could see Alessa visibly recoiling from the verbal attack, her arms crossed over her chest, her shoulders slumped and her eyes fixed on the floor. He could tell she wanted to shrivel up and die. But Patrick knew Alessa was the real thing. When his wife had asked her about the size of the diamond, Alessa had looked as if she were going to shit in her pants. She obviously had no idea how to answer such questions. Patrick knew Alessa couldn't have cared less if Remo had bought her a diamond chip instead. It was all the same to her. She wasn't worried about the size of the ring; she was marrying their son because she loved him.

Unlike Hannah, Patrick had noticed a change in Remo over the past year since he met Alessa. His son had grown and matured in a way that made him proud. He had bought a house to help get homeless people off the streets and accepted Lucy as his own flesh and blood. Patrick wondered why Hannah had become so bitter. After all, Remo was an adopted son. When Patrick and Hannah knew for certain that they couldn't have children of their own, it was Hannah who had convinced him that they should adopt. She had taught Remo to treat everyone equally, regardless of the person's background. She would say, "We're all just people and we should always help each other. Some people are just less fortunate than others, but we all have feelings, just the same."

Patrick missed the old Hannah. He felt sorry for Alessa now, as she stood awkwardly, waiting for the topic of conversation to change.

"As Remo said," Patrick intervened, "who cares how much he paid for the ring? When you're in love, it's worth every cent."

As Alessa's embarrassment slowly turned to anger, her face flushed. She wished the conversation would come to an end. Hannah had just told Remo she wasn't worth giving an expensive ring to, hadn't she? Alessa made a mental note: *first log of shit eaten; let's see how many I can swallow tonight before I hurl.*

Throughout dinner, father and son did most of the talking.

Finally, Hannah butted in. "Enough about hockey and the Flyers! Can we talk about the wedding now?"

Remo looked over at Alessa and noted that her eyes were locked down on her plate, as if she hadn't heard a word his mother had uttered. "Mom," he said, "we're thinking about something really small. We decided we'd have just you and Dad, Alessa's sister, Rosabella, Ebby and a couple of our friends. And we don't plan to wait a long time either. We thought we would get married in September."

"I picked September, because that's my birthday month and they thought it was a great idea," Lucy said proudly.

"I always thought September was a good month for weddings, but now that I know Lucy was born in September, I think it's a perfect month!" Patrick said with enthusiasm.

Unable to hide her disgust, Hannah pushed her plate away. Waving the fork she still held in her hand, she asked, "What's the rush? September is only two months away. Remo, I plan to have a few more guests at the wedding, other than the ones you just mentioned. Dad and I would like to invite some of our friends. I thought we could have it here in the backyard."

Remo looked at Alessa for some sign of approval. She, on her part, didn't want him to feel torn between his mother and her. She only wanted him to be happy. She could see how desperately he was trying to achieve a balance between his feelings for her and his devotion to his mother. He so obviously wanted to please them both. The truth was, Alessa couldn't have cared less if there was a wedding at all. She would have been just as happy to go to a justice of the peace and have a private celebration afterward. This ongoing battle just wasn't important to her.

"Hannah," she said, "we didn't give it that much thought, to be honest. If you'd like to have something here, I think that would be very nice."

Hannah wore her victory smile as she turned to Remo and said, "I'll do everything, son. You won't have to worry about a thing."

"That's great, Mom. Thanks," he replied, retreating from the earlier debate with relief. "Can you make sure Alessa has a say in some of this planning, since it is her wedding too?"

Hannah's lips drew together in a tight line, as if she were a child refusing to eat her food. "Of course I will," she told him. "She will need to pick the colors and we can work together on a menu."

Patrick watched his wife. He could tell she was happy because she was getting her way. But it hadn't escaped him either that Alessa had just surrendered to her future mother-in-law for the sake of maintaining peace, a fact that didn't appear to bother his wife at all. He knew Alessa had Remo's best interests at heart. It didn't surprise him that the girl had no passion for the things that were so important to Hannah. Patrick knew Alessa was a good egg, despite her sordid past, someone his son was lucky to have found.

As Hannah and Remo discussed the guest list, Patrick leaned over and nudged Alessa with his elbow. Surprised, but glad to have her future father-in-law's support, she knew she had made the right decision. Her spirits instantly lifted. Catching the silent and barely noticeable exchange between his father and Alessa, Remo was reassured that things would be fine.

Lucy broke into Alessa's thoughts by leaning over and asking her, "Alessa, can our color for the wedding be purple?"

Alessa laughed. "Of course, Luce," she replied, beaming. "Purple *is* our favorite color."

Lucy smiled back. "Yeah. Okay, we're good now."

Chapter Sixty-Seven

The rest of July flew by, as Alessa prepared for her final exams and went through the motions of planning her wedding with Hannah. She really didn't care who, how, where or when. So it was easy to let Remo's mother have her way. By early August, Hannah had completed the guest list. It covered everyone, starting from some of their close friends to casual acquaintances, and went up to a total of 100 people.

The night before Hannah was due to go to the printer for invitations, she called Alessa to finalize the list.

"Hi Alessa, this is Hannah," she said. "I'm going to the printer tomorrow for the invitations. I will need the addresses of your mom, your brother and your sisters. Do you have any other relatives we should be inviting?"

Alessa sighed heavily. She had known this topic of conversation would eventually come up again. "Actually, Hannah," she said, trying not to sound tense, "I'm only inviting my sister, Rosabella. I can give you her address."

Hannah, who had been waiting for this very moment, jumped at the opportunity. "Are you saying you're not inviting your own mother, Alessa?"

Alessa's patience was beginning to wear thin, "Yes, Hannah, that's right," she said crisply. "I don't speak to my mother. I've only talked to her once in the last four and a half years and it wasn't very pleasant."

Hannah was like a dog with a bone. "Alessa," she said in a voice reeking of disapproval, "no matter what happened between the two of you, she is still your *mother*. I couldn't imagine getting married without my mother being there at my wedding. What exactly happened between the two of you?"

The frustration was clear in Alessa's voice as she tried to close the subject. "It's a long, complicated story. For now, let's just leave it alone."

Hannah was furious at being blown off in this manner. "Alessa," she said in a harsh tone, "you are about to marry my son. I have a right to know what's going on. It's just unacceptable to me that you are being so disrespectful to your mother. Is this how you'll try to persuade Remo to treat me after you're married?"

Ding! Ding! Ding! Hannah had pushed Alessa's buttons and now there was no stopping the flood that had been dammed for a long time.

"Hannah," she said, throwing caution to the wind, "if you really need to know, I was raped, when I was seven years old, by my uncle who lived with us. When I told my mother about it, she didn't believe me. She allowed it to happen over and over again in her house. I finally ran away from home when I was sixteen years old. I went back a couple of months ago when my father died and found my mother to be the same heathen she had been when I left. There! Is that reason enough by your standards to justify not inviting her?"

Hannah was shocked. "Alessa, I can't believe what I'm hearing!" she exclaimed. "I should have been told about all of this before. I need to go now."

Even before Alessa hung up the phone, she knew that Hannah would call Remo and tell him in no uncertain terms that he was out of his fucking mind for deciding to marry her. Maybe he was making a mistake, Alessa told herself. After all, she wasn't exactly an innocent blushing, bride. She wasn't going to worry about Hannah anymore, though. She knew Remo would make his own decisions and she would let the chips fall where they may.

Alessa called Ebby to tell her what had just happened between Hannah and her. Ebby merely reinforced her own impression: first, there was no way Alessa would be able to change her future mother-in-law's opinion of her and second, while Remo loved his mother, he would make his own decisions.

Once their phone conversation ended, Ebby sat down at her kitchen table, wondering what made people like Hannah presume they were in a position to judge others. Meanwhile, Alessa went back to studying. Lucy was still over at a friend's house when Remo came home a few hours later. He walked over to Alessa and wrapped her in a warm, lingering embrace and he felt the tension in her body. He wasn't sure if she was so tightly wound up from her upcoming exams or it had something to do with her earlier conversation with his mother.

"How was your day?" he asked.

Alessa looked at him knowingly. "Well, aside from studying for exams, I talked to your mom today. I can tell from that look on your face that you did too."

Remo kissed her neck. "Ah hmm... So I see," he murmured. "I understand you told her about your uncle and your mother?"

Becoming aroused as he continued to kiss her neck, she said, "Ah hmm... I don't think I won her over."

Remembering that Lucy would be away for at least another couple of hours, Remo slid his strong, smooth hand under her shirt. Instantly excited, Alessa removed his shirt. She kissed his chest as he slowly took her shirt off and unsnapped her bra. Her nipples were hard. He bent to close his mouth over one, while unzipping her pants. Then he dropped to his knees and moved his lips down her body, kissing her inner thighs. Slowly, he removed her panties. Then his tongue found itself between her legs. She arched back against the kitchen table and he lifted her gently until she was lying flat on her back. His tongue continued to play between her legs and Alessa thought she would explode from the sensations it was causing within her.

Remo paused just long enough to make her want him more than the air she breathed. She reached out and grasped him, clinging tight, her body begging him to continue. As his fingers slid inside her, he leaned over her naked body and kissed her deeply and passionately. He licked her slowly from neck to navel and back down between her legs again till he was sure she couldn't contain her desperation. Then he thrust himself inside her. By this time, they were both so aroused that it only lasted a few minutes before they collapsed in a heap on the kitchen table.

After a moment, Alessa murmured softly, "Well, I guess I don't need to ask you what you said to your mother."

He nibbled on her ear. "Nope," he whispered. "That about says it all."

She ran her hand over his muscular abdomen. "You're the hottest man on earth. God, you turn me on!"

"You ain't so bad yourself," he quipped.

As they got dressed, they talked about their day. Hand in hand, they walked over to the kitchen counter to prepare dinner together. Alessa was content that no further words needed to be exchanged about Hannah. Remo had handled it and his mother knew his mind was made up. As Alessa was cleaning the lettuce at the sink, Remo walked up from behind and wrapped his arms around her waist.

"You're awful sexy the way you clean lettuce!"

Alessa laughed and went on with her chore.

"I love you, Alessa," Remo said. "I've never loved anyone in my life the way I love you."

Alessa turned to face him. Of course they had told each other many times before that they loved one another, but there was something pure and sincere in his voice this time.

"You okay?" she asked him.

"I'm better than okay," he replied, then bent down and kissed her gently.

"I love you too, Remo. I am a very lucky woman."

Remo turned the burners off on the stove and Alessa abandoned the lettuce in the sink. They held each other close, as they headed to their bedroom for Round Two.

Chapter Sixty-Eight

Alessa was relieved to finish her exams the following week. Then she started thinking about the wedding. It was early August and she would be getting married in less than a month. On a sunny Saturday morning, she was eating breakfast with Remo, when Lucy stumbled into the kitchen. Still half asleep, she asked, "What are we doing today?"

Alessa looked up from her breakfast, "Well, I thought we would go shopping for wedding dresses today."

Thrilled, Lucy squealed, "I can't wait! What time are we going?"

"We should be ready to leave at noon, okay?"

The child looked at the clock on the wall. It was only 8.30 a.m. "Okay, I'll be ready."

Lucy was going to be Alessa's maid of honor. Two of the girls who lived in the apartments below that Alessa was closest with had been chosen as her bridesmaids. One of the girls was seventeen years old. When she was fifteen, she had announced to her parents that she was gay. They had responded by beating her, claiming that God wanted them to beat the devil out of her body. When she recovered from the beating a few weeks later and told them it had made no difference and she was still gay, they had thrown her out of their home and told her to go live in the devil's playground with the other sinners. They were convinced she would be exiled to hell forever, never to see or know God. She was a sweet girl who was clear about her sexuality, but very confused about people and life in general. She had had a very religious, but stable childhood and when her parents threw her out, she had suddenly felt as if she knew nothing at all, either about people or about love. She had taken a bus into Philadelphia and had been living on the streets until the Outside Inn opened.

The other girl who had been selected as a bridesmaid was sixteen-years-old and had been severely abused as a child. Her mother had died of breast cancer when the girl was only four- years-old and she had been raised in a house full of men. The youngest of her siblings, she had been raped by every one of her family members—starting from her father to her three older brothers. She wore scars from cigarette burns on her arms and legs, all inflicted by her father. The men would also torment her with taunts about her being ugly and retarded. For a time, she actually believed she was mentally unstable. The day after one of her brothers let his friend have sex with her for an ounce of pot, she fled her home, knowing that she would never return.

Faced with the slimmest of chances, both girls, like Alessa, had found a way out of their predicament. These were the typical stories of many homeless teens. However, to survive such abuse without developing a heart of stone was rare. Usually, and understandably, these young teens were wary and on the defensive, always apprehensive that the world was out to hurt them. Like Alessa, though, both girls had come through, nurturing the hope that there were people with the capacity to love and care for other human beings. It was this thread of hope shared by all three that had made the girls instant friends.

Alessa first looked for Lucy's dress in the bridal shop, finding an inexpensive purple and white gown that was just the right style for an *almost* eleven-year-old. Satisfied at having made her first sale, the saleswoman showed them the matching gown for the bridesmaids. These dresses were also purple and white, but with variations to distinguish the maid of honor from the bridesmaids. None of the girls were picky. Their mission was to find dresses that looked good on them and cost as little money as possible.

Finally, the attention was focused on Alessa. The saleswoman sized her up and said, "I have a couple of dresses I think would be perfect for you."

The woman came out with three dresses and led Alessa to the dressing room. The first was in a mermaid style, form-fitting from the bust to the knees and flaring out at the bottom. The second was in silk, with a full lace overlay. It had a halter neckline and a straight fit down to the floor. Both dresses were beautiful and Alessa realized she and the girls might have a hard time deciding between them. She knew that if left to her, she would pick the cheaper one. The third dress had a heart-shaped bodice in satin that narrowed down to her navel. The skirt consisted of layer upon layer of the softest white tulle studded with small pearls and clear stones. The first two dresses had been stunning, but when Alessa put the third dress on, she felt as if she were in a fairy tale. She had never worn anything as beautiful and the dress looked absolutely perfect on her. The stones caught the light as she moved, creating an angelic effect.

The saleswoman studied her carefully before she spoke. "Yes," she sighed with contentment, "I knew this would be the right one."

When Alessa came out and posed for the girls, they gazed at her with their mouths open. None of them had ever seen a dress so elegantly simple, yet so exceptional.

Alessa looked at the saleswoman. "How much is it?" she asked tentatively.

The saleswoman inquired, "Well, is that the one you really like?"

Alessa hesitated, not wanting to commit to a dress she couldn't afford. "Yes, I love it," she replied. "But I need to know how much it costs."

The saleswoman seemed oblivious to her client's concern about the price. "It doesn't matter how much it costs," she replied merrily, then added, "because your new father-in-law, Patrick, is buying it for you. In fact, this is the very dress he thought would be perfect for you. He said it was going to be his gift to welcome his new daughter into the family."

Alessa began to cry and the others were too moved to hold back their tears. Lucy, however, looked a little disappointed until the saleswoman turned to her and said, "While Patrick didn't pick your dress for you, he said, he wanted to buy whatever you picked as a gift for his new granddaughter."

The child was instantly elated at the thought that Patrick had remembered her. Now she felt accepted.

When the girls got back to the car, Alessa looked over at Remo, who was pretending to be unaware of their presence, and said, "You knew, didn't you? That's why you brought us here."

Remo slid his hand down her arm. "Of course I knew," he smiled. "It was my dad's idea, though. He wanted to do something special for you and Lucy. He told me what he had done and where I was to take you. He loves you both, you know, and is happy for all of us."

When they got home, Alessa immediately called Patrick. The sound of his voice, as he answered the phone, made her feel connected to him. For the first time in her life, she felt as if she had a father.

"Hello Patrick," she said, then overcome by emotion, lapsed into silence.

Remo's father could feel how moved she was. He waited for her to speak again.

"Patrick," she began again, "I wanted to thank you for buying my dress and Lucy's. I had never expected that and neither had she. I can't describe how much it means to us."

Patrick choked up. After a small silence, he managed to say, "You're welcome, Alessa. I never had a daughter and now I do. Even better, I have a daughter who makes my son happy. You're a part of our family and I wanted to welcome you the right way. I realize things are hard for you with Hannah, but even she can't deny how happy Remo is with you and Lucy. Just keep that in mind the next time she says something crazy."

They both laughed at his comment about Hannah, knowing quite well that she was unlikely to change her views about Alessa and there would always be tension between them.

After Alessa had hung up the phone, she turned to Remo and wrapped her arms around him tightly.

He felt the turmoil within her and asked, "What's wrong?"

Tears streamed down her cheeks as she clung to him. After she had calmed down a bit, she explained, "Nothing's wrong. It's just that I never really had a dad and yours makes me feel so special. I'm crying because I'm happy. I am so happy!"

Remo held her and smiled at Lucy, who watched contentedly as the woman she loved the most in the world proclaimed her happiness.

"What do you say, Luce," Remo said, catching her eye, "should we go celebrate with some ice cream?"

Lucy jumped up at once. "Yeah, man!" she replied enthusiastically. "Let's go. I want vanilla with rainbow jimmies."

Alessa looked at her with a grin. "Of course you do! That's your favorite," she remarked.

Lucy skipped all the way to the car, with the two adults following close behind. Alessa thought about the events of the day and said to herself, "This was a good fuckin' day!"

Chapter Sixty-Nine

As the wedding day drew near, Alessa became increasingly nervous. It wasn't the prospect of marrying Remo that heightened her tension, but the thought of all the people who would be present at her wedding, watching her every step. The rehearsal dinner was in two days and they were all excited. They would be going to the church first. Afterward, they would have dinner at the Seven Stars Inn in Phoenixville. The restaurant had been in business since 1736 and it was there that George Washington and his army had retreated after the Battle of Brandywine. Remo had gone there once a year all through his childhood and he was excited about Alessa and Lucy dining with him at a place that had always been so special for him. He raved about the food and the history of the old restaurant that had sheltered many travelers from the time it had opened.

The rehearsal dinner was everything Remo had hoped it would be. They drove back to Philadelphia at the end of the night, bellies full and contentment in the air. They were happy and in love.

The next morning, they packed the car with all their wedding apparel and drove out to Patrick and Hannah's home. The florist and caterer were already scurrying about, getting things ready, when they arrived. As promised by Hannah, the color purple was throughout the house and the backyard. They had rented a large tent that was beautifully draped with fabric in purple, white and silver. Hannah was in all her glory, not because Remo was marrying Alessa, but because she loved to throw parties and this was going to be the ultimate party. As the guests began to arrive, Alessa, Lucy, Ebby and the bridesmaids climbed the stairs to the guest bedroom to get dressed. Alessa focused on getting Lucy ready first. When she had finished, she looked at Ebby who was in tears already.

"I can't believe you're crying already" Alessa exclaimed. "You're a nut job!"

Ebby told Lucy how beautiful she looked and the child felt very special as she primped before the full-length mirror. Ebby then turned to Alessa and said, "Well, you're next. Let's go, blushing bride!"

Alessa laughed. "Oh, please!" she said, "I'll probably burn in hell for wearing white on my wedding day. I'm hardly a blushing bride."

Ebby put an arm around her and led her further into the room where the wedding dress was hanging. After Alessa had put on her dress and her makeup was done, Ebby turned to her.

"I have something for you," she said. "Every bride needs something old, something new, something borrowed and something blue." She reached inside her purse and pulled out a strand of pearls. "These belonged to my mother. I wore them on my wedding day just as she had worn them on hers. So this is your 'something old'." Then she pulled out a small, wrapped box and handed it to Alessa who opened it and gazed in wonder at the small pearl earrings that lay inside.

"These are my gift to you—your 'something new'," Ebby said.

As rehearsed, Lucy stepped up to Alessa and took the blue sapphire ring Remo had given her off her finger. "And this," she said, holding out the ring, "is something borrowed and something blue."

Alessa felt as though she were a normal person now, someone other than herself. She looked from Ebby to Lucy and realized, once again, how lucky she was to have these two people in her life. She hugged them both. "Thank you," she said earnestly. "I love you both so much. I never want to lose this feeling. I wish I could feel this happy every day of my life."

Realizing she was close to tears again, Ebby got a hold on herself, straightened her shoulders and said briskly, "We better get going. They'll be starting in five minutes."

As instructed by his mother and her caddy girlfriends, Remo was already outside, waiting in the tent. "It's bad luck to see the bride before the wedding," they had warned him.

When Alessa came down the stairs in her bridal dress, even Hannah was taken aback by how beautiful she looked. The dress was perfect, she thought, examining it critically, something she would have picked herself. Patrick smiled up at the girls and as Alessa's eyes met his, she silently mouthed, "Thank you."

He gave her a slight nod of acknowledgement and appreciation, that spoke volumes about their new relationship, and turned to tell Lucy how gorgeous she looked.

For Alessa, it would be a moment frozen in time. Miraculously, she no longer felt nervous. On the contrary, she was charged with excitement and hope now.

Hannah's voice cut into her reverie. "Let's go. They're ready for you, Alessa."

Alessa reached the entrance to the tent, then stood aside, realizing there was no one to give her away. How pathetic, she thought, the old feelings of inadequacy threatening to come back and plague her.

Suddenly, Patrick was by her side. "I would consider it an honor, if I could walk you down the aisle," he whispered in her ear.

Alessa was grateful to be rescued. Hannah, on the other hand, visibly cringed. When Remo saw his father approaching him with Alessa on his arm, he was proud of them both. At that moment, he believed that they could all be one happy family. It moved him deeply to observe how beautiful his bride was and how affectionate his father was being to her.

The reception was fun and they all drank and danced. Alessa recognized that while Hannah could be a real bitch when she didn't get her way, she certainly knew how to throw a great party.

Although Alessa and Remo couldn't afford a honeymoon, they did take off the week following the wedding to hang out with each other. They had received 15,000 dollars in cash as wedding gifts from the people who attended the wedding and they decided to put it aside so that eventually, they would be able to buy another house for themselves to live in—some day.

One morning, midweek, when Remo and Alessa were sitting together on the front porch, drinking their coffee, they were surprised by the arrival of an apparently unknown woman. Watching her approach, Alessa assumed, at first, that she was just another of the many homeless people who often stopped by for something to eat or to use the bathroom. The woman seemed to be in her twenties and looked dazed. As she drew closer, however, Alessa realized that it was Sara, the young girl who had taken her to live with the other homeless teens when she found her standing outside the train station three years ago. Alessa knew full well that if it hadn't been for Sara, she would never have found Lucy. She sprang up from her chair and met the other girl midway. Alessa hadn't seen Sara since she had left with the others to spend the winter in Florida. The girl looked weathered and worn. By the way she was dressed, Alessa could tell she had been hooking herself. The dark circles around Sara's eyes and her withdrawn look also told her that she was using hard drugs. Alessa remembered that look only too clearly. It was the same one she had seen on Harlin's face in the last months before she fled from him.

Chapter Seventy

———————■———————

Alessa reached out to her right away. "Hi Sara!" she said warmly. "How have you been?"

"Do I know you?" the other girl asked, looking up at her with a vacant expression.

Slightly annoyed, but concerned, all the same, Alessa said, "It's me, Alessa. Remember, how we met at the train station and you took me to live under the bridge near Thirtieth Street Station?"

Sara sidestepped and would have fallen, but caught herself just in time. "Oh yeah," she said, apparently thinking hard to extract the memory from her foggy brain. "Yeah, I remember you. You and that little girl you took care of."

Alessa was overwhelmed with sadness at what Sara's life had become. This was the person who had befriended her in her hour of need and was indirectly responsible for why she was here today with Remo and Lucy, living the life she had dreamed of.

"Yeah, Sara, that's right," she said gently. "It's me, Alessa. The little girl was Lucy. She's still with me."

Sara suddenly dropped to her knees and threw up at Alessa's feet. Remo rushed over to help her up and together, they led the girl into their apartment. Alessa guided her into the bathroom and helped her take a shower. Between the vomit and the smell of filth from not showering for God knew how long, Sara was almost too ripe to be near. When Alessa helped her undress, she noticed all the track marks in her arms and legs.

"What kind of drugs are you shooting, Sara?" she asked, her face twisted with pity.

The girl's head dropped back, as though she were a bobble head, until she had regained enough control for her neck to be able to support her head again. Trying very hard to focus on Alessa, she said, "Yeah, I like heroin.

You got any, man? Listen, I ain't got no money, but I'll fuck you or your guy in exchange for some. I'll fuck you both at the same time, if you want. I give great fucking head. It doesn't matter to me. It can be a guy or a chick. You wanna fuck?"

Alessa eyes filled up. "No Sara, I don't want to fuck. Let's just get you cleaned up and you can eat something afterward."

Sara smiled a drugged-up, doped-out smile, "Hey man, whatever you say...*whatever* you want to do. You want to pay me to take some pictures of me in the shower?"

Alessa lost her temper. "No, what the fuck, Sara!" she snapped. "Just take a fucking shower!"

Startled by the vehemence of her response, Sara stepped into the shower obediently. When she had finished, she pulled the shower curtain back and looked at Alessa.

"Man, that felt so fucking good!" she exclaimed. "What did you say your name was?"

Agitated now, Alessa replied, enunciating each word carefully, "My name is Alessa and you know me. We've met before. You helped me a long time ago, when I had nowhere to sleep. Remember?"

Sara's grip on her towel slackened and the towel dropped to the floor. She was now standing naked in front of Alessa. It was quite obvious that Sara had had a rough life over the last three years. There were bruises between her legs and bite marks around her breasts.

"Nah, I don't remember you," Sara countered. "Maybe if you could loan me some money and I could get some dope with it, I would remember."

Alessa gave up and decided to feed Sara and let her sleep on the sofa. Maybe after some sleep, she would remember who Alessa was. Maybe the sight of Lucy would act as a catalyst. She had forgotten about Lucy. Alessa's stomach twisted, thinking of how the child might be affected when she came to know what had become of Sara. Although she was accustomed to being around drug users—after all, many of the homeless people they talked to used drugs—Lucy might be utterly disheartened to see Sara in this condition, precisely because it was Sara. Alessa decided to meet the child at school and talk to her about Sara before she came home. She wanted Lucy to make her own decision about seeing her old street friend.

After Alessa had gotten Sara into clean clothes, she led her into the kitchen. Remo was already making her scrambled eggs and toast. He had also made fresh coffee, hoping it would speed up the sobering process. Alessa sat with Sara as she tried to eat. She would pick up a shaky forkful and occasionally fail to deliver it to her mouth, spilling it, instead, on the floor. But she began to sober up ever so slightly, as the minutes went by. When she had finished eating, Alessa led her over to the sofa and told her to try and get some sleep. As soon as she had Sara as settled as possible, Alessa kissed Remo and left to get Lucy from school.

When Lucy saw her waiting outside the school, she asked, "What's wrong? Did something happen?"

Alessa explained how Sara had shown up at the house and that she was stoned on heroin. Lucy looked at her with the wisdom of a hundred-year-old woman. "So, you're worried how I will react to her?" she asked. "I mean, I feel bad for Sara and I still like her, but it's not like she scares me or anything. We know lots of homeless people who do drugs. It's fine. Did she remember you?"

Alessa shook her head. "No, she keeps asking me my name. We need to get back now. I left Remo there with her alone and she is really whacked out."

The moment they entered the apartment, Alessa saw Lucy take a deep breath and steel herself for the worst, growing into a different person in front of her eyes. Sara was sitting up on the sofa trying to convince Remo she would give him head in exchange for "a few bucks".

Lucy walked over to her and touched her arm. "Hi Sara," she said softly.

"Hey, I know you, don't I?" Sara asked. "You're that little girl that used to live with us, right?"

Lucy sat down next to her.

"Hey, little sister, you got any money you can lend me?" Sara went on. "This dude over here," she said pointing to Remo, "doesn't want to pay for n-o-t-h-i-n-g that I have to offer him! He's a real, fucking drag!"

Lucy stared at Sara with utter disgust, waiting hopefully for the person she once knew to emerge. But after a while she accepted that the real Sara wasn't in there anymore. At least, not right now.

Lucy turned to Alessa. "I think we should call Ebby and see if we can get her into a rehab," she said, trying to be practical.

Alessa patted the child on the back. She hadn't thought of it, but Lucy was right. There was no way they would be able to help Sara, until she got clean. In the state she was in now, Alessa thought she was repulsive. At the same time, she felt bad for her, knowing how hard it was to live on the streets. She understood why girls went into prostitution to survive, but was extremely disappointed Sara had turned to drugs. Alessa knew that most of the girls at the go-go clubs used drugs. Many of them had confided in her that if they didn't, they could never get on stage and let "all those pigs" grope them. Alessa had never needed to use drugs. She had grown up having sex, with nothing to numb her body or her mind. Maybe she had been lucky, she thought. Lucky to have been broken in, before her mind was fully developed, so that she had looked upon it as just a way of life.

Chapter Seventy-One

———————————————◼———————————————

Alessa called Ebby that evening to tell her what was going on. Ebby had warned her that drug addicts could be very unpredictable and that she should be careful around Sara. In the meantime, she assured Alessa that she would work on getting Sara into one of the county rehabilitation clinics.

The next morning, when Lucy woke up and stumbled to the bathroom, still groggy with sleep, to wash her face and hands, she saw a small bag containing some white residue, along with a syringe, lying in the sink. Startled, she jumped back and ran to find Alessa. Hearing a commotion in the kitchen, she stepped up her pace and crossed the hallway in a few strides.

Alessa, Remo and Sara were in the kitchen together. Sara was completely naked and Alessa was holding her by the arm as she tried to break free and lunge toward Remo.

"Come on, man!" Sara kept saying. "You can't find a ten dollar blow job as good as me out there! Come on, man! You can even fuck me!"

Shocked and disgusted by the sight, Lucy lost her temper. Without a moment's hesitation, she stepped in front of Sara and screamed, "Sara, stop it! You're acting like a whore! You can't act like this in our house. Either stop it or get the fuck out!"

Lucy's intervention startled Sara, but it probably surprised Alessa and Remo still more. Sara seemed to sober up for a moment, as she looked down at this eleven-year-old who had just called her a whore. Then she collapsed on the kitchen floor and lay there, exhausted. As Alessa sat holding her, Lucy quickly snatched up a blanket from the sofa and covered Sara with it. When they finally got her settled, she confessed that she'd found a little dope in a bag she had forgotten was with her and had figured she'd do it up. Sara was still out of it, but something about the things Lucy had said to her had brought her just a little closer to reality.

Ebby called later that morning to tell them that she had been successful in placing Sara in a rehab center. They could take her over any time that morning. Alessa explained what had just transpired, but as the effect of the drugs eventually wore off, Sara agreed to go. Alessa reflected that like her, Sara was twenty-one years old. Yet, their lives were so different now. She sent up a silent prayer to God, thanking him for having given her the chance to prove that she was a good and decent human being.

Early that afternoon, Remo and Alessa drove Sara down to the rehabilitation clinic. At her insistence, they stayed by her through the admission process. When asked, she readily agreed to give blood samples to test for STDs, including HIV and other venereal diseases she might have contracted on the streets. Sara admitted to having unprotected sex with men and women in the last eight months, when she had to turn to prostitution to make money. As Alessa heard her describe her drug habits and her experiences with prostitution to the psychologist assigned to her, she shared Sara's pain and regret. She knew that the psychologist was more interested in understanding if Sara was a risk to herself or to others in the clinic. It was something she had learned in school, an important aspect of her work when she dealt with any type of addiction.

It took over two hours to complete the admission procedures. By that time, Sara was far more sober than they had seen her since she arrived at their doorstep. She fully recognized Alessa now and grew frantic as the time for them to leave arrived.

"I totally fucked up my life, Alessa," she said. "Please don't hate me!"

Alessa held her tight. "I could never hate you, Sara," she soothed her. "I want to see you get better, though. By the way, this is my husband, Remo."

Sara looked at him, suspecting she might have said some pretty awful things to him in her drug-induced stupor, and felt her face flush with embarrassment.

"Nice to meet you, Remo," she said shamefully. "I'm truly sorry for anything I might have said or done."

Remo patted her on the shoulder. "Don't worry about anything," he reassured her. "Just focus on getting yourself better. Okay?"

As they drove back to the Outside Inn, Alessa told Remo how easily that could have been her, and not Sara. She reminded him about the time

Sara had helped her by taking her along to the group of homeless kids. Remo knew her well enough to understand that she didn't want him to despise Sara.

"Look," he said, "it's not like I haven't seen people on drugs before. We will visit her later and see what, if anything, we can do to help her through this."

Alessa relaxed in the seat next to him. "Some honeymoon, huh, Remo?"

He shrugged. "Well, at least we can say it wasn't boring. We still have three more days left anyway, so how about if we just enjoy the rest of our time together?'

Alessa leaned back into the car seat. "Sounds like a plan."

Chapter Seventy-Two

Remo and Alessa's next three days were filled with hanging out, drinking wine and enjoying each other's company. Lucy spent the last two days with them and they closed the weekend with a steak dinner. Remo fired up the barbeque grill and they splurged on filet mignon bought from a local butcher. They hadn't seen Sara since she entered rehab. The staff there informed them that she wouldn't be able to see anyone until she was fully detoxed, a process which could take five to seven days.

On Monday morning, while Alessa was reading a book in preparation for a class that would start that afternoon, the phone rang. It was the clinic telling her that Sara had come through the detox just fine. She had asked a nurse at the rehab to call Alessa and let her know she was getting better. She had also requested a visit from her. Alessa thanked them, showered and headed over to the clinic for a short visit before her class. Sara looked more herself now, the way Alessa remembered her, but she could see she was tired. Alessa knew she had been through a lot. Sara told her she would have to stay in bed for the next couple of days until she was eating normally and had regained some of her strength.

During the visit, a doctor came in to check on Sara.

"We got the results of your blood tests," he announced, then looked pointedly at Alessa.

"It's fine," Sara reassured him. "You can tell me in front of her."

"You've been very lucky, Sara," he continued. "You tested negative for HIV. However, you do have syphilis."

Sara looked confused. "So what does that mean?" she asked. "Can you give me something for it?"

The doctor explained it was a very common form of STD and he would start her on a course of antibiotics.

"Could I die from syphilis?" she asked with panic in her voice.

341

The doctor assured her she could not, but reminded her how lucky she was to have been spared something worse.

When he left, Alessa said, "You have a new start, Sara. You've been given another chance. Make the most of it, girl."

Sara dropped her head back on the pillow. "Alessa," she said, "I can't even tell you what I've done in the last eight months. I was stoned all the time. I don't know how, but thank God I stumbled on you. I probably would have died, if I hadn't."

Alessa stayed for a bit longer. When she got up to leave, Sara was overwhelmed with insecurity at the thought of being alone. "Will you come back?" she asked, the desperation evident in her voice.

"Of course I'm coming back," Alessa reassured her. "I have classes tomorrow morning, but I'll come back tomorrow afternoon."

Sara was suddenly alert. "You go to school now?" she asked incredulously.

Alessa laughed. "Yeah, I want to be a psychologist."

Sara sat up in bed. "That's so fucking cool!" she said softly. "You really made it. You're so lucky, Alessa. That's so fucking cool!"

Alessa looked away, feeling as though she had been far too lucky, while her friend had been far too unlucky, "Yeah. You'll make it too," she said gently.

Alessa made her way to school, remembering the desperation with which she had once wanted to change her life and wishing she could help Sara to turn her own life around. She thought about all the questions she'd once asked of herself: How would it happen? Could it even happen? Was she destined for a life where she would always want more? Oh yes, Alessa remembered the feeling well.

She didn't know what would be the right answer for Sara. Alessa, herself, had just kept moving forward with her life and, with some luck along the way, she had made it through. She had met people who, in one way or another, had helped her to pull herself out of the nightmare that had been her life.

That night at dinner, Alessa talked to Ebby about Sara. Ebby explained that she could probably get Sara into a halfway house after she had successfully completed rehab. Alessa was comforted by the thought that Sara would have a place to start her life over, once she got released.

With things settled, she stopped worrying about Sara and began to think about Christmas, which was fast approaching.

Chapter Seventy-Three

———————■———————

B y Christmastime, all the residents of the Outside Inn were in a state of feverish excitement. A local tree vendor had donated a Christmas tree to the house. It was set up in the foyer to enable all the residents to enjoy it. It was a magical time for all of them and Alessa savored the spirit of the holiday season. She wished people could be as kind all year long. The people on the streets seemed happier, laughed a little louder and made friendly eye contact with those who passed them. Alessa wondered what made people so different during the holidays. Maybe it was renewed hope, the promise of new beginnings?

During dinner with Remo and Lucy, she shared this observation about people changing for the better during the holidays.

"I think at Christmastime, people reminisce about their childhood and recall that feeling about anything being possible," Remo remarked. "Families are together a lot during the holidays and there is good food to enjoy. I guess it's all about feeling connected again."

Lucy added her two cents' worth. "I think it's because there are parties and everyone gets presents, but mostly, because we get to be with other people. Remember the first year, Alessa, when we didn't have anywhere to go and just stayed with each other? It was nice, but it made me feel sad too."

Alessa frowned, remembering how dejected she had felt back then. "You know, Lucy, I think you're right," she agreed. "Both you and Remo are right. It's all about being with other people and feeling like you belong."

The three of them would be spending Christmas Eve with Ebby and heading to Remo's parents' place on Christmas day. Alessa and Remo had bought modest gifts for each other and spent most of their Christmas savings on Lucy. Remo's father had given him 200 dollars to buy Lucy some extra things that she wanted. Not that the child really wanted much. Still, the couple had a great time spending the money to buy her things they thought she'd like.

Christmas Eve at Ebby's was just wonderful. The fire was roaring in the fireplace and Ebby had invited some of the staff from the Eliza Shirley Shelter where she worked. Alessa hadn't seen them in a long time and it was nice to catch up. They all knew of Alessa's progress.

"You're all Ebby ever talks about," one of the women told her.

On Christmas afternoon, the three of them drove out to see Remo's parents. Patrick and Hannah were hosting a much more formal party. Alessa grew nervous as dusk descended and they approached the house. Remo could feel her tension and started singing "Jingle Bells" in an attempt to lift her spirits and lighten her mood.

Alessa looked over at him. "I don't know what it is, but every time I'm going to see your mom, especially when I know her friends will be there, it makes my asshole pucker."

Remo burst out laughing at her choice of words. "Now *that's* a ladylike thing to say!" he teased.

Having heard every word, Lucy was giggling in the backseat. Before they knew it, all three of them were laughing, as they pulled into the long driveway.

The exterior of the house had been beautifully decorated with small white lights strung up perfectly around the trees and the bushes. An enormous wreath twinkled with lights in their front window. A smaller one, identical to the other, had been fixed on the front door. The doorway and windows had been trimmed with holly and fern. The place looked like a winter wonderland. The classic style in which the house had been decorated told Alessa that it was all Hannah's work. The interiors were more magnificent still. There was a large Christmas tree all lit up in the study. The ornaments had been tastefully arranged on it and Alessa wondered how Remo's mother could be so creative for her parties and yet so closed-minded, when it came to her daughter-in-law.

Chapter Seventy-Four

Hannah rushed over to embrace Remo and Patrick got up and walked over to Lucy and Alessa. He smiled at the child and asked, "Was Santa good to you this year?"

She beamed in her new jeans and sweater, then followed it up with a roll of her eyes. "Yes, Remo and Alessa were very good to me," she chirped. "I got a lot of great new clothes."

Patrick laughed at her mature answer and turned to greet Alessa. Hannah too finally acknowledged her daughter-in-law, but her greeting was mechanical, lacking in the warmth and love that her husband was so generous with. Alessa wished they had been closer. She wondered why the woman didn't like her. She knew Hannah wasn't happy that Remo had chosen her as his wife, but hoped she could see that her son wasn't suffering because of Alessa's past.

Having to pretend that everything was fine between them gnawed at Alessa. Hannah made no bones about disliking her daughter-in-law and persistently treated her as if she were shit stuck on the bottom of her shoe, shit that wouldn't come off. Hannah's bullshit was taking its toll on Alessa. She had been the more gracious of the two, as Remo had wanted her to be, but it did occur to Alessa that no one was expecting the same from Hannah. She could get away with behaving like the unreasonable bitch she was.

After a lavish Christmas dinner, Hannah announced that she wanted to take pictures by the decorated tree in the study. All the guests moved in and began milling about, refreshing their drinks at the bar and chatting excitedly.

"Let's get started," Hannah said. "First, I want to take a picture with just the family in it."

As Alessa and Lucy spontaneously took a step forward for the picture, Hannah looked over and said pointedly, "Remo, come over here, handsome. I want to get one with just the family."

Remo, who had been engrossed in conversation with one of Patrick's friends until his mother called out to him, hadn't noticed how Alessa and Lucy had stopped in their tracks when excluded from the family photo.

Standing next to his mother, he called out, "Alessa and Lucy, come on and join us."

They both stayed where they were, as if their feet had been bolted to the ground.

"Come on, honey," Hannah sweetly stated to her son. "Let's just get one with the three of us."

Oblivious to what had transpired minutes ago, Remo smiled for the camera and after the family photo was taken, joined one of his parents' neighbors at the bar.

At this point, Alessa and Lucy saw one of Hannah's friends approaching them. Alessa knew her to be a nice woman who was the mother of eight kids. So acceptance came naturally to her.

"Don't worry about Hannah," she whispered to Alessa. "Someday, she'll come around. And if she doesn't, well, then, from what I've seen, that's her loss."

Her words made Alessa feel less alone in the room full of people. She thanked the woman and moved to the bar to be near Remo. She got a glass of Merlot for herself and Remo made Lucy a Shirley Temple. The wine helped Alessa relax a little, but now being in the same room as her mother-in-law was like a thorn in her side. She was eager to love both of Remo's parents, but had begun to understand that Hannah wouldn't give her an inch. It was a sad realization for her, because she wanted nothing more than Remo's happiness. If only his mother could see that they both wanted the same thing! Alessa just couldn't understand Hannah's veiled hostility toward her, wondering, occasionally, if she wasn't plain jealous of her daughter-in-law, the woman with whom she now had to share Remo's love and attention. It was a sick thought, she felt, but couldn't reject it entirely whenever she saw Hannah fall all over Remo.

As Alessa and Remo made their way through the crowd of guests, stopping to greet and chat with some of them, she felt numb. Standing within earshot of Hannah, she overheard her bragging to her friends about how Remo had opened the Outside Inn.

"Isn't the name just so creative?" Hannah remarked. "My son really has a gift. Patrick and I are so proud of him."

Alessa's stomach flip-flopped. She wanted to stomp on her mother-in-law for deliberately leaving her out of the picture altogether. It wasn't that she needed credit for what she'd done. But Hannah's refusal to even consider the possibility of Alessa's contribution to something she was so proud of infuriated her. Remo's mother made Alessa feel the way she used to as a child—unloved, used and abused. No one seemed to have noticed and everyone was going about their evening, as though it were all perfectly normal.

For Alessa, the hours that passed seemed like an entire week and it was a relief to her when Remo asked if she was ready to go home. Lucy, in the meantime, had fallen asleep on one of the large leather sofas in the study. Remo hugged his parents' goodbye. Turning to embrace Alessa, Patrick sensed from her body language and her expression that something had upset her deeply. He wondered what he had missed, but suspected Hannah had something to do with it. Patrick couldn't understand why his wife disliked Alessa so intensely. He knew she was protective of Remo, but in all fairness, he had to acknowledge that her stubbornness in refusing to accept Alessa as a member of their family was beyond reason and cruel.

Chapter Seventy-Five

———————————■———————————

"That was a nice Christmas party, don't you think? Did you enjoy it?" Remo asked.

Alessa looked over at him and curbed the impulse to scream 'No, it was *not* nice! Your mother is a fucking bitch, a whore who goes out of her way to make me feel like I don't exist!' Instead, she said quietly, "Yeah, sure, it was nice."

Remo recognized that familiar tone right away. Something had obviously happened to upset Alessa. He himself had enjoyed the day and didn't want to ruin it by stirring up shit, but he needed to resolve whatever was bothering her just so she wouldn't be agitated for days. "What happened?" he asked. "Did I miss something?"

Alessa sighed deeply. She didn't feel like starting this conversation, but thought it was important for her to get it out and into the open. "Remo, it doesn't really matter," she sighed.

"What doesn't really matter, Alessa?" he retorted abruptly. "Why can't we ever go to my parents and just have a good time? Why do we always have to deal with this bullshit after we leave?"

Alessa was fuming by now. "Because," she enunciated clearly, "your mother treats me and Lucy like shit. That's why!"

She saw his grip tighten on the steering wheel.

"What did she do?" he finally asked.

"Well, let's see," she said, her voice dripping with sarcasm. "Did you happen to notice that Lucy and I weren't in the 'family' photo? Did that strike you as odd at all? Or, did you hear how she bragged to her stupid friends about you taking care of homeless people. It's as if I don't even exist! I even overheard her telling one of her friends that you and that particular friend's daughter had made such a cute couple and she wondered why that didn't work out. What the fuck, Remo? How much more shit do I have to eat?"

Having heard her out and recognized the anguish in her voice, Remo realized how Alessa was feeling.

"You're right," he said sympathetically. "You and Lucy should have been in the family photo. As for that girl I dated, she was a warthog. She was stuffy and boring. I went out with her twice. I never even had sex with her. So I really can't figure out why my mom said that to her friend."

"I don't really care if you had sex with the girl or not, Remo," Alessa told him. "You know that shit doesn't bother me. What bothers me is how your mother goes out of her way to make me feel like I'm just not good enough. I'm annoyed and since I promised you that I would take the high road, I feel like I have to put up with her bullying me in silence! So now, she's just gets to lay it on me as thick as she wants to and I have to suck it all up. I don't know if I can keep doing it much longer, Remo. Not only does Hannah treat me worse than ever, she has now begun to humiliate me in front of others. I have to keep 'eating shit', which makes me look like a stupid idiot who doesn't have the guts to stand up for herself. Since when did it all become my problem to keep the peace?"

Alessa began to cry, her tears coursing silently down her cheeks as she sat next to Remo. She was already exhausted from the daylong mental torture she had endured and now, to make matters worse, she and her husband were fighting over his mother.

"Why are you crying, Alessa?" Remo pleaded, dismayed to see how upset she was.

Her face was expressionless, as she stared out the car window and said, "Because God hates me."

Remo pulled the car over to the side. "Come here, you big baby," he said. "Of course God doesn't hate you. I know how my mom is and she's just proud of the things that I have done. She doesn't mean to be hurtful. She just can't see that I can love you both at the same time. She's a stupid idiot."

Alessa burst out laughing and clung to him as if he were a life raft.

"Look Alessa, I'll make you a deal," he said gently. "From now on, if you don't want to come with me to see my parents, you don't have to, all right? If it makes you feel this bad, you don't have to come with me. I want you to be happy and I certainly don't want Lucy growing up thinking she isn't a part of my family, because both of you *are* my family. Understand?"

Alessa sat back against the car seat. "I just wish it didn't have to be this way. That's all. Your dad seems to like me, though."

Remo laughed. "My dad loves you and Lucy," he said. "So does my mom. She just doesn't know how to express her feelings."

The objection to his last statement bubbled up within her, but Alessa decided to leave well enough alone. It had been a long day, with a less than great ending. As they drove the rest of the way home in silence, Remo thought about his mother. He wondered why Hannah was being so vicious to his wife. Whatever explanation he might have tried to pacify Alessa with, deep inside, he knew his mother was just being a bitch. He was torn, as he remembered how loving she had been to him as a child. They had done everything together. She was a real June Cleaver and now she had turned into Mommie-fucking-Dearest with the one person he loved most in the world. He didn't know how to reconcile the two startlingly different personas anymore. He was beginning to see how unfair it was to Alessa that she was expected to tolerate his mother's shit, but couldn't dish it back out for fear of hurting his feelings. Remo decided he would talk to his dad about it in the morning. Maybe Patrick would have an idea about tackling the problem.

Chapter Seventy-Six

Patrick wasn't surprised to receive a call from his son the following day. "I figured you'd call this morning," he said. "Alessa seemed pretty tense when she left here last night. What happened? Did she tell you?"

Remo let out a heavy sigh. "Nothing significant, Dad. Just a bunch of bullshit. Alessa and Lucy weren't in the 'family' photo. Mom gave me all the credit for the Outside Inn. It wasn't anything specific. It all boils down to how Mom treats her or, should I say, pretends she doesn't exist. Alessa and Lucy have had enough of that shit to last a lifetime. I just don't know what to do about it anymore and thought maybe you would have a solution."

"I understand, Remo. I've noticed what your mom's been up to. She isn't consciously *trying* to be evil. She just can't come to terms with the fact that you belong to another woman now. You were always 'her boy' and now it seems to her that you've found someone to replace her."

"Okay, Dad," Remo grunted. "But frankly, I find that a little creepy. I mean, Alessa is my wife and Lucy, my child. Neither of them is my mother. Yuck!"

Both men burst out laughing at the thought.

"Okay," Remo finally said, "so what do I need to tell Mom to reassure her that she's still important to me? Christ, women are a fucking pain in the ass!"

Both men laughed again, as if they had just shared a great secret, but it was all in good fun.

"Let me talk to your mother, son," Patrick suggested. "I'll call you back and let you know how things turn out."

Remo hung up the phone, still troubled by the thought that his mother stubbornly refused to admit how happy he was with Alessa and continued to make trouble for them. He just couldn't understand it. This was the same mother who had been loving and supportive all through his life. She had been fond of his friends, even the female ones. Of course Alessa was the first 'girlfriend' he had ever brought home, but still, Hannah was aware that he dated girls.

Alessa walked into the kitchen and broke into his thoughts. Remo noticed how beautiful she looked, with her hair tousled and her eyes still half-closed from sleep. He took her by the hand and silently led her back into their bedroom.

"Be quiet," he whispered, "we don't want to wake Lucy."

"Well, good morning to you too," she whispered, allowing herself to be led.

Later that morning, Patrick called his son to tell him that he had talked to Hannah. She had apparently got really pissed off, demanding to know why both of the men in her life were turning against her for Alessa's sake, and stormed out of the house.

"Sorry, son," Patrick said apologetically. "I think I just made it worse for Alessa. Now your mother thinks she's stealing *me* from her too!"

The two men laughed at the absurdity of it all and Remo promised his father he would call his mother later that afternoon.

After their conversation was over, Remo hung up the phone, wondering what it was going to take for his mother to lighten up and give Alessa a chance. He would just have to wing it, when he got her on the phone. Remo never did call his mother that day. Instead, he decided to get involved in the preparations for the post-Christmas party the residents of the Outside Inn had planned. Alessa helped to coordinate and they had plenty of food to eat from all the donations they'd received from local businesses. All the residents were there and by seven p.m. that evening, the party was in full swing. The residents of each apartment in the Outside Inn had decided to keep their door open and people milled about, moving from floor to floor, apartment to apartment, enjoying each other's company. They got along well. Many knew each other from the streets and the older residents always looked out for the younger ones.

Alessa thought it had been a great evening and a great idea. By the end of the night, Remo had forgotten about the problems between Alessa and his mother. Now he climbed the stairs to the third floor with his wife by his side. Having tucked Lucy in bed, they went back out to the living room for a mug of hot chocolate before going to bed themselves. They chatted about the day, feeling content about all the things they had done that had brought them to this moment.

"This doesn't seem real to me, sometimes," Alessa told him. "It's hard to believe that we have done all that we have in the short time we've been together."

Remo hugged her tight. "This is only the beginning," he said. "There is a lot more that we can do together. Lucy is thriving and we've gotten thirty-six people off the streets. We rock, don'tcha think?"

Alessa laughed. "Well, I was thinking more about how wonderful it makes me feel that we could help others. Like *they* rock, but of course, we rock too. Lucy is so smart, Remo. She is going to do great things when she grows up."

He leaned back into the sofa. "Agreed. We need to make sure that she keeps up the good work she's doing in school. You know, at first, I was a little apprehensive about raising her around all these strangers, but I can see now that she learns from them and they learn from her too. I couldn't ask for a better wife and daughter."

It was late and Alessa was finishing her hot chocolate, when the phone rang. Remo went into the kitchen to answer it. Alessa could hear his voice begin to rise and went to see who was on the phone.

"No Mom, that's *not* what's going on," she heard Remo say in exasperation. "You're being paranoid. Dad and I just thought that you could be a little nicer. You could be a little more accepting of them. Alessa and Lucy are my family and if you don't accept them, then you don't accept me either."

Remo held out the phone and looked at Alessa. "She hung up on me."

Infuriated, she asked, "What was *that* about? What did you two guys do?"

Remo explained how he had talked to his father and the two men had agreed that Patrick would confront Hannah about the events that had taken place on Christmas Day.

Alessa started to shake. She said through clenched teeth, "I don't want your mom being nice to me, just because you and your dad tell her she has to be nice. If she hates me, then fine, she can hate me! Now she's *really* going to hate me, because she's going to think I am pitting you against her. What the fuck were you thinking? God, Remo, I don't need this fucking bullshit in my life!"

Remo was now irritated both with his mother and Alessa. He didn't know what he was supposed to do to make things better between them. Finally, he picked up the phone and called his mother back. When she answered, he could tell she was crying.

"Mom?" he said, treading carefully, "all I'm saying is that it makes it hard for us to visit you and Dad, when you treat Alessa and Lucy like they don't belong."

"You know what, Remo?" Hannah screamed, "*you* were the one who tied yourself down with that lost cause and now I'm suddenly supposed to like her! Well, I'll tell you honestly that she certainly wasn't what I had in mind for you. I always saw you with someone strong, someone with a career and a family, for God's sake! Not some lost soul, whose family won't even associate themselves with her!"

Remo's face turned red. "Alessa's family is a pack of morons! She struggled to get through her childhood with those lousy people. Why would *you* want to make it hard for her to be a part of our family? I thought we were better than that, Mom. I thought you raised me not to judge others and to be open-minded. Why, all of a sudden, did that change?"

Hannah was openly crying now. "Because I thought that when you finally married, I would gain a daughter too. Alessa isn't like a daughter at all. She doesn't *know* how to be a daughter. She sure knows how to be a stripper and a prostitute, though, doesn't she? I know *everything* about her. And I had to find it out from our neighbors, of all people! How do you think that makes me feel? My son married to a prostitute! What the hell were you thinking? Did you think I would never find out? Of course you didn't, because you knew I would never agree to you marrying a whore!"

Remo willed himself to stay calm, as she ranted on, "Did she tell you all of this earlier? Or are you just beginning to find out about it now, like me?"

"I already knew," he told her quietly. "She told me everything on our first date, long before I fell in love with her. She told me so that I could make an informed decision before we got serious about each other."

"Well, then, how could you have stayed with her?" Hannah retorted sharply. "She had sex with men for money, Remo! She danced *naked* for them! God only knows what diseases she might have! And how exactly did she 'find' Lucy? None of this makes any sense to me. I just don't understand what you see in her!"

Remo said with authority, "Then, Mom, you're blind. I have to go now. It's late and I need to get some sleep. We can talk again tomorrow, but I want to tell you now that nothing will change how I feel about Alessa and Lucy. Nothing you can say or do will stop me from loving them. Good night, Mom."

He turned and looked at Alessa. She was exhausted. Alessa felt sorry for him too. She knew this was ripping him in half and he felt like shit.

"Your mom found out about my dark past, huh?" she asked.

Remo sneered, "Yeah, that stupid motherfucker who used to get lap dances from you at the club must have said something to someone and it got back to my mom. Maybe I should tell her about her neighbor's little fantasy, about how he likes to go to strip clubs and dress up in diapers when he's getting a private lap dance!"

"No, you won't!" Alessa snapped. "It's nobody's business. Just because we are going through a rough time doesn't mean I want to destroy someone else's marriage. Okay?"

Remo dropped his head. "Yeah, fine. I won't tell her anything about the neighbor. Let's go to bed. I'm thoroughly worn out and just want to sleep."

Chapter Seventy-Seven

———————————■———————————

Remo wasn't in much better spirits the next morning when he woke up.

Lucy picked up the vibes immediately. "What's wrong, Remo?" she asked. "Did something happen?"

He looked at her with deep affection. "No, Luce, I'm just in a bad mood this morning. It's something to do with work," he lied.

Relieved that he wasn't annoyed with either her or Alessa, Lucy went back to eating her eggs. She was very caring and perceptive for an eleven-year-old. It was only natural that she should be so. After all, she had been exposed to a lot in her short time on earth. Ebby had always told Alessa that Lucy was a special kid. She was smart, funny and had strong instincts.

Shortly after breakfast, Hannah called to talk to Remo again. He could tell from her voice that she was more settled than she had been the night before. He figured his father had talked to her about her rude behavior. Hannah promised Remo she would do her best to be kind to Alessa, but added that she still wasn't happy with his 'situation'. He considered this a progress of sorts, even if it wasn't exactly what he had hoped for from her. He understood that what she really meant was nothing would change. His mother was only promising to be kinder to Alessa in an effort not to lose her son. Still, he had to give her a chance to try.

When he returned to the kitchen, Alessa and Lucy were washing the breakfast dishes.

"I was thinking that we needed a vacation," Remo remarked. "When I was a kid, we used to go to Wrightsville Beach in North Carolina. I thought we could plan a summer trip. What do you guys think about that?"

Lucy was instantly charged at the thought of a vacation. "I think it sounds great!" she chirped. "What do we do there?"

Remo laughed. "We go to the beach, silly! We can get boogie boards and ride the waves. It's so much fun. So what do you think?"

The two of them looked to Alessa for approval. Alessa had never been to North Carolina. The furthest she had ever gotten was Atlantic City, which she had visited with her grandmother when she was a little girl.

She smiled at them. "Okay, fine, but Remo and I need to discuss how we're going to pay for this trip first."

Remo gathered her up in his arms. "Don't you worry," he reassured her. "I have it covered. My contract with my company is up and I can ask for a bonus to sign on for another three years. It won't be a problem. If they refuse, I'll find another place to work, where they will gladly give me a signing bonus. My company knows I can leave any time I want to. I happen to be very much in demand, ya know. They also know my clients will move to wherever I go so they can continue to work with me."

Alessa frowned at him. "Oh, good. A great therapist and humble too!"

"It's settled then. We can go see a travel agent today and find out what they can offer us. We'll book our air tickets and rent a condo—hopefully, one right on the beach!"

Lucy jumped off her chair. "We're going on an airplane? I've *never* been on an airplane!"

Alessa's faced was shrouded in worry. "Neither have I. The thought makes me a little nervous."

Remo's face puckered as if she were crazy. "There's nothing to worry about. Flying is easy and it only takes about an hour by plane to get there from Philly."

They piled into the car later that afternoon and went to a travel agent. They had decided to go away for their vacation over the week of July Fourth. The agent had found them a two-bedroom condominium at Station One on the beach. Remo wanted this to be a very special experience for Alessa and Lucy. They were in high spirits when they arrived back at the Outside Inn. Lucy flew out of the car in her eagerness to announce to some of the residents that they were going on vacation. For her, it was as if Christmas was never going to end and she loved every minute of being a part of their family. It warmed Alessa's generous heart to see her that way.

Later that evening, Ebby went over to their apartment for dinner. Alessa had made chicken francaise, a new recipe she had whipped together herself. The four of them polished off the meal and after Alessa and Ebby had finished the bottle of wine they were drinking, they moved to the living room. Remo and Lucy went off to read in their respective bedrooms, while the two women sat and talked. Alessa gave Ebby a blow-by-blow account of Hannah's behavior at the Christmas party. She told her about the fight Remo had with Hannah and eventually finished by sharing their vacation plans. Suspecting that Remo's mother was determined to be judgmental and would probably never change her mind, Ebby was cautious in her advice to Alessa. She fought off the impulse to suggest that Alessa tell her mother-in-law to go fuck herself, because she knew that Remo's feelings were involved as well and didn't want to worsen an already prickly situation. She encouraged Alessa, instead, to take her husband up on his suggestion and not attend any more functions where Hannah would be present.

Alessa looked saddened by the advice. "I feel bad, Ebby," she confessed. "I think I should be with my husband when he visits his parents. Besides, I am always happy to see Patrick. He has been very nice to Lucy and me."

"You're right, you're right," Ebby agreed hurriedly. "But if you continue to subject yourself to Hannah's nastiness, you're going to have to learn how to blow her off and not take things personally. Otherwise, you're not helping anyone."

Alessa agreed and finished with, "You know I can't stand that fucking bitch, right?"

Ebby laughed. "Well, she treats you like shit. So I'm relieved that you feel the way you do. Just because you have to eat shit doesn't mean you have to become shit."

The two women laughed and hugged each other.

Ebby turned serious. "Alessa, I need your help with something," she said. "A couple of days ago, I had a teenage girl come to the shelter. We think she's about sixteen years old. We haven't been able to get her to open up and talk to us. She was in pretty bad shape when she turned up at our doorstep. She had definitely been beaten and judging by the way she was dressed, we are pretty sure she was into prostitution. The thing is, she won't really talk to any of us. Normally, after a couple of days, we can get them to open up, but this one just sits and cries. I was wondering if you would come by the shelter tomorrow and give it a try."

Alessa was touched that she had been asked for help. "Of course I will," she assured her, "but she might not talk to me either, Ebby. I'm willing to give it a try, though. What time should I be there?"

Happy that Alessa had agreed to help, Ebby said, "Let's meet tomorrow at ten a.m."

The next morning, Alessa was both excited and anxious as she headed to the Eliza Shirley Shelter. She wanted so badly to be able to help the girl. Yet, even though she had gained a lot of confidence over the past two years, the moment a fresh challenge presented itself, Alessa always doubted herself and her capabilities. Ebby knew differently, though. She knew Alessa was the only person who could come even within a shot of breaking the girl's silence.

Chapter Seventy-Eight

As Alessa climbed the steps leading to the entrance of the Eliza Shirley Shelter, she remembered the first time she had gone there under very different circumstances and was grateful to be returning to the place to provide someone help instead of seeking it herself. The staff was delighted to see her and after she had greeted each of them in turn, she went into Ebby's office.

Ebby looked up from her desk. "You ready?"

Alessa took a deep breath. "Yeah, I'm ready," she said. "I don't want you to come with me, though. Just tell me where I can find her."

Ebby was surprised, but pleased as well that Alessa was so decisive about her approach in handling the girl.

Alessa found the teenage girl alone in the day room, sitting on a small love seat with her legs drawn up against her chest and her forehead resting on her knees.

Approaching her cautiously, so as not to startle her, she came to a halt a few feet away. "Hey," is all she said.

The young girl looked up. Tears were streaming down her face. "Hey," she responded.

Alessa approached the love seat and asked, "Can I sit here with you?"

The girl said indifferently, "Doesn't matter to me."

Alessa had no way of knowing that the exchange between them in that first minute, brief though it was, was more than what the staff had been able to get out of the girl in the four days she had been at the shelter.

"I'm Alessa," she said. "I lived here for a short time a couple of years ago. I had to get away from this asshole that was making me fuck everything with three legs. He was a scary dude, but I was safe here. Are you staying here now?"

Curious, the girl looked up. "Yeah, why?"

"I was just wondering, is all. What's your name anyway?"

The girl looked at Alessa with disdain and a hint of wariness. "Why? You writing a fucking book?"

"I wish. But no, I'm not writing a book. I'm just trying to be friendly. If you don't want to talk, then fine. Fuck it," Alessa answered nonchalantly. She got up from the sofa abruptly, secretly irritated with the girl.

The girl sensed her annoyance. "No, wait!" she said. "My name is Regina."

Alessa turned to face her. "Okay, Regina. Well, I'm going to split now. Nice talking to you."

Regina jumped up from the love seat. "Look, man. I'm just scared. I didn't mean to be a bitch, okay?"

"Okay, whatever. But you know, most people who come here are scared. I mean, if you're here, the odds are good that your life is pretty fucked up. It's not like this place is home to movie stars and athletes. So why *are* you here?"

Regina sat back down on the love seat. Alessa sat down next to her.

"If I tell, that motherfucker will kill me," Regina said. "I just need a few days to hide so that I can get the fuck out of Philadelphia. You know what I mean?"

Alessa rested her head on the back of the love seat. She let out a big sigh as she stared at the ceiling. "Yeah, I know what you mean...unfortunately."

Regina looked at her and tears began spilling from her eyes. "I don't know *what* I'm gonna do! I'm so scared all the time! I hate myself!"

Alessa rolled her head sideways so she was facing her. "We're all scared sometimes, Regina. It ain't like you're alone. When I came to this shelter, I was sure the guy—I don't know what to call him, really, he was sort of my pimp, but really my girlfriend's brother—was going to kill me. Anyway, he was pounding heroin into his arm like crazy before I split. Motherfucker! I hated him! I was scared, scared shitless. I had no idea what I was going to do. I couldn't ask my family for help, because they were just as bad as the asshole I was running from. So I came here. They helped me here, Regina."

"Yeah, like how? How did they help you?" the girl asked, and Alessa noticed the first glimmer of hope in her voice.

Alessa sat up straighter. "They talked to me a lot about what was going on. They contacted the local cops to let them know that that monster was looking for me. It was mostly the talking that helped. They seem all straight and shit, but they know what's going on with people like us."

Regina leaned in closer, feeling a connection with Alessa from the moment she had said, "People like us." It made her feel less isolated from the world.

Alessa focused hard on her and dove in. "So what's your story? What happened to you?"

Regina hesitated, silence hanging in the air like a dark cloud. Finally she spoke. "I was taken three years ago. I was walking home from school and this van pulled up. Someone grabbed me and shoved a needle in my arm. When I woke up, I was in some kind of old basement. There were other girls and boys there too. We all had a chain on one ankle that was bolted to the floor."

Holy Christ! Alessa thought. *Now how the fuck am I supposed to respond to this?*

"Who were these people?" she asked, trying to remain calm. "Did they do anything to you?"

"I don't know who they are, really. But after a while, they gave me new underwear and then..." Her voice trailed off and she seemed to close down, as if she were afraid someone other than Alessa would overhear her.

Alessa moved closer and put her arm around the girl. "It's okay, Regina," she said soothingly, "you don't have to tell me anything you don't want to. Okay?"

Regina clung to her. "I'm just scared is all. I'm really scared. They know where my family lives. I'm afraid they'll kill them."

Alessa talked the girl into having lunch with her. She filled the empty silence with her own story about being homeless and how she had met Lucy. Regina never asked her how she had become homeless or got into prostitution. She just listened intently, trading her own dark world for Alessa's, even if it was just for a short time. For the first time in three years, Regina had found a way of escaping her private demons for a while.

Chapter Seventy-Nine

———————————

After lunch with Regina, Alessa met Ebby back in her office and gave her as much of the girl's story as she had divulged.

"Jesus, Alessa!" Ebby exclaimed when she had heard her out. "I need to call the police. Her family needs to know she's alive."

Alessa grasped her by the shoulder, just as she was about to pick up the telephone. "Not yet, Ebby," she cautioned her. "I need to find out what her family was like, before we get in touch with them. For all we know, she was abused by them too. We don't want to send her back to a fucked-up situation. I want to take her home with me for a couple of days. She can sleep with Lucy. She said there were other kids being kept in leg chains where she had been. We need to help them. Okay?"

Ebby was clearly uncomfortable with what Alessa was demanding of her. Now that she knew the girl had been kidnapped, she was conscious of her legal obligation to call the police. However, as Alessa had pointed out, her moral obligation was to obtain a clearer understanding of the girl's history with her family and potentially gather enough information to save the lives of other innocent kids. Ebby finally conceded that while she was taking a huge risk, Alessa was right.

"Okay, Alessa," she agreed, "but only two days. They can close the shelter down, if they find out that we withheld information on a kidnap victim."

"You're a cool fucking chick, you know that?" Alessa said, poking Ebby in the belly.

"Yeah, sure! I'm cool all right! I'm not going to be so cool, though, when they shut the shelter down because I made a bad decision," Ebby remarked wryly.

Alessa went back to the day room to find Regina lying on the love seat in the fetal position. As she approached, the girl looked up with an expression of sheer terror.

"It's okay, Regina," Alessa reassured her. "You're going to be fine. I was thinking that maybe you could come and stay at my house for a couple of days. Would you like to do that?"

The girl quickly accepted the offer. Alessa called Remo to come and pick them both up. As she gave him a brief explanation of the recent developments, he silently questioned the wisdom of what they were about to do for the same reasons that had worried Ebby. However, Alessa was so sure of what needed to be done that he did not argue with her.

"Pull up in the back, Remo. I don't want to take her out the front," Alessa told him.

Twenty minutes later, he was driving back to the Outside Inn with Alessa and Regina. When they arrived at the apartment, Alessa gave Remo a look he recognized well. It meant that he needed to make himself scarce.

Before he left, he turned to Regina. "Well, welcome to our home," he said warmly. "We are happy to have you here with us for the next couple of days. I need to run some errands. So I'll be back later."

Regina didn't respond. She merely stood in the middle of the living room, her arms crossed over her chest. After Remo's departure, it was obvious to Alessa that her guest's tension was beginning to subside.

"Remo would never hurt you," she told the girl. "He's my husband."

Regina sat down on the sofa. "I just don't really like boys anymore," she said. "They hurt me."

Alessa plopped down next to her. "How did they hurt you?" she asked. "You were telling me that the men who had taken you away gave you new underwear. Then what happened?"

Regina spoke so softly Alessa had to strain to hear her. "They took me upstairs. I had to stand there, while these old men bid on me."

Alessa was shocked. "What do you mean they 'bid' on you?"

Regina looked down at the floor. "Whoever paid the most money got to have sex with me. This ugly, disgusting pig paid the most. He said, 'I'd take a second mortgage for some of that untapped pussy.' Later, the other kids who had been there longer told me what that meant. It meant that it would be my first time having sex with anyone. And the first time sucked. It hurt really bad and I bled on the mattress. When that fucking pig saw the blood, he smiled and shoved his dick in even harder. He kept saying, 'Give me more of that untapped pussy, girl!'"

Alessa felt sick to her stomach. It was the familiar feeling she thought she had left behind her long ago. "It's really fucked up that a grown man would do such a disgusting thing to a kid or anyone else for that matter!" she exclaimed. "You know that, right? You understand that what they did to you was wrong and it wasn't your fault?"

Regina shook her head from side to side. "Maybe, but how about all the other times?" she said. "I was sucking guys' dicks so that the men who ran the house would feed me. There was no food or water, if you didn't 'perform', as they put it. Every day that I was there, men would bid on me. It was weird. You didn't want to have sex with them, but you knew if you didn't do a good job of it, no one would bid on you and you wouldn't be given anything to eat or drink."

Alessa walked into the kitchen and poured them each a glass of lemonade. She handed one to Regina. "What about your family?" she asked. "I mean, were you happy, before they took you away?"

The girl was crying openly now. "My family was great. My mom and dad made everything so much fun. I have an older brother and we were like best friends. When they first took me, I would pray for my family to find me. But after I started being a whore, I didn't want them to find me anymore. I was too embarrassed about the things I was doing."

Alessa was relieved to hear good things about Regina's family. "You aren't a whore, Regina," she said firmly. "You were kidnapped and forced to do things. You had no choice."

"That's not what they told me. They told me all the time that I was a whore and my job was to sell myself to the highest bidder. 'That's what whores do,' they would say, 'they sell themselves.'"

Alessa tried to comfort the young girl. "Well, that was a bunch of dickheads who told you that, Regina. I need to know something: how did you get away from them?"

Regina sat up straight, as if to brave her demons. "On the last bidding war, this guy who had always wanted me won. He told them he wanted me back in his hotel. At first, they wouldn't allow it, but then I saw him give them a handful of money and they agreed to take me over there. When I got to the hotel, the man who had won me told me to take a shower and wash real good. When I came out in my towel, he gave me something really sexy to wear. He told me it was a present. It was sheer and you could see my body through it. It had a thong and was really short, so you could see my ass. This guy wasn't as rough with me as the others usually were."

Alessa's body tensed at what was coming.

"Anyway," Regina went on, "I put it on and he gave me some wine to drink. After two glasses, he took his underwear off and told me to suck his dick. So I did. After a while, he had me lie down on the bed and took my thong off. He dipped his fingers into a jar of Vaseline that was sitting next to the bed and starting sticking them in my crotch. It felt really good. No one had ever done that to me before and it was the first time I felt that way. He could tell I liked it and started to kiss my tits. I had never really wanted to fuck any of the men who bid on me, until then.

"When he pulled his fingers out, I thought I would die. I wanted them in me so much, because the other kids, especially the boys, used to talk about orgasms, but until then, I didn't know what they were. I figured that this was what they must have meant and I mean, if you have to have sex with somebody you don't know, you might as well like it, right?"

Alessa nodded to assure Regina that she wasn't judging her.

"So I took his hand and put it back between my legs. He was really happy and asked me if I liked what he was doing. I told him I did and so he put his fingers back inside me. A few seconds later, he told me to suck his dick again and I did. Except that this time, I was really into it, because I wanted him to fuck me so I could feel good too. He was moaning and saying how good it was. After a few more minutes, he had me get back up on the bed and he stuck his fingers in the Vaseline again and shoved them inside me. I felt awful about feeling so good, but I couldn't help it."

Regina stopped to take a deep breath. "Finally, he spread my legs out wide and stuck his dick in me. God, it felt so good! I was overcome by this wonderful feeling. It was like I had taken drugs or something. My head was swimming and I wanted to feel that way forever."

Alessa wasn't expecting all of this and was a bit shocked at Regina's description of her experiences. At the same time, she found the girl's candor an encouraging sign.

"After that," Regina continued, "he ordered room service and let me order anything I wanted from the menu. I got a burger, fries and a milkshake. I hadn't eaten that much food in three years. I was in fucking heaven! We talked a lot that night. I told him I wanted to stay with him forever and he said he would see what he could do, but wouldn't make any promises. The next day, he was on the phone and I heard him say he wanted me to stay with him for good. Then he added, 'I can go as high as a hundred thousand, but that's it.' After he had hung up the phone, he told me I could stay with him for six months. But I would have to go back when my time was up, because they wouldn't let me stay with him for good. The guilt eats me up, though, Alessa."

Confused, Alessa asked, "Guilt about what? You have nothing to feel guilty about!"

Regina wished the earth would open and swallow her up. It was evident that she felt great shame over what she was about to confess next.

"I have a lot to feel guilty about," she said. "I enjoyed having sex with him. He always gave me orgasms. It turned him on to see me come. So he was really good at making sure I did. I know I should have hated it, but I didn't. And that makes me feel guilty. Like I had asked for it."

Alessa thought intently about it, beginning to understand how Regina might feel responsible for the dilemma she had been in. It was confusing enough for adults, let alone for kids and teenagers.

"Regina, it doesn't matter that you had orgasms," she told the girl. "If you hadn't been kidnapped and forced to have sex with all those men, you wouldn't even be here today. What they did to you, all of them—including the man who was nice to you—was wrong. You're only a child. You should have no guilt whatsoever. It just proves to me how strong you really are."

Chapter Eighty

Alessa consoled Regina as best she could, telling her how sorry she was for all that the girl had been through.

"Well," Regina said, feeling braver now. "It was staying with my master for six months that helped me get away. So it wasn't all that bad. I mean, he treated me pretty good and all. I was allowed to shower every day and I got to eat what I wanted. He didn't let me out of the hotel room, but he did let me watch television."

Alessa asked, "Did you ever think about running away from the hotel room when he wasn't there?"

"No, I knew they would find me and bring me back."

Alessa was confused. "So how did you know they wouldn't find you this time?"

Regina blushed. "I didn't, but when my master told me they were coming to get me, I decided I would rather die than go back there."

"Why do you call him your master?" Alessa asked curiously.

"Because he never told me his name. He told me to call him master. So I did."

Alessa wished all the bad people could burst into flames and disappear from this earth. There were so many who inflicted so much pain.

"Anyway," Regina went on, "I found the name of the shelter in the phone book and went there. Then you showed up."

"We need to let your parents know you're okay. They have probably been searching for you since you went missing. Okay?" Alessa asked.

Regina shook her head. "Not yet. You said I could stay here for a couple of days. Can we call them after that?"

Alessa agreed, but reminded her that after two days, they would have to contact her parents.

That night, she called Ebby to give her the information she had gleaned from Regina. Ebby was sad for the teen, but not surprised. She had stopped being surprised by the horrors people laid on other people.

Alessa felt they should contact Regina's parents the next day. "She wants the two days here that I promised her," she explained. "She is going to need therapy, though. She has a lot of guilt and shame over what happened to her in the last three years. From what I gathered, she comes from a pretty wholesome family and she's afraid her parents won't want her back now. I know they are going to be thrilled to know she's alive and safe, but they need to take this really slowly with her."

Before they hung up, Ebby cautioned her. "Listen, you need to be careful, because we don't know if these guys *will* come looking for her. I think you're okay for tonight, but tomorrow, we get the police involved. In the morning, I need you to get as much information as possible about the location where she was held. There are other kids still in there. Regina is one of the lucky ones."

Ebby was pleased that Regina had been able to escape her captors. She was happier still that Alessa had proved her right by getting the story out of the girl. She knew Alessa was going to be a great therapist one day. She had a way of gaining people's trust by just being herself. Once Regina was back with her parents, Ebby planned on telling Alessa what a fine job she'd done handling the whole situation.

The next morning, Remo made breakfast for the four of them, while Alessa talked to Regina again in her bedroom. Lucy was unaware of the reasons that had brought the girl to their home for two days and Alessa intended to keep it that way.

"Regina," Alessa now began, "we need you to describe the place where those men kept you after kidnapping you. It's important, because there are other kids trapped there too. We want to make sure that the police return them to their parents and that they catch the men who did this to you."

The girl looked like a deer caught in the beam of headlights. "But if they find out I snitched on them, they will kill me and my family."

"No, they won't," Alessa said firmly, sitting close to the girl. "The police will protect you. This is a chance for you to help the others. You want to help them, right?"

Regina didn't hesitate. "Yeah, I do," she said, "but I don't know where the house is. The only thing I know is that it's on Dauphin Street."

Alessa's palms were instantly moist and her skin felt like it was on fire. She had the irresistible urge to run and hide some place, where no one would ever find her. Then she reminded herself that Harlin was still in prison and Dauphin Street was one of the worst areas in the whole city anyway.

"Do you remember any of their names?" she asked quickly. "You know, of the men who kidnapped you?"

Regina shook her head. "They always called each other 'dude' or 'man'. They never used names. I do know what they look like, though, at least the ones who watched us at the house and a couple of the clients who did the bidding."

While they were all in the kitchen eating breakfast, Alessa got up and went back into the bedroom to call Ebby and tell her what she had found out.

Ebby detected the note of panic in Alessa's voice right away. "Alessa," she said gently, "it's going to be okay. Harlin is serving a full sentence in prison. He won't be released for another year. I'm sure he has moved on by now anyway. But you need to relax, because if Regina senses your fear, it will only scare her further."

Alessa started to cry. "It scared the shit out of me when Regina mentioned Dauphin Street. I haven't thought about it in a long time. It just freaked me out, that's all. Don't worry, though. I'll keep my shit together in front of Regina. When will the police be coming over?"

"I want you to bring Regina back to the shelter to meet the police," Ebby told her. "We don't want to establish any connection with where you live or leave any trails that can be followed. Truth is, we don't know who these people are or what they are capable of. They may have other houses, like the one Regina was in, all over the city. So I want you to bring her back here at two o'clock this afternoon. I will call the police as soon as you get here."

Alessa always felt better after talking to Ebby. Somehow, it made her less afraid. "Okay, Ebby," she said, steeling herself for what lay ahead. "We'll be there at two."

After they hung up, Alessa showered and dressed. When she got back into the living room, Remo was playing Monopoly with Lucy and Regina. They all looked up as she walked in.

Remo could tell there was something going on. "What's up, Alessa?" he asked.

Alessa looked at Regina. "We need to be back at the shelter by two o'clock today. The police are going to come and talk to you. Then they will contact your parents. Today is a big day for you, Regina. You're going to be back with your family again."

The girl smiled at the thought of seeing her family. "Okay, Alessa."

"Come on. Let's go take a look in my closet and see what you can wear for your homecoming."

Chapter Eighty-One

Regina was so nervous she puked twice before the police arrived at the shelter. After talking with her for over an hour, the police detective who was questioning her told Alessa and Ebby that they were in the process of contacting her parents. Less than an hour later, Regina's parents, Cliff and Beth, arrived at the shelter. Alessa and Ebby watched the tearful reunion, both feeling content about having been able to make a difference. Despite the tiny glimmer of hope they'd struggled to keep alive, Regina's parents had feared she was dead. As they hugged and kissed the daughter they hadn't seen in three years, the love and warmth they all had for each other was obvious. Alessa knew how lucky Regina was to be so loved and wanted by her family.

Cliff and Beth hugged and kissed Alessa too, after they heard about her role in getting their daughter back to them.

"We will never forget you," Regina's mother told her gratefully.

Alessa felt a bit embarrassed over the fuss they were making, but understood that this was an emotional moment for them. It wasn't often that a child, missing for three years, was returned to her parents. They would all have a lot of healing ahead of them. The city assigned a social worker to help them get through all the hard discussions that would enable the family to recover. Cliff and Beth were briefed on what had happened to her so there would at least be an understanding that she would be emotionally traumatized for a long time.

Meanwhile, Remo had been waiting in the staff break room. Alessa joined him after Regina had left with her parents.

"Hello, gorgeous," he said, as she came in. "How did it go?"

Enjoying the feeling of victory, Alessa said, "It went very well. Her parents were a little intimidated when they heard she had been a sex slave for the last three years, but Regina is strong and actually pretty rational. I'm sure they will all be just fine."

Remo gave her a bear hug. "Good. Now let's go home. You need a little time to process all of this too. Ebby told me that Regina mentioned Dauphin Street. That got you upset, right?"

Alessa hugged him tighter. "Yes, it did. Everything about that hellhole scares me. I just panicked a little bit."

With his arm securely around her, Remo guided her out of the shelter. On the drive back home, they talked about Alessa's fears. Remo assured her there was nothing to be afraid of. It was such a shady part of town, he said, it was hardly surprising that they were able to keep those kids captive without anyone coming to know.

"What about the other kids?" he inquired.

Alessa told him the Philadelphia Police Department had undercover cops already working on it. They had been watching a couple of drug dealers over the past three months and had a pretty good idea where the house might be located. The police had, in fact, seen an unusual number of men of different ages and from different walks of life entering one particular home on a regular basis. The police had assumed these visits were drug related, but now suspected they might have something to do with these kids who are being held captive.

The next couple of days at the Outside Inn were quiet. The phone rang on the third evening after Regina had returned to her parents. It was Ebby.

"They busted the house on Dauphin Street," she said. "They arrested fourteen men that the police believe were buyers and sellers of these kids. Alessa, they rescued twelve children between the ages of seven and eighteen from the house. All those kids are free now. It's just an incredible ending! It's what makes my job so rewarding. With your help, Regina saved *twelve* other kids today!"

Alessa was happy to hear about the rescue. She ran into the living room, bounced into Remo's lap and relayed the news. He too was genuinely happy for all the kids and their parents. It was a great ending to a horrific ordeal and he was proud that Alessa had been a part of bringing it all down.

In the weeks that followed, Alessa was glad to return to her normal routine. She was back in school and loving every minute of her education. Things at the Outside Inn were working well. They managed to make it through a winter that had brought a lot of snow and kept them extra busy on the weekends, providing food and drink to the many homeless people throughout the city. It was a peaceful time for all of them. Spring was a welcome change from the slow winter months that had passed. Lucy was all fired up about their approaching vacation, while Alessa was excited that she would finish college in September. She was already thinking of where she would work, once she got her bachelor's degree.

Regina visited with them two Saturdays a month. They would spend the day at Clark Park, a short distance from the Outside Inn, where they interacted with the homeless. Cliff and Beth knew how close Regina was to Alessa and believed the outings would be good therapy for her. The girl had started to heal and often talked to Alessa about how happy she was to be back with her family.

"Not once did they make me feel ashamed or responsible for all the things that had happened to me," she told Alessa one Saturday afternoon, while handing out soft pretzels to the homeless. "They keep saying that they are just grateful that I have come home. I didn't realize how much I had missed them, until now."

Alessa was proud of the progress the girl had made. Remo and Ebby, for their part, were proud of the woman Alessa herself had become.

By early May, Lucy and Remo were talking constantly about their trip to Wrightsville Beach. They both wanted to rent a jet ski and go on the ghost walk of Wilmington, North Carolina. Other than that, the plan was to spend time on the beach and enjoy dinners out. Alessa just sat back and let the two of them enjoy planning everything. She was perfectly content doing nothing and didn't want to invade their turf and stake a claim on their shared exhilaration. By mid-June, however, she had joined in the excitement of going on vacation. They were leaving in two weeks and were all pumped up by a sense of anticipation, but the intensity of Lucy's enthusiasm was hard to match.

The morning of the trip arrived. The child was up at the crack ass of dawn, getting a shower and packing her carry-on bag for the flight. Even though Remo had explained it was a very short flight to Wrightsville Beach, Lucy insisted she needed to take along at least three books and some snacks for the plane ride.

As they boarded the plane that morning, they were all brimming with excitement. And just as Remo had said, the flight was over in no time at all. In Wilmington, they rented a car from the airport and covered the distance to Wrightsville Beach in a quick fifteen minutes. They entered their rented condo at Station One and Lucy immediately ran out on the balcony off the living room.

The balcony offered a panoramic view of the ocean. Directly below them was a swimming pool for Station One guests. Remo, Alessa and Lucy gazed at the people strolling on the beach and lazing in the sun. There were kids on boogie boards and families playing volleyball and football.

Lucy just about came out of her skin, as she turned to the two of them. "Can we go to the beach now?" she asked, barely able to contain herself.

Remo smiled at her indulgently. "How about if we unpack first? Then we can put our suits on and head down to the beach?"

Lucy darted in like a rocket to find her bedroom and unpack her suit-case. An hour later, they were sitting on the beach in chairs Remo had rented for the week. It was an incredible first day and Alessa felt as though she were leading someone else's charmed life. She had never been surrounded by so much beauty and happiness. The ocean was vast, the sound of the waves soothing and she was with the two people she loved most in the world. That night, they went to the Oceanic for dinner and ate out on the pier, where a band was playing live music. Lucy ate the cupcake of the day, a chocolate affair, topped with chocolate icing, and proclaimed it to be "the best cupcake anyone had ever made". Afterward, they strolled barefoot on the beach. It had been a great day and Alessa realized blissfully that she had a whole week of great days ahead of her.

Wrightsville Beach was a great little town. The people were friendly and everyone seemed happy there. Remo, Alessa and Lucy rented bikes, one morning, and rode them up and down the small island. They shopped at the local grocery store within walking distance of their condominium and ate pizza at Vito's. Alessa had a feeling she'd never had before, a feeling of complete freedom. As they participated in different enjoyable activities that week and Remo reminisced about his own childhood, Alessa realized how much fun she had missed out on as a kid and envied him for it. She was, however, enormously pleased that Lucy was getting to enjoy her childhood the way Remo had enjoyed his own.

They loved the jet skis and the ghost tour was fun, especially since it was topped off with ice cream at Kilwin's, where they made their own waffle cones in the front window. People stood in line and Lucy told Remo,

"I think we picked the right place. Look at all the people waiting to get ice cream!"

Remo reveled in watching the two of them in such a relaxed and happy frame of mind. They were great together. Each of them understood and loved the others deeply, not because they had to, but because they really wanted to. They spent July 4th watching fireworks on the beach in front of their condo.

The fireworks lit up the sky and were reflected in the water below. Remo had never felt so much love for another, as he did during that week. Having the two of them in his life was the greatest gift anyone could ever have given him, he thought.

On their last night there, they dined at Osteria Cicchetti, an Italian restaurant in Wilmington that had a warm ambiance and great food. Later, they walked across the parking lot to Boombalatti's, where they made the best homemade ice cream any of them had ever tasted. Lucy was in heaven. She was having the greatest time of her life; they all were.

The next morning, a little wistful that their vacation was over, they vowed to each other to return the next summer. They arrived home on Saturday and Alessa called Ebby, as soon as she got in, to tell her about the vacation. Remo and Lucy remained on vacation time. They both took naps that afternoon and when they got up, insisted they were still on vacation. So they all went out to dinner.

They relived the past week over the meal and stopped for ice cream on their way home. It had been a truly magical week for all of them.

Lucy told them over ice cream, "Do you realize this will be the first year ever, since I was born, that I can actually write about my summer when I go back to school? You know, teachers always make you do that and I had just been making stuff up. Now I can write about it the way it really was, just like the other kids do."

Alessa hugged the child tightly. "You're a great person, Luce. I love you very much, more than anybody in the world."

Lucy threw her a mischievous grin. "Even more than Remo?"

Alessa became very serious. "Yes, even more than Remo."

Remo pretended to be offended, but quickly said, "Who in their right mind wouldn't love you the most, Lucy? You're the best person we know."

Brimming with contentment, Lucy reached up, hugged them both and yelled out, "Group hug!"

They all put their arms around each other and laughed.

Back home, Lucy was tucked into bed and Alessa and Remo went into the living room to have a glass of wine.

"Remo, I can't thank you enough for this past week," Alessa told him. "It was the best week of my life. I've never felt so good. It was the most amazing first vacation ever!"

Remo moved closer and kissed her deeply. "And you are the most amazing person I've ever known. I love you. I love you both."

Chapter Eighty-Two

The next year flew by and before they knew it, it was July and they were celebrating Alessa's twenty-third birthday at the Devil's Alley on Chestnut Street. Lucy was beside herself with glee, when her burger came out with onion rings stacked on top and filled with French fries. Ebby joined them and it was a quiet, but fun evening. Before dessert was served, Regina and her parents joined them too. It was all Alessa could have wished for. The rest of the summer flew by and before they knew it, they were getting Lucy ready to go back to school. She was excited about turning thirteen and Alessa was planning a party at their apartment with her friends from school.

A week before Lucy's birthday, Cliff and Beth drove Regina down as usual to Alessa's apartment so she could spend Saturday with them. Alessa, Lucy, Remo and Regina walked down to Clark Park to meet the customary mix of students, families and homeless people. It was eighty-two degrees and sunny, unusually warm for mid-September in Philadelphia. Alessa and Regina sat on a bench, while Remo and Lucy walked around the park, handing out soft pretzels and juice to the homeless.

It had been a whole year since Regina returned to her parents. She had evolved so much, both physically and mentally, that Alessa found her completely transformed. They had remained friends and she was pleased with the girl's rapid progress. They talked about a boy in school that Regina had a crush on. The girl was nervous about dating anyone in her school, since they all knew what had happened to her, but couldn't help sharing with Alessa her feeling that this particular boy was different. He was kind of a "geek", as she put it, but was always very pleasant to her and treated her with respect. He was, in fact, one of the few kids outside her close circle of friends who talked to her as though she were just a regular teenage girl.

Then, without warning, Regina's entire body language changed in mid-sentence. Alessa saw that she was distracted and tense.

"What's wrong, Regina?" she asked, alarmed. "Why do you look so scared?"

The girl could barely speak. She was whispering now, as if she were afraid of being overheard. "That woman over there, by the black car, is the one who used to feed us in the house where they had kept me locked up."

Her heart thudding, Alessa followed her gaze and almost threw up. The woman Regina had been referring to was someone she knew, someone she had loved. Thoughts raced through Alessa's mind, Regina must be mistaken. How could this be? Alessa found it impossible to believe.

There, standing next to a black Mercedes, was Tasha, Harlin's sister and her only friend from the time she had lived in North Philadelphia. Alessa froze. She felt as if the world had stopped spinning. Everything around her seemed to have gone dead silent.

She felt Regina tugging on her arm. "I'm scared, Alessa. I want to leave right now."

"Me too, sweetie," Alessa replied gently. She panicked as she scanned the park, her eyes wildly searching for Remo and Lucy, but unable to see them anywhere. Just before she lost complete control over herself she spotted the two off in a remote corner talking to people. Alessa pointed out where Remo and Lucy were and urged Regina to run to them and tell them to go back to the Outside Inn immediately and call the police. "Tell the police you saw a woman from the house on Daulphin Street. Do it! Do it now!"

Having got the girl safely out of the way, Alessa stood staring at Tasha. If she really were the person who had fed the kids being held in the basement of the house from where Regina had fled, surely Harlin had something to do with it. Even from a distance, she could see that Tasha looked worn out and ragged. Life had not treated her well over the past five years; that much was clear.

Alessa started to move away from where Tasha was, but stopped short as she felt the cold metal of a gun against her neck. Remaining out of her field of vision, the gunman ordered her to turn and walk toward the street. Alessa obeyed, heading for Tasha and the Mercedes, quite aware by now that the man with the gun was one of Harlin's boys.

As she approached her former friend, the girl who had helped her escape from her prison just five years ago, Alessa was desperate to reach out to her and plead for help once again.

"Tasha," she cried out, "what's going on? What's happening?"

Tasha seemed nervous and wired, acting as if Alessa hadn't said a word, as she slid into the car's passenger seat.

The gunman opened the back door and snapped, "Get in, bitch!"

It wasn't until Alessa leaned down to get into the car that she saw the man sitting there. Harlin stared at her grimly, his expression one of pure venom. It was clear that his rage against Alessa for fleeing his clutches had not subsided. The realization that she was in grave danger wrenched from her gut a small, involuntary whimper. Harlin reached over and grabbed her by the hair, pulling her face to within inches of his own.

"You thought you would fuck me over and I would forget?" he snarled. "You stupid, fucking bitch! Because of you, I spent five years locked up. Then you turn around and have my house busted! Do you know how much money you cost me?"

Alessa feared she would lose control of all her bodily functions, as she fought hard against the sheer terror that threatened to overwhelm her.

Harlin pushed her away from him. "See my boys over there? The ones next to your faggot husband and those dumb kids you been helping?"

Alessa looked back into the park and noticed two of Harlin's boys standing not ten feet behind Remo, Lucy and Regina. Her heart was beating, as if she had just finished running a marathon.

She gulped in the car's stale, smoke-filled air and begged, "Please, Harlin. I'll do anything you want me to. Just leave them alone. They have nothing to do with this."

"I don't give a fuck 'bout what you say!" he sneered. "All I know is, you ruined my life and now it's payback time."

He tapped the driver's seat from behind and as they pulled away, Alessa turned to look back at Remo, Lucy and Regina with panic and fear. From the frantic look on their faces, she could tell they were looking for her. She watched in horror as Harlin's boys began walking toward them. Then the car sped off and all Alessa could visualize was her world crumbling to pieces. During the drive back to North Philadelphia, not once did Tasha turn around to look at Alessa. As if in a drug-induced coma, she kept her eyes fixed on the view from the front window.

Chapter Eighty-Three

As they turned onto Dauphin Street, a petrified Alessa cringed at the memories evoked by the familiar surroundings. The car pulled up in front of a row home, a couple of blocks from where Harlin used to live. One of his boys came around the car, opened the door and yanked Alessa to her feet. Another gripped her by the arm as he pushed her toward the front door, with Harlin and Tasha following behind. The blood in Alessa's veins turned to ice as she stepped inside. Harlin's old gang was in the living room. They all looked up and started laughing and high-fiving each other when they saw her. Then Harlin grabbed her by the hair and shoved her down a long hallway into a bedroom.

Alessa noticed that the room's only window had been painted black and bars had been mounted on the inside. There was a small mattress on the floor and a single black light bulb hung from the ceiling. The room was dim and stank of death. Harlin slammed the door shut behind him and flung Alessa down on the mattress. He stood in front of her and dropped his jeans, then his boxers.

"The first thing you're gonna do is suck my dick. And bitch, you better make it good!" he growled. "Make sure it's the best fucking blow job you've ever given!"

Alessa did exactly that. She would do anything not to piss him off. She knew that if she angered him in any way, Remo, Lucy and Regina would pay the price.

When it was over, Harlin got dressed and left the room without uttering another word. Alessa lay back on the soiled mattress, curled herself into a ball and cried her heart out. When she had exhausted her tears, she began to pray. She prayed passionately to God to keep her family safe. She prayed that she would get out of this somehow. And finally, she prayed that Harlin and all those who were involved in his wicked activities would die.

Since she had no way of telling the time, Alessa figured that a few hours must have gone by before she heard the door being unlocked and looked over to see Tasha enter. She was carrying two pieces of dry toast and a glass of water.

"You need to eat," Tasha told her.

With tears streaming down her face, Alessa gazed begging her. "Tasha, you have to help me," she pleaded. Please!"

Tasha's face was devoid of all emotion. She looked like a zombie in a cheap horror movie, as she turned to face Alessa.

"Listen," she said, "I helped you once and it cost me everything. After you left, Harlin turned me out to make up for the money he would have earned through you. My parents couldn't even protect me from him. When he was sent to prison I thought I could stop hooking. As soon as he was locked up, some guys from a rival gang killed my parents. I got stuck in this motherfuckin' neighborhood, doing every man that Harlin's boys could find on the street. I did my time. Now, it's your turn, bitch. You should never have sent the police to bust the old house. Harlin was making plenty of money off those dumb, fucking kids and then you had to go and ruin it. So now you'll just have to deal with it. I ain't your friend and I don't give a fuck about you!"

Alessa could see the pain in Tasha's face for all that she lost and suffered.

With that, Tasha turned and left the room. Alessa's mind was racing. She couldn't believe this was happening to her again. How had it come to this? Why did history keep repeating itself? Why had God picked her, of all people, to dish out so much unhappiness? The only thing that kept Alessa breathing was her desire to get back to Remo and Lucy, where she belonged.

The next morning, Harlin came into the bedroom, switched on the light and stood over her. To Alessa, he looked like a giant monster. Before her eyes could adjust to the sudden glare of the light bulb, Harlin reached down and seized her by the neck of her shirt.

"You and me are gonna have a talk," he declared ominously.

Alessa felt like a rag doll as he yanked her up into a sitting position.

"Tonight, there's gonna be a party and you're the guest of honor," he announced with sadistic delight, flinging some exotic lingerie at her so that it hit her in the face before falling into her lap. "You're wearing this and when the party starts, you're on the auction block. See, after what you did, bitch, I have to set up my business from scratch and you're the only one I have at the moment to put up for auction. You're gonna shower and you're gonna make people want to bid on you. You understand?"

Alessa nodded in agreement. When Harlin had left, she trembled with fear. This couldn't be happening again. She was no longer the child whose uncle had raped her. Nor was she the teenager who had danced in the nude and offered sex for money. She was an educated woman who had put her life together. She sat on the mattress all morning, reliving the good times in her life. She thought of Ebby and how much she loved her. She imagined what it would be like when she and Remo grew older. She thought about Lucy and how lucky she was to have her. She savored the happy moments, trying to regain her resilience. Alessa was in survival mode again. She needed to do whatever it took to get her through this new ordeal so she could go back to her own people, to those she loved and who loved her.

She had no clue as to where Harlin's men would take Remo and Lucy. Maybe they too were in this very house? Her next thought made her break out in a cold sweat. She was so spooked it felt like her skin would peel away from her body. *What if,* she mused with a shudder, *they planned to sell Lucy like they had sold Regina? Oh my God! Regina! What were they going to do to her?*

Hours passed as Alessa sat and worried. Sometime in the afternoon, the bedroom door was unlocked and Tasha came in with a peanut butter and jelly sandwich and a glass of water. Alessa snatched it from her and gobbled it down. She looked up at Tasha when she was finished.

"Please, Tasha. Please!" she begged. "You have to help me. I don't deserve this and you know it."

For a moment, Alessa caught a glimpse of the old Tasha she had once known. Her hopes soared as she saw her face soften for a fraction of a second. But within an instant, the expression of cruel indifference was back.

"I ain't gotta help nobody, but me," Tasha flung back at her. "Fuck that shit! You gonna need to help yourself. You better do what Harlin tells you to or you ain't makin' it outta here alive. Got it?"

"Yes, yes I got it," Alessa said, retreating. But she couldn't help asking, "Please Tasha, where are Remo and Lucy? Are they okay?"

"I don't know nothin' about them and you just need to forget about them anyway. That life you had is over. This is your new life till Harlin says you can have a different one. Unless you want him to beat you, you better just do what he tells you to do."

Tasha walked out of the bedroom and locked the door behind her. Alessa sat there for hours. She didn't know how long she waited, because she couldn't see out the window. She didn't even know if it was night or day. Finally, she heard someone unlock the door again. Tensed up, she immediately went and sat on the end of the mattress. The door opened and Harlin walked into the room. She could see he was high. He gripped her arm and yanked her up from the mattress. He dragged her into the bathroom and ordered her to strip. His creepy gaze made her skin crawl as she undressed. She stood in front of him with her arms folded over her bare breasts.

"Bitch, when I tell you to get undressed, I don't want you hiding your tits or nothin' else from me!" he snarled. "You stand with your hands at your sides."

Alessa immediately dropped her arms to her sides. A feeling of humiliation consumed her. Harlin pushed by her and turned on the shower. Then he motioned for her to get under it. Harlin watched her as she stood under the water. He kept the door to the shower open so he could see her every move. "Wash up that pussy real good and get all that funk outta your hair. You smell like shit."

Alessa washed, hoping she could wash away her very existence. When she was finished, Harlin handed her a towel. Walking her back into the bedroom, he said, "I'll be back in twenty minutes. You better be done up right and wear that outfit I gave you this morning."

Alessa quickly dried herself and applied makeup, using the cosmetics that had been placed in the room while she was showering. She put on the sleazy lingerie Harlin had got her and sat on the mattress waiting.

Harlin came back into the room and approached her. "Stand up," he commanded.

As Alessa stood there, staring into his eyes, she searched for a tiny morsel of compassion, but could find none. The man who had once saved her from being murdered after she had been brutally raped was now the most evil monster she had ever set eyes on.

Harlin stepped closer, grasped her ass and pulled her body into his so their torsos were touching. "You remember what I said about tonight? If you want to see that pathetic white-trash family of yours again, you better do what I say."

Alessa seized the moment. "Please don't hurt them, Harlin," she whined. "Are they are okay? Where are they? Please let them go!"

Harlin stepped back. "'*Please* don't hurt them, *please* let them go, are they *okay?*'" he mimicked, mocking her. "Listen, bitch, I ain't here to help you. Just shut the fuck up!"

Just then his sister walked into the bedroom. She was carrying a pair of the "fuck-me" boots Alessa used to wear when she danced.

"They're here," Tasha announced matter-of-factly.

Chapter Eighty-Four

Alessa walked into the living room to find at least fifteen men there. Ranging in age from eighteen to sixty, they watched her as she approached the small platform set up in the middle of the room. The lights in the room were low so she could just make out their faces, but their expressions were so fucking horny Alessa could tell that they could barely keep their pants on. Circling her like untamed beasts, each of them studied her breasts and her ass to make sure they were firm. None of them touched her, but their piercing stares were like knives plunging into her flesh.

The room was silent, until Harlin spoke. "Okay," he said, "who's going to give me a bid?"

No one said a word. Then a short, fat white man in his mid-fifties complained, "Listen, this bitch is too fucking old. I didn't come here for this! You got anything younger? How fucking old is she anyway?"

"She's seventeen," Harlin lied.

All the men began to grumble, knowing that Alessa was much older than that.

The short, fat man said, "We're looking for that untapped stuff, man. Bring us something around thirteen or fourteen and we'll get some bids on the table."

Relieved, at first, that they were rejecting her, Alessa took a while to grasp what they wanted: children. She couldn't believe her ears and wished she could have killed all of them on the spot. She could see Harlin growing angrier by the moment, because no one was buying.

"Listen, this is what we got tonight," he said sternly. "We are putting our lineup back together. We'll have some younger ones by this time next week. I know this bitch ain't as young as you like 'em, but she has some experience."

Harlin walked over to a table in the corner and turned on music. He walked back and looked at Alessa. "Show them," he demanded.

Alessa began to dance to the music. Half the men left the room, while the rest watched the show. When the song was over, Harlin looked at the remaining men.

"Well?" he asked,"who's gonna give me a bid?"

The short, fat man spoke up. "Like I said before, she ain't young enough to bid on. I'll give you fifty bucks, but I want her all night in that room of hers. I need more than one fuck, if I'm gonna pay anything."

The other men nodded in agreement, but no one offered more than 50 dollars. Harlin pulled Alessa down off the platform. "Fine," he said. "Here, take her back in the bedroom and do whatever you want. If the bitch gives you any trouble, just yell."

Alessa was crying quietly as one of Harlin's boys led the two of them back into the bedroom. Once inside, the fat little pervert sized up Alessa's body without ever making eye contact with her.

"I'll tell you what," he said. "Since we're doing an all-nighter, let's take this in steps. First, I want you to undress me."

Alessa walked over to him and began unbuttoning his shirt. He held her hand still for a minute as he removed three big, smelly cigars from his pocket. He put the cigars on the floor next to the bed.

"I'll need them for later," he explained.

When he was standing completely naked in front of her, Alessa felt sick with revulsion. He was so fat that he had male breasts. A roll of flab from his stomach overhung his pelvis so that all she could see was the head of a short, fat, rampant penis. He was already rock hard by the time Alessa had undressed him and he sat down on the edge of the mattress and told her to undress slowly. Alessa was twenty-three years old and had a stunningly beautiful body and as she began to remove her clothes, one by one, she could hear his breathing quicken. She took off her bra first and the moment she did so, the man sprang to his feet and put his smelly mouth on her breasts. As he licked and sucked on them, Alessa wanted to bash his brains in. After several minutes, he withdrew and ordered her to take the rest of her clothes off. When she did, he stepped right up and jammed his fingers into her crotch. Alessa wanted to scream out in pain and humiliation, but knew the consequences would be worse than what this filthy piece of trash was doing to her.

The man had Alessa lie on her back as he invaded every inch of her body. Then he picked up an unlit cigar and told her to turn over and lie on her stomach. He crawled over her and dragged her body up from the waist so that her ass was raised. Then she felt him force his unlit cigar into her vagina, moving it back and forth inside her, the act turning him on more and more with each thrust. Finally, he pulled the cigar all the way out and inserted it into his mouth, licking it as if it were a lollipop. When he was done, he tossed the cigar onto the floor and plunged his penis into her rectum. Alessa groaned in pain, which just turned him on more.

When he was satisfied, he lay down next to her, picked up the cigar and lit it. Without looking at her, he said, "Not too bad for your age. We are going to have some real fun tonight."

By morning, Alessa didn't care if she lived or died. When Harlin came in to get her, she was barely able to walk to the bathroom with him. Harlin merely shoved a towel into her hand and ordered her to shower.

Once that was over, he escorted her back to the bedroom that was now hers and said, "Tasha will be in with food. After you eat, get some sleep. You look like shit and we ain't gonna make no money with you looking like shit and being an old hag. You're useless!"

He locked the door behind him and left her standing there in a towel. Alessa had endured a lot in her early years, but she knew that the previous night had been one of the worst in her life. She had to find a way to escape and get back to Remo and Lucy.

Chapter Eighty-Five

When Tasha came in with food, Alessa begged her for help again. "Tasha," she said, starting to cry, "do you know what that sick pig did to me last night? Please, Tasha, help me!" Alessa's chest heaved with sobs.

Tasha sat down on the mattress next to her and put an arm around her shoulders. Alessa clung to her as if she were a life preserver.

"Please, Tasha," she begged, "at least find out for me what they've done with Remo and Lucy. Please? I just need to know. I need to know that someday, I can go home to them. Please, Tasha!"

Tasha lingered for a moment longer, but made no promises to help her. She gave Alessa a quick hug and said, "I need ya to understand that it's either you or me and when you live on these streets, you need to do whatever is necessary to keep yourself safe. Ain't nothing personal. Just a matter of survival."

That night, after Alessa had carried out Harlin's instructions and put on her lingerie, he didn't take her out to the living room. Instead, the door opened and he stood there with a man in his early twenties. He was skinny, with long, stringy hair. As he reached out for Alessa, she could see the dirt under his fingernails. His breath smelled of whiskey.

Harlin looked at her. "He paid for an hour," he explained. "Since no one will bid on your old ass, from now on, you'll just give them whatever they pay for. Give him whatever he wants."

Four days had gone by since Alessa was brought to the house on Dauphin Street. She was now their resident whore. Men would come in and Harlin would tell her how long she had to spend with each of them.

On the fifth night, Tasha sat down for dinner in the kitchen with Harlin. She looked at her brother and said, "Listen, Harlin, she's crying all the time. She wants to go home and be with her family. I know you ain't lettin' her do that now, but I need to tell her something, before the bitch goes crazy on ya."

Harlin smiled. "Okay, Tash. Fine. She don't need to worry no more about going back to her family, because they're all dead. We killed that faggot husband of hers and that stupid little whore kid she thinks is her daughter. So you tell her we're the closest thing to family she's got. If she does what we want her to do now, I'll let her help with the young girls once we bring them in here. She's too old anyway. Ain't nobody willing to give me any real money for her."

Tasha sat looking at him, her mouth hanging open. "They're both dead, Harlin?"

Harlin slammed down his fork. "That's what I said, ain't it?"

Picking listlessly at her food now, Tasha realized that her brother, the man she had once loved, but had long ago come to hate, was completely toxic. She realized that Alessa's family had died in vain. For she knew in her heart that Alessa would have done anything to save Remo and Lucy.

As she tried to fall asleep that night, Tasha couldn't stop the tears. She thought about how close she and Alessa had once been. In fact, Alessa had been the only real friend she had ever known. Tasha knew she needed to tell Alessa the truth so she could come to terms with it and move on.

The next morning, when she entered the room, Alessa was sitting on the mattress and staring at the blank wall. She looked up at Tasha and gave her a feeble smile. Tasha sat down next to her and took her hand.

"I talked to Harlin about your family," she ventured tentatively.

With hope surging through her, Alessa turned swiftly to face her. "Oh my God!" she exclaimed, overjoyed. "Thank you so much! Are they okay? Where are they?"

Tasha looked at the floor. "They ain't with us no more."

Alessa screeched in alarm, "What do you mean by 'not with us'? What have they done to them?"

"I mean they're dead."

A primal sound, almost like that of a wounded animal, soared up from deep within Alessa. Her grief seemed to be emerging from her very soul. Tasha couldn't bear to watch her suffering. The woman who was once her friend, sobbed and screamed until she was spent. Then she just stared into space. Her eyes were blank and her mind seemed lost in some other world no one could reach. Tasha sat with her into the early evening, rocking her and trying to console her.

"It's gonna be okay," she soothed. "Harlin said that once he gets some young girls back in here, you can help run the house. You don't have to be a whore no more. He said you're too old for it anyway. Guess it pays to get old, huh?"

Tasha's words penetrated Alessa's mind, but she remained silent. There was nothing anyone could say to make her feel human again.

When Harlin checked in with his sister, she explained that things were fine. "But the girl needs a night off," she cautioned him. "She needs to grieve."

Tasha stayed with Alessa that night, holding her, while she cried in her sleep. When Alessa woke up the next morning, she wondered for a moment whether it hadn't all been a bad dream. Then she rolled over and saw Tasha asleep next to her and she knew it wasn't. She burst into tears all over again. She had lost the only man she had ever loved and the only child she would ever have. She thought of their innocence and how she had brought this on both of them. She wished a million times she could relive her life and bring them back, but knew she couldn't. All she had now to keep her company was this dark room and the evil people who lived and played in this house. Everything she had achieved and the people she had loved had been destroyed in a single moment. Her grief now turned to hatred for Harlin. Hatred so intense and real, that Alessa felt her heart had turned to stone and would never feel love for another human being again.

Chapter Eighty-Six

That night, Harlin opened the bedroom door to find Alessa sitting on the floor next to the mattress. She looked more like a robot than a human being. Her eyes were blank and staring into them, Harlin was pleased by what he saw: she had finally come to realize that she was a puppet in his hands, to be manipulated as he wished. Maybe, from now on, he wouldn't have to see that stupid look on her face, the look that suggested she was hoping for something that would never actually happen.

"Let's go," he said abruptly. As Alessa stood up to follow him, he stopped her sharply with a gesture. "Put your lingerie on," he commanded.

This time, Alessa undressed in front of him without a trace of self-consciousness, as though she no longer felt ashamed or embarrassed to strip before a man. She put on the lingerie and, without Harlin even reminding her to do so, stepped into her high heels. She was like a zombie and Harlin liked it. It made his life a lot easier now. He led her out into the living room and Alessa was surprised to find no clients waiting for her. She was alone with Harlin.

He turned to her and while taking off his shirt, announced, "Tonight is *my* night for a little pussy. Just you and me. You ain't gotta do *no one* else tonight!"

Alessa faked her relief, as though he were doing her a favor by offering himself as the sole client for the night, and acted like the naïve girl she used to be when they'd first met. But deep in her heart, there was nothing but hatred for him, a hatred so intense she wished he would die. As she stood waiting for him to take his pleasure, Harlin reached behind to put his gun on the sofa. Then he took off his pants and boxers. Naked, he told her to turn on the music. She obeyed his command and went back to him on the sofa. He yelled, "Dance!"

As he moved his hands down her body, a soft moan issued from his lips. He slid her thong off and pulled her into himself. Grasping her by the hips, he lifted her and brought her down slowly to rest on him so that he was inside her. Alessa slowly gyrated up and down. Harlin's breathing became labored and she began kissing him. He kissed her back lustfully, as he had never kissed anyone before. Between moans, he mumbled incoherently, "We'll make this work."

When he came, his arms went around her waist and he clung to her, as if for his very life. Then he opened his eyes and a chill went through him; his own gun, now gripped in Alessa's hand, was pointing steadily at his temple.

His face twisted in rage. His voice was threatening, as he snarled, "What are you going to do with that, bitch?"

Without a word, Alessa pulled the trigger.

As Harlin sprawled on the sofa, half his skull gone, she stared down at him expressionlessly. Then she said, "Blow your fucking brains out, *bitch*!"

Leaving him there, Alessa went back into the bedroom. She flung off the lingerie and put on the jeans, tee shirt and sneakers she had been wearing the day she had been abducted from the park. She sat on the edge of the mattress, reflecting on the precious moments she had shared with Remo and Lucy. She paid a silent tribute to her love for them and begged God's forgiveness for being the cause of their deaths. She thought about her life and how empty it would now be. She realized how impossible it would be for her to go on without them. She needed to be with them. Then slowly, she picked up Harlin's gun, placed it against her temple and pulled the trigger.

Chapter Eighty-Seven

———————◼———————

The police arrived just as the second shot was fired. Tasha was standing in front of the house.

"She's in there," she told them.

A police officer asked, "Are you the one who called the police?"

Tasha nodded. "She was the only friend I ever had. Harlin killed her family and I knew she wasn't gonna make it without her husband and her kid."

The police entered the house and found Harlin dead in the living room where Alessa had left him. They moved through the house quickly and found Alessa in the bedroom. She too was dead. Meanwhile, a firestorm of police and flashing lights outside the house was attracting attention from people in the neighborhood. On the front steps, Tasha sat wrapped in a blanket, being questioned by the police. She looked up, as a man and an older woman, neither in uniform, approached the front door. The policeman who was talking to her blocked their entry into the house.

"I'm sorry, sir," he said politely, but firmly, "no one can go in there."

Remo looked steadily at the officer. "I'm Alessa's husband," he said.

Tasha started screaming. "No, you can't be! Harlin said they killed you and your kid!"

Remo looked at her. "I have no idea what you're talking about."

Two policemen now approached Remo and Ebby. They took them off to one side where an officer verified their identities. Then, with deep sorrow in his voice, the policeman said, "I'm sorry, sir. Your wife is dead. It appears that she shot herself in the head after killing the man who had abducted her."

Ebby let out a gurgling cry of anguish before the words finally exploded from her lips. "Oh my God!"

Remo had fallen to his knees and was bent over with pain. "No, no, no!" he whispered to himself in a voice raw with torment.

The two of them sat on the pavement, holding onto each other and shuddering with grief as a crowd gathered, silenced by the sight of their crippling anguish.

Hours later, the police drove Remo and Ebby back to the Outside Inn. At the apartment, Lucy was sitting on the floor playing Monopoly with one of the young residents who had agreed to look after her. They both looked up and Lucy was startled by the expression on Remo and Ebby's faces. Remo rushed to the girl and gathered her up in his arms. Ebby stood beside them, as he explained that Alessa was dead. Lucy cried from the depths of her being, clinging to Remo as though she would never let him go. Ebby wrapped her arms around the two and the three of them stayed there, huddled together, united in their sorrow.

Later that night, as the three of them sat together, Lucy asked, "Why did Alessa have to leave us? Didn't she know that we would find her?"

Remo moved closer. "The man who took her away told her he had killed us both. I don't think she wanted to live without us, Luce."

By two a.m., they were all exhausted. Remo went to his room to get some sleep. Ebby lay down next to Lucy in her bed and they slept in each other's arms. In the morning, when they appeared in the kitchen, an invisible shroud of gloom seemed to have descended on them. The apartment seemed a vast, empty vacuum, devoid of life. All that could fill it were mere memories—of the woman who had changed their lives.

The Final Moments

—■—

Despite their bereavement, routine matters clamored for attention. Remo had to go to the morgue that morning to identify Alessa's body. This dreaded formality, mandatory for the police investigation to get underway, would serve as a sort of closure for him. When he arrived at the morgue, the coroner led him to the room where Alessa's body had been laid out. A large bandage camouflaged her head where part of her skull was missing. Her face was pale and serene, as though relieved of all the troubles that had plagued her throughout her life. Remo approached her for the last time. Part of him expected her to sit up and give him that radiant smile that had been such a comfort in his life for years now. Gazing down at her face, he told her how much he had loved her. There would never be a better wife for him, he told her, nor a more loving mother for Lucy. He stayed with her for an hour, stroking her hair and kissing her cheek. She would be cremated that afternoon and he knew this would the last time he would ever see her.

Heartbroken and alone, he wondered how he would live through the day, as he turned to her for the last time and said, "You were the love of my life. No one will ever take your place. You saved me, Alessa. You saved so many of us."

Then the coroner gently led him away.

Over the next three days, Remo and Ebby discussed the funeral arrangements, as Lucy sat listening to them in silence. They were going to have a mass at the local Catholic Church and Remo's dad planned to buy a plot for Alessa in a Philadelphia cemetery so they could bury her ashes there.

"I don't know why you are doing this," Lucy suddenly butted in, her eyes filling with tears. "This is *not* what Alessa would have wanted. I hate you both! How can you not understand?"

Remo and Ebby were shocked at her outburst, but realized, instantly, that perhaps they hadn't paid enough attention to her feelings.

"What is it, Luce?" Remo asked gently. "What would Alessa have wanted us to do?"

"Alessa would have wanted her ashes scattered under the bridge where the two of us used to live," Lucy managed to mumble between muffled sobs. "She would have wanted to be there, because she always told me it was living there that had changed her life forever."

Remo and Ebby conceded that the girl was right. Lucy had been an inseparable part of Alessa; sometimes, it had seemed as if they were one and the same person.

Remo put his arms around her. "You're absolutely right. That's what we're going to do. Okay, Luce?"

The girl nodded and buried her face in Remo's chest. There was something she had to know right away, but was apprehensive about asking him, in case she faced rejection.

"Remo?" she said tentatively, "Are you and me still going to live together or do I have to live somewhere else?"

Remo was taken aback. "God no, Lucy! You and I will always be together. We're family. Even without Alessa here, you and I will always be family."

Now that she knew for sure that she and Remo would get through Alessa's death together, Lucy let her defenses down at last and allowed herself a good cry.

They scheduled a time to scatter Alessa's ashes under the bridge near the train station. They informed the residents of the Outside Inn, who had been devastated to learn of her death, so that they could attend. Alessa's sister, Rosabella, had been called. She would be coming with her daughter, Eva. Patrick, Hannah and Sara would be there, as would Regina and her parents.

As they drove down Thirtieth Street to the bridge where Alessa's ashes would rest, people were lined up on both sides.

"Great," Remo remarked, "there must be an event taking place here today. We'll park here and walk the rest of the way. We're only about four blocks away."

He, along with Lucy and Ebby, walked the four blocks, holding the urn that contained Alessa's ashes. They realized quickly there wasn't an event in the city that day. The people that lined the street, reached out to them—homeless people, business people and others who had come to pay their respects to Alessa. So overwhelmed were the three of them by the love and devotion she had inspired in so many during her short time on earth that they cried and held onto each other as they moved toward the bridge. Lucy led them to the spot where she and Alessa had slept, years before.

Remo's parents were both there, waiting. Patrick put his arm around his son, while Hannah hugged Lucy. There was no room to move, as people gathered around them.

"I want to thank you all for coming here today," Remo began. "Alessa would never have expected so many of you to be here today. Nor did she realize how many lives she had touched. We will all miss her and the magic that she had managed to retain within her, in spite of all the hardships she lived through." He paused to look around him. Everyone was weeping by now and Remo could not contain his tears either, as he grieved openly for the woman he had loved.

"Alessa once told me," Ebby said, "that her only wish in life was that someone would miss her when she died. She was alone at the time, with no one in her life. But since then, all of you have filled her life with joy. I imagine her now, looking down from heaven and saying, 'Ebby, can you fucking believe it? Look at all the people who will miss me!'"

The crowd laughed at this well-remembered image of Alessa who had been known as a potty mouth and proud of it too.

Finally, it was Lucy's turn. The crowd gazed at her, overwhelmed by the grief of the thirteen-year-old as they watched her mourn, feeling the pain of her loss. But the young adolescent was the most eloquent of them all.

"Alessa believed that our names meant a lot," she said. "She told me my name meant 'light'. She used to say I was the light that had showed her the way." Lucy paused to compose herself, then continued. "She also told me that it was her grandmother who had given her the name, 'Alessa', when she was born. It means 'defender of mankind'. That's what her grandmother believed she saw as she looked into the baby's eyes and glimpsed at her soul. Alessa loved to tell me that story. It was the only happy memory from her childhood. And she defended and saved so many of us. She was the only mother I ever had, the best mom I could ever have asked for. I'm going to miss her for the rest of my life."

As the crowd bowed their heads to pray for Alessa, they were all aware she was watching over them.

After they had scattered the ashes, Remo turned to Lucy and took her hand. He reached up into the tree that towered above them and rubbed the brass plate that had been mounted on the tree trunk. Then he lifted the girl so she could rub her hand across it too. Ebby looked up to read what was written on it:

Alessa - Defender of Mankind
The Greatest Mother, Wife and Friend

Continue Reading...

Read the beginning of Paige Dearth's second novel...

W H E N
SMILES FADE

The Seed Is Planted

———————————— ∎ ————————————

"**E**mma! Get your ass down here, you stupid little bitch! What the fuck did I tell you about not living like a pig?" Pepper screamed. Panic-stricken at the thought of what would happen next, Emma rushed her younger sister, Gracie, over to the bedroom closet and pushed the tiny child inside. Before shutting the door she said, "Don't move or make any noise." Then in a softer whisper she warned her younger sister, "You have to be really, really quiet. I'll be right back. I promise."

That was code for "be invisible." Gracie obeyed her older sister, tears of fright silently dribbling down her cheeks.

Emma rushed into the hallway and stopped to look at her mother, who was standing just inside her own bedroom. "What the hell did you do now?" she accused. "How many times do I have to tell you to do what you're told? You brainless idiot!"

Gracie listened from the closet to the rapid patter of eight-year-old Emma's feet as she ran down the stairs. There was an eerie silence during which she unconsciously held her breath. Then the first blow was struck. Followed by others. Gracie cringed at her older sister's muffled shrieks of torment as she imagined the scene downstairs with telling accuracy. Emma, she knew from past experience, had once again been transformed into her father's punching bag. She wondered why their mother didn't go and help Emma. Resisting the urge to run downstairs, Gracie stayed hidden upstairs in the bedroom closet as she was instructed, waiting for the beating to end, scared that her father would come for her after he was finished with her older sister.

Down in the kitchen, Pepper Murphy lurched around, unsteady on his feet. He towered over his young daughter, contemplating her stricken face for several minutes and deriving a sickening enthusiasm and fresh energy from her growing terror. She stood before him, whimpering from the fear that was planted in her heart, wishing, as always, that her father's love for her would overpower his fury. That never happened. When she had worked herself up into a frenzy of fear, Pepper punched her in the eye. Emma lost her footing and hurtled back into the doorframe. Almost immediately, her face began to swell at the site of impact.

Snatching her up by the collar of her shirt, Pepper slapped Emma across the face with such force that he split her lip open. Blood gushing into her mouth and down her chin, she watched as her father walked over to the stove and turned on the burner. When the cold black coil began to glow a scorching orange, he shut the burner off and stood glaring at his daughter. Her body involuntarily shook as she wondered what he was going to do to her. Huddled in the corner of the kitchen, Emma wished the walls would open so that she could crawl inside of them and find the needed protection from her father's wrath. "Please, Daddy. Please don't hurt me. I'm sorry," the child begged.

His eyes bored into hers, undeterred by her fear and pain. Emma watched in terror as the corners of his mouth curled up, until he was smiling like a sadistic monster. She trembled visibly in anticipation of what was to come. Her father suddenly pounced on her. Grasping her by the arm, he dragged her, kicking and screaming, over to the hot burner. Then he seized her left hand and ordered her to unclench her teeny fist. After she opened her hand, Pepper slapped her palm down on the hot burner in one swift movement, holding it in place for a couple of seconds and letting the young, tender skin boil and blister from the intense heat that still remained. Then he bent down, his face close to his daughter's, and snorted, "Oink! Oink! Oink!" into her ear.

All through the ordeal, Emma's shrills of agony sliced through the silence of the house. Valerie lay on her bed upstairs. Her mind filled with raw horror as she imagined what would happen to her if Pepper killed the child and was sent to prison. She prayed that he wouldn't take it too far this time. She didn't give a thought to the suffering that her older daughter was enduring at the hands of her husband. It was as if she had ice water running through her veins in place of blood.

As Emma collapsed on the floor, Pepper stood over her threateningly. Speaking in a tight, cold voice, he said through clenched teeth, "You are a worthless piece of shit. I don't know why I just don't kill you right now. I'm giving you another chance to act like a human being. You can forget about eating dinner tonight. I don't see why a little pig like you should be fed. Consider yourself lucky that I don't beat you to death." He began to leave the kitchen, but turned back at the doorway and bellowed, "You better have this place cleaned up before I get home from the bar!" With that final warning, Pepper grabbed a beer from the refrigerator then stormed out of the kitchen and left the house.

Emma remained sprawled on the floor, paralyzed by the depth of her own despair, her eight-year-old mind trying to recover from what her father had just done to her. Then she scolded herself for failing to wash that one dirty fork that Valerie had left in the sink when she had gotten home from school. Maybe if she had washed it, none of this would have happened, she tried to rationalize, looking for some reason why she deserved such harsh punishment. She sat staring at her blistered, deformed palm. The pain the burn caused was only secondary to her overwhelming despair at being unloved.

This year of her life was when Emma became acutely aware of the possibility that Pepper might actually kill her. The years prior had been hard for her, but now that she was getting older her thoughts and senses were on high alert and she could no longer deny them. She grappled with finding different ways to behave that would stop the abuse, not because she was afraid of dying, but because she was afraid to leave Gracie alone with her parents.

After Pepper had burned her hand on the stove, she did everything in her power to fly below his radar. She made sure to clean the house after school every day and took special care in making his meals. But nothing lightened his fury. It was a Wednesday night and Emma was sitting at the kitchen table doing her homework after she had finished cleaning up from dinner. Her father staggered back into the kitchen to get himself another beer. He opened the can and took a long, hard swig. His head hung as if it were too heavy for his neck to hold as he eyed her with disgust. "I don't know why you bother with dat school shit; you're never gonna 'mount to nuttin' no matter how hard you try," he babbled through his drunken daze.

Emma looked up at him, her heart pounding in her chest. "My math teacher thinks I'm really smart. She told me that if I wanted to, I could be an accountant someday," Emma said, hoping to make him feel proud of her.

Pepper stomped over to the table and picked up one of her pencils and thrust the point into her forearm. The pencil stood at attention as she looked on in shock. She quickly yanked the pencil out of her arm and ran to the sink to wash off the blood with soap and water. "See dat! Now you're not so worried 'bout pretending like you understand anything in those books of yours. Let that be a lesson not to leave your stuff all over my kitchen table. Now get this shit out of here!" he bellowed.

Pepper was tireless in his violent treatment of Emma. To her, the slaps, punches, and kicks came from a bottomless pit of hate that burrowed deep in her father's soul. The endless bruises he left on her made Emma feel hopeless and ashamed. Alone in the bathroom, Emma would study the wounds and scars that Pepper gave her. She was consumed by her sense of loneliness and lack of power to change her circumstances. She was completely at his mercy and knew he could do whatever he wanted to her, regardless of how broken she became.

It was a warm morning in August and the two girls were jumping rope in the backyard. Pepper got annoyed because they were making too much noise while he was nursing a burning hangover with vodka. He flung open the back door and stood holding his aching head. "You two shut the fuck up. You hear?"

They immediately went silent and stood perfectly still. He turned and went back into the house, and Emma was lulled into a false sense of security as they began running through the yard, playing tag. Moments later, the rotted screen door burst open and Pepper barreled down the cement steps into the yard. He grabbed Emma under her arm and pulled her into the house. She began to plead with him, knowing she was in for something terrible. "I'm sorry, Daddy," she cried, "I swear, we'll be quiet. okay, Daddy? Please don't hurt me," she cried.

Pepper grabbed the soft flesh under her upper arm and pinched as hard as he could. Emma went to her knees as she tried to get him to release his hold. He dragged her into the living room where there was an old wooden trunk. "You want to disobey me? Well then, there is a price for that," he said calmly.

Pepper pushed the glass vase filled with dusty plastic flowers off the chest. It slammed to the floor and shattered into a million pieces. Emma's eyes bulged as she frantically wondered what he was going to do to her. As her father lifted the lid to the trunk, she shrunk away from him trying to run and escape. He lifted her around the waist, her feet flailing as she tried to break away from his tight grip. Her movements made it impossible for him to get her legs into the trunk. Growing more irrational by the moment, he clamped his teeth on her shoulder until he could taste her blood in his mouth. Then he twisted her arm behind her back until he heard the pop as it dislocated at the shoulder. With excruciating pain in both shoulders she stopped fighting and sank into the trunk. After he slammed the lid shut and locked it, he left her and went to find Gracie. Ignoring her own painful injuries, Emma's gut twisted as she heard her father slapping Gracie around the living room. I wish I were a superhero, she thought, so that I can break out of here and help my sister.

Inside the trunk her body was twisted in an unnatural position. Her legs were folded at the knees behind her and her torso was bent at the waist so that her nose touched her knees. There was not enough room in the small space for her to reposition herself, and after a couple of hours her limbs went numb.

After the first twenty-four hours had passed and he hadn't let her out, all she wanted was to die. She reveled in the idea of leaving her measly existence and finally being free of her tormentor, believing that death was a much more appealing option than her current living conditions.

During her imprisonment, every so often her father would flip the trunk on different sides, smashing her dislocated shoulder and twisted body against the walls of the wooden box. Two days later, when he finally opened the lid and let her out, Emma could barely walk.

She literally crawled, with Gracie's help, over to the sofa where she lay for another four hours. Finally she managed to get to her feet. As she headed toward the foot of the stairs to go up to her room, Pepper put his foot in front of her. Unsteady on her feet, she crashed down onto the floor. She broke her fall with her hands before her face hit the floor and she scurried like a wounded animal to get away from her father. He stood over her and began to laugh. He laughed so hard that tears streamed down his face as his daughter watched him, humiliated and defeated.

Then, without warning, her stomach twisted into a tight knot as disgust for her father overcame her anguish. She felt a surge of hatred so profound that no one could stop it from taking complete control of her. It shook her entire being. Emma grappled with an idea so horrifying that it took her a while to accept it: she now believed that her father was the devil himself in a man's body. This conviction would mark a new beginning for her, eventually determining who she would become. The seed had been planted.

Chapter One

———————————■———————————

It was a cold November night a little more than a year later and the temperature had dipped into the low thirties. The family was having dinner in the small, dimly lit kitchen. Valerie's eyes were fixed on her plate as Pepper grumbled about his boss and how much he despised the man. That evening, like most others, his drinking had started before he even got home and only ramped up the moment he walked through the front door.

Emma had just spooned some peas onto Gracie's plate. The six-year-old reached for her glass of water and accidentally caught her father's freshly opened can of beer with her small arm. Pepper erupted. His face looked like a twisted mass of bumpy, pulsating flesh as the veins in his temples stood out and he turned bright red. Clenching his fists, he put them up against Gracie's dainty face and yelled, "You fucking little whore! You spilled my beer! You're an idiot, just like your sister!"

Without warning, he yanked the terrified child out of her chair and flung her down on the floor. Before she could recover from the shock, he bent down and slapped her in the face, sending her flying across the kitchen floor. Her body seemed weightless, like a rag doll, as she tumbled head over heels and landed on the other side of the room. Pepper trudged over to her, buried his fingers in her hair, and closed his fist over a handful of strands. Then he pulled her upright until she was standing. Gracie's face twisted with pain as she let out a bloodcurdling shriek.

Her father ground his nose against hers. "You fucking maggot!" he yelled. "I never wanted you! You belong to that stupid bitch over there!" He gestured toward Valerie. As Pepper released his daughter's hair, she fell back to the floor.

Stunned by what had happened, Emma ran to her little sister. She desperately hoped her mother would protect them, even though Valerie

417

had proven time and again that she wouldn't. She now snapped at her father. "Why don't you leave her alone? You bully!" she screamed.

Outraged by what he considered to be the ultimate form of disrespect, Pepper snatched a frying pan from the top of the stove and whacked the side of her face with it, knocking her unconscious. When Emma woke up, she found herself lying on the cement steps that led from the back of the house into their small yard. Dressed only in the jeans and sweater she had worn to school that day, she felt the cold seeping into her bones, clearing the cobwebs of confusion that had clouded her mind. Emma picked herself up and knocked softly on the back door.

Pepper, who had been waiting for her to wake up, immediately flung open the door, startling her. "You think you're smart?" he snapped. "You think you can talk to me like that? Nobody tells me what to do in my house! Tonight, you'll sleep outside and learn never to talk back to me, girl!"

After he had slammed the door in her face, Emma huddled into herself, trying to keep warm. The wind slashed through her worn clothing, increasing her desperation to find shelter. Afraid to go too far, she decided to seek refuge on their front porch. There, she remembered, was a broken down sofa that had never made its way to the trash.

Mrs. Tisdale, her elderly neighbor who lived across the street, was looking out her window as Emma made her way to the front of their row home. The old woman watched the child move slowly up the front porch, trying to step as lightly as possible so that the creaky boards wouldn't betray her presence. Then her eyes widened in alarm as the little girl crawled under the worn cushions on the sofa and completely vanished from sight.

Mrs. Tisdale kept her eyes glued to the sofa for more than fifteen minutes before she put on her coat and went across the street to find out what the hell was going on. She approached Emma with great care, so as not to startle her, and gently lifted the cushion covering her face. "Child," she murmured, "why you out here in the cold? Where's your mama?"

Her eyes red from crying, Emma replied, "My father is making me sleep outside tonight. He was hitting my little sister and I yelled at him to stop. So he hit me with a pan and put me outside. This is my punishment."

"Well, I'll be dipped in shit if a little child like you is gonna sleep out here in the cold!" the elderly neighbor said in a huff. "Come on, baby, you sleepin' at my house tonight."

Emma's body stiffened with resistance. "No, Mrs. Tisdale," she protested, "I have to stay here so I can get up in the morning and get out back before my father goes to work. If he finds out I didn't stay on the back steps during the night, I don't know what he'll do to me."

Mrs. Tisdale gave her concern due consideration. "Okay then," she conceded, "you'll come sleep at my house and we'll set an alarm so that you can get up before he does. That way, you can go back on those steps before that bastard goes off to work. okay, baby?"

Comfortable with Mrs. Tisdale's proposition, Emma dug herself out from beneath the cushions and followed her across the street. Once inside her own house, Mrs. Tisdale wrapped Emma in a warm blanket and made her a steaming cup of cocoa. The chocolaty milk warmed her insides, filling her with a sense of security. Emma was grateful for Mrs. Tisdale's kindness as she lay, warm and cozy, on her neighbor's sofa waiting for sleep to provide a temporary release from her life.

This was the first real encounter that Emma had with Mrs. Tisdale. From here on the relationship grew, and over time, the girl came to rely on her for the support she needed to make it through each treacherous day. Mrs. Tisdale was well aware of how Pepper treated his two daughters. As a result, she tried to compensate by showering the children with the love their parents couldn't seem to find for them. Mrs. Tisdale failed to understand how Valerie could allow her husband to beat their own children. If it were her husband, the old lady told herself, she would surely have set things right. Hell, she thought, I'm gonna try my best to set things right and I ain't even married to that no-good dirty, rotten bastard.

Chapter Two

————————————————————◼————————————————————

A voluptuous black woman, Mrs. Tisdale had short salt-and-pepper hair that fell about her head in large curls. Her eyes were such a light brown that people mistook her eye color for hazel. Her bright smile lit up her jolly face, and her hands, although extremely large, gave Emma tender comfort when she needed it most. Mrs. Tisdale's loving ways filled the girl with joy, and when the old woman laughed, a rumbling sound rose from deep within her belly, making the child's heart soar and offering her a temporary reprieve from the darkness that enveloped her life.

From the time she had gotten to know Emma, Mrs. Tisdale often brought up the issue of Child Protective Services, explaining to the girl that they offered a way out of her predicament. The old lady wanted to alert them so they could take Emma and Gracie away from their brutal father, but the child had pleaded with her to keep the secret. Not understanding how the system worked, Emma feared that they would take her away and leave Gracie at home to become the new target of Pepper's abuse.

"Mrs. Tisdale," Emma had sobbed, "it won't be any use. My mother will just stick up for my dad and tell them I'm lying."

Against her better judgment, Mrs. Tisdale had let it go. Instead, she had turned to prayer, asking for peace and love to be bestowed upon Emma.

At home, Emma lived in fear, but with Mrs. Tisdale, she always felt safe and secure. Life was sweet with her elderly neighbor, regardless of how short-lived those moments of happiness were. When Pepper was at work or drowning himself in booze at the bar, the child helped Mrs. Tisdale fold clothes and do small chores, listening intently to the stories the lady shared of her own youth. Emma would pretend that her neighbor was her real mother, knowing that if she were, her life would be very different.

In the neighborhood, Mrs. Tisdale was regarded as a tough old black woman. Nobody in Norristown fucked with her. She had three grown sons.

They were big and they were mean. When it came to protecting their mama, they were ruthless. Her sons were always nice to Emma, because their mama had explained to them, "The poor child has to put up with brutal beatings from her papa. He's a sorry excuse for a father. We need to give her as much lovin' as we can, so she knows people care for her. Otherwise, she's likely to turn out just like him. Children become what they know. You hear me now?"

Rather quickly, Emma secretly began to wish that Mrs. Tisdale's sons would stop Pepper from hurting her. But just like Valerie, they never came to her rescue. Emma had no choice but to carry the burden of her sickening youth alone.

Chapter Three

Pepper Murphy's mother had died in childbirth, leaving his alcoholic father to raise the boy. The man often beat his small son, berating him time and again for killing his mother. The boy's destructive temper evolved over time, fueled by his anger and helplessness as he endured daily rounds of abuse from his father. When he was still a young boy, Pepper had taken to hiding behind bushes and cars and either throwing large stones at other children as they walked by or whacking them on the back with thick tree branches. He did these things in an attempt to release his own anger.

In middle school, he acquired quite a reputation as the class bully; he would hit and verbally abuse his classmates for no good reason, leaving them defenseless and humiliated. As a young teen, Pepper's explosive anger at his peers escalated to intolerable levels, often leaving his weaker prey with scars and bruises from his boiling rage.

By the time he reached high school he was drinking and smoking and had only a couple of close friends. However, when he entered eleventh grade, Pepper's shop teacher took a liking to him. The teacher realized that with some encouragement the boy could be saved from the fate that he was heading toward. He thought Pepper could someday be a talented home builder, a dream of Pepper's from the time he was small and had used his homemade wood blocks to build houses.

Pepper's whole attitude changed with the positive attention he received from his shop teacher. He made the teenager believe that he could actually do something good so that he would become a man that others respected. For the first time in his life, Pepper was filled with optimism. He quickly became likeable to many of his peers. He enjoyed the last two years of high school—making new friends, going to parties, and becoming the guy that all the girls wanted as their boyfriend.

When he graduated from high school, he had big plans of setting up his own construction business with his closest friend. They talked with excitement about getting contracts for building houses for a large company. The two friends mapped out how they would start out with smaller construction jobs before branching out to build homes on their own. They agreed to save a portion of their earnings from each job to purchase their first company truck.

Only four months after they graduated high school, the two young men signed their first contract. They believed that all of their dreams were coming true. "We need to celebrate! We're on our way to the big time," Pepper boasted. "Let's go to the bar and have a few beers."

They had only been at the bar for an hour when Pepper raised his beer. "Here's to building houses, buddy!"

As they banged glasses and chugged their beers, a beautiful woman named Valerie walked in front of them. Pepper and his friend stared at her, along with every other man in the bar, as she made her way over to a table of friends. That was the night Pepper and Valerie first met.

Pepper and Valerie were almost immediately infatuated with each other. Her beauty stirred a sexual hunger in him that he couldn't control and she was smitten by his apparently strong, protective nature. The two made an attractive couple. Pepper was tall and full-bodied and his intimidating stature matched his burly character. Pepper's jet-black hair and thick, dark eyelashes set off his blazing green eyes. His full lips complemented his long, slender nose, and his rugged features and square jaw made him appear fearless.

Valerie was equally attractive, but what she possessed in physical beauty she lacked in brains. She had long, straight blond hair that fell to her shoulders like strands of golden silk. Her eyes were stunning, almost royal blue, and her pale pink pouty lips were plump and inviting. She was tall and thin with full breasts, a tiny waist, and curved hips.

Valerie's parents had died suddenly when their car slid off of a bridge on an icy winter night two days before Christmas. She was just thirteen-years-old with no other family, and spent the next five years of her life being raised in various foster homes. She carried an unrelenting resentment towards her parents who died and left her alone. Moving all the time annoyed the shit out of her and she hated having to adjust to new families and different rules.

By the time she was fourteen-years-old the other foster girls had taught her how to use her body to get men to do whatever she wanted. These girls influenced her into being manipulative and self-absorbed. Her mannerisms and good looks often created tension between each of her foster parents. The men took her side while the women resented that she stole all of the attention that rightfully belonged to them. Valerie lied and cheated to her foster parents, teachers and anyone else who stood in her way. The once sweet child had grown into a despicable young woman. Finally, when Valerie turned eighteen, she and another girl who she knew from foster care moved into a cheap, rundown apartment over a pizza shop in Pottstown.

Pepper and Valerie were inseparable at first. He took her to the movies where they sat in the very back row, kissing and groping each other. When the weather turned warmer, Valerie made picnics with egg salad sandwiches, potato chips, and homemade blueberry pie. They would spread a blanket out in Valley Forge State Park where they ate their lunch and talked about how much they liked being together. Since their conversations lacked substance, they spent most of their time together kissing and sexually teasing one another.

They had been dating for six months when, after Pepper had one too many shots of whiskey, he forced himself on Valerie against her will during one of their usual make-out sessions. Valerie was devastated that he had stolen her virginity. When she found out she was pregnant with Emma, she threatened to tell the police that she had been raped by him if he left her.

When Pepper turned to his old high school shop teacher for advice, he told him in no uncertain terms, "Good men take care of things when they make mistakes. If it's true that what you did was a mistake then your only choice is to marry her and raise the child together."

Pepper's attraction to Valerie had always been a physical one and he had never planned on spending his whole life with her. But between his shop teacher's advice and her threat of lying to the police, he grudgingly agreed to stay with her. Pepper, for his part, was forced to work on an assembly line at the local auto factory in order to feed his new and unwanted family. Abandoning his friend and the dream of his own business made his heart heavy and filled him with bitterness.

By the time Emma was born, Pepper already resented the baby who, he firmly believed, had destroyed his dream and stolen his life. It was inevitable that she would never know a father's love. She only knew the man as a large and frightening creature she had to please at any cost. But no matter how hard she tried, she was never successful. She clung to the only option available to keep his violent temper at bay—obedience. It might, she hoped, help to lessen the intensity of the physical and emotional pain he caused her.

Despite her dismal circumstances, Emma was still a sweet-natured child, respectful toward everyone she met. People took to her easily, and those who knew her well sensed a deep sadness about her. They couldn't help being moved to pity. A beautiful girl, she seemed to have the perfect combination of her parents' good looks. Blessed with her mother's blond hair and her father's piercing green eyes, she was taller than most nine-year-olds, her height alone leading people to believe that she was older than she actually was. She worked hard every day to keep her spirit intact in the unhealthy, dysfunctional place she knew as "home." While her father abused her physically and emotionally, her mother constantly blamed her for Pepper's rotten temper. "The two of us were doing fine," Valerie would explain as if it were really true, "until you came along and ruined everything we had."

Three years younger than Emma, Gracie was an average looking girl with curly black hair and deep-set brown eyes. Her nose, a bit too large for her long face, merely accentuated the thinness of her lips. Although far less attractive and more timid than her sister, Gracie was equally sweet-natured. The child's only asset in life was her sister, who acted as her protector and was the only one to stand between her and their heathen father. As Emma grew older, she often spared her younger sister from their father's beatings by pushing herself forward as a buffer. When Gracie was old enough to understand her sister's sacrifice, her emotions were set in turmoil between guilt and love.

The so-called Murphy family lived in a small home on Chain Street in Norristown, Pennsylvania. They lived largely on bare essentials; sometimes even those were lacking. Their row home was a run down shack that appeared on the verge of collapse. The wood porch had rotted and its roof was supported by four-by-fours sloppily nailed in place to prevent it from crashing down. The floorboards creaked when walked on, their mushiness giving a bit beneath their feet.

Inside, the once white walls were yellowed from Pepper's chain-smok-
The long shag rugs were old and so matted down with overuse that

their fibers felt perpetually soggy under their bare feet. The furniture was secondhand with pieces of foam peeking out from the ripped upholstery in several places. The absence of adequate lighting made their home feel like the inside of a cave; but for the glare of the small television that stood on a battered table, there was almost no light at all.

Valerie and Pepper earned so little money that putting food on the table took great effort. The family rarely owned anything new and relied on handouts that were offered at local churches. Of the little that the couple earned, a major chunk went toward supporting Pepper's addiction to booze. The financial strain that the couple lived under only brought more tension into the home. Pepper knew they were destined to be poor white trash and for this he despised his family.

Emma and Gracie were submerged in dreariness day after day. They didn't enjoy the small gestures of affection like most other children that didn't cost anything to give, like a hug or a tender pat on the back. With no relief from their dismal circumstances in sight, they clung to each other to save themselves from the misery that threatened to swallow them alive.

Made in the USA
Coppell, TX
07 March 2021